"Fans of Sylvan's Shadow World series won't be disappointed by this tale. The saga of vampire mates Miranda Grey and David Solomon is one roller-coaster ride featuring complex plots, intrigue, and devastating emotions. Sylvan is slowly revealing more of her overarching conspiracy plot, promising spellbinding drama to come!" —*RT Book Reviews*

"This series is getting more interesting by the book."
—*Mystifying Paranormal Reviews*

PRAISE FOR
SHADOW'S FALL

"Dianne Sylvan is truly a remarkable storyteller. With the ability to bring her characters to life and make their hearts pound with action, readers will salivate for the next installment of the Shadow World series." —*Nocturne Romance Reads*

"The third Shadow World urban fantasy is a great, exhilarating entry with several stunning twists, including a fabulous, shocking cliff-hanging climax . . . Fast-paced with backstabbing and betrayal, *Shadow's Fall* is superb." —*Alternative Worlds*

"*Shadow's Fall* is an exciting, well-executed third installment to Ms. Sylvan's wonderful Shadow World, and I now wait impatiently for the fourth installment." —*Smexy Books*

"Exceeded my expectations since the last book! It was awesome and mind-blowing." —*Mystifying Paranormal Reviews*

"Sylvan continues to impress with her ability to wring emotions from her readers and give us the right balance of action and romance . . . It's the true talent of a writer who can have her readers feeling the same things as her characters along with them, and Sylvan's highly developed characters do just that." —*SF Site*

continued

PRAISE FOR
SHADOWFLAME

"I absolutely loved this book! . . . Fans of vampire books every-where, I have found the next big thing, and it is the Shadow World series by Dianne Sylvan. The twists and turns that Syl-van placed in this book kept me flying through the pages . . . Queen Miranda is one of the strongest female characters I have come across, and hands down this series is going to be sensa-tional! I cannot rave enough over this one . . . *Shadowflame* gave me all the high-impact action, romance, and gore that I want in a book." —*Fresh Fiction*

"Dianne Sylvan's writing is captivating. She creates a world that will suck you in from the get-go. Her writing style is fluid and unrelenting. *Shadowflame* follows the same near-flawless writing style that book one did . . . I enjoyed the suspense and Dianne Sylvan's creative way of keeping readers on their toes." —*Nocturne Romance Reads*

"Miranda was the sort of heroine I enjoy reading about; she didn't just suddenly fall for David, she made him work at gaining her trust . . . The overall book was refreshing." —*Night Owl Reviews*

"If you thought *Queen of Shadows* was fantastic, you are going to be blown away by *Shadowflame* . . . Dianne really knows how to rip your heart out and get you feeling everything the characters are feeling as you read." —*Urban Fantasy Investigations*

"Dianne Sylvan has truly created a vampire world that I would want to be a part of for years to come . . . A phenomenal book from beginning to end." —*Mystifying Paranormal Reviews*

"Dianne Sylvan is the queen of emotional storytelling. She takes the story exactly where she thinks it needs to go, even if it's not pretty . . . I loved it." —*The Spinecracker*

PRAISE FOR
QUEEN OF SHADOWS

"Sylvan's powerful debut is packed with startling action, sensual romance, and delightfully nerdy vampires . . . [Her] compelling take on vampirism, her endearing characters, and a complex, unabashedly feminist plot will have readers hungry for a sequel." —*Publishers Weekly* (starred review)

"*Queen of Shadows* pulled me in . . . Dianne Sylvan's rich, dark, sexy reimagined Austin is filled with people I want to visit again and again . . . Sylvan's got voice, doesn't miss a beat, and rocks it all the way to the last note . . . Looking for a new addiction? Go no further."
—Devon Monk, national bestselling author of *Stone Cold*

"Dianne Sylvan has created an original take on vampires that I thoroughly enjoyed, and I'll be looking for her next book with great anticipation. She's a skilled and talented storyteller who definitely knows how to deliver one hell of a book!"
—Angela Knight, *New York Times* bestselling author of *Master of Darkness*

"Dianne Sylvan is an incredibly talented writer. She draws the reader not only into the story but into the very marrow of someone who is starting to question their grip on reality . . . *Queen of Shadows* concludes with a great flourish, leaving the reader euphoric." —*Sacramento Book Review*

"Well written . . . The relationship between the empath and the vampire makes for a strong Shadow World thriller that will enthrall the audience with a sense of awe, as supernatural Austin comes across [as] realistic through the filters of the flawed lead protagonists." —*Alternative Worlds*

"My favorite book of 2010 so far . . . Moving, well written, suspenseful, and sensual, this is a novel you won't want to miss."
—*Fantasy Literature*

Ace Books by Dianne Sylvan

QUEEN OF SHADOWS
SHADOWFLAME
SHADOW'S FALL
OF SHADOW BORN
SHADOWBOUND

SHADOWBOUND

DIANNE SYLVAN

ACE BOOKS, NEW YORK

THE BERKLEY PUBLISHING GROUP
Published by the Penguin Group
Penguin Group (USA) LLC
375 Hudson Street, New York, New York 10014

USA • Canada • UK • Ireland • Australia • New Zealand • India • South Africa • China

penguin.com

A Penguin Random House Company

SHADOWBOUND

An Ace Book / published by arrangement with the author

Ace Books are published by The Berkley Publishing Group.
ACE and the "A" design are trademarks of Penguin Group (USA) LLC.

For information, address: The Berkley Publishing Group,
a division of Penguin Group (USA) LLC,
375 Hudson Street, New York, New York 10014.

ISBN: 978-0-425-25984-9

PUBLISHING HISTORY
Ace mass-market edition / April 2014

PRINTED IN THE UNITED STATES OF AMERICA

10 9 8 7 6 5 4 3 2 1

Cover art by Gene Mollica.

To my mother:
for golden summers, Jell-O fingers,
and endless slumber parties;
and for knowing I was your daughter
the first day we met

Prologue

TEL AVIV, 2003

The earth shook.

There was nothing to do but run.

Avi did not run. His sword flashed in the night, and he and Elite 7, the only other survivor of the Prime's personal guard, fought back-to-back, keeping the enemy busy while the others escaped the Haven. There seemed to be a thousand of the adversary, their blood spattering the pristine walls and centuries' worth of treasure passed from one Signet to the next. Whoever was behind this would have a lot of stains to wash out of his new carpets.

"Go!" Elite 7 shouted. "Get the women to safety! I will hold them off!"

He wanted to protest—there would be no leaving this hallway for 7 if Avi left him to fight alone—but they both knew the mind of their Prime, and knew that in the absence of a Queen, he valued his wife and her two sisters above all else in the Haven. The Prime would want them delivered to the safe house, and he would not have trusted anyone to the task but his Second.

"For God's sake, Avi, go!"

He caught Elite 7's eye. *"Shalom aleichem,"* he said.

Elite 7 smiled at his old friend. They had greeted each other the same way for eight years . . . and said farewell the same way, too. *"Wa-laikum as-salâm."*

He returned the smile. Only then did he run.

The world was on fire—smoke was thick in the air, leaving his lungs burning as he crossed the compound amid flying crossbow bolts and flaming arrows. Servants, Elite, anyone caught by surprise would be cut down mercilessly . . . and they had *all* been caught by surprise. No one, not even the intelligence operatives he had trained himself, had any idea this was coming. Their Prime had ruled for four decades without a single challenger—more than any other leader could say in this part of the world.

The women's apartment was on the far western side of the main building. He angled away from the Haven's main concourse and took a side corridor the enemy wouldn't know about unless they had memorized every meter of the property's layout.

Before he could reach the door, a sword swung toward his throat; he spun around, meeting it with his own blade, hitting hard enough to knock the weapon out of his opponent's hand. Another quick stroke took the invader's head.

He looked up and saw three more coming toward him. "I do not have time for this," he said.

For all their ferocity and overwhelming numbers, these would-be Elite were nowhere near skilled enough for the second in command of Israel. He had them all down inside ninety seconds and was at the door in another ten.

He jerked the door open, twisted inside, and shut it, slamming down the steel security bar. "Geveret Amit," he said, "you and your sisters must come with me now—"

He turned . . . and froze.

The cozy room was a shambles, furniture broken and curtains ripped down. The window had been shattered, leaving shards of glass everywhere. And all around him, lying headless or with hilted stakes jutting from their chests, were dead men, none of them Elite.

The women were gone.

The devastation, however, was not what gripped his attention.

At the far end of the room, in the only upright chair, a man sat calmly watching him, wiping blood from a blade. Dressed in black leather and almost certainly American, he was completely unaffected by the blood and death all around him.

The Second knew why without doubt: He had killed all of these men himself.

"Ah, there you are," the man said. Even sitting still he had the preternatural grace of their kind . . . a very, very powerful one of their kind. His pale eyes swept the Second from head to foot and back up again, his expression one of a certain provisional approval. "The women are safe," he stated in flawless Hebrew. "You should be far more worried about yourself."

He stood. Normally, the Second would have laughed—this was hardly an intimidating figure—but there was such strength in his young-seeming body, and such great age in his eyes, that a towering giant would not have been half as frightening.

"Avishai Shavit," he went on, sheathing the blade. There were at least four other visible weapons and signs of half a dozen more under his coat. "We have a mutual friend in the Mossad. He speaks highly of you."

He had to mean Director Dagan. "Who are you?" he finally asked.

"I may be your salvation," was the answer. "The men who have murdered your Prime will hunt you down and leave your head on a pike outside these gates before they will risk you making a play for the Signet yourself. One way or another, you have to leave Israel."

Avi made a sardonic noise. "Yes, I figured that much out already. And?"

A slight smile. "You are fearless in battle—I was watching. You've been in military intelligence your entire life. Second in command is as high as you can go unless a Signet takes you, and you know, in your heart, that you are not a Prime. You are, however, exactly what I'm looking for."

There was a pounding outside the door. They had to know their men were dead by now. "To what end?"

"You have heard the whispers," he said. He didn't seem to notice the people trying to break down the door. "When a despot falls dead in the middle of dinner from no discernible cause . . . when Death comes like a thief in the night where no mortal hand could reach . . . you hear someone say it, and someone else call him a fool, because no such thing exists."

Avi stared, nodding slowly. "I have heard."

"Then you know exactly who I am."

"There are many warriors greater than I. Why go through all this trouble just for me?"

"You mean this?" He gestured at the bodies. "You will soon learn, if you accept my offer, that this, for us, is no trouble at all. Now . . . if you would like to hear more, I suggest we take our leave of this mess and go somewhere more private."

"How do you propose we do that?"

A smile, amused but also sinister, leaving Avi uneasy . . . but also intrigued. "One moment." The visitor drew a mobile phone from his coat and, when the other end of the line picked up, said only, "Activate."

Beyond the door, a half-dozen piercing screams went up, screams of terror and agony that were all cut short, a strangled silence left in their wake.

"What did . . ."

The man met his eyes, and again Avi had to steel himself against an instinctive ripple of fear. "Lesson one," he said. "Do not ask questions whose answers you don't really want to know." He opened the door and looked at the Second. "You have nothing to lose, Avishai Shavit. Will you come?"

He did not hesitate. "I will."

"Good. Follow me."

"What do I call you?"

His quiet, commanding voice held all the authority of a Signet—and all the warmth of the Arctic. "You will call me Alpha."

PART ONE

The Eight of Pentacles

One

Just another night at the office.

The venue's stage door swung open and several black-clad security staff emerged, trying to clear a path from the door to the car waiting nearby. Dozens of cameras clicked, lights flashing. A cacophony of voices erupted that drowned out even the sounds of nearby traffic. A moment later, a curly-haired redhead bobbed through the crowd, politely refusing interviews.

"Miss Grey! How are you feeling since you recovered from the shooting?"

"Miss Grey, have you started work on your second album yet?"

"Miss Grey, is it true that the man who shot you was killed while in police custody?"

She kept walking, letting Minh and Stuart keep the way open, until she'd passed through the reporters and hit the small knot of fans that had managed to get to the door before her guards blocked anyone else from entering the alley.

Most of them were bright-eyed young women who reminded her so much of herself . . . when she was mortal . . . before she'd gone insane.

These were the people who had given her a career. She

made a habit of pausing with them for just a moment to sign a few CDs and give a hug captured on a phone camera—the image would be blurry, but with the chaos they would blame the phone itself. It wasn't much of a stretch; Miranda almost never got a decent shot with her own phone, and hers was ten-years-beyond-state-of-the-art by virtue of her being married to the Fanged Wondergeek.

Finally with a parting smile she took pity on her body-guards and headed for the car. Harlan held the limo door open for her and she slid in, dragging her guitar along with her onto the seat.

As pretentious as she'd thought it was the first week, she had to admit the limo was a comfortable way to travel; the Lincoln had thrown a rod or something and had to go to an actual mechanic for a change.

The car pulled away from the curb, and she reached into her coat pocket for her phone. The usual patrol status reports were coming in: situation normal.

"Straight to the rendezvous, my Lady, or did you need to stop along the way?"

She had already fed tonight, but as the high from the show began to abate, already her body was whispering pleas for more blood, and she was starting to get that itching, gritty feeling in her veins. Just thinking of fresh blood caused her stomach to lurch painfully.

Miranda sighed. "Stop before we leave downtown, please."

She'd expended a lot of energy performing tonight. That must be why she was hungry again so soon; she was just getting used to being back onstage. Modulating her energy was different now—on the one hand she was stronger, but on the other, working her empathy through her new power was taking some adjustment. All of that extra power could burn out quickly, leaving her exhausted, if she got it into her head that she was invincible.

But even as she told herself she was just tired and over-worked, she wanted to curl up and weep . . . because she knew it was a lie.

A few minutes later Harlan pulled over. "I believe this area should provide a nice selection," he said.

"Thank you. I'll be back in fifteen minutes."

It was a warm, humid night at the end of July, a little cooler than average for this time of year but still growing steadily more oppressive. She and David had both switched to light-weight coats made for rain rather than cold—there were few other ways to walk around town concealing a sword, but their usual leather was a bit much for a Texas summer.

Tonight, though, standing on the sidewalk surveying the scene, she felt a chill move through her.

It had been only ten days since the attack on Hart's Haven, less than a month since she had become . . . what she was now. Since that first night, since she had woken as this new creature and discovered she had killed someone, she had known that all of this new power had come with a price. She could run faster, fight harder, sense things beyond the percep-tion of even the strongest vampire. A stake to her heart would no longer kill her. She could track a lawbreaker across the entire city without breaking a sweat, and she knew there were other changes she hadn't discovered yet.

But true invulnerability was impossible. If they were now this strong, this hard to kill, there had to be an equal and opposite consequence.

She left the car and made her way down the street toward a crowded corner where a steady stream of humans crossed from one side to the other. Drawing near, she moved back behind a building and peered around the corner at them, feel-ing . . . what, exactly?

Distant. Alien. *Hungry.*

The distance between her and the mortal world had grown so much in such a short time. She still had friends among them, but night after night she watched humans walking by, completely unaware of the creature whose eyes were sweep-ing over them, and she felt every inch of that distance, felt a final separation from their ordinary lives . . . lives that were so fragile, so easily ended.

A pert young Indian-American woman in a business suit caught her eye, and she bent her will against the girl's, pulling her from the river of mortals and into the darkness, away from her kind, away from everything alive and familiar.

Miranda took the girl's arm and steered her back against the wall, careful not to hurt her or get her tripped up on the human's insanely impractical heels. The girl's face was a vacant neutral, her consciousness wrapped in shadow so it would never occur to her to struggle.

But if she did struggle . . . if she tried to run . . .

Miranda's teeth dug into her lip. She imagined the girl bolting, shedding those stupid shoes and running as hard and fast as she could . . . running for her life . . . she imagined giving her a head start, holding on to the wisp of her scent, and then running after her . . . *chasing her.*

All of this worrying about injury and tending to their prey's memories was nothing but a conceit to civility—what her body craved as much as blood was to *hunt*, to bring the girl down and tear open her throat under the open sky and feel her heart shudder to a stop as her blood soaked into the . . . ground . . .

Miranda cried out and stumbled away from the girl, nearly losing her hold over the human's mind. She wanted to tell the girl to run away as fast as she could, but was that to save her, or to revel in the bright salt-sweet adrenaline that would infuse the girl's blood?

Before she could panic at her own thoughts, she pinned the girl back and roughly turned her head to the side to take what she had come for.

She understood, though she tried not to think about, why her teeth had changed. The second pair enabled her to get a harder grip on a human's throat, and caused more damage, four punctures instead of only two. More blood would flow faster . . . she could finish in half the time. Lions and wolves had more than two pointed teeth. Their teeth were designed to tear flesh; a human's were comparatively flat and dull. This new design made her a more efficient predator.

It had been tricky, but she'd figured out how to change the angle of her head so that she wouldn't dig in with the second set. The girl gasped and struggled feebly, but Miranda tightened her hold over the girl's mind and froze her in place. *Don't fight. Please don't fight. You'll only make it harder to stop.*

The girl tasted so young and innocent . . . and as she wandered back into the teeming masses of humanity, her hand reaching up to touch her neck, then running absently through her disheveled hair, the Queen watched her from her hiding place, letting the blood run through her body and satisfy her . . . *for now* . . . and wondering, with an aching heart, how much longer she would be able to let them walk away.

Every weekend in Austin, families gathered beneath the metal shelters of city park pavilions and held barbecues, birthday parties—piles of gifts, balloons, piñatas, a cooler of beer for the adults. Laughter and the shrieks of young children would fill the air; the little ones would run back and forth from the tables to the playground. By the time they went home everyone would be sweaty and tired on a hot, humid July night, but they would be smiling after a day with their friends and family.

They would have no idea that only two nights before, a corpse had lain on its back atop the same table where the children would sit with their feet swinging and their faces sticky with ice cream.

The pavilion's lights were all on, and the whole park was swarming with police uniforms. A pair of overworked homicide detectives oversaw the scene.

One of the detectives, a redheaded, freckled man whose face looked like it would be far more comfortable in riotous laughter than grim determination, looked up from his notepad at the officer who had called for his attention. "What?"

"Um, Detective Maguire, there are some . . . people . . . here to see you. They said you called?"

Maguire nodded. *Here we go.* "Right, let them through."

Once upon a time, a routine security detail for an eccentric celebrity's *Rolling Stone* interview had blown Maguire's horizons wide open. He didn't expect to cross paths with the Signets again, but not long after, a bizarre murder caught his attention even though he wasn't yet in Homicide. As soon as Maguire saw the body, he knew what they were dealing with, and his investigation brought Maguire back into the sights of a vampire . . . lucky for him, a vampire whose help would get him promoted to detective and help him solve half a dozen cases since, when cause of death was more Halloween than homicide. The prince of the city, ruler of the entire South, genius, warrior, and diplomat . . . and somehow Maguire . . . and his daughter . . . had come to call his people their friends.

The officers within the vicinity, as one, froze in the middle of whatever they were doing as someone rolled back the yellow tape to let in the strangest people most of them would ever see in this city—and that was saying something in a place like Austin.

Four black-clad individuals surrounded a central figure, a man in a long black coat, wildly out of place this time of year. They were all pale and sharp-eyed, instantly sizing up every potential threat.

They stuck close to their fifth member, who walked like a man who was used to getting his way; in fact, when one of the officers started to protest their presence, the man fixed her with his deep, shadowed blue eyes, and she went stark white, stammered, and moved out of the way.

Maguire held back a smile.

"Detective." David Solomon, Prime of the Southern United States, gave him a nod of acknowledgment. "You called?"

Maguire was a decorated military man who had been a beat cop for ten years and a detective for six, and as good as he was at being intimidating, he would never understand what it was about the Prime that commanded attention so completely. Other vampires were plenty scary, but they didn't make everyone stop and stare like God had just walked into the room.

"I need you to have a look at this," Maguire said. He gestured at the table where the ME had already arrived and was preparing to take the body back to the morgue.

"Is it an Alpha Seven?" Solomon asked, following him over.

"I don't think so—it's a little weird."

A raised eyebrow. "Coming from you, Detective, that's disturbing."

"Yeah, tell me about it."

When they reached the table, the Prime drew up short. "Son of a bitch."

"What is it?" Maguire asked.

Solomon stood over the body, his face unreadable, looking down at the man who had been left there—a white-blond young man in his mid to late twenties. The body was badly beaten, and one wrist looked to have been slashed, but there was no obvious cause of death unless it was exsanguination; odder still, the ME hadn't been able to estimate a time of death, because it appeared to her that the body had been kept in cold storage that delayed the onset of decay. The wounds suggested a battle or crime of passion, but keeping a corpse in a fridge suggested something else altogether.

But what had caused Maguire to call the Haven, what gave him a feeling of unease he couldn't shake, was what lay on the man's chest: a heavy chain, an amulet, set with the shattered remains of some kind of stone.

"This is definitely out of your jurisdiction," the Prime said.

"I was afraid you'd say that. What do you need me to do?"

Solomon reached down and picked up the broken amulet. The ME and several of the Crime Scene Unit people started to dive toward him, each probably ready to yell something about disturbing the evidence, but Solomon merely held up his other hand, and they all fell silent.

He ignored the police completely and stared at the amulet for a minute, troubled.

Maguire moved closer so they wouldn't be as easy to overhear. "Is that what I think it is?"

"A Signet, yes."

Something in his face made Maguire ask, "Did you know this man?"

The Prime looked at Maguire. "He killed me."

"Holy shit—that's the guy? Well, do you know who killed him?"

Solomon made a slow circuit around the table, eyes narrowed. "I know exactly who killed him," he said. "I just don't know what they gained from it."

"Is there any point in an autopsy?" Maguire asked quietly.

"Do not let them do an autopsy," Solomon said firmly, pitching his voice just loudly enough for Maguire to hear. "Do whatever you have to do to make this body disappear—get it out in the sunlight and have the paperwork misplaced. I don't want the medical examiner running tests. I would take it, but I fear that would create more questions than a clerical error. You should have called me before the rest of them got here."

"I would have, but I wasn't the first one on the scene,"

Maguire replied. "Somebody called it in to 911. They sent one unit and the officers called the cavalry. Trust me, I would have left it to you."

"Someone called it in," the Prime repeated thoughtfully. "Someone made sure the body was found before dawn burned it away."

"Huh. You're right. And that means—"

"They wanted me to see it." Solomon nodded to himself, then said, tucking the Signet in his coat, "This is all I need, Detective. I leave the rest to you."

"Great. This should be easy." Maguire gave him a wry grin. "Glad to have you back in the world, Solomon."

He smiled at Maguire—the sort of smile that made Maguire doubly glad the Prime was on his side. "I am glad to be back. Good night, Detective."

He nodded to his Elite, who fell back into step on all sides of him, and the five vampires walked away, leaving a scene full of detectives, officers, and medical examiners staring at each other with wide eyes.

Silence on the other end of the line.

After a moment David asked, "Are you all right?"

He heard her take a deep breath. "Yes. It's . . . it's really not a surprise. Now we know for sure."

"I'm sorry," he said. "I know you cared for him."

Across the country, in her new Haven in New York, Prime Olivia Daniels laughed a little, and he could practically hear her shaking her head. "Only you would feel bad that the man who murdered you was murdered. Have you told the others?"

"Not yet. I wanted you to know first."

"Thank you. I appreciate that."

"Is there anything I can do for you?" he asked.

Now he could hear her smiling. "Not unless you can alter time, speed up the harvest, or teleport me off this rock," she quoted.

David couldn't help it—he laughed, surprised. "Did you just *Star Wars* me?"

"You're not the only nerd in the world, you know."

Despite the situation, he was grinning as they hung up. He

looked across the bedroom to where Miranda sat cross-legged on the bed with her laptop; she was giving him a knowing look.

"What?" he asked.

Now she smiled. "Nothing. I just think it's cute that the first female Prime in Signet history has a crush on you."

"Wait . . . what?"

She giggled at the look on his face. "Oh, come on—you really didn't know?"

David shook his head. "I never thought about it."

Miranda was still laughing. "Don't look so panicked, baby. It's just flirty. Not a big deal."

He tried to come up with something to say that would assure her she was wrong, but contradicting an empath about emotional matters was like trying to tell him how the Internet worked.

Olivia was a strong and extremely attractive woman, of course—not conventionally beautiful, perhaps, but he really had no use for convention. She had seen him through a violently painful transformation and taken care of him when he had no memory of who he was. He really did enjoy talking to her, but he'd assumed it was because she was a new Prime and he liked helping her get settled. But now that he thought about it . . . *oh hell*.

"I really do think it's cute," Miranda told him, this time without laughing. "There's nothing wrong with you being attracted to somebody. People are going to be hot for you no matter what—I mean, you have *seen* you, right? If I got uppity every time that happened, I'd never have a moment's peace. And let's not forget this link we all have as part of Persephone's Circle; I'm sure that factors in. We've all got some weird emotional attachments to each other, but really, all either of you wants is a friend."

He half smiled. "That's true. And . . . she reminds me so much of Faith, sometimes, it's almost uncanny. Except I don't think Faith would ever have been comfortable as a Prime, constantly in the spotlight—and Olivia is taking to it remarkably, like a cat to a keyboard."

"You know, if you would work with your empathy a little instead of ignoring it, you would have figured it out yourself."

David sighed. "I don't want empathy, Miranda. I saw what it did to you—what it still does to you even now that it's under control. I prefer to be a coldhearted bastard whenever possible."

"Oh, yeah, right." She rolled her eyes.

"Just do me a favor . . . if at any point you think Olivia is starting to feel like Faith did, or if I start acting that way . . . tell me. I never want a situation like that again."

She smiled a little sadly. "Would knowing about Faith have changed what happened?"

"Probably not. But at least we could have been honest with each other and gotten everything out in the open. I of all people know what a bad idea it is to repress feelings for someone, especially when jealousy is involved."

"True."

She looked tired again, he noticed. They had both been feeling run-down the last couple of days and it was wearing on them emotionally as well as physically; they'd actually had a fight, of sorts, over the thermostat that dusk. He felt feverish and nauseated; she was freezing. They'd both realized how silly the argument was, but it was a sign of a larger problem; neither of them was feeling well, and it was getting worse, and though he kept hoping he was wrong, he had a sinking feeling that—

Just then his phone vibrated in his hand, and he looked down at the text message that had just come in. "Speak of the devil."

Call me.

He held the phone up where she could see the screen.

Miranda frowned. "That's the first we've heard from him since we got back from New York. Before that I was talking to him almost every day."

"I know. Whatever's going on over there . . . I'm almost afraid to find out." He stared at the phone for a moment longer before hitting call.

"Yes?"

"Are you all right?"

"Fine," Deven lied. David hated how flat and worn down he sounded. "Everything's fine."

"Then why did you text? I haven't heard from you in days."

"I don't know . . . I guess I just wanted to hear your voice . . . to hear something normal."

"What does that mean?"

"Nothing, nothing. How are you?"

"Actually, I was going to call you anyway. Detective Maguire called me to a crime scene earlier—someone left a message for me in a public park."

"What kind of message?"

David took a deep breath. "Jeremy Hayes. Dead. With his Signet shattered."

"Well, that's one way to get your attention. Have you told Olivia?"

"Yes. I called her first. She's all right—a little rattled, but like she said, it wasn't exactly a surprise. If the artifact Hayes stole from Hart was exactly like the Stone of Awakening, it stands to reason it had a similar ritual attached to it. Hayes would have been far too convenient a target for Morningstar to resist—he had a Signet, he was badly injured, and he delivered the artifact right to them."

"The question being, of course, assuming the ritual accomplished the same thing as the Awakening, draining all the power from Jeremy, what did they do with that power? The Awakening used your life force to bust the lock off Persephone's cage, but what was Morningstar trying to open? And why were they so keen for you to know it?"

"I don't know. But they didn't leave him in Olivia's territory, where I presume he was killed, and they didn't return him to Australia. They brought him here to my backyard."

"Which would indicate they know you're supposed to be the general of our little army. Lucky you."

"I don't like any of this. I don't like being the one in the dark." David didn't add that was exactly what Deven was doing to him, but he was pretty sure the sentence's double meaning was clear.

"Trust me . . . there are some things you're better off not knowing."

Finally David couldn't stand it anymore. "What the hell is going on over there, Deven? Why won't you tell me what's wrong?"

A pause. Then, "Would you believe me if I told you I was dying of ennui?"

David rolled his eyes. "Very funny."

"Yes, it's hysterical. I have to go . . . kiss Miranda for me."

"Deven, wait—"

"Good-bye."

David had to resist the childish urge to throw the phone. He dropped it on the sofa cushion and put his head in his hands.

He could hear amusement in Miranda's voice. "So . . . tell me again: Which one of you is the unstoppable force and which is the immovable object?"

"I've never known anyone so frustrating in my entire life." He ran his hand back through his hair. "Have I ever thanked you for not pissing me off every time we're in the same room?"

"You two must have been very entertaining as a couple."

"Mostly when we weren't having sex, we were killing people or beating each other up."

"Oh, now, I know that's not a hundred percent true. It might make you feel better to think of it that way, but he left you way too screwed up for it to have been that simple."

"I suppose you're right. But still, we did spend an awful lot of time angry. That's one of the many, many things that sets you apart—you and I have fought, but usually over things that matter, not just because you're a contrary little dick."

Miranda chuckled, closed her computer, and walked across the room to sit down next to him. "I'm worried about him, too, but . . . you can't help someone who doesn't want to be helped," she said, pulling his head to her shoulder and leaning back into the cushions. He sighed and lay against her chest, listening to her heartbeat for a moment with his eyes closed.

"This is what I'm supposed to lead," he said tiredly. "You and I, who don't even know what can kill us anymore. Jacob and Cora, who don't have a single outstanding psychic ability between them. Olivia, who doesn't have a Consort and therefore leaves an empty space in the Circle for however long she's on her own. Jonathan, a precognitive who keeps everything he sees secret. And Deven, an assassin in desperate need of Prozac. We're doomed."

Miranda chuckled. Her fingers wound through his hair, rubbing gently, energy moving through her to help soothe the headache she knew he had. "Don't be such a drama Prime, baby. You know this whole mess has barely even started. We'll get there."

"I hope so." He surrendered to her talented hands, saying quietly, "I just wish I knew what we're supposed to do, or when, or why . . . or anything."

There was a smile in her voice, but it had an edge to it. "Be careful what you wish for," she said.

Jonathan was standing in the doorway, watching as he ended the call. "What was that about?"

Deven reached over to the nightstand and left his phone there, sighing. "Jeremy Hayes is dead."

"Well, yes, we figured that."

"No, I mean he's *dead*. They found his body. Morningstar made sure David saw it. They left his broken Signet so we'd know how Jeremy died."

"Damn," Jonathan said, shaking his head. "And we still have no idea what that Widget he took from Hart was really for."

"I have a feeling it didn't conjure kittens and cotton candy."

The Consort laughed. He looked the Prime up and down and said, "You look a little better tonight. How long have you been awake?"

"About three hours." Deven looked over at him and saw that he was holding a glass of blood in one hand and a foam takeout cup with a straw in the other. "Is one of those for me?"

"Both. Room service," the Consort answered with a grin. He held up the glass. "Fresh tonight, O positive."

He took the glass and Jonathan stood beside him, one hand resting reassuringly on the back of the Prime's neck, while he drank it slowly, fighting off intermittent moments of dizziness. It did help—by the time he was done he felt more alert, and the spinning had stopped.

Deven gestured at his other hand. "What's in that one?"

Jonathan smiled and held it out. "A slightly melted but nonetheless delicious peanut butter hot fudge milkshake from Goodall's. I considered using it to extort sexual favors, but you've had such a rotten week I changed my mind."

Deven shook his head, smiling in spite of himself, and reached out with both hands to grab the cup; he drained half of it much faster than he'd drunk the blood.

"Slow down or you'll get brain freeze," Jonathan told him.

"What's the situation out there?" Deven asked between slurps.

"Dull as tombs, thank God. I spoke to Murdoch earlier tonight; there was a bit of a territory skirmish in Los Angeles between the Blood Kings and the Silver Bullet gang. They're going to be a problem eventually, but their recruitment rate is so low it could be a year before a significant incident."

The Prime nodded through his weariness, trying to concentrate. "The Blood Kings are like cockroaches; once they've infested the area they're damn near impossible to eradicate without nuking the site from orbit. But Murdoch knows that, so if he can't manage it he'll call for more swords."

"Agreed. Regardless, we've probably got a few months before anything breaks there. Now, assuming things go tonight like they have been, is there anything you need me to take care of while you're down?"

Deven thought about it and shook his head, but then said, "There is one thing I need."

"What?"

"Kiss me."

Jonathan smiled, thrilled at the rare request, and sat down next to him on the bed, pulling him close and enthusiastically doing as he'd been asked. "How's that?" he gasped as they pulled apart.

Deven leaned on his shoulder, inhaling deeply; he wanted to wrap himself up in Jonathan's smell—whiskey, cigars, leather-bound books—and hide from everything. "Perfect. Thank you."

Jonathan kissed him on the nose. "You taste like a Reese's cup."

There was a soft knock at their suite door, and Deven tensed. He and Jonathan exchanged a look.

"Are you ready for this?" Jonathan asked.

"No. But what choice do I have?"

Jonathan rose and went to the door; Deven braced himself, for what he knew was coming.

Their houseguest stood in the hallway, waiting patiently to be admitted, the door guards on either side staying as far away from him as possible without actually leaving their posts.

He wore an odd hybrid sort of outfit that was a little modern, a little medieval, and would probably pass unnoticed out in the city unless someone looked closely. His auburn hair was once again braided, leaving most of it to fall in a shining curtain down his back but keeping the rest out of his fair, gentle face.

Those dark violet, luminous eyes seemed to see past edges and walls, and *into* everything. No one in the Haven was able to make eye contact with him for more than a second; they were all afraid of what he would see.

Deven was no exception.

The Elf swept into the room and bowed to the Pair. "Good evening, my Lords."

And again, as happened every time Nicolanai came into the room, Deven couldn't breathe for a moment, and something in the sound of the Elf's low, musical voice made a tremor crawl from his heart outward. The Elf had a strange effect on everyone, though, whether Elite, servant, or Signet.

"Have you noticed any changes from the last session?" Nico asked, getting right to business, removing the outermost layer of his outfit—a long coat made of some slightly sheer fabric whose sleeves and lower hem almost shimmered like water—and draping it over a chair.

Deven shook himself out of whatever the hell it was that kept happening whenever he saw the Elf, and said, "No. Nothing."

Nico nodded, turned to Jonathan. "And you?"

The Consort moved to his usual chair by the bed, crossing one ankle over the other knee. "Actually, I have—from this end of the bond he seems more stable. It's subtle, but it's there."

"Good." Nico approached the bed, and Deven moved over. "I must warn you: After tonight's session there will be much greater alterations."

"What exactly are you doing?" Jonathan wanted to know. "You haven't been very forthcoming with the details so far."

Deven had to smile at his tone; Jonathan was not enjoying watching any of this and didn't entirely trust the purple-eyed stranger who had shown up promising to fix whatever was sucking the will to live out of his Prime . . . especially since so far there had been no visible results and the process was, to put it mildly, unpleasant.

"You have not asked," Nico replied reasonably, moving into the position he'd taken last time, sitting cross-legged up on the bed near the pillows. "Think of the universe as a giant interconnected web of energy. Each person consists of a smaller web within it, its threads connecting with many others. Among my people I am known as a Weaver—I have the ability to see and manipulate those threads."

"Then how would you describe what's wrong with Deven?"

"Entropy," Nico said frankly. "A vampire's soul is different from a human's, but it was made from a human's, and one characteristic both share is a limited life span. You simply aren't made to live this long. Essentially the Prime is falling apart as if he had already died, but he hasn't, and the dissolution is driving him mad. In most deaths the body and mind die together. Not so here."

"So what's the cure?"

"I have been sifting through his life thread by thread and, at each intersection, welding him back together. But all of this work will be for naught if there is insufficient energy flowing through the web to hold it together. Because he is already connected to you, I am hoping to open that connection a little wider, so that he can draw more energy from you—enough to support the matrix I have created." Nico paused, then said, "I assumed you would not object."

"No, I don't object," Jonathan said, at the same time Deven asked, "What will it do to him?"

Nico smiled slightly. He was a very serious . . . person . . . not given to a lot of laughter, though he did have a quick and occasionally cutting wit when he allowed it to show. Deven found himself contrasting the Elf with Jonathan, who was nearly the polar opposite; Jonathan loved to laugh and smiled more than anyone Deven knew, even after being stuck with Deven for sixty years. That was part of why their Pairing worked despite its obvious issues—Jonathan knew how to make his Prime smile.

"I cannot say for certain," Nico said. "It will not be a great drain on him—as a Pair you already share much of your energy, after all. He may barely even notice, or it may make him feel weak for a while. Once the flow settles in and you are both used to it, you should be relatively unaffected."

"Wait . . . have you done anything like this before?" Jonathan asked.

A fluid shrug. "Yes and no. My people do not have bonds like yours, and we are not subject to age—even though your bodies do not age, your hearts clearly do. But we do have our own similar problems, and I have repaired many of those." He saw the doubt on Jonathan's face and added, "This is what I do, my Lord. I am among the most powerful of my kind. I promise you I will not leave this house until I am sure your Prime will survive."

Nico hadn't referred to the other Elves much in the ten days he had been here, and Deven was dying to ask him all the questions that he'd been carrying around since he was a child . . . but after the Elf was done with him he slept for at least two days without moving, and on the third day he was so emotionally raw that he didn't even want to leave the bedroom.

"Let us begin," Nico said.

Deven took a deep breath. "All right." He cast another glance over at Jonathan, who gave him an encouraging smile.

You can do this. Think of Jonathan . . . if you live, he lives. It's not so bad. You've hurt much worse . . . many times.

He lay down on his back with his head in Nico's lap. For a moment the proximity overrode his dread, and he stared up at the Elf, taking in his breathless beauty. Deven had never seen anything like Nico—he *almost* looked human, even forgetting the ears and eyes, but everything from the way he walked to the curve of his lower lip held some starlit mystery that reminded Deven that while vampires had once been human, Nico had never been; he had been born what he was, a species that didn't even live on this plane.

"What are you looking at, my Lord?" the Elf asked quietly, and to Deven's surprise there was a spark of mischief in his eyes that was, goddamn it, insanely attractive.

"Um . . . the . . . I . . . that vine-looking mark next to your eye," Deven finished lamely, gesturing up at Nico's face. "Is that henna?"

"You mean, is it temporary? No."

"You got a tattoo on your *face*?" Jonathan asked, amazed. "You're tougher than you look."

Now Nico did smile. "If that was a compliment, thank you. It is the mark of my mother's family. We are matrilineal. Once there were a hundred in our family line; now there are three: my mother, my brother, and I."

"You have a brother?" Deven asked, surprised.

Nico placed his hands on Deven's temples, pressing lightly, eyes drifting closed as he began to pull power from wherever it was Elves got theirs. "I do indeed, a twin. Now, try to relax . . . I will do my best to minimize the discomfort."

Deven shut his own eyes with a sigh that turned into a pain-filled gasp as the Elf took hold of the frayed threads of Deven's being and began to pull them apart.

He's dead. Hart is dead.

She had been saying it, both aloud and in her head, for more than a week now, and it still had not sunk in. In fact, the more she said it, the less sense the words made.

Cora was glad it had been Miranda. She remembered the night of the Council ball, asking Miranda if it was easy to take a life, and Miranda's answer that there were things worth dying, and killing, for . . . That night had been on Cora's mind a lot in the last ten days. It was much more satisfying, if that was the word, that Hart had been killed by someone who understood the depravity of his crimes and would know exactly the kind of monster she was destroying. Just any assassin wouldn't do.

Cora really had no idea what to make of how she was feeling. Jacob, too, had been concerned about her. He told her if she wanted to talk, she need only say so, but if she didn't, he understood.

She had smiled, her heart gone warm with love for her husband.

She thought about the last time she and Jacob had attempted lovemaking—they had succeeded several times since returning from Texas, each time a little easier for her, but just as often, she froze in the midst of things, flashbacks running rampant in her mind, causing her to strike out, screaming.

That had happened many times in the last three years. She had spent decades as a slave to Hart's lusts, and those decades had taken their toll. She had feared when she first met Jacob that she would never be able to bear his touch at all; they had made a lot of progress.

She wanted her husband to touch her. She wanted it more and more every night, and things were getting better . . . but now . . . would it be easier, knowing Hart was no longer out there raping young women to death? She had never been afraid that she would end up back in his clutches, not really, and yet . . . just knowing he existed, somewhere across the ocean, crouching like a toad behind fortified walls . . . as long as he was in the world she could never fully let out her breath.

His harem had been freed not long before by the traitorous Jeremy Hayes. She would probably never know if they had all survived, or if they had any chance at healing. She doubted many of them had the blessing of a man like Jacob or the friends she had found to help them learn to live with what they had endured.

She had spent a lot of time at prayer and on her yoga mat lately—more than usual—asking for God's help for those girls, and trying to make sense of things.

"Why am I not happy about this?" she asked God one night, sitting in her cozy yoga studio in front of the altar she had built. Taking inspiration from Lali, her first teacher, she had set up the room as a place of prayer and meditation as well as physical activity.

She didn't expect God to speak back, of course. If God were in the habit of doing so, he would have answered her when she lay on the floor of the harem freezing and starving, the constant terror of what would happen again over and over carving ragged gouges in her heart.

She could not know the mind of God. If she had been released from the harem at any other time she might never have met Jacob. She certainly wouldn't have been in Austin at the precise moment she needed to be to find inspiration in Miranda Grey, to stand up on her own two feet and walk out of that room. She might not have become the person she was becoming, and Cora had found that she *liked* that person, and her life, very much.

She had seen what happened when someone of deep faith endured years of misery and turned his back on God. It was not a fate she would ever have desired.

She thought of Prime Deven, who suffered more from the death of his faith than he ever had at the hands of others. She could feel, sometimes even across the ocean, the pain he was in—a consequence of the strange connection among them all, she guessed. She wished she could sweep the Prime up in her arms and promise him that God had *not* abandoned him— that Deven had closed the door, and only Deven could reopen it. She had to get through to him before it was too late.

She pondered calling him, just to see how he was. He probably wouldn't confide in her—she was fairly certain Deven had never confided in anyone—but she had to at least offer. They had spoken a few times since he gave her her Nighthound Vràna, so it wouldn't be entirely novel for her to call now. She could perhaps use the pretense of asking his advice about the dog. As thorny and cold as he could be, every time she had ever called, he had stopped whatever he was doing and given her his full attention.

As if the thought had been a hand stretching over continents, she abruptly stopped midprayer—she could feel him right now.

What . . .

An intense wave of energy washed over her, the likes of which she had never felt before; it felt nothing like a vampire's power, although it was just as ageless and far, far stronger. It held the scent of green growing things, and it was redolent of healing, of rest.

It was certainly not Deven's energy, but it was twining through his like a climbing vine. She felt—or saw—it strengthening and supporting everyplace it moved. The two energies seemed to wrap around one another effortlessly, as if they had been made to join this way.

The image of a darkened bedroom came to her mind. Next to a great bed sat Jonathan in a chair, watching the bed intently with his chin resting on his fist. On the bed itself, she saw Deven lying on his back, eyes closed, fingers twisted in the comforter and clenching in pain every few moments. And sitting with him, the Prime's head in his lap, was . . .

What in the name of . . . ?

Her presence did not go unnoticed. The third figure "looked" at her, and she gasped and tried to flee back into her own body, both because the power before her was so alien and frightening . . . and because it was familiar.

"I know you," she whispered to herself. "How do I know you?"

"Peace, child," came a gentle, accented voice. *"I am a friend."*

Cora didn't know if it would work, but she spoke back across the miles: "What are you doing to him?"

She felt him smile. *"Buying time . . . but return to your home, young one, before your mate loses his mind with worry. You and I will meet again soon enough."*

Cora let go of the vision, suddenly desperate to do as he said, and flew back into the room with a cry to find Jacob kneeling in front of her, his hands on her shoulders as he called her name.

"Good God, Cora, what happened?" Jacob asked, pulling her into his arms. His relief was palpable all around her. "I felt you . . . disappear."

She was shaking slightly. "I do not know exactly," she said. "I was meditating, and . . . then I was in California."

He peered at her curiously. "Doing what?"

She took a deep breath. "Witnessing something frightening . . . or, possibly something wonderful . . . I really have no idea which."

Jacob kissed the top of her head. "Try not to do that again, all right? I prefer having you here."

She smiled at him. "May I use your phone?"

"Of course . . . may I ask . . . ?"

She took the device from him and scrolled through his contacts until she found the number she was looking for. "I doubt he will answer, but . . . I need to speak with Jonathan."

"Stop," Deven panted. "That's enough."

"Hold on for one more moment . . ."

"I can't. It's too much. Please, Nico." His voice nearly cracked on the last two words, so bent by the strain of what they were doing that it would have been a relief to break down completely.

The Elf withdrew, and the sudden absence of his psychic touch left Deven shaking and weak. He pulled away from Nico physically, turning onto his side and almost curling into a ball. Despite being drenched in sweat, he was freezing.

"Why is it hurting him?" Jonathan demanded, moving out of his chair to sit down on the side of the bed and place a comforting hand on his Prime's shoulder. Deven threaded trembling fingers with his and held on for dear life. The Consort looked like he wanted to throttle the Elf. "I thought this was supposed to be healing."

Nico turned his wide, dark eyes on Jonathan, and surprisingly, the Consort looked away. "Healing is not always a matter of pleasure," Nico said. "To return a dislocated limb to its socket requires intense pain, does it not?"

"It's all right," Deven murmured, shutting his eyes for a moment. "It took me seven centuries to fuck myself up this badly. It can't be fixed in a few days."

"On the contrary," Nico said, "You are doing very well. Thankfully your Elven blood enables me to connect with you on a deeper level—otherwise this might take months. At this rate you will be back to your life in another week at most."

"Should I feel different?" Jonathan asked, frowning.

"Not yet. It will take a day or so for the stronger energy flow to become established—until then, my Lord Prime, I expect you will feel weak and possibly sick, but once the energy is moving as it should, things will improve quickly."

"I feel all right," Deven started to say, but as he tried to sit up, dizziness hit him full force and his arms gave out, dropping him back to the bed on his face.

Nico moved out from under his head and turned him onto his back. "Just rest," he said, squeezing Deven's hand. Deven fought the urge to grab on to his hand and keep him there, like a security blanket.

Deven saw an odd look pass over Jonathan's face while Nico tucked the Prime in, but the Consort merely asked, "Are there a lot of Weavers where you come from?"

"No," Nico replied. "And even fewer with my strength. Weaving has always been a rare gift. As you can imagine, directly touching energy this way is difficult and takes many years to learn."

"Is your brother a Weaver?" Deven asked sleepily, burrowing into the pillows, his mind and body both completely exhausted.

He could hear Nico smiling. "No . . . Kai is a Bard, and a powerful one."

Deven tried to frame another question before he lost consciousness, but he felt Nico's hand on his face, and the Elf said kindly, "Rest, my Lord. I promise we will talk later when you are stronger."

That was all he heard.

Nicolanai rose gracefully from the bed, not at all rumpled from nearly four hours cross-legged. Whatever material Elves made their clothes out of, it was amazingly wrinkleproof. "Stay close to him," he said. "He will have nightmares again."

Jonathan nodded. "Call the guards at your door if you need anything. Don't hesitate."

"I will not."

The Consort started to speak, then stopped, but the Elf paused and turned his head back toward the bed, waiting, and Jonathan finally said, "Thank you."

Nico turned back and stared at him, his eyes penetrating. "You should not thank me yet. I gave you my word that he would survive, and he will, but there may be consequences to this we cannot anticipate."

"But at least he's acting like he wants to try to get better," Jonathan told him. "Now perhaps he'll fight for his own life instead of just giving up."

Nico stared down at Deven for a long moment. "There is little enough left of my people, so few traces of our time here . . . to think that someone with such a high calling, such power, could be cast down and condemned and learn to value himself so little . . . perhaps my kinsmen are right that we should have sealed off the Veil forever and not set foot here again."

"Oh? What do your kin think about you being here, then?"

A faint smile. "Only two of them even knew I left."

"You sneaked away? Why?"

"Why did I have to sneak, or why was I willing to?"

"Both. Either."

Nico sighed. "A great many prophecies pointed toward a day when we would have to return to the mortal world to aid in saving it. I believe that day has come. Others disagree. Vehemently." He allowed himself another small smile, this one wry. "I expect to be in a fair amount of trouble when I get home."

Jonathan's eyebrows shot up. "What, you mean they'll punish you?"

Something surprisingly dark and fierce crossed the Elf's face as he glanced down at the sleeping Prime. "They can try."

With that, he left the bedroom, closing the door silently behind him.

Jonathan stared after him for a moment before he was able to shake himself out of the spell the Elf seemed to cast over everyone he laid eyes on. The guards at the guest suite were utterly terrified of the Weaver, though they didn't say so; no one had any idea what to make of him, but they all knew he was incredibly powerful, ethereally beautiful, and very, very weird.

He told himself it was the Elf's strangeness that bothered him, not the way Deven reacted to him . . . like all of a sudden the Prime really *was* a seventeen-year-old, tumbling headlong into a new romance, all tongue-tied and nervous whenever the Elf was near. In all their history together Jonathan had never seen his Prime genuinely attracted to anyone besides David, and that had been going on long before Prime and Consort met. As far as he knew Deven and David's courtship had involved less blushing and stammering and more writhing and screaming.

And while Jonathan was perfectly willing to step back and let Deven have an outside lover, that didn't mean he wanted a front-row seat to the proceedings . . . but Nico could be good for him, if they didn't let their fears get in the way, which was probably what would happen, knowing Deven. Jonathan hadn't been lying when he said he would give anything to see his Prime happy.

The Consort fished his phone out of his pocket to leave on the bedside table with Dev's and noticed that Cora had called; he smiled. He had a feeling he knew exactly what she wanted. It would have to wait, though—by now it was midmorning in

Prague, and besides, at the moment Jonathan had only one goal in mind.

Placing the phone down carefully to avoid making noise, he kicked off his shoes and stretched out on the bed at Deven's side. He drew the inert Prime into their favorite sleeping position—Jonathan forming a solid wall against Deven's back, giving him the feeling of safety he craved—and kissed him on the ear, sighing . . . so much was changing. He knew the Elf would succeed; that much was easy to predict. But for how long?

And at what cost?

"Stay with me," he said softly into Deven's ear. "You stay with me, and I'll stay with you, and . . ." He could hear the catch in his own voice, and fell silent for a while, just listening to Dev breathe.

Holding his Prime tightly, as if he could hold on hard enough to keep the world from tearing everything apart, he closed his eyes and lay waiting for Deven to scream himself awake.

Two

On the night of the new moon, the newborn son of the Goddess of Death killed a mortal without a single pang of remorse.

The new moon before that, he had been wandering around a stranger in his own life, with only partial memory of his own transformation from an ordinary vampire into something more. He had been home, restored to his Queen, but only partway, until the night she joined him across the divide.

The new moon before that, he had been murdered.

The human wasn't exactly what he'd been hoping to find, but the hunger that had been growing for the last two days had at last overridden sense and reason and he was grateful he'd maintained enough control to find a drug dealer—one who sold to high school children and extorted sex for meth from the girls.

He would do.

For two nights David had fought it, had denied it. Until waking up tonight he had held on to a slim and fading hope that it would go away. But deep down, he had known what was really happening. Just in the last twenty-four hours his new senses had all dulled, which seemed counterintuitive given that those senses were supposed to make them better hunters . . . but it wasn't about that, this time. It was a warning.

An order.

Do what you were made to do. All of these gifts, all of your power, is meaningless unless you surrender to your nature. Do it . . . and everything will come back. The pain will fade. Do it.

It wasn't the first time he had heard that voice whispering in his mind—that voice like feathers across a moonlit sky. He couldn't say for certain if the voice was his own subconscious or that of Someone Else, but really, even if there was a difference, it didn't matter. Once he would have doubted it was real, but in the last few months he had lost the luxury of doubt.

By the time he got into town that night his entire body felt like it was on fire from the inside—it was a vampire's hunger times ten, coalescing into physical agony that nearly had him clawing at his skin.

It would only get worse. He knew it would only get worse.

He'd expected the human's death to soothe the pain and calm the shaking, but he was unprepared for the blast wave of satisfaction, pleasure, and *purpose* that hit him as soon as the body hit the ground. Every cell burned, but now with power.

In that moment nothing else mattered. The world fell away. He wanted to kneel down and kiss the dead man's slack mouth to thank him for being such a reprehensible sack of shit . . . finally the man's oily, poisoned life had shown the world its meaning.

He didn't kneel. Since taking the Signet he had knelt to no one . . . except to the being who had brought him back from death . . . which was how he'd ended up in this situation in the first place.

He held his hand out over the body and made it disappear. No fuss, no muss.

When he returned to the car, Harlan immediately noticed the complete 180-degree shift in his behavior—the Prime who had gone into the city to hunt was short-tempered and exhausted, with dark circles under his eyes, and couldn't concentrate long enough to frame a full sentence. The Prime who walked back was the one they all knew.

"You must have found quite a meal out there," Harlan said. "You looked like hell, Sire, if you don't mind me saying so."

David smiled at him as the driver opened the door of the limo. "I feel much better, Harlan, thank you."

The initial wave of energy left him giddy as it passed, and he leaned back and closed his eyes as the car pulled away to head for their second rendezvous, cataloging each difference, extrapolating a timeline based on how he felt now compared to how he had felt an hour ago.

It was difficult to know for sure how often this would happen—there was one set of numbers if he went from his own death, another if he went from the onset of his transformation, and another if he went from Miranda's, which was when his own had finished.

But looking out the tinted window and up at the cloud-smudged sky, it occurred to him the math might not matter so much as the timing. The Awakening had to be performed on the new moon. Tonight was the new moon again. There had been one between those dates, but at that point Miranda hadn't come across and his own transition hadn't been complete.

Miranda.

Now, for the first time, he thought about the meaning of his actions from her perspective—he had been so desperate to make the pain stop that he had set all of that aside, telling himself he'd feel guilty later, once he didn't want to die.

He still didn't feel guilty. He had removed a predator from the streets who got children hooked on a degrading, disgusting drug and fucked fifteen-year-old girls just because he could. The world would not suffer for his loss . . . and there were plenty more where that came from. Humanity always provided.

Miranda was not going to see it that way.

The rest of their Circle had not shown any signs of Miranda's gift, but he had a mild case of empathy, and he knew its purpose as much as he knew why they had more fangs. Empathy, just a touch, enabled him to find evildoers and know without a doubt what he was killing. A compassionate concession on Persephone's part, perhaps, to their modern sensibilities—vampires had been created to control the human population, but the law set down by Primes like David kept them from fulfilling that purpose, whether out of fear of exposure or a sense of morality. By and large the Shadow World lived in denial of the reason it was created.

And thus the Thirdborn took on the sins of the entire vampire race.

He was rehearsing what to tell her in his mind when the car pulled over and, a moment later, Harlan opened the door and Miranda practically fell inside.

Her condition astonished him. He figured she would look tired, but in the few hours since they had gone their own ways, he to Hunter Development and she to a meeting with her management, she looked like she'd lost ten pounds and had the drawn, sallow face of a vampire who hadn't fed in weeks. Starvation took a long time to kill them, and it was a gruesome way to die.

"Good God, Miranda . . ." He reached over to her and pulled her close. She felt as insubstantial as an autumn leaf. Her skin was far cooler than it should be, and he took her hands and tried to rub life back into them, though he knew it was futile.

Her eyes were red, as from crying, but also dull from overwhelming emotions that had turned into numbness. She looked from her hands up to his face.

"That's all you had to do?" she asked softly.

He didn't have to ask what she meant any more than she had to ask what he'd done. "Yes."

She drew her hands back and put them over her face. "I don't think I can do it."

He didn't want to make it harder, but he knew she would prefer the truth even if it was terrible: "You have to."

"It's not fair." The words could have sounded petulant, but they mostly just sounded resigned.

"It's perfectly fair," he replied gently. "We knew there would be consequences. We both accepted them to regain our life together."

She sat with her face in her hands for another minute, and he could feel her trying to balance two impossible lives, asking herself if the heavier one was worth its weight.

Finally she lifted her head. Her face held sadness, but also the beginnings of determination—she was Queen. She would do what had to be done to fulfill her role in their world. Death had never stopped her before and it wouldn't now. "Will you come with me? I don't want to be alone."

"Of course I will." He put his hands on her face and looked into her eyes, letting her see how much better he felt, how much better *she* would feel. They had work to do—work that might save far more lives than the two of them could end—and they couldn't do it if they starved themselves into rabid animals. If it got to that point she would no longer know herself, or him; she would lose everything that made her Miranda and become a twisted thing with only one goal: to kill, over and over, until someone put her down.

She closed her eyes, took a deep breath. "Okay."

He leaned in and kissed her, then reached over to hit the buzzer and ask Harlan to stop the car.

Searing pain—a hot iron this time. "Confess!"

He could hear the ragged ruin of his own voice, hoarse from screaming: "I'm not a demon. I never hurt anyone. I'm not a demon . . . please . . ."

As the long hours passed and he still maintained his innocence, they grew impatient. Those hours, and the days and days before of torment and blood, were nothing, nothing, compared to the day they began crushing his hands . . . one finger at a time, then the palm . . . that was what would cause the systemic infection that only becoming a vampire could save him from. It was a kind of pain that would never leave him; seven hundred years later he would still wake screaming from phantom agony in both hands, and they would ache for hours afterward.

"Confess!"

The horrible, dull crunch of bones slowly breaking—

Deven fought his way out of sleep with a cry of terror, striking out with all his strength . . . but the assailants were invisible, made only of memory.

He'd been having nightmares about the past for seven centuries, but over the years they'd become more vague, events blurring into each other as the memories became less distinct. Having the Elf mucking about in his psyche had triggered something, though, and brought those memories roaring back. Usually having Jonathan next to him helped immeasurably; the Consort's presence soothed him, gave him distance.

Tonight Jonathan wasn't in bed. That was a bit odd; Jonathan had been very diligent about staying with him as much as possible while he slept after the healing sessions. There must have been some sort of disturbance that called him away.

Sunset had passed an hour ago, leaving the air in the Haven soft and faintly ocean-scented as the wind blew in from the coast. The metal shutters covering all the windows stood open, bathing the bedroom in a gentle blue light. Gradually, the cool air and peaceful silence carried away the nightmare.

Finally, he climbed out of bed and found clothes. Most likely Jonathan had been roused by one of the Elite; he had been running himself ragged managing the territory while Deven slept off repeated Elf hangovers. Luckily Jonathan was an excellent organizer, leader, and strategist. Really, when it came down to the night-to-night work of the Signets, Deven was a bit on the useless side; he had always preferred . . . to . . .

He paused, frowning, shirt halfway on.

Something was different. Something . . .

He held up his hands, rubbing them together—they felt different. They were stiff from clenching them hard in his sleep, and they felt . . . they *felt*.

The fugue state he'd been walking around in had given way to sudden clarity: After weeks of feeling like he was shrouded in fog, growing more and more physically numb and bowing beneath the weight of his history, it felt like the moon had come out and pierced the gloom, throwing everything into sharp relief.

Heart pounding, he reached out along the bond to find Jonathan, but as he'd suspected the Consort was in town. He must have left right at sunset to have arrived in the city already; whatever was up, it was important. Deven grabbed his phone and sent Jonathan a message: *Call me when you can.*

For the first time in two weeks the Prime emerged from the suite looking like himself—blades, coat, piercings, and all. He even yanked out a hair to check the dye job and deemed it fit for another week. With Ghostlight returned to her usual place on his hip, he strode down the hall, smiling.

The guards he passed looked genuinely relieved to see him; there was no telling what the rumor mill had been generating to explain why their leader had become a shut-in while the Pair entertained a pointy-eared weirdo.

Curious as to whether there was an energetic connection between himself and Nico, he expanded his awareness to try to find him. Sure enough, the Elf's presence glowed softly in his mind—not in the rooms they'd given him, but nearby.

He found Nico in a long hallway, staring at the wide array of weaponry on display there. The Elf's expression was one of apprehension and sadness, but when he sensed Deven approaching, he looked up and smiled.

The world spun off its axis for a moment under the beauty of that smile, but he shrugged off the reaction impatiently.

The Elf was dressed in a more Tolkien-esque robe and cloak this time, the cloak a deep blue with silver embroidery around the edge and a carved silver crescent moon clasp. The Elf's hair, unbound, fell all the way to his waist, shining like silk. He was wildly out of place before a wall covered in weapons. The outfit would have looked much better in an old-growth forest, or a castle of carved marble . . .

. . . *or on my bedroom floor.*

Damn it.

"Good evening, my Lord," Nico said, bowing. "You seem to be feeling better."

"I am," he replied, returning the smile. "I feel like myself again."

Nico's gaze swept from Deven's head down to his feet, then back up; the way his eyes lingered was just a little longer than a cursory examination called for. Was that appreciation in his gaze, or just analysis? The Elf was maddeningly difficult to read.

"You must be cautious," Nico advised him. "I know you feel well, but you are still fragile—try not to exert yourself too much either physically or psychically until after I have finished my work. I would hate to see you fall back into that darkness again."

"So would I." Deven gestured at the wall and said, "I wouldn't have expected to see you in here."

"I have wandered around most of the buildings and the grounds in the two weeks I have been here—trying not to frighten anyone," he added a bit wryly. "I saw these . . . implements . . . and wanted a closer look, although . . ."

"Jonathan calls this the Gallery of Pointy Things," Deven said. "The previous Prime hung all these disgusting old animal heads on the walls—no one would walk down here in the dark because of all the beady glass eyes staring at them."

Nico approached a pair of Damascus steel swords that Deven had picked up in India and lifted a hand as if to touch one, but then thought better of it. "You are . . . very creative when you wish to deal death."

Deven almost laughed at the disturbed expression on his face, but said only, "I take it you don't have warriors where you come from."

"No. Elves are a pacifist people; we live our lives so as to cause the least harm possible. We seek out peace and cooperation, not destruction." He lowered his gaze to the sword Deven wore.

Dev drew the blade and held her out in both hands for him to look at; Nico actually touched the hilt, lightly, then ran his fingers along the sword's spine, and that touch made Deven feel like his own spine was melting. *What the hell is wrong with me?*

"This carving is lovely," Nico said. "Gaelic, is it not?"

"Yes. It's her name: Ghostlight."

Their eyes met, the Elf's gaze penetrating. "It suits you."

Unsure whether that was a compliment, Deven resheathed the sword.

Nico looked at Deven, eyes troubled. "How do you do it?"

"Do what?"

"Reconcile who you are with what you do."

"I don't," he replied. "I think of my healing ability as just another attribute, not a sign that I'm part of anything bigger."

Nico lowered his voice to where the nearest guards wouldn't overhear. "And the Red Shadow? How do you reconcile contract killing with being a healer?"

"How did you—"

"I have spent three nights inside your mind, my Lord," Nico said. "I know a lot more about you than you probably want me to."

Deven turned away, uncomfortable under his scrutiny. "I was born with this blood, and I suffered for it. Your people fled the human world; I was left here alone to fend for myself, and I chose to become powerful enough that no one else could hurt me. Once you've lived the life I have, in the world I've had to live in, then you can judge my decisions."

"I meant no offense," the Elf said, taken aback by the coldness in his words. "I only want to understand. This world is . . . I was unprepared for what I would see here."

"It's easy to see nothing but ugliness." Deven took hold of the Elf's arm and drew him along by the wrist, down the hall to one of the back doors of the Haven. "Let me show you something."

The Haven was situated to the west of Sacramento proper, and its primary residence was designed to mimic a Mediterranean villa; it had courtyards and fountains that flooded in moonlight, all of which closed up tight at dawn. His favorite feature, however, was a wraparound terrace that stretched along the entire back length of the building, allowing access from any adjacent room. The terrace looked out over a wildlife refuge where the trees seemed to go on forever.

He led the Elf out onto the balcony, up to the wall that surrounded it where the view was finest.

Nico smiled, eyes sweeping out over the valley. He closed his eyes and took a deep breath. Deven had done the same thing many times over the years; something about looking out over the forest and breathing its air felt like sustenance, assuaging a different hunger than did blood.

They stood there for a while in companionable silence, Deven leaning on his elbows on the wall, Nico with his arms crossed. Overhead the sky was ablaze with stars in the black bowl of the night; distantly he could hear the city, but facing west, all was peaceful, the noise blending into the night symphony of crickets, frogs, and wind through leaf-laden trees.

"This is beautiful," Nico said.

Dev nodded. "One day I'll have to take you to the giant redwoods. You'd love it there—it's like a living cathedral. Sometimes I sneak off for a night and go listen to them talk."

Nico gave him a slightly surprised, speculative look. "You can hear them?"

"Well . . . I . . ." Deven cursed himself mentally for saying anything. There were parts of him he never revealed to anyone, not even Jonathan—and yet in the course of a ten-minute conversation with Nico he'd already let something slip that no one on this earth had ever known about him. "Never mind."

Sensing his discomfort, Nico turned his gaze back to the view and let the matter drop.

It occurred to Deven that this was the first time he'd really been alone with the Elf, at least when he was coherent. The thought actually made his stomach twist around itself with uncharacteristic nervousness. Meanwhile, the part of his mind that was able to think rationally was flabbergasted that of all the attractive males he'd ever met, less than half a dozen had ever affected him at all, and no one had ever turned him into a gibbering idiot like this.

It was ridiculous. He was Prime, not some hormonal teenager. *Pull yourself together, for fuck's sake.*

"I did not mean to judge you, earlier," Nico told him quietly. "I have often wondered . . . how differently would things have turned out if my people had fought back instead of hiding? The thought of killing another creature sickens me, but when something precious is threatened, how is it more righteous to run away rather than to stand your ground?"

"I must say I didn't expect to hear that from you."

Another smile, this time smaller, touched with some regret, from what source Deven couldn't imagine. "I am known for saying unpopular things."

Their eyes met again. *God, those eyes . . .* They had their own gravitational pull, and his heart was spinning in orbit around them.

"We're not . . . related, or anything, are we?" Deven asked suddenly around the tightness in his chest.

As if he were expecting any question but that one, the Elf laughed. "No, we are not. As I understand it, you have the blood from your grandmother, who was of a different family line than ours."

"Right. I never met her. My parents didn't exactly invite her round for Christmas dinner." A thought arose that had never before occurred to him, and he asked, "Is she still alive?"

"She is indeed."

"Where?"

"In Avilon, one of only three Elven sanctuaries that survived the Burning Times. We sealed the Veil—the barrier that shields Avilon from the mortal world—not long after you were born, so she assumed you died at the hands of the Inquisition like so many of our part-human kin."

A flash of the nightmare he'd woken from earlier appeared in Deven's mind, and a violent tremor ran through him, the memory of that time crystal clear and horrifically close for a moment. The intrusion was so harsh and unexpected that it left him feeling weak—as the Elf had warned, he wasn't completely recovered, and before he could brace himself against the wall, his knees gave out.

He fully expected to crack his skull on the tile floor, but Nico acted with near-vampire quickness and caught him, gently lifting him back up with an ease that surprised the hell out of the Prime. Nico's willowy body held far more strength than he would have believed, and while he inwardly cursed himself for displaying such vulnerability, he sagged against the Elf for a moment, trying to ground . . . all the while noticing how solid Nico was, how warm . . . and how everywhere they were touching felt like it was electrically charged.

Deven rubbed his hands together against the phantom pain—for a moment he could feel it again, the radial breaks from the center of his palms, the unbearable pressure just before the bones splintered. That stench he had tried so hard to forget . . . human filth, blood, putrefaction, burning flesh . . . pushed cruelly into his mind.

Nico took his hands lightly, drawing them apart to stop the compulsive motion. "Breathe, my Lord . . . you are no longer in that place, or that time. This is your home and you are safe."

Deven felt Nico reach into himself and offer a light current of energy, which the Prime took gratefully. The weakness faded, the world righted itself, and he laid his head on Nico's shoulder. For just a moment they stood there, holding on to each other.

Deven thought back to the last time something like this had happened, but this time he had no painful history with the person holding him. That night had caused so much suffering that it was hard to think back on it with anything but shame . . . but the memory of that stolen moment in David's arms still brought a stab of longing for what had once been beautiful . . . out of reach now, forever, which was absolutely a good thing for everyone concerned.

Before Deven could speak, the Elf drew back and led him over to one of the seating areas on the balcony, gingerly helping him sit down on a chaise longue and lean back into the cushions. The loss of contact was almost physically painful.

Nico moved back to stand at the wall again, putting a few feet of distance between them.

"I did die at the hands of the Inquisition," Deven said after a while. "I was dying on the floor of my cell, rotting from the inside out from infection, when a woman came to the prison and bought my freedom. She knew I wasn't going to survive, so she brought me across—but doing that to someone already so weak should have killed me outright. She couldn't even keep me unconscious for the transformation because I would never have awoken. I don't know how I lived through that night, but I did."

As he thought of Eladra and his years with the Order of Elysium, dizziness washed over him again with the onslaught of guilt, and he fought as hard as he could to push it away where it couldn't destroy the tenuous balance the Elf had given him.

There was sorrow in Nico's face as he said, just loudly enough to carry, "You have a strong heart."

"Either that or I was too afraid of hell to die." He didn't really intend the words to come out as bitterly as they did, but the thought of Eladra brought the reasons for his mental breakdown back to the forefront of his mind, and it was hard, after all of that, not to get caught up in the emotions that went with it. He looked away from the Elf and shut his eyes a moment.

He didn't hear footsteps, but Nico crossed the balcony and sat down beside him, and Deven felt the pressure of a hand on his forehead.

The pain vanished.

"Whatever the reason you survived," Nico said, "I am grateful you did."

The undeserved compassion, even affection, in the Elf's voice was almost too much, but he managed to keep himself centered and said, "I should keep you around so you can zap me every time I get upset about something."

A smile. "I would not normally intervene—difficult emotions have their place—but I am concerned that in the state you are in, dwelling too much in the past will shatter the energy matrix and we will be back at the beginning. I know how difficult the process has been for you and wouldn't put you through that again unless I had to."

"We need to change the subject, then."

"I think it would be wise."

"All right . . . tell me more about your home, Avilon . . . where is it?"

"Between," Nico said. "It once existed here on earth, but when we were threatened with extinction, the Elders drew the Veil around it, essentially removing it from ordinary space and time. To leave it, or to return, one must cross through the Veil, an act requiring tremendous power now that the old portals are gone."

"Did you know why I was calling?" he asked.

"Not at first. The Speaking Stone was in the Temple, locked away in a back room; no one had laid eyes upon it in decades. But the Acolytes were helping to move some old archives and artifacts from one room to another, and they found the stone, glowing red and pulsating. No one in the Temple knew what to do with it, so they brought it to me."

"It just happened to be found when I was calling you? That's one hell of a coincidence."

Nico looked at him, amused. "Do you honestly believe in coincidence, my Lord?"

He had no answer for that. "Then what happened?"

"As soon as I touched the stone I could see you, and as shocked as I was to find out you existed—probably the only creature left on earth with enough of our blood to have our eyes—I knew immediately what was wrong, and I knew I had to help."

Deven stared at him, unbelieving. "You were willing to leave your home and come to this world you knew nothing about, all alone . . . and then stay here for weeks to fix a broken-down vampire whose entire life has been devoted to death . . . just because I'm one quarter Elf?"

"Not just because of that," Nico answered.

"Then . . . why?"

The Elf lifted a hand and brushed his fingers across Deven's lips. There was a touch of humor in his eyes, but his voice was full of a sudden vulnerability that made Deven shake inside. "Is it not obvious?" he asked softly.

They stared at each other, so close together he could hear the Elf's heart racing, and Deven almost, almost let himself sink into what he knew could very easily happen . . . but he shook his head, turning away from Nico, away from those damned eyes.

He felt it clearly: The Elf was hurt. "I am sorry," Nico said.

"I can't," Deven told him, trying to keep the words gentle. "It isn't you, it's . . . all the memories you've stirred up seem to have one common denominator: I hurt people. I've done nothing but cause Jonathan pain for sixty years. He'll say he doesn't mind—and the truth is he probably doesn't . . . but I mind. I have so many deaths and so much suffering on my conscience already."

With a deep breath, Nico rose and stood silently until Deven looked up at him.

The Elf was smiling regretfully. "Well done," he said.

"Well done?"

"I thought, after spending so much time in your mind, that you could not surprise me." Nico reached down and touched Deven's face, fingers slipping around to his lips before he withdrew the hand, stepped back, and bowed. "If you have no more need of me, my Lord, I shall retire."

Deven nodded, not entirely trusting himself to speak, but before he had much time to consider any possible fallout of the last few minutes, he heard a familiar footfall approaching, and Jonathan called, "What happened?"

Dev had no idea what to say. The Consort joined him, his face concerned; his hazel eyes fell on the still-open door from the terrace into the guest suite, and Deven felt himself flushing with undeserved shame.

"You weren't answering your phone," Jonathan said a bit sternly. "I was starting to freak out a little."

Deven groped in his pockets and sighed. "I must have left it in the bedroom—I'm sorry, love."

Jonathan leaned forward and kissed his forehead, and thankfully he didn't push the issue. "Well, aside from that . . . you look like you're feeling better. You look like you again."

Deven nodded. "That's why I texted, to tell you how well the magic was working. What were you doing in town, anyway?"

Jonathan frowned. "There was a . . . weird disturbance. Normally it would have been strictly an Elite matter, but they thought it was far enough from the ordinary that they called for one of us to evaluate the situation."

"What situation?"

"Just after sunset two vampires, a couple, were walking down McMillan Boulevard and were attacked. One was killed; the other managed to escape and run for it until she found a patrol. The attackers followed her and went after the Elite as well. There was a pretty bloody battle, but we were lucky—none of ours was killed, though there were some significant injuries. Two of the attackers went down, but the rest got away."

"So . . . was it a gang we know, or something new?"

"Oh, it was new, all right." Jonathan looked like he could scarcely believe his own words, and after the next sentence it was clear why: "The attackers were human."

Dev gave him a quizzical look. "Humans that could keep up with a vampire on the run and then take on an Elite patrol and live to tell the tale? How does that happen?"

"The Elite who fought them said they were way stronger and faster than humans are supposed to be—as fast as vampires."

"That's impossible."

"It gets worse."

"Of course it does."

"The Elite patrol leader found these on the bodies." Jonathan reached inside his jacket and took out a plastic baggie, handing it to Deven.

He stared down at the bag for a long minute before he said, "Get David on the phone."

Miranda didn't remember the first human she had killed as a vampire. She'd been in the grip of her transformation to Thirdborn and the whole day was a blur. She knew it was a woman who had killed her own baby, and afterward the Queen had given the woman's husband an anonymous donation to help him move on. She knew that gift for what it was: blood money. She didn't know how else to atone.

It was, as David had said, depressingly easy to find another one like her.

Once upon a time the combined misery and evil of the human world had assaulted Miranda's mind as men had assaulted her body, and since then she had stayed away from minds like theirs, feeding only on perfectly average women, those who were healthy and wouldn't suffer for it.

She no longer had that privilege.

"Slowly, beloved," David murmured in her ear. "Don't make yourself sick."

Her Prime's hand pressed against her back, reassuringly strong, as she pressed against the body she had pinned to the wall. Blood flowed freely from the four perfectly round holes she had punched in the woman's throat, and this part, at least, was familiar. Prime and Queen both kept a hard hold over the human's mind, stilling her struggles. She might feel some pain, but essentially her mind was already asleep and would not awaken. It was a kindness the human didn't deserve; she had scammed dozens of elderly people out of their savings, leaving them penniless and often homeless.

Miranda paused and looked over at her husband, who was watching her, his eyes still black, desire there that should have disgusted or at least frightened her. The first time she'd seen his eyes change she had been afraid, but now . . . the intense emotion and power that brought about the blackness affected her in a very different way than it had before. She gestured for him to come to her, to wrap his arm around her waist and hold her, whispering encouragement into her ear. Being so close to him set her skin on fire, made her want him so badly . . . but more important, his added power helped her keep the human from fighting without losing her own focus. She didn't want to make anyone suffer.

This was it: the point of no return. Her heartbeat fell into sync with the human's, signaling that if she didn't want to cause permanent damage, she had to stop.

She didn't stop. She couldn't. It was too late to go back to what she had been before. She had accepted all of this, knowingly or not, the minute she lay down with David and bared her throat to his teeth.

She had read that when people died, as in hospital rooms, it was a quiet, gentle thing, a sigh out, eyes drifting shut, machines flatlining the only loud sounds in the room.

To her kind, it was a little different.

The woman's death erupted from her as if her soul were exploding out of her body in its desperation to win free of her life. Perhaps her soul went somewhere and perhaps it didn't, but her death, that last burst of energy, rushed out through her veins and into the Queen's mouth—it filled her body, her mind, with the deep, hell-dark energy of the woman's last moment. Miranda drank it in, shut her eyes, and standing there with blood still trickling from her mouth, the Queen was at last renewed.

She gripped the woman's shoulders and kept her where she was until the last drop of blood had hit Miranda's tongue, and with a hard swallow, she finally let the human drop to the concrete in a lifeless heap.

She was crying, but she had no idea whether it was from sorrow or joy; relief, sweet and hot and black shot through with red, surged through her, her cells washed in that darkness, carrying healing and an almost sexual enjoyment through her body. Her vision sharpened again, sounds became clearer.

Her shields were restored to their normal strength. She hadn't even realized they were wobbling until that moment. No wonder she had felt so horrible, if her empathy had been creeping up on her against her knowledge or will.

She had let it go too long. Another night and her shields might have collapsed, her sanity falling with them—and this time it might not come back.

She stared at the body for a minute. *I hope the money was worth it. Better luck next time.*

Breathing deeply, she looked over at her husband, who gave the corpse a faintly disgusted look and waved his hand over it dismissively to banish it.

He saw her watching and inclined his head toward the nearby Dumpster. "We're going to have to think of a better place to put them," he said. "One or two will probably pass unnoticed, but two every month increases the odds of someone seeing a body in the trash."

He spoke so casually, as if it were any of his myriad logistical operations and just another problem to solve.

Miranda pulled her sweaty hair back from her face and held it with her hands for a minute. "This is our life now," she said quietly.

He came to her, held her close. "We'll make this work," he said. "I think . . . I think it will come again every new moon."

"How do you know that?"

"I can feel it," he replied with a sigh. "And I don't think we should wait until we're losing our minds next time—we pushed it too far. Technically the new moon was yesterday afternoon; if we'd given in last night we could have avoided this misery. We don't have to get to that point, if we just . . ."

"Kill people," she finished for him. "Every month for the rest of our lives."

He didn't try to justify it, or make it less awful, which she appreciated, even though she knew he was far more okay with it than she was. Three hundred fifty years did offer a certain perspective that she, still young enough to be alive by human reckoning, still lacked.

She knew there had been a time when he'd taken human life as wantonly as many vampires did. Most of them realized over time that it was unnecessary and would lead to discovery and death at the hands of Hunters, but a few kept going until they were taken down either by the Hunters themselves or the Signets. In "civilized" vampire society, killing humans was looked at as a silly phase the young went through that wasn't sustainable for the Shadow World as a whole. Most of the Signets who had no-kill laws did so not because of a love for humanity but because they didn't want Hunters infesting their territories.

"I guess it's a good thing we're above our own law," she said tiredly. She didn't feel guilty . . . at least not yet. She was in a strange emotional place that was sort of like shock, except not numb—*detached*, more like. She felt detached from what she had done. Was that how it was supposed to work? Did becoming a killer mean she would no longer care? Was she condemned to devolve into a sociopath?

David seemed to sense her confusion and paused, kissing her forehead and telling her, "We both know you're never going to become a mindless killer, Miranda. You're not capable of not caring. That detachment you're feeling may keep you sane until you can make peace with this."

She stopped and stared at him. "I got off on it, David. Where am I supposed to find peace in that?"

He didn't have an answer for her.

They started walking again, and he let out a breath and returned to the previous subject. "I can talk to Maguire about finding prisoners—Texas does love its capital punishment, and death row is always a busy place."

They had, at last, reached the car, and he waved Harlan away so the driver wouldn't have to come around the limo—a much bigger pain than circling the Lincoln—and opened the door himself, settling Miranda into the seat as if she were an invalid. She didn't complain; it felt good to be fussed over, to be treated like a treasure instead of . . .

She closed her eyes. *Don't think about it yet. Let it be until you've rested. Just let it be.*

Miranda curled up against her Prime and let the rhythmic motion of the car lull her into the first peaceful sleep she'd had in days.

PLEASE COME. HE'S ASKING FOR YOU.

The words on the screen wavered in front of her eyes. The longer she stared at them, the less sense they made. English seemed to have a short life cycle in print—after a few minutes the words broke apart in the mind until they were unrecognizable and lost all meaning. If she stared at a word too long, she started doubting the spelling. "Please" . . . what did that even mean?

Her hands were shaking on the keys. She couldn't keep her fingers there any longer.

Her eyes fell on the sterile package on the other end of the table and the vial of clear liquid sitting beside it, unassuming, innocuous. From this distance it could have been anything. Whatever was in the vial could be something as harmless as vitamin B12, or it could be the difference between life and death for its recipient.

In her case that was only metaphorically true.

As always, the shame crawled its way up her spine and clamped its jaws around her throat. The litany began: *How could you? How could you? He's an old man. An old dying man. How could you?*

He doesn't know the difference, her other internal voice, the one she imagined as a petulant child in a dirty pinafore, wailed. *I need it and he doesn't! There's no way anyone could find out. What difference does it make?*

You'll lose your license.

Oh, who the fuck cares?

She had to smile at that. The little girl in her mind loved to curse. She'd started cursing, in fact, after George told her about his secretary—such a cliché. He moved out, and the little imaginary girl stamped her foot and threw things.

Six months later, alone in the house she'd grown up in with an old man she barely recognized as her father drooling and raving in a hospital bed in the room that had once been her mother's art studio, Mari knew something had to give.

It wouldn't be long—a month, at most—before the old man shuffled off his goddamn mortal coil and finally got out of her life. She couldn't hide here much longer. There would be estate sales, paperwork . . . what she really wanted was to take a gas can to the property and burn it down with his corpse inside. No fuss, no muss. A modern Viking funeral. It should be so simple. As it was, the indignity of death wasn't enough for Americans—no, after you died all the possessions you had worked your whole life to collect were sold off, stored, dumped in the trash, anything to get them out of the way of the living who would move into your house and erase your existence.

One of these days she would die, too, and Jenny would be forced to observe the ritual of sorting, culling, trashing. Mari had left the seven-year-old with George for a couple of weeks, since she was out of school and Mari didn't want to force her to deal with a mean old man who pissed himself and looked like a haunted-house ghoul. Jenny sounded happy on the phone—absentee father figure guilt equaled lavish attention and a lot of fun trips. That was fine, for now. Mari hated a lot of things about George but knew he'd take good care of their daughter.

She realized she had been staring at the vial for several minutes and wrenched her eyes away, but they landed somewhere else she didn't want them to: the copy of *Rolling Stone* that had been lying there since she had returned to Rio Verde to pose as a one-woman hospice crew. She had most of the magazine's glossy insides memorized, but nothing so well as the cover.

A woman with ridiculously gorgeous red curly hair falling all around her shoulders stared with intense leaf-green eyes at the camera like some modern-day Medusa daring people to meet her gaze. She wore black, tight leather that showed off the milk-and-honey of her complexion, including thigh-high boots and a corset top providing a perfect laced-up frame for her breasts. She wasn't posing provocatively; she was just standing there, one arm resting on the side of the black acoustic guitar that hung around her shoulder. And right there between and above said breasts was that weird necklace she never seemed to take off, the huge ruby on a heavy antique silver setting.

She was smiling with a hint of mischief and a lot of humor. Mari didn't remember her smiling at all when they were young.

The headline beside her read: *Miranda Grey Bares Her Teeth: The* Rolling Stone *Interview.*

She couldn't take it anymore. She lurched up out of her chair, nearly knocking over her laptop, and seized the package and vial, dropping back down into the chair with the items clutched to her chest.

It wasn't any different from vaccinating a toddler. She tried to think of it that way. She was giving that imaginary little girl in her head a vaccine against reality.

The ritual was calming: roll up her sleeve, run her fingers over the skin to find just the right spot. Her veins were in abominable shape after six months of this, but at least there was no one around to notice, and when she left the house she wore long sleeves even in the Texas heat.

Open up the syringe packet. Watch the clear liquid fill the syringe, then flick the air bubbles out. It was the same kind of magic that warded off chicken pox and polio.

The old man was on about twenty different drugs, a great many intravenous, and given his condition there was no reason for the hospital to bat an eye at a little extra morphine here and there. At this point if he wanted to spend his remaining days in an opiate coma, who were they to say no?

Nobody was watching anyway. This was Rio Verde—the people here had known her since she was born. They whispered about her mother, but they knew Mari and her father were normal people, stable people. They were a family of doctors and lawyers.

And Miranda.

Mari hadn't spent enough time in town since arriving here to really get a sense of how people felt about their local-girl-done-good. The local teenagers were probably fans, wearing holes in her CDs and dreaming of a day when they, too, could get the hell out of this town and make something of themselves.

Miranda looked too much like Marilyn for people's comfort. She always had. In the brief period between Marilyn being dragged off to Austin to the hospital she would later die in and their father moving them all up to Dallas for a fresh start, people had seemed wary of Miranda, reluctant to look her in the eye. There had been no love lost between Miranda and Rio Verde.

Or Miranda and Marianne.

The plunger shot home, and within seconds her racing thoughts began to slow down. It felt as if someone had cracked an egg on her head and a sweet burning trickled down over her body, sending her fear back under its rock and her shame a mile away.

She was glad she'd finished writing the e-mail already. Typing right now would be hilarious.

Would it work? Would curiosity, if nothing else, draw the

prodigal daughter back to this dismal hole in the world? Did Miranda have anything to say to her dying father, or anything to say to her sister, who might as well already be dead?

Mari found herself hoping Miranda wouldn't reply. She nearly deleted the draft altogether. She could tell him she'd sent it. She could keep putting him off until it no longer mattered. He was barely lucid for five minutes at a time, and she had always been a skilled liar.

The doorbell rang; UPS was due to bring another shipment from either the mail-order pharmacy or the medical supply company. Marianne stood, her hand still on the keyboard, tempted . . . so tempted . . . to hit delete.

But seeing the vial next to the ripped-open package and used needle brought a touch of the shame back, and with a heavy sigh, she hit send.

She couldn't deny a last request . . . although whose it was, she wasn't sure.

The tarot cards were pissing Stella off.

She sat cross-legged in front of her altar, going through her usual ritual, asking the cards to help her decide what to do with herself: Go back to school? Get a new job? Stay at Revelry a little longer?

The problem was, after her adventures with the Signets, she was no longer content with the idea of hanging out doing nothing for the rest of her life. She wanted to do something important. She just had no idea what that might be.

The cards, however, were not interested in her little human problems. She tried to do the reading three times, laying the cards out in the Celtic Cross pattern most Witches favored, but every time, the cards gave her absolute crap, a jumble of random symbols that would take Cirque du Soleil–level acrobatics to connect to each other. None of the cards she pulled made any sense.

Finally, she threw her hands up in exasperation. "Fine!" she said to the empty air. "Forget my damn question. Just tell me what you think I need to know."

She shuffled and cut the deck again and didn't bother with

a layout this time. She pulled six cards and turned them over one by one.

The first card was the Queen of Swords. The red-haired woman in the picture stared out at her, a dare in her eyes, a blade in her hand.

"Oh, damn it. Damn it, not again." Stella glared at the museum replica statue of Persephone in the center of the altar. "You're hijacking my reading to tell me something about Miranda, aren't you. You know, that's really rude."

Second card: the Two of Swords, which usually had to do with someone whose heart was closed off, living in denial of something or blocking emotion. Its image was of a hooded male figure wearing a black cloak, holding two swords crossed in a way that was just as likely to slice off his own head as protect him from assault.

Something about the way the figure stood reminded her strongly of Prime Deven. She almost laughed at how appropriate the card was for him.

The center card . . . Stella frowned at it, not sure what to make of it: the Eight of Pentacles. Normally it symbolized dedicating oneself to knowledge, becoming involved in something that consumed you . . . but she felt, with a combination of certainty and dread, that the card's traditional meaning was irrelevant here. As with the Queen of Swords card, what mattered was the picture.

A spider sat patiently in the center of a web of glowing threads; around it, the web's intersections formed eight circles to suggest the Pentacles themselves. As soon as she saw the image, her Sight went temporarily haywire—suddenly her mind was spinning, knowledge flooding into her mind in a massive wave of light that coalesced into a handful of words:

He's here.

The Spider . . . he's here . . . it has begun.

When she'd had a chance to ground, she said to the statue, "Seriously? Didn't things *just change*? What else could possibly . . . you know, strike that last bit."

As if to answer her unfinished question, the fourth card was the Ten of Swords.

A man lay on the ground run through with ten swords. The

scene was desolate, bloody, and just looking at it made Stella's skin crawl. It was the card of grave misfortune . . . or sacrifice.

"Miranda's already sacrificed enough," Stella said, growing angry. "Can't she have just a little while where things don't fall to shit? No offense, Lady Persephone, but you're being kind of an asshole."

The fifth card wasn't all that comforting either: the Devil. Bondage, slavery, willful ignorance . . . giving up one's free will to an addiction, lust, or darkness. It wasn't always a purely negative card, but in this context it was hard for Stella to see it any other way.

At least the last card wasn't so dire: the Wheel of Fortune, the card of destiny. It was a vague ending to the reading, but at least it wasn't covered in blood or chained to a wall.

The question was, should she tell Miranda about the cards? Stella wasn't getting any real urgency from them—they might be a long-range warning. And what would she tell Miranda if she did call her? She hated to make the Queen worry about the future unless she knew without a doubt that she understood the meaning.

After sitting there staring at the cards for a while, Stella decided to hold off—she'd meditate on the reading for a day or two and see if she could get any clarity.

"So, what was the point of all that?" she asked. "A string of cards that make no sense together—that's why you stole my reading?" She paused, looking down at the center card, that crazy burst of intuition that had hit her when she turned it over. "Or . . . is there something I'm not getting?"

She wasn't expecting an answer, and she didn't get one, but for the rest of the night all she could think about was the Eight of Pentacles, and the thought kept repeating in her mind: *He's here . . . it has begun.*

Three

"It has begun."

The flat black stone gleamed in the pool of light cast just above it. In that circle of light, an image had formed, as if he were staring at his reflection in a still pond; but the face staring back, while similar to his own, definitely belonged to someone else.

"And you are sure it's him."

"Yes," Nico said. "I'm afraid so."

A world away—literally—the person in the mirror shook his head. *"That is not what I wanted to hear, brother."*

"Nor did I particularly want to say it." He smiled affectionately at Kai, who, despite being his twin, seemed both years younger and eons older at times. "I had hoped I was wrong . . . that Lesela's prophecy was in error . . . but I think I knew all along it was true."

"To hell with the prophecy," Kai said, his violet eyes— almost as unusually dark as Nico's own, and yet another reason they had been whispered about their entire lives—fierce and protective. *"Come home, Nico. These creatures are not worth your life."*

Nico looked away. "There is far more at stake here than my life. I will not condemn this world for my own sake."

"What has that world ever done for you, or any of us?" Kai demanded. *"The mortals tortured and burned our family and drove us from our homes—and the vampires fed their way through entire clans on the Inquisition's payroll. We owe them nothing."*

Nico told his brother firmly, "I shall return when I am done, and we will see what happens after that. Nothing is written in stone—and even stone erodes with time."

"What do you want me to tell Lesela?"

"Nothing yet. She already feels guilty enough that her prophecy sent me here. If she knew who else was involved she would blame herself even more."

Nico and Lesela had been lovers once, not too long ago, and were still close friends. The gift of Prophecy was as rare as the gift of Weaving and carried with it similar responsibility, so they shared the feeling of being different from their kin. Seven centuries ago Lesela had foreseen the attack that would drive the last Elves from the human world, but even she had not seen what she would leave behind . . . one of the last precious remnants of a time when Elves and humans had loved each other without fear . . . her grandchild. That loss still haunted her seven hundred years later, but as Nico had said, Lesela had believed that child long dead.

Would she really want to know that she was wrong?

"You could have done your work in one night and come home two weeks ago," Kai pointed out. *"Why do you linger?"*

"I don't know vampire energetic anatomy well enough to work that quickly."

Kai snorted softly. *"I rather doubt this boy's energy is the anatomy you're staying around for."*

The Weaver couldn't help but laugh at that. That was Kai: powerful, beautiful, and frequently infuriating, often mercilessly blunt. Despite the rumors that had dogged them since birth, Kai had never wanted for admirers or lovers of whatever number or gender he was in the mood for. Most Bards had a similar allure, but Kai's talent and beauty seemed to double the usual allotment. The closest earth term Nico had encountered to describe his twin would be "rock star."

Nico had been quite content to dwell in his brother's shadow. Kai was remarkable looking for an Elf—black hair, dark eyes, an intensity surrounding him that drew others to him irresistibly. Despite how the vampires here stared at him, Nico was perfectly average among his people, except for his abilities as a Weaver, which had far outstripped those of his most advanced teachers before he had even come of age.

He had told Jonathan he was one of the strongest Weavers, but that was not the full truth. He was in fact the most powerful Weaver in all of Avilon, perhaps anywhere. He would have been perfectly happy to spend his life without anyone ever knowing that.

It seemed the Goddess had other ideas.

Kai sighed, bringing him back to the present moment. *"So tell me, is he at least worth all of this wailing and gnashing of teeth? You have not said much about him."*

It took Nico a moment to find words. "I think . . . once you dig down past the self-loathing and fear, the soul within is lovely . . . almost blinding in its light. And I expect the others to be the same—there is tremendous potential for good among them, and a nobility that still amazes me."

Now Kai rolled his eyes. *"I do not speak of glorious destinies here, Nico."*

"I know. But I do not know what to tell you otherwise."

"Of course you do. You are just afraid to admit it . . . for now. But I will humor you, as I know how much stress you are under with all of this."

Hoping to change the subject, Nico asked, "How is Mother? I assume she knows where I am by now."

"Angry as a hive of bees in a hailstorm. She will have several handfuls of choice words for you when you get back."

"And the rest of the Enclave?"

"Not much better. There was talk of sending someone to collect you, but it turns out you're the only Weaver strong enough to build a portal, so basically you can come and go as you like and they can do nothing about it except annoy me." Kai grinned.

He'd been afraid of that. The ruling council of Avilon was mostly made up of older Elves who had survived the Burning Times—most of them scarred on the inside and many on the outside from the horrors they had endured and the loss they had suffered. To them, earth was a cesspool and humanity a cancer, and the Elves had no business ever returning. He didn't disagree, exactly, but he knew there were things worth protecting here.

Unbidden, the memory of that moment on the balcony flooded his mind, and he gripped the edge of the table hard, trying not to get lost in it.

As usual his brother intuited what he was feeling even across an entire dimension. *"Prophecy or no prophecy, you cannot help what soil your heart plants itself in,"* Kai said, his voice losing its edge. *"You have a choice what to do, but not how to feel. Don't be so hard on yourself."*

"Easy for you to say," Nico replied with a weak smile. "You don't have the fate of three races pivoting around whom you sleep with."

A smile and a sigh. Nico knew that Kai hated feeling helpless; from their childhood it had always been he who took care of Nico, who got them into trouble and then took the blame himself, who gave his smaller, gentler brother first pick of the cookies he filched from the House of Bakers. *"Go to bed, Nicolanai. You look weary and I know holding this connection isn't helping. Get some rest."*

"I shall. Blessings, brother . . . and try not to worry. I'll be home soon."

"You had better be."

As the light disappeared and the stone became just a stone again, Nico shut his eyes tightly against the longing—he wanted to go home. This place was wrong, and he was wrong in it; he missed the serenity, the simplicity, of life in Avilon. Even this far from the city he could smell what he knew to be engine exhaust and pollution. He was surrounded by the kind of creatures that had eaten many of his kin.

Suddenly restless, he rose and walked over to the door that opened onto the balcony.

Perhaps this place still had that industrial smell, and perhaps it was not the forest of his birth, but it was a forest nonetheless, and he greeted it silently with a sigh, feeling some of the tension release. He leaned on the wall, just breathing it in. The forest here responded to him sleepily, but it had a long memory, and once, his people had walked here. The land always remembered.

Again, he thought of the last time he'd been out here . . . of catching Deven when he collapsed, feeling that slender body against his for just a moment. The fire that had raced up between them had sent his senses reeling, had driven him to say, in a roundabout way, what he was aching for . . . they had been inches apart when Deven pushed him away . . . and it astonished Nico how much that rejection hurt.

That was the moment he knew without doubt that Lesela's vision had been true. He had tried so hard to deny it—to think that he was simply here to help and then go back to his life— and even though he had felt the attraction the second he had laid eyes upon Deven outside the church, he had pushed it away, hoping . . . praying . . . that it would fade . . . that he would go home, and never have to return here to face what Lesela had said he would face.

In a scant two weeks, in spite of every dark and violent thing he had learned about the Prime and the dozen layers of pain and guilt Deven wore like a shroud, in spite of everything that should drive the Weaver away from such a creature, in spite of what was to come, Nico had fallen in love with him, and in losing his heart, changed the fortunes of everyone . . . *everyone*.

He was still leaning on the wall with his head in his hands when he realized he wasn't alone.

Starting, he turned toward the flicker of movement in his peripheral vision. "Good evening, my Lord," he said, bowing.

The Consort smiled. "Good evening."

He was a handsome but imposing man—though Elves were stronger than they looked, Jonathan could easily have snapped Nico in half like a twig—but gifted with surprising good humor considering the life he led. Nico could sense that he, too, had a touch of the blood, but it was very far back, and searching out his actual family line would be intrusive to say the least. It was barely more than a trace; at most he would have stronger-than-usual psychic abilities.

"If I am disturbing you," Nico began, but Jonathan waved his hand.

"No, no, I just needed some air."

They pondered the view in silence for a while, but eventually Nico could feel the Consort's eyes on him. He waited.

"If you're waiting for my permission, you have it," Jonathan said. "He and I have an understanding—we always have. He's just never acted on it."

"And why should he now?" Nico asked.

Warmhearted as he was, the Consort could still be menacing when he wanted to, and he towered over Nico by several inches. "Are we really going to play this game?"

"I do not—"

"You and I both know it wasn't just some glowing rock that brought you here. Whatever prophetic impulse you're acting on, pay me the respect of owning up to it."

Nico sighed. He turned toward the view again, fear evaporating and weariness taking its place. "My people by and large fear and hate this world," he said. "We have hidden for so long that many of us have forgotten what we were made for. A Prophet's word did send me here. And though I want to be of service to this world as I have been called to do, I was not ready for . . ."

Jonathan chuckled softly. "You weren't ready for Deven."

"Not at all."

"You came here thinking it would be straightforward work, only to find yourself crushing a bit on your patient."

Nico shook his head, smiling at the absurdity of the conversation. " 'Crush' is not exactly the word for it," he said. "More like 'pulverize.' "

The Consort nodded sympathetically. "I've been there. It was the quintessential thunderbolt, love at first sight. At that very moment, if you'll pardon my language, I knew I was well and truly fucked."

He met the Consort's gaze. "Are you unhappy?"

Jonathan chuckled. "I suppose from the outside our relationship doesn't make a lot of sense. I certainly wouldn't have guessed, before I came to California, that I would end up bound to a spiky little warrior with more demons than a Halloween party."

Nico frowned. "I do not understand the reference, my Lord."

"Not important. But I don't think 'happy' is the right word for this life. 'Content' might be better. Except . . ." Jonathan looked reluctant to say anything else but went on anyway. "There are so many things I wish I could change. So much I wish I could do for him. I envy you your power."

The Elf had to smile at that. "Say you saw someone you cared for about to drown in a river, and you had the ability to dam that river so he would live——but you also saw that if you did, the river would not feed the fields around it and hundreds of people would starve . . . or you saved him from drowning and the next day he knocked over a candle that burned down a house with ten other people in it . . . how would you choose what future to create?"

"Then how do you ever act at all? I'd be paralyzed with fear over the consequences."

"In this case the cost of not helping far outweighed the other potential outcomes . . . but still, being able to Weave is no guarantee of wisdom. The chessboard has no boundaries, and every move tips the fortunes of worlds."

"All right," Jonathan said, "I take it back. I don't envy you."

Nico lowered his eyes. Jonathan had no idea. "Nor do I envy you. I see a thousand possibilities before the fact, but you see a single reality after," he said after a moment. "It would be a heavy burden."

Now Jonathan was the one who looked away. "Over the years I've learned a lot of things I wish I could forget."

Nico shook his head and smiled a little, returning his gaze to the forest, taking solace from the soft rustling sound of the canopy of leaves. "So have I, my Lord," he said softly. "So have I."

David sat staring at his laptop screen, one hand absently scratching his lower lip while he considered what he was looking at.

"You're sure they were human."

Deven sounded a good ten times more energetic than he had during their last conversation. "Yes. We had multiple reports from the scene and the blood we recovered was definitely human—I smelled it myself."

"Send me all the forensic details you have from the scene."

"Sending now."

David continued to stare at the image while the files down-loaded. He'd seen the same thing several times already, but this time, the implications were alarming.

Two earpieces, both alike in dignity: identical in design and construction to all the others associated with Morningstar. One of those first earpieces had been left in New York when the Order harassed Hart, whom Morningstar mistakenly thought had been recruited by Lydia and the Order of Elysium; another came from outside Stella Maguire's apartment when an agent of Morningstar ransacked it—searching, David believed, for Miranda's Signet, though how Morningstar had known to hunt down Stella was still a mystery. In both cases the person who lost the earpiece was definitely a vampire.

And now these two, taken from the bodies of two humans who fought like vampires and nearly took down some of the most fearsome Elite in the world.

"Do you think they're still hiring vampires, if they've got humans who can do this?" Deven asked.

"My guess would be no. There are few ordinary mortals—even trained Hunters—who can fight a vampire face-to-face, so they brought in what they hated most in the world until they found a way to come at us themselves. Most likely they killed any vampires they still had on the roster . . . but a better question is . . ."

"How the hell they did it," Deven finished for him. "The answer is pretty obvious, don't you think?"

"I'd wager the death of a Prime would be enough to create superhuman warriors."

"But how many?"

"It can't be a limitless supply. We need to know more about what we're dealing with here; there might have been other sightings of these people in other territories that nobody's talk-ing about."

"True. No vampire is going to want to admit he got his ass handed to him by a human."

Behind him, David heard Miranda enter the bedroom, remove her sword, hang it up, then sit down on the sofa to pull off her boots with a sigh. It was a little early for her to be back—dawn was three hours away. She was supposed to be in the middle of a training session with Bax.

Finally, they hung up, leaving David once again staring at the earpieces, not at all happy about where this might be leading.

Miranda came up behind him and put her hands on his shoulders, rubbing them as she peered down at the screen. "Those things again? Oh, goody."

He smiled, enjoying her talented hands. "Oh, it's much better this time." He related the incident in California to her, and their suspicions that Jeremy's death had been the catalyst for whatever magic had given Morningstar this lovely new thing to play with.

She digested the story for a moment, then said, "I'm not sure what's worse, the thought that they made hundreds of vampire hunters, or that they could only make a few."

"What do you mean?" he asked, turning his chair to look at her.

"Well, if Jeremy's death let them create, say, only twenty vampire hunters, what do you think they're going to do when we've killed all twenty?"

David blinked at her. "Damn. I didn't even think of that. This could go very badly very quickly." He shook his head. "On the other hand, the fear of being ritually murdered might convince the rest of the Council it's in their best interest to help us track these people down."

Miranda sat down in his lap, and he wound his arms around her gratefully. "What's wrong?" he asked after a moment. "You skipped your session with Bax, and you feel troubled."

She bit her lip, and he could sense a complex knot of uncertain emotions. "I got an e-mail . . ."

He gave her a questioning look. "Go on."

Miranda took a deep breath and just blurted it out. "It was from my sister," she said. "My father's dying. She says he only has a couple of weeks. He wants to see me."

The abrupt mental shift from Signet business was a bit jarring, but his emotional reaction to hearing anything about her family tended toward violence anyway. These people had abandoned her to her madness, just as they had her mother. Since then, Miranda had heard from them three times at most, always a cool and distant e-mail from Marianne, always wanting something.

"He can go fuck himself off a cliff," David said.

Miranda looked taken aback, for a second, by the vehemence of his words, then chuckled. "That's very sweet of you, baby."

"Did your sister have any further details, or was it just a summons?"

The Queen's eyes were on the wall across from the desk where their weapons hung. "It's some kind of cancer," Miranda told him. "He's holed up in Rio Verde, with her playing nursemaid."

"I thought they moved to Dallas to get away from your mother's memory," David said.

"They did. We lived in Rio Verde until I was nine, then moved to Austin, and after they put her away, Dad headed to Dallas. That's why I've always considered Austin my hometown even though I wasn't born here. But a couple of years ago he moved back to Rio Verde—to the same house." Miranda paused, then said, "She said please. She's never said that to me before."

David leaned forward and kissed the skin just above her Signet. "You're going, aren't you," he said.

"It's a last request," Miranda said. "How can I deny a last request? Plus . . . it's just one of those things I think I have to do. They're the only thing left that links me to my history. I don't want that history, but . . . I just have to see the house one more time, look them both in the face."

"All right. Rio Verde's five hours from here—we can get there and back in one night, but it'll be pushing it."

"I want to go alone," she told him. "I'm a big girl. I can handle it."

"Out of the question," David replied. Her eyebrows shot up, no doubt a precursor to her pointing out, quite rightly, that he wasn't the boss of her, but he added, more gently, "If you don't want me to go, I won't, but you must at least take a pair of guards. The thought of you being alone and something going wrong—"

"David, it's a town of eight thousand people. I'll be there for a few hours. What could go wrong?"

He frowned. "You do realize that by saying that you've already damned your luck."

"Yeah, probably. If it will really make you feel better, I'll take Minh and Stuart. I can go Friday—I don't have a show."

Their eyes met and held. "I know I can't protect you from getting hurt," he said. "I know it's not my job. But I can't help wanting to keep you safe, even from things I know you need to do. I would cheerfully dismember anyone who made you unhappy."

She grinned. "And I love you for it, which is kind of twisted."

He put his arms around her again and grinned back. "Remind yourself periodically over the next century or so that you said it, I didn't."

Amy's Ice Cream on Sixth was an odd touchstone in Miranda's life. Every time she sat down—always at the same table—she was a different person, living a different version of her life. What she ordered was never the same, but the place itself had barely changed in the time she had become a part of the Shadow World.

The first time had been her first date with David, though "date" was a bit of a misnomer. She was still human then, and though they had both felt the growing connection between them, she'd had no idea she would end up taking him to bed that very night.

She smiled to herself as she spooned up another bite of her ice cream. She'd been a cheap date—a sundae and a little Shakespeare was all it took.

That night was the beginning of the end of her humanity. Now, after death, war, infidelity, forgiveness, and still more death, she felt far more secure in her relationship with David than she ever had before, and certainly more secure than she would have expected three years ago. Despite all that had happened and all that still could, she had no regrets.

Yet now she had to step back in time and revisit the years before Austin, before she became what she considered the *real* Miranda. She would have said they wouldn't recognize her now in Rio Verde, but given her celebrity status, they probably would.

That didn't mean they'd see her, though. For her whole life, people had looked right through her. Marianne was the "good daughter," the medical professional, smiling out from a cheerful

Christmas card with her societally approved white-bread family all in matching reindeer sweaters.

Marianne had never been the kind of sister one confided in, or giggled with over boys as a teenager, but when they were children, they had known how to talk to each other. Adolescence followed by their mother's madness killed that sweet, young knowledge between them. Miranda wasn't really interested in rekindling a relationship, but still, she hoped that Marianne would remember that time of their lives when every day was a golden-hued summer and they had run through the sprinklers on chubby legs.

Behind her, she heard the creak and shudder of the ladies' room door being shoved open, and a moment later Stella slid back into her chair with a grin.

"You okay?" the Witch asked, her smile fading.

"Yeah," Miranda said. "It's been a weird week."

"No kidding. Where were we?"

"The Eight of Pentacles."

Now, Stella bit her lip as she dug through the tarot deck in her hands and came up with the card in question. Stella held it up: a spider in a web with eight circles of light in its threads.

"When I pulled this one I got this crazy surge of intuition, and all I could think was, 'The Spider is here.' Do any of your people go by the name Spider?"

Miranda shook her head. "Not that I've ever heard of. But given the rest of the cards"—she picked up the Devil card, which Stella had already explained—"can we assume this Spider person, or thing, is responsible for the badness that's about to go down?"

"I didn't really get an enemy vibe—just a gigantic portentous vibe. Even if he is responsible, it's not because he's a bad guy. Kind of like how Deven's always doing really bad things for good reasons."

"He?"

"Yeah. It felt male. Beats the hell out of me."

The Queen considered everything Stella had told her for a moment, then shook her head. "Your cards are dicks."

Stella laughed. "Most of the time they behave pretty well. You're just lucky, I guess."

Miranda's eyes fell on the Ten of Swords, that horrible

image of bloody death . . . a card of sacrifice, Stella had said. Instantly the memory of the woman she had killed flashed in Miranda's mind. Was that what the card referred to? Taking a human sacrifice once a month essentially in Persephone's name?

She could only hope that was the worst it might mean.

Stella picked up the cards one by one and returned them to the deck, wrapping the deck in a piece of black velvet and stowing it in a bag before she returned to the last few bites of her own ice cream.

Miranda, whose hot fudge sundae had been deceased for several minutes, said, "I'll be right back." She headed for the restroom; the ride back to the Haven was about forty-five minutes but felt like an eternity if she'd had a thirty-two-ounce Dr Pepper like tonight.

The Amy's restroom was painted in bright cartoon images of cows wearing scuba gear and swimming with perplexed-looking tropical fish. She smiled at the artwork—it helped her avoid looking in the mirror while she washed her hands. Perhaps in another decade it would stop being so weird not to have a reflection, but right now it left her deeply uneasy, as if by not appearing in the mirror, she didn't really exist.

As she yanked a paper towel out of the dispenser, something—a noise? a smell?—made her pause and train all her senses beyond the restroom door.

She could feel Stella at the table waiting for her, and the two employees behind the bar attending to the only other customer in the place. Only weeks ago the fact that the customer was human would have let her dismiss him as a threat, but now . . .

Miranda opened the door silently and leaned her head around.

She sighed.

It was a ninety-year-old man. She might still have suspected something amiss, but the clothes he was wearing and his stooped posture made it pretty clear he was unarmed.

Still, the vague feeling of unease remained, and Miranda knew it was time to leave. She couldn't tell if Stella noticed her edginess or not, but the Witch followed her outside without comment.

"We're about a block down," Miranda said. "I told Harlan

to wait on a side street since there's not exactly room for a limo here."

Stella laughed. "I've never really understood the point of limos. There are fancy cars that don't take up nearly that much space or use that much gas."

"It's purely for show," Miranda replied with a smile. "Our other car worked just fine and was a lot easier to maneuver. The limo doesn't use that much gas, though—it's a hybrid like all our vehicles."

As they walked, Miranda kept her senses on alert and her hand on Shadowflame. Her eyes moved from shadow to shadow, her new vision allowing her to pierce the darkness and pick out details half a block away if she concentrated. Meanwhile she swept the area with her empathy looking for the usual emotions she'd find in an attacker: hatred, anticipation, fear, bloodlust. This early in the night there were still plenty of humans about . . . and now she had to worry about them, too. Any one of the people they passed could turn out to be Morningstar.

She was relieved to reach the empty parking lot where Harlan was waiting.

"Good evening, my Lady, Miss Stella," he said, bowing and holding the door open. "Where to?"

"Stella's apartment," Miranda replied.

Almost the second the limo started to pull out onto Sixth, a wave of foreboding hit the Queen. She started to tell Harlan to stop and back up—

—but before she could speak she caught movement in her peripheral vision, something huge speeding toward the—

The impact was as loud as it was violent, the sound of crushing metal and tires squealing almost overwhelming Stella's screams as the limo flew sideways and flipped over, throwing both women around in their seat belts like rag dolls.

Miranda could feel the cabin shrinking around her, and without thinking, without worrying if she had the strength or the ability, she seized Stella's arm with one hand, reached through to the driver's seat with her mind, and flung Harlan as hard as she could through the windshield to throw him clear as she and Stella vanished from the car.

* * *

Déjà vu. Noise blaring everywhere—sirens, shouting voices.

She opened her eyes and immediately regretted it. "Fuck me running," she groaned.

Stella, who was staring into the Queen's face, let out an anguished breath. "Are you okay? Are you hurt?"

Miranda shook her head and forced herself to sit up. She *was* hurt, but not badly—she had a splendid variety of lacerations and contusions, and her ankle felt broken, but it took only a moment to heal as she sat there in the middle of Sixth Street surrounded by the scattered and smoldering debris of the limo.

The car itself was on its back like some sort of stranded beetle, blocking the entire street. It was bent in a slight V where it had been hit. There were police cars, fire trucks, and an ambulance already on the scene, and she saw a team of paramedics running toward her bearing trauma equipment.

"I'm okay," she said. "Take Stella and check her out."

Stella tried to protest, but Miranda leaned hard on the paramedics' minds to make them ignore the Queen and devote their attention to the human. Stella didn't appear to have a scratch on her, but they needed to rule out internal bleeding.

Miranda was still mentally numb, but she got to her feet, an anxious thought filling her mind. "Harlan!"

She headed back toward the wreck, looking for any indication of a body.

There, about fifty feet away from the car—she saw something moving under a tree.

She fully expected to find him dying, but amazingly, he was alert and leaning back against the trunk. He looked dreadful—though certainly not as bad as he should have after going through a windshield—but she could tell he was going to be fine.

"Thank . . . God," he panted. "Couldn't see you from here. Called for help—ours and theirs. There are two teams en route and the Prime's on his way."

"Just relax," Miranda said. She smiled. "Consider yourself off duty for the night."

In the distance she heard car doors slamming—a lot of car doors.

Mere seconds later David was at her side. "Are you all right?" he asked, pulling her into his arms. "I mean, I know you're all right, but . . ."

"I'm okay," she replied. "We need to get Harlan some blood and rest."

"Mo's on his way over—he stopped to check in on Stella since they've got her at the ambulance already."

David knelt to make sure Harlan wasn't badly injured; the driver was bloody and battered, but as Miranda had thought, he didn't seem to have any truly grave wounds. "How the hell was he thrown clear?" David asked as he squeezed Harlan's shoulder with a reassuring hand and stood back up.

"I did it," she said. "I grabbed Stella and Misted but I couldn't reach Harlan physically, so the best I could do was throw him through the windshield."

"You didn't throw him through the windshield," David said, shaking his head. "I walked by the car on my way here. The windshield is shattered but still in place, no body-sized holes."

"How is that possible?"

"You must have Misted him, the way I've done with bodies—it stands to reason you would be able to."

Miranda swallowed hard. "I guess so."

Mo and his team arrived and clustered around Harlan. Mo had come prepared; he had bags of blood for both of them. Miranda moved around the back of the tree where she wouldn't be seen and drank half of her bag, letting the blood move through her and take care of the last few injuries. Then she gave the rest back to Mo.

"Give this to Harlan, too," she told the medic. "He needs it way more than I do."

Hand in hand, she and David walked back toward the limo, where a dozen or more police officers were already swarming. One of them started to command them to leave, but David raised an eyebrow at him and he went back to what he was doing without saying another word.

Miranda watched her Prime examine the wreckage; he didn't touch anything but walked around the entire car, and she could see him analyzing every detail. At one point he bent and picked something up off the ground.

When he returned to her, she saw he had Stella's purse. "Stella was on the passenger side, right?" he asked, handing her the bag.

Miranda shook her head. "Driver's."

He frowned. "Are you sure?"

"Yeah, why?"

David gestured at the driver's side of the car, which was bent in at a scary angle. "That's the side that got hit. Even if you Misted before the car rolled, she should have been at the very least badly injured or more likely killed."

"She's not hurt at all," Miranda said, suddenly realizing how strange that was. She turned toward the ambulance, where the EMTs had Stella sitting on a stretcher with an oxygen mask over her face, and walked over.

Stella gave her a thumbs-up, then lowered the mask and smiled weakly. "I'm okay," she told Miranda before the Queen could even ask. "I don't even have a bruise. They said it's the damnedest thing they've ever seen."

Yet another car pulled up onto the scene, one she recognized as Detective Maguire's. Miranda smiled. The poor man—this was the third time he'd been called in to a disaster that his daughter was either involved in or witness to. As if, being a parent, he didn't have enough to worry about without vampires getting involved.

Miranda returned to where David stood and told him the Witch's condition.

"None of this makes sense," he said. "Look at the tire marks here—whatever hit you was enormous, like a dump truck, and it kept pushing the limo until it flipped. But then it backed up and left the scene. Whatever it was, it hit Stella's side dead-on at . . . forty-two miles per hour. With that much momentum she should have been squashed like a bug on impact, but she doesn't have so much as a hair out of place."

"Do you think it was Morningstar?" Miranda asked.

He looked confused, a rare and unsettling sight. "Why would they do this? They would have known a wreck was unlikely to kill you unless something sheared your head off or you bled to death before you could heal, and at your strength, in the middle of the city where help is always nearby, those are slim odds. Why do something so big and public with so little chance of success when they haven't even tried attacking Austin with their new warriors yet?"

Miranda's eyes fell on the stretcher again. "It wasn't about me," she said. "It was about Stella."

"There are much easier ways to kill a human."

She felt that little intuitive tug at her mind. Stella had been the channel for Persephone's power at the solstice. She was growing progressively stronger. Persephone had told Stella that getting involved with all of this would change her life, and now Stella had not only survived what should have been a fatal crash, she had miraculously come through completely unharmed.

"They weren't trying to kill her," Miranda said softly. "It was some kind of test. They were watching . . . waiting to see if she was hurt. They know something that we don't know."

"I'm afraid they know a lot of things we don't know," David said, meeting her gaze. "I'll go talk Maguire out of shooting us both."

Miranda returned to the stretcher. Stella had been freed of the oxygen mask and was sitting wrapped in a blanket, her feet swinging back and forth while she waited for the paramedics to clear her.

The Witch saw the look on Miranda's face, and her own face changed; for a moment she looked much older.

Stella's voice was grim, but accepting. "I'm going back to the Haven, aren't I."

Miranda nodded.

The Witch sighed. "Damn," she said. "Pywacket's going to be so pissed."

"This is Lieutenant Neelesh—emergency code four-two-four—my team is under attack! We have heavy casualties—I repeat, code four-two-four, the Pair is in imminent danger—"

A blade sang through the air and opened his side, sending him to the ground in a rush of his own blood. Around him he could hear the rest of his team trying desperately to fight their way to the Prime—but no one had seen this coming, no one had been prepared for an ordinary-looking group of mortals to suddenly fall upon them like demons. They had taken several of the attackers down, but more kept coming, putting themselves between the Elite and their Signet, cutting him off from aid.

Neelesh wrenched himself up onto his hands despite the agony in his side and tried to get back to his feet. He would not die in a pool of blood on the streets of Mumbai, not like this. He saw an opening and bolted for it, summoning all the strength he had left to reach the Prime.

He was close, so close, when he felt the stake bite deep into his back with such force that it knocked him back to the ground.

He could no longer think through the pain, but loyalty still drove him, and he tried, with unresponsive limbs, to rise again.

A pair of boots entered his vision, and he heard a sword being drawn.

The last thing he saw was the Prime falling back against the side of the car, a stake jutting from his chest . . . and just as the world went dark, he heard the desolate, wailing death shriek of the Queen.

Four

Australia was still in chaos, a dozen gangs ripping each other's throats out to try and take charge. In the Mideastern United States, once ruled by Joseph Kelley, things weren't much better: Someone had claimed the Signet only to die two days later, and now the continuous warfare Kelley had battled his entire tenure had erupted into violence that was claiming both human and vampire lives.

And now, Varati.

In the sixty-plus years Deven had ruled the West, he had seen three Signets lose their bearers. In the past *two months* four Signets had died. McMannis, Hart, Kelley, Varati . . . five, if he counted David. All but one had been directly linked to Jeremy Hayes, but it was still alarming, and this last one . . .

The reports were still sketchy. All anyone knew for certain was that the Indian Pair and their entourage had been taken out in full view of the Shadow District of Mumbai, caught by surprise . . . by humans . . . and not the small group that had shown up in California, but more than a dozen, all of them faster and stronger than any average vampire, and able by sheer numbers and shock value to overwhelm the Elite bodyguards Varati had with him.

India's warriors were not amateurs. They weren't equal to Deven's or David's, but still, to overpower them would have taken a skill level far beyond most vampire gangs, beyond that of a great many lower-shelf Elite. Even accepting that it was magic, Deven couldn't conceive of such a thing. Not once in seven centuries had he seen a human successfully attempt to fight an Elite—the average vampire Hunter was much smarter than that and worked within the limitations of the human race, using projectile weapons and traps rather than face-to-face combat. There really weren't that many Hunters, and they usually worked alone, so most Primes ignored them unless they became a nuisance.

This was something altogether different.

India was still in a state of shock, and violence hadn't erupted yet. Red Shadow intelligence was that a member of Varati's Court was poised to make a move on the Signet but was waiting a few days to let any warring factions take each other out first.

Word had gone out to the entire Council about Morningstar and what they might be capable of, but the other Primes were proving themselves no smarter now than when they had met in Austin; some denied it was even possible, others insisted Morningstar had no reason to come after them. Only a few heeded the warning and increased security.

The others were in for a nasty surprise.

Sacramento was, as usual, quiet that Thursday night. For the first time in a long time, the Prime took to the streets himself. He generally preferred anonymity, remaining an unseen and whispered-about presence, but subtlety had flown out the window when Morningstar started attacking Primes in public. He knew better than to think his presence would scare Morningstar away, but hopefully at least a few of their thugs would recognize him and it would be made clear that they were being watched by the Signet. If nothing else he might learn something.

Jonathan had not liked the idea. Not a surprise. If Varati, his Queen, and a cadre of their Elite had been massacred by these people, a single Prime without any guards would seem an easy target.

Deven smiled slightly. A great many people far more powerful than these lunatics had fallen bleeding to the street because of such assumptions.

He was feeling remarkably well that night, which probably accounted for some of his bravado—he'd had another session with Nico, and this time instead of being drained for days, he'd immediately felt like another veil had been stripped from his eyes and every cell in his body had been infused with new life. Two weeks ago he might have been afraid to go into battle, but now he was out looking for trouble like a spry young vampire of 250.

Thinking of the Elf nearly made him falter, though. They were pretending nothing had happened that night on the balcony . . . but Nico haunted his thoughts, and it was all he could do not to seek out the Elf's company, even just to talk. Deven tried telling himself they could be friends, and that friendship was better than nothing, but though Deven had many faults, lying to himself was not generally one of them. If he let himself feel any affection for Nico at all, it would only get worse. The Elf would be done healing him soon, and then he would leave, and Deven would never see him again. That was what he wanted.

Deven nearly snorted. So lying to himself was one of his faults after all.

There were few humans out so late, and even fewer vampires on the hunt. Word had gotten out about the strange new threat in town, and most were staying close to home until they heard from the Signet that it was safe again. At least so far Morningstar didn't seem to have any interest whatsoever in humans . . . but just to be safe, Deven sent out warnings to all the mortals he was aware of who associated with the Shadow World. He knew a few weapons artisans, a forensic expert or two, and of course key members of every city and state government in the West.

As he walked the thought arose, unbidden, of the last time he had prowled the streets . . . the night he had fallen to his knees outside St. Anthony's like a proper penitent . . . the night he had first looked up into those dark violet eyes that promised such peace. He had craved that peace so deeply in that moment . . . but now what he craved from the Elf was a little less peaceful and a little more elemental.

Damn it . . . stop thinking about him. Stop.

He was near one of his favorite spots in Sacramento, a large dance club similar to the Black Door in Austin; it was a hunting ground established by a member of the Court in order to create a safer space for feeding, for both vampire and mortal alike. Having some form of regulation over public hunting was key when it came to keeping a territory quiet; the vampires felt free to drink from humans, but the clubs were an attractive place to find healthy specimens without the risk of exposure.

It was well known that the Prime hunted there, which made it that much more popular among law-abiding vampires. He frequently partook of both the local cuisine and the local Ecstasy.

He was about five blocks from the club, deep in the dark heart that beat within every city, when he heard something.

He paused, looked around, analyzing. Empty street corner, three-story buildings on all sides, one streetlamp, two alleys that dead-ended. Well within range of the nearest motion sensors, and four minutes from the nearest patrol route, where a team would pass by in approximately two minutes. Depending on the situation it would be possible to run either back the way he'd come or straight ahead. The best way to escape, however, would be to Mist.

He stood right where he was and waited.

They emerged from the darkness, all dressed in black, and he watched them curiously for a moment as they emulated, but didn't come close to matching, vampiric grace or menace. They were all armed much as the Elite would be, with swords and stakes, knives of various kinds.

Deven let them surround him, looking from one to another, calculating their relative strengths and weaknesses; strangely, they all had very similar facial expressions, not quite blank but not entirely there, either.

Theory: The magic that gave them their strength put them in some kind of trance or otherwise worked its will over theirs. Who, then, was their puppeteer?

Finally, there were twelve Morningstar surrounding him . . . but they didn't make a move. They were waiting for something.

"Good evening," came a deep male voice.

Deven turned toward the sound slowly, one hand on the hilt of his sword.

A man emerged from the alley, and right away his appearance set off warning bells in Deven's head; he was dressed as a priest, all in black with a clerical collar. Short, fine brown hair crowned his head, over a pale, somewhat sickly-looking face with calm, intelligent brown eyes. Aside from the outfit he was perfectly ordinary, not at all threatening, the very image of an approachable and sympathetic clergyman.

Deven said nothing but continued to wait. The human would keep talking; they always kept talking.

"You must be the Prime of this territory—O'Donnell, is it? Of Irish descent."

Deven held back a snort. "You got Irish from O'Donnell? Genius."

"I hear you were once a man of the cloth like myself."

Deven smiled slightly. "I suspect it was a different kind of cloth."

His smile was returned. Again, Deven was surprised; he had expected anyone associated with Morningstar to be a raving lunatic, but this man was perfectly composed, even friendly. Usually a human who knowingly faced a vampire—let alone a Prime—was either craven or crazy, trying to escape or seized with suicidal bravado. "I am called the Shepherd," he said.

"Are you the leader of this Order, then?"

The Shepherd shook his head. "I am one of many around the world guiding our soldiers to their destinies."

"What destiny would that be, besides pissing me off?"

Another smile, smug; this Shepherd thought he had the upper hand, whether through knowledge or numbers.

It was cute.

"Surely you understand that vampires have to die," the Shepherd said reasonably. "It is our sacred task to wipe the stain of your existence from the earth. Your Circle, however . . . we have something very special in mind for you."

"I'm flattered," Deven said. "But Varati wasn't one of our Circle."

"That was a test run. We will eventually destroy the entire Council, felling them one by one." The Shepherd walked in a slow circle around Deven, perhaps to be intimidating. "But beyond the fact that you are all deviants, sodomites, and idolaters—"

"Deviants and sodomites?" Deven asked, feigning incredulity. "I have no idea what you mean."

The Shepherd obviously heard the sarcasm but started to say, "Leviticus—"

"Oh, fuck Leviticus," Deven said. "Get creative. Come on, I'll help you—I promise I've done much worse things than suck cock. I've killed hundreds of people. I've tortured, done a bit of maiming. I've cursed the name of God more times than I can count. I helped a man commit adultery—great big gay adultery, at that. That should be worth an honorable mention, shouldn't it?"

The Shepherd clearly had not been expecting the conversation to take this particular turn, but he didn't react until Deven stopped talking. "Beyond the fact that you are all deviants, you are also the only thing standing between our holy work and the destruction of the demon you call Persephone."

"Aha," Deven said, nodding. "Now we come to it. You were the ones who banished her in the first place, and now that she's returning, you want to do it again while there's still distance between her and us."

"Until your Circle is complete, she is vulnerable. Our first mission is to stop the formation of the Circle."

"And how do you plan to accomplish that?"

The Shepherd took a few steps back and made a quick gesture. "We'll start with you."

Dev looked around at the humans surrounding him. They were all drawing their weapons, preparing to spring.

A dozen superhumans, one Prime.

No contest.

They came at him from all sides, twelve against one, and he dropped flat on the ground so that their blades clashed into each other rather than meeting flesh. It was a cheap trick, but it almost always worked on people who dove into a fight rather than coming in slowly. The adrenaline of attack overrode self-preservation. He rolled to the right, hitting two in the knees and taking them down, using their bodies as a springboard, backflipping and spinning to take two heads in one stroke, with a third on the follow-through.

The remaining eight attacked in pairs, each from a different side; Deven met each blade with his, driving two pairs back toward the nearest wall.

They were good. They were very good. Whoever had trained them had been a master . . . but not an adept . . . and certainly nothing like the Alpha.

Another head hit the ground with a dull thud, its associated body not five seconds later. The humans were fast—fast enough to challenge him, which he liked. It was so hard to find warriors of his caliber anymore. Their style was a pastiche that wasn't terribly elegant but was quite effective. One of them even showed some creativity in her attack strategy—so they weren't just running through a program but could adapt.

He coaxed them all into a circle again and stood at the center, fighting them all at once. Another faltered, just for a second, just long enough for Ghostlight to slip in past his guard and slit his throat.

And there, Deven realized, was the problem with Morningstar's plan: These humans might be fast and strong like vampires, but they were still mortal. Their leaders had sacrificed a Prime to imbue them with strength and then neglected to supply them with Kevlar.

Another man went down with a gurgle of blood, and Deven braced his foot on the body to pull the sword out of the man's chest. Five to go.

He focused his attention on the one that seemed strongest. They fought along the alleyway just long enough for Deven to memorize his moves and then throw them back at him—the human favored a one-two-three combination that he used over and over, and it was child's play to take it, reverse it, and use it against him.

Three . . . two . . . one . . . and the man got close enough that Deven seized him by the shoulders, spun him around, and broke his neck.

Deven turned back to the remaining three and pointed at them with Ghostlight's dripping blade. "This is your last chance," Deven said. "Leave my city now and abandon this foolish quest, or die here in the street choking on your own blood."

He didn't actually mean it, but he wanted to see if he was right, and he was—whatever was driving them would drive them until they killed their target or fell dead themselves. Kamikaze soldiers . . . not good.

They all three attacked at once, and he immediately shifted back into the power-dance sight that he shared with David—he could see their actions a split second before they were made. It was hard to do with two opponents, and nearly impossible with three, but he specialized in the impossible.

He dodged a punch, then used one human's momentum to fling the other across the alley. When she got back to her feet and came at him again, he passed his shorter blade into his right hand, leaving the left free, and hit her so hard in the chest her sternum shattered and nearly got his hand stuck in the crisscrossing bones of her rib cage. She barely had time to scream—there was no more air in her lungs, no way to cry out, only the last wet sounds of her heart sputtering still.

He jerked free of her, letting the body fall to the ground in a heap. As he dropped her, he turned toward a faint noise and threw the knife; it hit the man coming toward him, the force flinging the human backward several feet before he fell down dead.

They'd saved the best for last, and this one showed no signs of tiring. Dev and the human circled around each other, blade on blade like the clanging of bells, until Deven snaked in and sliced open his arm. The human jerked backward but didn't fall. As he regained his balance, Deven lowered his sword, spun, and kicked the man in the side of the head, knocking him to the ground unconscious.

An eerie silence fell once the sounds of battle and the groans of the dying were hushed. Deven stood over the bodies, looking around for the Shepherd, but it was no surprise the man was gone.

He stared down at the last one left alive as he sheathed Ghostlight and took out his phone.

"Dispatch, I need a prisoner retrieval team to these coordinates, as well as a crime scene analysis and body disposal team. Have interrogation room six prepared."

"As you will it, Sire."

"Also send a message to the analysts to get me a copy of the sensor readings for this block for the last two hours."

"Consider it done, my Lord Prime."

Before he could even lower the phone it was ringing, and he didn't have to look to know who it was. "I'm all right."

"What the hell were you thinking?" Jonathan demanded, his anger almost as loud as his fear.

"I was thinking, 'I'm surrounded, so I'd better kill these bastards.'"

"You should have Misted out of there. You didn't need to fight."

"Of course I did. Morningstar needed to see that we're not all so easy to kill, and our people needed to see that Morningstar isn't invincible. They're enhanced humans, but they're still humans. And now we have solid data to look at and one of theirs we can question. I'd call that a win."

"Damn it, Deven . . ." Jonathan trailed off; he didn't have much of an argument, and he knew it, though Deven could hear how scared he had been.

"I'm sorry, darling," Deven said, looking up to see the two vans pulling up to the scene. "I have to go—we can talk more when I get home."

Jonathan hung up without answering, something he often did when Deven's behavior infuriated him beyond words. By the time Dev got back to the Haven the Consort would be calmer, halfway through a bottle of Woodford Reserve, and would be able to put emotion aside and listen to reason.

While he waited for the Elite teams to get the scene under control and drag the still-breathing human to the van, he made another call.

Miranda answered without preamble, "What's going on? It feels weird over there."

"Hello, love . . . is David in? I have some news about our pest control problem."

"He's in the shower—what happened?"

He smiled. "You'll never guess who I met tonight."

Miranda had to leave after the screaming started.

She knew better than to sit in on the interrogation, but still, part of her was morbidly curious; she knew her husband was an accomplished torturer and had no doubt that Deven was similarly gifted, but there was something especially horrible in what they were doing tonight that made her want to hear at least a little bit of it.

"For the record, this is pretty messed up," she said. "Torture by conference call?"

David, surrounded by his monitors with the sensor network, a Signet territory map, and other information on the four screens at his workroom desk, had queued up a recording program directly in front of him and was setting it up. He looked over at her, his eyes hard. "Then leave," he replied, not harshly, but firmly. "If you don't think you can handle it, it's better if you're not here; you might unintentionally make a sound or speak and alter the dynamic."

David brought up another window, where there was a read-out of vital signs: Deven had attached sensors to the prisoner's body so they could pay attention to heart rate, pulse, temperature.

Despite the nausea she already felt in her stomach, she tried for a joke. "What's the strategy—good vampire, bad vampire?"

David smiled and shook his head. "Assuming Dev still does things the same way as he did in the forties, right now the prisoner is chained wrist and ankle against the wall, just a few inches off the ground to put additional pressure on his joints and eliminate the sense of stability of being on the floor."

"So, no table full of torture implements to show the guy and scare him?"

"Not necessary. The scariest torture implement will be the one doing the talking." David lifted a finger to his lips to quiet her and turned up the volume, crossing his arms to listen.

Miranda heard a chair scrape over the ground, the creak of leather. "You're an excellent warrior," Deven said. He was calm, his tone light, and Miranda tried to imagine him in all his Goth regalia, all five foot four of him, 150 pounds soaking wet . . . he'd scare the ever-loving piss out of the mortal just by sitting there.

"I met your boss this evening before I had the pleasure of meeting your team," Deven went on. "He didn't really fit the profile of a fanatical religious type. Trust me, I know them when I see them."

As he spoke, the human's heart rate was rising. Miranda

shot David a quizzical look, and David pressed an image into her mind of Deven toying with a wicked-looking knife as he spoke, repeatedly drawing the blade along his thumb to raise a line of blood that closed as the human watched.

"What shall I call you?" When the human didn't immediately answer, Deven added, "You're going to want to talk to me. I just singlehandedly killed eleven of your compatriots—you saw me do it. Do you think for one second you aren't just as disposable to me? If you don't talk, I'll find another who will. If you do, I will show you mercy."

There was still no reply, but a few seconds later Miranda heard something whistle through the air and impact hard in the wall; the human's heart rate went through the roof and he whimpered before he could stop himself. "West Twelve," he blurted.

"I assume that designates where you're stationed and your standing within the garrison."

A long moment of silence passed, the only sound the human's heavy breathing. Clearly whatever mystical abilities he'd been given didn't include withstanding intimidation. Whenever David questioned a vampire, it often took hours; Miranda suspected this would take maybe twenty minutes at the rate it was going.

"All right, West Twelve," Deven said. "Here's how this is going to go. I could sit here for hours, winning your trust, being sympathetic, and gradually prying pieces of information from you without you even realizing it. But to be honest, I'm terrible at that. My teachers were always so disappointed, but I prefer a more direct approach."

The chair scraped again; footsteps approached the far end of the room where the man was hung. There was an odd noise that Miranda figured was Deven yanking the knife out of the wall. Then the Prime's voice grew quieter, but deathly serious, all levity gone.

"You're going to tell me everything you know about the Order of the Morningstar, the Shepherd, and whoever pulls his strings. And you're going to be thorough and detailed and not try my very limited patience."

Miranda silently willed the man not to argue, not to try and be a hero. Just talk. Just talk, damn it.

"A-and what if I don't tell you anything?" West 12 asked.

Deven answered with a question of his own. "Did you know that human blood tastes better when it's infused with heightened emotion—lust, anger, fear? Some of us are junkies for one or another. One of the most popular things to charge blood with is pain. And pain and fear together . . . it's like candy, and I for one have a bit of a sweet tooth."

Miranda heard the human struggling in his chains, and a low hiss told her that the Prime had extended his teeth—a surefire way to terrify just about any human. It was an atavistic fear that even those familiar with vampires would try to get away from.

Miranda closed her eyes and could practically see it: Deven took the knife in his hand and drove it into the human's arm, almost all the way through. The human screamed . . . then screamed again when Dev clamped his mouth on the wound and sucked hard.

She didn't visualize whatever happened next: The scream went on, punctuated by begging, promises to talk, and more screaming. She knew why. There were so many places on the human body to cut and drink from, so many that hurt so much worse than the throat, especially if the vampire used his influence over the mortal mind to drive that pain and fear up to a fever pitch. Deven would carefully avoid any major organs, but he knew exactly where to place the knife, what angle to press it in at, what speed to pierce the skin.

Despite his words, she knew he hadn't learned the method from a mentor. He had learned it by experiencing it himself.

Miranda pushed herself up out of her chair and stumbled from the room, having just enough presence of mind to close the door quietly so the slam wouldn't distract anyone. The man's terror, beyond reason and civility, had dug its claws into her heart, and it drove her down the hall, away from David's workroom, toward the music room.

David had been right, and she'd been an idiot. She had no business in that room. Needless to say her curiosity was satisfied.

She forgot, sometimes, what they were capable of. Even now. She knew David wouldn't feel a shred of guilt no matter what horrific sounds the human made before Deven finally showed him that final second of "mercy" and broke his neck, slit his throat, or stabbed him in the heart; David would simply sit there listening, evaluating the human's words for nuances and details, supplying a question here and there . . . so very civilized. And he would probably listen to the recording several more times without caring one whit about the suspect's life.

She also knew, without having to ask, that he felt no guilt over the lives they had taken on the new moon. He had been the first to surrender to the need, but even then, she suspected he had only really resisted in the first place for her sake. It didn't scare her—she had known who he was long before she relinquished her humanity. Primes, he had told her once, were required to do things that no one else could, no matter how ugly the task.

She couldn't judge him for it. She, too, had killed, both humans and vampires. He had found her that first night in the alley bleeding and barely sane, surrounded by the corpses of four men. She had used her empathy to hurt her enemies in ways a sword couldn't, and she would most likely do it again . . . no, she *would* do it again.

Miranda reached the music room and closed the door behind her; she sank onto the piano bench, shut her eyes, and grounded herself, breathing slowly and deeply, and the panic faded, as did the shame—yes, they were killers . . . both of them. This wasn't really about torture; it was about what she had done and would have to do again. No, she wasn't okay with it. But the facts were the facts, and she was going to have to find a way to live with it. They had too much to do; there was too much at stake. The means were monstrous but necessary, even though the ends were still undefined.

And she was going to keep telling herself that until she believed it.

Deven finished scrubbing the blood from under his fingernails and emerged from the bathroom, stretching idly.

"That was pretty much a bust," Jonathan said from his chair, where he sat reading. "I suppose it was too much to ask for the guy to know all their plans."

"He was just a foot soldier. If we really want to know their inner workings, we need to question the Shepherd."

"How do you propose we do that?"

Dev reached for the clean T-shirt he'd left on the bed and pulled it on. He'd already showered once tonight, after the fight, and was very careful not to get any bloodier than he had to in the interrogation. He'd gotten away with stained hands and a few smears on his shirt; not bad.

"No clue," he replied. "I think it's safe to assume this was a test—they had a few casualties with Varati and wanted to see what they'd be up against with a fight-trained Prime. Varati was a good ruler, but he was no warrior. His Second was responsible for the Elite's skill in battle. Whether they killed me tonight or not, they would learn something valuable about us, just as we learned about them."

"I'm sure your reputation preceded you," Jonathan said wryly.

"Even if it didn't, it's following me. I have no doubt the Shepherd watched the whole thing and then reported back to Crazy Fucker High Command."

Jonathan shot him a familiar look. "Oh, you mean he called you?"

"You're still upset with me for getting into it with them, I see."

"You could have been killed, Dev."

Deven sighed. "I seriously doubt that." He picked up the knife he'd fought with from the desk where he'd sat to clean it and strapped it back in place. He felt dangerously exposed unless he had at least three weapons at all times—one for each hand and a backup. "I've fought against much more formidable odds than twelve to one, especially considering they were human. At no point did I feel remotely in jeopardy—and even if I had, I could have Misted out any time I liked."

"As if you would." Jonathan shook his head. "I thought you'd shaken the suicidal tendencies thanks to the Elf's handiwork."

"I came home without a scratch, Jonathan—how much less suicidal could it have been? It was a calculated risk. I wanted to learn exactly how strong they are, and I did."

"To hell with how strong they are," Jonathan snapped. "I almost lost you to an emotional black hole and just when I get you back, you start courting death again. You can't expect me to just sit back in silence while you stalk around town getting into fights that could kill us both."

"What do *you* expect?" Deven demanded. "In all the time you've known me, have I ever walked away from a fight? Did you think that the Elf would magically turn me into some kind of pacifist or something more acceptable to you? *I'm never going to change, Jonathan.* I've told you a thousand times you cannot fix me. Stop trying."

They stared at each other for a minute. Jonathan lowered his eyes first, staring off into the cold fireplace with a slow shake of his head, and the anger Deven could feel radiating from him faded back into worry, then sadness.

The emotion reverberating down the bond between them was more painful than a stab wound could ever be. He crossed the room and knelt in front of his Consort's chair, taking his hands and kissing them softly. Their eyes met again, apology written in both hazel and lavender.

Deven smiled up at him. "That makes, what, five hundred times we've had that argument?"

It took Jonathan a breath to smile back. "At least."

"It's as silly now as it was in 1952."

"Yes . . . but I'm still right."

Deven rested his head on Jonathan's knee for a moment. "Tell me what you want me to do."

"I want you to want to live," he replied.

Deven was about to reply when his phone chimed, and one of the Elite said, *"Sire, your presence has been requested by the Weaver . . . somewhat urgently."*

The Pair frowned at each other. "I'm on my way," Deven said. He stood, squeezing Jonathan's hands as he did so, and said, "I wonder what's wrong."

Jonathan leaned back, looking defeated. "I'm sure whatever it is, you can solve it by taking your clothes off."

Deven froze, eyes narrowing. "What?"

Chagrin. "Nothing, baby, I'm just in a bad mood." At Deven's raised eyebrow, he added, "I mean it. That was a cheap shot, and I'm sorry." He held on to Deven's hands for a second, looking down at them and then up into his eyes. "I love you just as you are," Jonathan said. "The worst of you and the best. I just wish you could see what I see in you . . . how amazing you are."

Deven looked away, suddenly aching. "I don't deserve you."

Now, Jonathan grinned. "Probably not. But neither I nor the Elf deserves you either."

He looked back at his Consort with a sigh. "Jonathan, nothing is going to happen between us. I don't want it to. Sure, I'm attracted to him, but who wouldn't be? But it's nothing . . . I mean it."

Jonathan's grin turned into a laugh. "Oh, darling, you're adorable when you're stupid. Now go see what's going on . . . I'll be here whenever you get back."

Despite Jonathan's return to his upbeat manner, as Deven walked down the hall toward Nico's room, he found himself deeply troubled by the entire conversation. It wasn't the argument, really—as he'd said, they'd had the same one many times before, and it was never going to be resolved. When they'd first Paired, it had been bitter and lengthy; by now they had it down to less than two minutes. Most of the time Jonathan supported his Prime's methods, but once in a while he lost patience with Deven's arrogance and recklessness. Deven didn't blame him.

No . . . this was something else. Ever since the Elf had come into their lives . . . no, now that he thought about it, it had started before that, right at the same time Deven had begun to break down after he murdered Eladra.

Was it possible that Jonathan was breaking down, too, thanks to the bond? That the dissolution of Deven's life force had seeped along the bond to Jonathan and was still damaging him even though Deven himself was better? Perhaps Nico could help him, too, if that was the case. If he didn't, eventually the problem would echo back to Deven again, an endless feedback loop that destroyed them both piece by piece.

Or perhaps that wasn't it either. The imbalance in Jonathan's behavior reminded Deven very strongly of how the Consort had acted after he foresaw the events that led up to the Awakening . . . and also when he'd Seen, years ago, that the flame-haired woman who had burned her way into David's heart would be swallowed by dark water. However those visions had ended up, Jonathan had suffered from that knowledge, and it seemed he was suffering again. He hadn't said anything about a precog episode, but it wouldn't be the first time he kept one to himself.

"Good God," Deven muttered. "What's going to go wrong now?"

He reached the guest suite, where the Elite who had called him still stood guard and opened the door for him as he approached.

He felt uncharacteristically nervous as he stepped across the threshold. He had no idea what the Elf wanted, but since that night on the balcony Deven had stayed away from him as much as possible, coming into contact only during their healing sessions. That was all the intimacy he could bear.

"Nico?" Deven walked through the suite, and though the light in the bedroom was on, the Elf was nowhere to be found. The door to the terrace stood ajar, and he went to it and stepped outside, calling again.

The Elf stood facing away, silhouetted against the shadows below and the starlit night above. He didn't answer.

"You called," Deven said. "Is everything all right?"

Nico turned toward him, and Deven took a step back—fury, pure and smoldering, was written in every line of the Elf's body. *"What did I tell you?"*

Bewildered, Deven just gaped at him. He'd never seen Nico angry; in fact he'd only ever seen him implacably calm, except that one moment when they had nearly kissed. Wrath shone from his dark eyes, and it was as attractive as it was disturbing. "I don't understand," Deven managed.

"I told you that the work I had done was still fragile," Nico said. "I told you not to exert yourself physically or emotionally because it could undo everything I had done and send you back into the abyss. And what did you do tonight?"

"How did you know—"

"I felt it." He cut Deven off. "We are still connected. I felt you seek out violence—and do not tell me the enemy came after you. I know you went into the city looking for a fight. I felt your bloodlust, satisfaction at the kill, over and over. And then that lust heightened when you took the renewed strength I had given you and used it to torture a man to death."

"I wasn't aware that your help came with strings attached," Deven said icily. "I thought you were here to help *me*, not what you could make me into. You and Jonathan both think you can tame me like some unruly horse and teach me to canter on command. You're both wrong. I will do my job as I see fit, and neither of you will raise a hand to stop me."

"Oh?" Nico crossed his arms and moved closer, anger turning to steel both in his voice and in his eyes. "And if I do, what then? Will you torture me, too?"

Deven glared up into his eyes, knowing his own had gone silver. His teeth extended slightly and he forced them back up, but not before Nico saw them and paled a shade. "Was that a dare?" Deven asked in a cold, quiet voice.

A moment passed where the only sounds were the forest beyond and the hard, angry breathing of vampire and Elf. The world hung suspended for a few seconds, the night around them waiting.

Then Nico seized him by the shoulders and hauled Deven against him, his mouth covering the Prime's with such intensity that Deven was, momentarily, too stunned to respond. Between one heartbeat and the next his paralysis broke, and he grabbed the front of Nico's shirt and kissed back until they were both completely breathless, practically clawing at each other in the frantic need to touch.

This time, Nico was the one to push away; he released Deven with a gasp and backed up to the balcony wall. "I am sorry," he panted. "I should not have done that."

"Not your fault," Deven said weakly. "I make everybody angry."

There was anguish in the Elf's dark eyes. "I am not angry," he replied. "I am afraid."

"I scare a lot of people, too." Deven smiled, though his heart felt sick and shaky. "What . . . what are you afraid of?"

Nico turned out toward the forest and said nothing for a minute, seeming to draw strength from the view. His long-fingered hands, pressed flat on the wall, clenched for a moment and then fell helplessly to his sides. He searched for words a while before answering.

"I am afraid of you," he admitted, sounding relieved to get the words out. "Afraid of what I feel when I am near you.

Afraid to leave this place without telling you the truth." He met Deven's eyes and said very quietly, "I ask nothing of you—I only want to know you, in whatever way you will allow. I will happily accept friendship, if you would accept mine . . . but with the work we have done together I cannot lie to you . . . I love you. I am terrified of what you are, of what may come, but I love you all the same."

The world spun. In all his long life he'd heard only a handful of men say those words. Jonathan had first said it in wonder, only a few hours after they'd met; David had said it almost shyly, then again and again, the first night they lay together. Both times Deven's heart had reeled from it, and from the realization that he loved them, too, though in both cases he'd waited to say it back until they'd been together long enough that he was no longer so scared of losing them.

He knew the Elf was waiting for him to say something, anything. It was such an overwhelming, confusing barrage of feelings, he sagged back against the wall, unable to entirely comprehend it: *He loves me. I am loved . . . by yet another, when I don't deserve any of it. Why do they keep loving me? Why don't they see what I really am?*

Nico was watching him, and asked softly, "Is it so difficult to believe?"

The question opened a great chasm of sorrow in his chest, and he said, barely at a whisper, "Yes."

That seemed to decide something for the Elf, who came to him silently. Arms wrapped slowly around him; Nico kissed him gently on the lips, then leaned so that their foreheads touched. In that moment Deven felt something so rare and precious his eyes burned: peace.

Oh, how he wanted to stay . . . to let the Elf lead him by the hand into the cool dark of his room, and let him prove his words over and over again all day . . . but another part of him, just as adamant, refused.

With a reluctant sigh, he drew away. Nico smiled a little wistfully but let him go without complaint.

"Tomorrow," the Weaver said. "We shall have one last session—by then you will be as healed as you can be. I will stay a few days after that to ensure the matrix is stable."

Deven nodded. "Very well."

They stared at each other for another minute; then Nico said, "Your Consort is a lucky man, to have such loyalty."

It started as a laugh but ended up sounding strangled. "Jonathan deserves better," he said as he turned to walk away. "So do you."

Five

"Tell me the truth," Miranda said, her eyes on the shadowy shapes passing by the car window. The glass had a new special coating David had created that enabled them to leave the house in the last hours of daylight without the massive headaches they got from sunlight through normal UV-blocking tint. "Please. Why won't he talk to me? Did I do something? Is it too weird to be close to me with David back?"

Jonathan chuckled. "No, sweetheart, that's not it at all—it has nothing to do with you. And I would love nothing more than to tell you everything, but I can't—not without talking to him first."

The Queen sighed. His assertion didn't make her feel any better. "Yeah, okay."

"I can tell you this much . . . it was bad. Very bad. I wasn't entirely sure he was going to make it."

"What?" She sat up straight. "Not make it as in *die*? What the hell, Jonathan? How could you not ask for help?"

"We did, just . . . not you. Someone came to help us, and I think it worked."

"Someone . . ." Miranda gripped the phone tightly. "That's all you can say."

"Well . . . okay, do you remember what he told David about finding someone to help rebond you two?"

"Right, something about a magic stone and calling people with Elven blood, like a really badass Witch." She raised an eyebrow. "You found a badass Witch?"

"Heavy on the badass, not so much a Witch. He calls himself a Weaver—it's a pretty specialized craft."

"Is this guy . . . are you sure he's on our side? There's nothing weird about him?"

Jonathan laughed outright. "Oh, darling, you have no idea. But trust me, whatever our side is, he's on it."

Miranda heard something in his words that he probably hadn't intended. "What aren't you telling me?"

"It's nothing, really . . . I'm pretty sure he's in love with Deven, is all."

"That's nothing? You sound awfully calm about it."

"Why shouldn't I be?" A note of exasperation entered the Consort's voice. "Why does everyone think I'm lying when I say I don't mind him having lovers?"

"Because we're not talking about a shag-for-sport, if there's love involved. It upset you when he slept with David, even though you knew that was coming. This time it's not even someone he has a long history with."

He sighed. "I want him to be happy."

"That wasn't an answer, Jonathan."

"It wasn't meant to be an answer, Miranda." He paused, then said, "It doesn't bother me."

"You sound bothered."

"I said it doesn't bother me—I didn't say I wasn't bothered. Right now, it doesn't matter—Dev's fighting it, trying to do the right thing by me, and I'm trying to think of it as sweet rather than ridiculous. You know him—his answer for everything is either denial or bloodshed. But there are things that could happen, events that might unfold. I don't know exactly what." He spoke over the question she was already forming. "I don't know whether it's going to turn out to be good or bad. But I know that whatever it is, this is how it starts. I can't say I'm all that enthusiastic about the possibilities. You know the kinds of things I see . . . they're almost never good, at least, not at the outset."

She leaned back in her seat, biting her lip, feeling a sudden urge to cry for no real reason. Jonathan was right—his pre-cognitive visions had foretold terrible things, even though at least one, her own death, had ended well for her. "Are you sure you can't tell me what you saw?"

"I would if I could."

Miranda closed her eyes and forced herself to say, "Okay. If you get any more details, let me know. After everything we've all been through together I really don't like being kept in the dark."

She could hear him smile. "You'll be the first to hear about it. Be careful tonight. The only thing worse than vampire drama is family drama."

"I'll do my best. I'll talk to you later."

After she hung up, she took a deep breath, wiping impa-tiently at her eyes. What the hell did Jonathan think he was doing? He should have known better . . . but she wasn't sure whether it was the fact that he had flat-out lied to her, or the thought of him carrying the weight of whatever was coming, that brought tears to her eyes.

She knew perfectly well he'd seen more than he said. They all knew that Jonathan's precog gift was startlingly clear. Sometimes what he saw had a different meaning than it appeared to at first, and sometimes the images were jumbled, but he always saw in detail.

Miranda started to call David, but even as her finger pulled up his number, Minh said from the front seat, "Rio Verde, my Lady. We'll be at the address you gave me in five minutes."

"Oh, hell," she muttered, then louder, "Thank you."

It would have to wait a couple of hours. She wasn't sure which she wanted to deal with less—her sister or Jonathan's doomsday predictions. Both made her stomach hurt and her heart feel heavy. Neither promised a good day's sleep nor any sort of satisfaction.

She took another deep breath to try to ground out some of her anxiety. This at least would be over with soon. By morn-ing she'd be home again, in Austin where she belonged.

Miranda got out of the car and stood in the driveway for a minute, staring at the house, feeling . . . she wasn't sure what.

The house looked the same, and not. The property was a

little shabbier overall, though the lawn was still perfectly manicured. The same black mailbox she had run to every afternoon to grab the bills and circulars for her mother was still on its brick pedestal by the road. Even the house numbers still hung where they always had, though they had rusted: 2219.

Minh and Stuart disembarked behind her and waited for her orders. She gestured for them to follow—she intended to have them wait outside but knew David would have a coronary if she left them in the car altogether. With everything they'd been through, she was a lot less likely to dismiss his concerns for her safety than she would have been in the past.

She had two knives under her coat, just in case. She hadn't wanted to wear Shadowflame into such close quarters where there would, no doubt, be awkward questions, but hell if she was going anywhere unarmed. If she did, David and Deven would *both* have coronaries.

Rio Verde hadn't stood the test of time very well. The town was in a slow and steady decline since Paragon Petroleum had closed up shop and withdrawn to Houston. Young people didn't move here anymore . . . except for her sister.

She rang the bell; no answer. She frowned and tried again. Still no answer. They knew she was coming; she'd gotten an e-mail from Marianne that very morning verifying the time.

Miranda was just about to take out her phone when she heard the deadbolt shoot back and, a second later, a pale face peered out at her.

They stared at each other: the prodigal daughter, the good daughter. Marianne looked like she had aged a hundred years—she was thin and worn-looking, with dark circles under her eyes and a dullness in both her eyes and hair. Marianne hadn't inherited their mother's coloring; she had their father's olive skin, brown eyes, and brown hair. Still, once upon a time Stephen Grey had been a handsome man, and Marianne had a sort of classic beauty Miranda had envied throughout their teenage years. Now, though . . .

"Oh, you're here," Marianne said vaguely. "Come in."

Something in her tone set off warning bells in Miranda's mind. "Wait . . . are you all right?"

Marianne looked at her again, and for just a second Miranda saw something in her eyes that made the warning bells double in volume and echo throughout her being: *fear.* "Yeah, fine. Come on in. He's awake."

Taking a deep breath, Miranda turned back to her bodyguards. "Minh, stay out here and keep watch. Stuart, with me."

Marianne stepped back to let her into the house, and as she lifted her arm to open the door her sleeve fell back. Miranda didn't allow her reaction to show, but she knew what she was looking at. Track marks.

Right then Miranda wanted to be anywhere but in that house.

Marianne ushered her into the living room. Miranda looked around, swallowing her unease, trying to digest the strangeness of the sight before her. It felt like she'd stepped back in time. The room was exactly as she remembered it, down to the photographs hanging over the fireplace. She saw her own face, and her mother's, all around her, frozen at different points in time, the frames filmed with dust.

Behind her Marianne shut the door and locked it, startling Miranda.

"How are George and Jenny?" Miranda asked, unable to stand the weird silence any longer.

"George is in Plano," Marianne replied. "We're separated."

"I'm sorry to hear that."

"Don't be," Mari said flatly. "He's an asshole."

Miranda had to laugh at that. "Well, yeah, but I wasn't going to say so."

"Jenny's . . ." Marianne took a deep breath, and Miranda saw that flicker of fear again. "She's in second grade now."

"Is she living with George, or with you?"

"Right now she's . . ." Marianne shook her head, denying what Miranda couldn't guess. "She's fine. Come on, let's get this over with while he's still lucid."

Miranda followed her through the living room into the hallway, past what had once been their bedrooms, to the extra room that had served as Marilyn's art studio once upon a time. Miranda could smell antiseptic, and the closer they got the stronger other smells grew: that indefinable odor of old age, and another that she recognized as that hospital smell of sickness and soiled linen. She could hear monitors beeping quietly.

Marianne stood back and let her go in first. Miranda had to force herself; she was beginning to understand what a colossal mistake this was. She shouldn't have come. What did she have to prove to these people?

"I'm sorry," Marianne said softly behind her. "I'm sorry."

Miranda turned back to her. "What?"

Marianne was crying, melting back against the wall. "They have Jenny. They have Jenny. I'm sorry."

The Queen felt something thud into her back.

She spun around and felt another impact, this one in her shoulder. The pain hit a few seconds behind as a third, then fourth, then fifth shaft struck her torso.

Crossbows. It must be—

She didn't have time to finish the thought, and she didn't have time to draw a weapon. Someone moved up behind her, something struck the back of her head, and she knew no more.

"You are without a doubt one of the oddest men I've ever met," Olivia noted.

David smiled. "Why do you say that?"

"Tell me everything you're doing right at this moment."

"Well, I'm talking to you, and I'm creating a comparative data matrix from sensors in Sacramento and those in Austin as well as from observational data from the attack on Varati in Mumbai so we can get a better idea of the physical limits of Morningstar's thugs—in a few minutes I'll have the first stab at an upgrade for the sensor network that can register that specific variety of human. I'm also refining the software that runs the camera I used for Miranda's *Rolling Stone* interview. And I'm reverse-engineering the earpieces to see if any of the technology will be useful for my own communication system."

"And?"

"And what? Oh, right—I'm also working my way through a pint of Rocky Road."

Olivia was laughing. "I rest my case."

"I'm not odd," David replied. "I'm just busy. Three hundred fifty years is enough time to develop a lot of hobbies. I collected stamps for a while."

The scanner in front of him beeped, and he set aside the mostly empty pint and returned his attention to the earpiece. He'd examined several of them since all this had started, but most had the same kind of explosive charge hidden inside as the first one he'd opened; he'd finally worked out a way to disable the charge, but the first two times the laser hadn't been calibrated exactly and he'd destroyed them. This time it seemed to be working—steady as his hands were, he was having much better luck using an automated mechanical arm he'd borrowed from Hunter Development to do the cutting.

He heard someone speak to her, and she sighed and said, "I have to go—we've had Elite trials going on all evening and my First Lieutenant has a group of finalists for me to look over."

"Good luck," David told her. "Call if you need anything."

"Will do."

As he hung up, David paused to check on the computer running the comparison matrix of Morningstar data; it was still happily plugging along. It had taken a couple of hours to write the program itself, but actually running it took no effort on his part except to keep an eye on it for glitches.

He started to return his attention to both the laser and the ice cream—

—and between one breath and another, pain lanced through his body, a dozen burning points of entry he recognized immediately as crossbow bolts at close range. He tried to stand, but the pain was so intense none of his limbs were cooperating, and only through all of his will did he manage to grab the edge of the table and avoid hitting his head.

The room swam in and out of focus. He couldn't think—he knew that it wasn't he who was injured, and the intensity of the pain told him he wasn't catching echoes from New York, Prague, or Sacramento. So far his awareness of the others' emotions and pain had been minimal—and he was fine with that—but that meant there was only one place it could be coming from. Miranda.

Terror overwhelmed the pain. She was five hours away. By the time he reached Rio Verde, even breaking every speed limit in Texas, it would be too late to stop whatever they had planned for her.

Sinking to his knees, he groped for the phone. Miranda's phone went straight to voice mail; he changed contacts.

It didn't even finish the first ring. "What the hell is happening over there?"

David ignored the question. "Tell me you have a Shadow operative closer than five hours to Rio Verde."

"Shit, David, I don't even know where Rio Verde *is*. Give me a minute."

He closed his eyes, trying to breathe, trying desperately not to panic. She was alive; she must be. The pain from the bolts was still screaming at him, but it hadn't gotten worse. They most likely had shot her down and then dragged her into captivity.

"The closest I have is Houston," Deven said. "That's still three hours out."

"That's two hours closer than I am. Send them—please. I don't know what else to do."

"I already gave the order. What could have happened to her in that crappy little town?"

"It has to be Morningstar." David grabbed the table again and dragged himself to his feet. He picked up the phone with one hand while calling Harlan on his com. "Elite Five."

"Yes, Sire?"

"This is an emergency," he said. "Have the second Escalade out front in five minutes."

"As you will it, Sire."

The guards outside the workroom gave him looks that were both quizzical and worried as he half-staggered past them. The only thought in his mind, *Get to Miranda*, played on repeat so loudly in his head it crowded out the pain.

He had no doubt that Deven could feel his rising panic. "Keep breathing," Deven said. "She'll be fine—she can take care of herself."

"It's going to be too late," David panted. He reached the front doors of the Haven, where Harlan already had the vehicle waiting. There was so much they could do to Miranda in five hours . . . assuming they didn't just kill her . . . she was in pain . . . He had to have faith that whichever Shadow operative Deven had sent could save her.

"Just get on the road," Deven commanded. "I have an idea . . . let me call you back."

"But what—"

Deven hung up before David could finish the question, and David climbed into the SUV, saying, "We're going to Rio Verde. I want you to get there as fast as possible."

"Yes, Sire. On our way."

Harlan had the car on the highway in less than ten minutes. By then the pain from the crossbow bolts had become a continuous low-level ache, but he knew better than to think Miranda was safe—most likely she was unconscious. It gave him the clarity of mind to call the Houston satellite garrison and order a team of Elite to head for Rio Verde as well. He didn't know what they would be driving into, but he had to assume he'd need reinforcements.

After that there was nothing he could do but wait and send as much reassurance down the bond as he could, trying to reach her even if she couldn't reply, just to let her know help was coming, and no matter what darkness her attackers had dreamed up for her, she wasn't alone.

Six

The Queen woke alone.

At first, nothing made sense. Her body hurt; she had felt that variety of pain before, and knew it for what it was, but when she focused on one of the wounds, she couldn't heal it. When she tried to move her arm, agony stabbed through her wrist, forcing her to lie still and bite down on her tongue to stop a scream. And though she could smell the metal-and-petrochemicals reek of a warehouse of some sort around her, directly above the night sky was exposed.

Think, Queen. Think. How long have I been out? What happened?

Marianne. Marianne had sold her out to Morningstar—Miranda had figured out that much before she lost consciousness. The Order had Jenny and threatened to harm the child if Marianne didn't lure Miranda into the ambush.

The room began to solidify around her. She tried to focus on the details to help her ignore the pain. It wasn't a warehouse—not big enough, and the floor was dirt, not concrete. It smelled like it had once held large machinery. But why she'd be able to see the sky, she didn't . . . know . . .

Oh God.

She was in a cage, or rather, a pen with eight-foot sides, open at the top. The ceiling of the building had been partially removed in a square about the size of the pen. She was on the ground, on her back, directly beneath the hole . . . staked to the ground. Up above her, the night was beginning to pale.

They were going to burn her alive.

A deep, instinctive fear shuddered through her, and before she could stop herself she tried to jerk her arms free, but the wood shafts nailed through them holding her on the ground sent such pain through her body that she cried out. She felt the wood penetrating her arm, separating tendon and bone, injuries that would cripple a human at the very least. She moaned softly and tried to hold still.

The sound seemed to summon whoever was guarding her. She heard bootsteps approaching the cage. She finally turned her attention to the rest of the room and counted at least ten others by sound and scent. She didn't look at them; she didn't want them to see her afraid.

They were all standing around the steel bars staring down at her. She could feel their disgust, their loathing—to them she was human-shaped vermin they were entitled to exterminate. They watched her with all the compassion of a collector pushing pins through a dead butterfly.

Now that she was finally in the same room as they were, she could feel the difference between them and ordinary humans; the magic on them that gave them the ability to fight vampires had a signature to it sort of like a scent and sort of like heat, but not quite either.

She wanted to fight. She wanted a chance to save herself. But the longer the stakes held her wounds open, the weaker she felt; wood itself would no longer kill her, but no wound could heal if there was still something in it. She was bleeding slowly onto the dirt. It took a while to kill a vampire with exsanguination but it was possible, depending on the size of the wounds and the time involved. Right now it was a race to see how she would die: by blood or by fire.

The murmur of conversation rose and fell around her. She tried to pick out individual sentences, any kind of information she could save for later, but her mind was simply too addled to make sense of it. Their sense of triumph was obvious, though, as was their anticipation. They were excited about watching her die.

Finally she heard someone speaking English quietly off to one side: "Why aren't we using this one?"

And another voice: "The Shepherd says she's part of the Circle; they're too much of a threat."

"Too bad. It's kind of hot, now that I look at it—if we had a party before dawn the Shepherd would never know."

Miranda's entire body went ice cold.

"Shut up," the other snapped, then said in a low voice, "You start saying shit like that and they'll call you a sympathizer— and when it comes time to kill all of *them* off, you'll be first in line."

"Yeah, whatever. What are we supposed to do with the woman and the kid?"

"Orders are to kill them as soon as it's dead. The only way to be sure we destroy them for good is to wipe out the bloodlines."

Strange . . . as she listened to them talk, trying with all her will to hang on to their words so she could remember them because she knew they were important, feeling her body growing weaker with each passing minute, feeling the first hint of dawn touch her skin and redouble her fear, she felt something happening . . . in the corner of the room, behind the two men, something was . . . wrong . . . no, not wrong, just . . . strange . . .

It felt almost as if the air and the earth in that spot were turning to water, and then into light. Behind her closed eyes she could see a soft glimmer beginning to build, first just around the edges of an oval-shaped space in the shadows, then expanding, like someone slowly swinging a door open.

There was a blast of wind—cool, damp wind, scented with evergreen and the faint taste of the ocean—nothing like the air around her. The light grew absolutely blinding; then, as quickly as it had come, it faded, and the night was as it had been.

"Did you feel that?" one of the two men asked.

The second started to reply, but all Miranda heard was a sputtering, gurgling sound. A few seconds later she heard the telltale heavy thud of a body hitting the ground.

Her consciousness was fading in and out, but she heard a familiar voice snap, "Cover the child's eyes."

The next few minutes were a cacophony of men yelling, weapons being drawn, and the silvery swish of a blade—through the air, against other blades, and into flesh. Miranda managed to turn her head toward the noise and saw steel catch the light, moving so fast the humans barely had time to get their hands on their own swords before they were down.

They had clearly not been expecting an attack, believing their location secret and that there was no possibility another vampire could try to rescue her in time.

Within minutes, they were all dead.

She heard chains rattling and then falling to the ground. "Get out," the voice she knew came again. "Room two twenty-one at the Verde Inn—you'll be safe there." Then, a child's cry of fear, and footsteps running away—one adult, carrying a lighter burden.

Miranda lifted her head slightly. She had to know what was happening.

Something struck the gate and it flew off its hinges, slamming into the far side of the cage.

A shadow fell over Miranda, and a glowing green light caught her eyes. Her relief was so profound she laughed weakly, the sound strangled by tears.

"Be still," Deven said gently, kneeling beside her. "This is going to hurt."

"Where's . . ." she panted.

"He's four hours away. Dawn is coming—we need to get somewhere dark."

The first stake came out and she screamed, back arching against the pain. It felt like it was flaying her open from the inside. The second nearly made her black out. By the time it clattered to the ground, she was sobbing.

She had been staked and shot before, but it was nothing like this—these were thicker, rammed deep into the ground, and the wood they were made of had barely even been sanded. It scraped against the inside of the wounds and left a fire of torment in its wake.

"Breathe . . . just breathe."

Desperate for something to cling to, she wrapped her fingers in his coat and held on for dear life. If the stakes in her wrists were agonizing, the ones in her legs were beyond that;

she hadn't known her body could feel that kind of pain without dying. They had been rammed in at an angle, through her calves. Worst of all, there were still more—several of the crossbow bolts had been left in her, though they'd been broken off in back.

"I can't . . ." she half panted, half sobbed.

"You can, Miranda. I promise you can." Deven carefully lifted her shoulders up off the ground and leaned her against him. With one hand, he reached up and unsnapped the studded leather collar he was wearing. "Here," he said, tilting his head, offering his neck. "Bite down."

She didn't have time to question it—he didn't give her time. He started pulling the bolts, in rapid succession, getting it over with as fast as possible. On top of everything else, the crossbow bolts had barbed heads.

Her teeth tore into the skin in front of her, dark blood spilling into her mouth, ripping deeper with every stifled scream. He didn't even flinch.

The last bolt came out, and he put his hand on the back of her head, encouraging her to drink. Vampire blood wouldn't do her much good physically, but just the act of feeding helped soothe some of her panic. She had never fed on her own kind, except for David, and that had only been either to turn her into a Thirdborn or in the course of sex. It surprised her how similar to David Deven tasted—like two vintages of the same wine.

"We need to get out of here," he said, looking up at the sky, which continued to lighten. She watched the holes in his neck—not the neat punctures they usually left, but ragged tears from all four teeth—close up and disappear.

"Sorry . . . about that," she said.

Deven kissed her forehead. "Barely a scratch." They had perhaps an hour before the sun was high enough to hurt them. "I think we're on the edge of town—we might be stuck here for the day. Let's see if we can find someplace a little more comfortable."

"You don't have a car?" she whispered. She didn't have the strength to summon her voice.

"No . . . I'm on my own. I was the only one who could get here fast enough."

"Wait . . . how *did* you get here? There's no airport."

"I'll explain later." Straightening, he picked her up off the ground and carried her out of the pen. Just getting out from under the open sky made her feel far less afraid.

The next quarter hour or so faded in and out, but when she opened her eyes again, she could smell hay, and the same earthy animal stink as in David's stables. Here, though, the smell was old and faded, just like the machinery smell in the other building. Nothing but owls and mice had lived here for a long time.

Miranda looked around curiously; most of the barn was far below. They were in a hayloft. Usually a place like that would have gaps in the planks that let sunlight reach in, but up here, whoever had built the place had taken extra care to keep the wind and rain out to protect the hay, and it was comfortably dark, especially since Deven had found a faded canvas tarp and was basically making them a hay fort to block out any remaining sunlight.

Miranda couldn't lie there and not help; she forced herself up and grabbed a small bale, stacking it near the entrance. It looked almost like a little house, or like the stable in a Nativity, the thought of which would have made her laugh if she hadn't been so tired.

"We need three Wise Men," she said.

He lightly squeezed the back of her neck, a surprisingly reassuring gesture. "We'll have to settle for two badass Signets. Go inside and get comfortable. I'll get a look at what our defenses are and whether there's an animal or, if we're really lucky, a human around we can get you fed on."

Miranda had to move slowly; the wounds were still deep, and without feeding she couldn't heal them completely and stay conscious. She knew as soon as Deven had made certain their defenses he'd come to her aid; they didn't have time for her to lie around whimpering. She spread another tarp over the floor of their tiny hideaway and pushed and shoved the hay beneath into something resembling pillows, then sank back into it with a grunt.

"We're on an abandoned farm outside town," Deven said, returning from his recon. "According to my phone there's nothing for miles—I'm barely getting a signal. If there are any Morningstar left on the property, they're biding their time. I called David," he added before she could ask, reaching down to pull off her boots. "He knows you're all right. He may have already tried to call you. I persuaded him to stop at a motel and come the rest of the way close to sunset—otherwise he'd be stranded in the car for twelve hours losing his mind. Now, just relax . . . let me take care of this mess."

He held his hands above her body, moving them slowly over her; she felt healing energy sighing softly into her, bathing each wound in warmth and leaving a slight vibration behind. As the pain abated she was able to watch him more closely, and the difference in his energy from the last time they'd met was amazing. He was clearer, even stronger, and his power flowed almost effortlessly where, back when he'd healed Kat, it had taken twice as long and had knocked him out for most of a day. He had, since she'd last seen him, tapped into something fathomless.

She remembered what Jonathan had said about the "Weaver" who had helped them. Whatever this guy was, he was powerful . . . frighteningly so.

They settled in together to wait out the sunlight, Miranda's head resting on his shoulder. The barn creaked softly in the wind, and though she could feel the sun burning outside, she felt protected; the quiet, broken by the droning of insects and the passage of birds overhead, coupled with the warmth to take some of the horror of the night away.

"Okay," she said. "Tell me how you got here so fast."

"A really big slingshot."

She elbowed him in the ribs. "I'm guessing it had something to do with your new friend," Miranda said.

"How did you . . . never mind." Deven sighed. "Yes. He has the ability to create portals from place to place. It's hard work, though, and doing it on such short notice to an unfamiliar location wiped him out. I'll have to take a plane back."

"Does this miracle worker have a name?"

"Nico."

She reached up and touched his Signet, silent for a moment, before saying quietly, "You really were dying, weren't you."

"Yes."

"Why didn't you tell us?"

"Because you couldn't have done anything . . . and because

I don't think I really wanted to get better." He shut his eyes for a moment. "If Nico hadn't appeared out of nowhere determined to help, I probably would have just given up."

"Even if it meant taking Jonathan with you?"

"I didn't want to punish him, too, but by then, all I wanted was for it to end. I would never have killed us on purpose, but if I could just lie back and let it happen . . . you have to understand . . . after everything I've destroyed, it was no less than I deserved."

Miranda felt tears burn her eyes. "You can't really believe that." She knew, though, that he did, and the hollowness of such a thought, along with the memory of a time when she'd have been perfectly happy for him to die, filled her with such sadness, when she was already feeling hurt and vulnerable, that she turned her face into his neck and wept.

She heard an affectionate chuckle. "Don't cry, love . . . you can't be rid of me that easily."

She lifted her head. "It's not just that. It's been a really shitty day, and . . ."

"You wish David were here."

She nodded, sniffing. "I never should have come here. I don't know what I was thinking. It was stupid."

Deven used the hem of his shirt to wipe her eyes. "Seeking love is never stupid. No one is immune to missing those they've lost."

They were silent for a while; Miranda knew she should sleep, and her body was craving it, but her mind wouldn't be still. She kept remembering the terror of waking up staked to the ground . . . of feeling the sky lighten overhead, knowing that she couldn't free herself . . . thinking that after everything, she might die alone on a filthy floor and never see David again . . .

"You're projecting, my Lady."

"Sorry . . . I'm just so tired of this constant feeling of impending doom hanging over my head. I just want a little time to pass without fighting for my life or being afraid of whom I'll lose next."

"I wish I had comforting words for you, but . . ."

"I know. It's far from over. I just have to suck it up and deal. It just . . . it hurts."

"If you dwell too much on your sorrow and fear, you'll end up on the ground with a dying heart," Deven said. "Trust me, Miranda . . . you don't want that. Just deal with what's in front of you, and trust your own strength. Take solace in what you love."

"I am," she said, tightening her grip on his hand again. "Take your own advice."

The sun was well up outside by now; the main part of the barn was run through with shafts of light that kept the hayloft from being as dark as she might have liked, but still, it was safe and warm.

Her phone rang. It took a moment of groping with the ache in her arms, but she found it in her pocket. "Hello?"

"Thank God you're safe." David's voice crackled and skipped from the poor signal.

"Hey, baby. Where are you?"

". . . motel about an hour outside Rio Verde . . . be there as soon as I can. Have you fed?"

"No. Not a whole lot of people wandering around the barn. But I'm okay for now."

"I'll have some with me when . . . get there. You only have to last until sunset."

"I'll be fine."

Most people wouldn't be able to hear the rough edge of worry in his voice, but she certainly could as he said, "Tell Deven he'd better take good care of you or I'll yank his piercings out . . . and I won't start with his face."

"Understood," Deven said, leaning toward the phone. "Now stop pacing around your room and go to sleep."

"Fine . . . both of you get some rest. We'll all be home soon."

"How are you really feeling?" Deven asked after they hung up. "You don't sound fine."

She drew a shaky breath. "I'm hungry. It's getting harder to ignore. I'll make it until sunset, but I'm probably going to get good and bitchy pretty soon. Distract me . . . tell me more about this Nico of yours."

"He's not mine," he said a little too quickly. She peered at him curiously, taking a moment to read the surface emotions she could sense; he was unusually open at the moment, and what she saw surprised her. At the look on her face, he added, "It's not like that."

"Are you sure?" she asked. "It feels like that to me."

He toyed with one of her curls for a while, then said, "He told me he loves me."

"And what did you say?"

"That it's not going to happen. I care about Nico . . . God knows I do . . . there's a connection between us that runs deep. He understands something about me no one else ever could. But the fact is, I can count the actual relationships I've had in my life on the fingers of one hand. Of those, the only one that didn't end in misery was Jonathan. I know that no matter what, he'll never leave me. He's my North Star, my constant. I don't care what he says—he might honestly be okay with it, but I'm not. And Nico says he loves me now, but he'll be gone in a few days, and if I indulge in what seems like a harmless dalliance, I'll have to live with the damage I cause to the one heart that truly matters. I don't think I'm that powerful a healer."

She nodded slowly. "I agree and I disagree," she said. "I agree that Jonathan feels more than he claims to about the whole thing, even though I don't think he's aware of it. I think he would go to his grave defending your right to be with whomever you wanted. But I disagree that anything with you and this guy would be a dalliance. I can sense it . . . if you ever let yourself feel for him, he'd have you for good. So it's best, I guess, that you don't . . . of course, emotions aren't really subject to choice. Only actions are."

Deven didn't say anything to that, just shook his head.

Miranda began to feel sleepy; exhaustion pulled at all her limbs, the strain of the night's events finally overriding her hunger—or, perhaps, she was being helped along in that direction by the subtle yet noticeable current of energy that was still flowing through her.

Well, that was one way to change the subject.

With a sigh, she turned her face into Deven's shoulder and closed her eyes.

Deven looked down from the stacked hay bales where he perched, trying to get enough of a signal on his phone to check in with David. How did people in this backwater plan a battle?

Down in the barn the light was beginning to turn watery and blue. Another hour and the sun would be far enough down that it was safe outside. Best guess, David was about an hour away. The timing was a bit troublesome.

They were in the safest possible place in the event of an attack; the only way up, assuming one couldn't climb the walls or jump fifteen feet, was the single rickety ladder. Easy enough to defend. He had a full complement of weapons, and though Miranda hadn't brought Shadowflame she had at least two blades on her that he'd seen.

Miranda stirred and woke. "Everything okay?" she asked with a yawn.

"Looks like we may have company," he replied. "David got his Morningstar-sensing scanner thing up and limping; he's pretty sure there's a fuckload of them headed out here. They'll probably arrive right before he does, so we might have to fend them off for a few minutes."

"How many is a fuckload?"

"More than an assload, less than a fuckton."

She laughed and pushed herself to her feet. She still looked exhausted, even after hours of sleep. She needed to feed, soon, or her strength reserves would burn out. As it was, he wasn't optimistic that she'd be able to fight. It was a testament to her newly won strength that she was upright at all after being staked to the ground all day.

"I don't get it," the Queen said. "If they had more people, why didn't they just come get us during the day?"

"I don't know. I know that they brought these people in from Houston, so it took a few hours to mobilize the troops and make the trip, but for some reason they still don't seem to want to attack during daylight. I guess that's the next mystery to solve. For now, gift horse, mouth."

Miranda took up her knives from the hay bale where all their weapons were waiting and buckled them on, then pulled on her coat. Deven hopped down and joined her to do the same thing, but it took him a lot longer as he had fourteen weapons total—seven he'd taken off and left on the hay bale so he could curl up with Miranda without poking her somewhere unfortunate, and seven he'd kept on.

The Queen grimaced. "I might not be much good in a

fight—my arms feel like they're made of lead. I thought you healed all of that?"

He looked her up and down. "I can't really help the fatigue because it's hunger-based. Not even I can draw blood from nowhere. I was conservative with the energy because I was worried that too much would have you unconscious for days. But I can deal with residual pain; come here."

She did, and he took both of her wrists in hand and concentrated on them for a moment. As she watched, his eyes darkened from lavender to deep violet, then faded back again as the pain in her arms faded. She didn't remember ever seeing them do that before.

Miranda started to step back, but suddenly Deven froze, tightening his grip on her arms. She turned her head to look out at the barn. "What . . ."

There it was again: a car door slamming.

The sun was still half an hour up. It wasn't David.

"They're here," Miranda said softly.

He listened hard and with a sinking heart counted the doors: two, four, eight, twelve. Assuming eight passengers per vehicle . . . Focusing even more, he counted the quiet sounds of boots on the dry, hard-packed ground outside.

Miranda shook her head, frowning. "How many?"

"Thirty."

She paled. "That's a fuckload."

"How many can you take?"

"Last time I was in a group fight I was against a dozen, but they would have killed me if David hadn't appeared. Right now? Not that many. You?"

"In straight combat I could take out around fifteen without much trouble. From up here, with only one way to reach us, if there are no crossbows I can deal with them all."

"We have to assume they'll have at least a few arrows." The Queen crossed her arms, standing on the edge of the hayloft, narrowing her eyes. "Let me handle those. I can concentrate my strength on the most strategic targets."

He started to say something, but a loud noise startled them both into silence.

Another vehicle had arrived outside, this one with a deafening diesel engine, and as it came to a stop there were a series of clanks, a grinding sound . . . and then another engine roaring to life, along with the shrill beep of something big backing up.

"What. The hell. Is that?"

He ignored the Queen for a moment and stared across the barn at one of the thin gaps in the slats; it only afforded an inch or two of the view, but what he saw was something truck-sized and yellow-orange being maneuvered toward the barn.

"It's a bulldozer," Deven said. "They're going to bring the building down."

Seven

Miranda just stared at him, while outside the beeping and engine grinding continued. "You can't be serious."

"What else do you think it could be?"

She looked out over the barn, evaluating the waning light and scent of the air. "Twenty minutes until sunset," she said. "What happens if we're exposed to dusk this late?"

Deven didn't seem afraid, but then, she wasn't sure he was capable of fear; truth be told he didn't even look particularly worried, just irritated. "Dawn and dusk are kind of a gray area. Right now a good long exposure, say a full sixty seconds, would kill us . . . and if you thought those stakes hurt, you're in for a much more unpleasant surprise."

Her heart was pounding—she remembered that brief moment in Stella's apartment when she'd been exposed. She stepped back, and again, wanting nothing more than to dive into the hay and curl up in a ball.

"It definitely won't take them twenty minutes to knock down the walls," she said.

"Probably not. Hitting a few load-bearing beams would make short work of a shack like this."

She made a helpless gesture. "Why the hell aren't you worried? How can you be so calm?"

The Prime raised an eyebrow. "I don't know if you knew this, but the Queen I'm trapped in here with is a telekinetic empath."

"But I can't move something I can't see!"

"And your empathic gift can't penetrate a barn door?" He gave her a somewhat weary smile. "How disappointing."

Miranda shot him a look of annoyance but grounded herself and reached out toward the world outside. She tried to ignore the continuing sounds of the humans outside revving up the bulldozer and turning it so it faced the barn door; she extended her senses slowly, touching each mind she felt to give her an idea of the size of the crowd.

Deven's count had been right: thirty.

"Weird," she murmured without losing the vision. "Their minds are . . . I don't know, it's like they're all copies of the same mind. They aren't exactly a hive, but they all have the same emotions . . . the same programming."

She followed the sounds of the engine and looked for the person closest to it, the driver. Pushing a surge of power toward the man, she loaded it with the most disruptive thing she could think of: panic.

Run. They're going to kill you. Run. Run!

She heard a scream, and a commotion; the driver all but fell off his seat and bolted. To her shock, she heard a familiar click and whistle—they shot him.

Another human was already climbing into the driver's seat. Miranda pulled her energy back from the first man and threw it hard at the second. He, too, leapt from the seat and ran, and he, too, fell with a crossbow bolt in his back.

A third human started to replace him, but before Miranda could ready another hit, she heard someone bark, *"Forget the walls! They've got an empath! Move in!"*

Miranda looked at Deven. "That leaves twenty-eight."

Before she even got the sentence out, a wave of nausea and exhaustion hit her—already weakened, she'd overextended her gift. She didn't have the energy to take down all of them that way—she had to pace herself.

The barn door shuddered, then splintered, falling off its hinges to the ground. The light that flooded in was bright enough to make her head pound, but she'd managed to stall them just enough that it was no longer genuinely dangerous.

From here on out, it was a fight to the death.

What seemed like a hundred uniformed humans poured into the door, some armed with crossbows, others with swords. The first arrows were already flying before the whole unit had even crossed the threshold.

Miranda ducked one that came at her head. Beside her, she heard Deven draw his sword.

"Stay up here as long as you can," he said. "They can only come up the ladder single file—you can knock them down from there."

"But where are you—"

Without another word, he jumped off the edge of the hay-loft; her heart crawled up into her throat as he spun in midair, slicing open the throat of the closest human before he'd even landed.

A group of soldiers rushed him, and two were down in mere seconds. Meanwhile others kept firing up at her, and four more humans ran for the ladder, trying to scale it as quickly as possible. They were, she noticed, remarkably fast, just as she'd heard; she had never seen humans move like that. Up until that moment she hadn't entirely believed it was possible.

Miranda made for the ladder. The first man reached the top, and she seized him by the shirt collar and hauled him up with her, letting the slowly mounting hunger she'd been fighting off all day have its way with him. The second soldier made it to the top, but without lifting her mouth from her prey's throat, she wrenched herself around and kicked the ladder hard, sending it, and the three humans attempting to climb it, to the ground in a heap.

His blood hit her system like dynamite—and, with only a split second's thought that she was going to kill him one way or another, she kept drinking until he stopped fighting her, until that rush of death flowed into her body and renewed every single tired, aching cell. She didn't have time to truly enjoy it, though.

She shoved him off onto the fight below and, smiling, wiped the blood from her mouth. She felt awake again . . . awake, alive . . . and spoiling for a fight.

The Queen backflipped, pushing herself off the hayloft's edge with her hands, and hit the ground rolling sideways until she was upright; the knives were in her hands, and the one in her left had already slammed into a human's chest.

She looked over at Deven, who seemed to be enjoying himself. He had another five dead, strewn about the ground like fallen leaves.

Another bolt zipped past her ear. She reached out with her mind and caught it, then turned it around and sent it back to its rightful owner; the muffled scream told her it struck home. As she engaged two others, she glanced over to see how many crossbows they had left: three. Deciding on the easiest way to incapacitate them, Miranda grabbed the first one with her power and broke his fingers. He doubled over in pain, dropping his weapon.

She had to bring her full attention back to where she was, though, as her two opponents had intensified their attack. Miranda jumped back over a body and took the dead woman's sword.

Distantly she heard a series of noises that her brain interpreted as car doors.

"More of them?" she called to Deven, too distracted to try to sense outside.

Deven flashed her a grin. "I don't think so."

She parted the head of one of her opponents from his shoulders and turned to the door just in time to see the most welcome sight she'd had all day: her Elite.

More than a dozen black-clad vampires swarmed into the barn. The humans had to abandon their quarry and turn around to face their attackers, and for a moment they seemed evenly matched.

Then a man in a long black coat walked into the barn, his blue eyes on fire with wrath, power seething around him like the eye of a hurricane.

Miranda felt the humans' fear breaking through their programming, but they had nowhere to run. They were blocked on one end by Miranda and Deven, on the other by David, and on both sides by Elite . . . but they didn't surrender. In fact, they seemed to become even faster and stronger the more desperate their circumstances.

A vampire woman snaked her way through the crowd to the Queen. She had a sword in her hands. "My Lady," she said, loudly enough to be heard over the din of battle, "I believe you left this in the SUV."

"Minh!" Miranda pulled herself back into normal reality, took Shadowflame from her, and tossed the sword's sheath back into a pile of hay where she could retrieve it later. "You're all right—how's Stuart?"

"Dead," Minh replied. "The bastards left me unconscious on the driveway when they made off with you. Stuart was still inside, staked. He must have tried to save you."

Anger rose hot and bitter in Miranda's throat, and she snarled and closed on another soldier, Shadowflame flashing through his jugular and carotid with a spray of blood.

She looked around the barn for David. She could feel him in her mind, close enough to ease the growing anxiety of being so far from her Prime, and saw him off to one side of the fight, a human pinned back against the wall as David drank from him. She frowned—it was kind of an odd time to feed.

When he let the human drop, he met her eyes across the room, and they smiled at each other, adrenaline twisted around happiness at being reunited.

David's eyes flicked past her for a moment, and she saw his expression change, his smile fading into alarm.

It happened so fast. She spun in the direction David was staring, fear choking her at whatever could possibly be bad enough to make him react that way . . . just in time to see Deven fall.

David couldn't even move—Miranda, who was closer, was beside Dev in seconds. David saw blood, far too much of it, and the Queen had gone white as she eased the Prime onto his back. It wasn't immediately clear what had happened, but one thing was clear: It was bad.

David felt the room around him slow down as his mind kicked into high gear. He counted the remaining humans: They were down to six. They were all within thirty feet of him. Close enough, and few enough, for a more direct approach than a fair fight. He calculated how to divide his power to reach them all at once. Normally six would be too many for this . . . but this time he had something he normally didn't have to work with.

Rage.

Teeth pressing into his lower lip, the room gone red with the desire to make them pay, David seized all six humans and, his hands closing into fists, reached into them with his mind, took hold of all six hearts . . . and made them explode.

They had just enough time to scream.

The Elite froze, watching with fascination as their remaining half-dozen enemies fell to the ground simultaneously. As soon as the humans stopped moving, everything became eerily silent.

He shook himself out of his paralysis and made for the far end of the barn, joining Miranda just in time to see her pull a throwing stake from Deven's chest and another from his side.

"It's not a heart shot," she reassured David, though her voice was tense at the sight of the wounds. The chest shot wasn't that bad; it started to heal immediately. The side stake, however, looked like it had been in there a while, and the amount of blood was almost frightening. He had to have been wounded early in the fight and just ignored it—a very Deven thing to do.

"Idiot," David scolded him gently. "You're supposed to pull those out."

"New piercing," Deven replied, pale and shaky from blood loss. "You don't like it?"

"My turn to hurt you," Miranda told him. "Take a deep breath."

Deven didn't make a sound when she pulled the second stake . . . but he did pass out.

Miranda looked past David to the scattered bodies he'd left strewn about the ground. "If it had been me lying here, would you have been angry enough to do that?"

Their eyes met. He looked for emotion behind her words, but empathically he sensed nothing amiss; she just wanted to know. "No," he replied. "I would have ripped out their hearts with my bare hands and shoved them down their throats."

She smiled. "I probably shouldn't find that romantic, should I."

The Pair rose simultaneously, and David gestured to one of the lieutenants he'd brought. "Very carefully get him to the car. Give him one of the blood bags in the cooler. We'll be there momentarily."

Four Elite clustered around the inert Prime. David took Miranda's hand and drew her off to the side, where they'd be out of the way while the other Elite stacked bodies and prepared to burn down the barn.

Miranda threw her arms around him, and they held on to each other for a long time, neither speaking. All the fear he'd been carrying since he'd felt the first crossbow bolt hit her finally fell from his shoulders, and he felt like he could fly.

"I love you so much," he murmured, touching his forehead to hers. "I've never been so scared."

"You, scared?" she smiled. "Too bad I was half-dead and could barely feel you—that must have been something."

He held her chin in his hand and examined her. "You're a mess."

"So are you. Did you by any chance look for Marianne? I have a few questions for her."

David nodded. "She is currently holed up in the Verde Inn—I have surveillance on her. I also had a room reserved for us; we can make it back to Austin tonight if you want to deal with such a long drive after such a crap day, but I thought you might at least want a shower first, and I rather doubted you'd want to go to your father's house."

Miranda frowned. "I never did see him. There's nobody there to take care of him."

David met her eyes. "Your father is dead," he told her gently. "After you were taken and Stuart was killed, Minh searched the house for some clue as to where they'd taken you, and she found him in his hospital bed along with an empty vial of morphine and a syringe hanging out of his IV. Either Morningstar killed him, or Marianne did."

"They had her daughter," she mused. "I want to be angry with her for selling me out, but . . . what else could she do?"

Before David could reply, there came a voice: "Sire . . . there might be a problem."

The Prime lifted his chin, indicating the Elite should go on.

"You said when we came in that there were exactly thirty

humans. There are only twenty-nine bodies. And one of their vehicles is gone—they must have bolted during the chaos."

He nodded. "Noted, Elite Forty-six. Thank you for the report."

Miranda looked quizzical. "Aren't you concerned that one of them got away?"

Smiling, he said, "He didn't get away." He took out his phone, pulled up a map, and showed her the green dot moving rapidly down the interstate. "He's taking us on a little trip back to Morningstar HQ."

"You put a tracker on him? Or on the car? How can you be sure he won't find it?"

"He won't unless he goes through a metal detector." David took her hand again and led her outside; the Elite could handle things from here. As they walked, David took a small case about the size of a mint tin from his inner coat pocket and showed her its contents: three tiny flat devices only a few millimeters long, with an empty slot where a fourth had been. "It's currently residing under his skin, like an ID microchip in a dog."

"How did you get it in him? There wasn't exactly a lull during the battle."

He grinned. "Each of them has a strip of temporary adhesive on the back. It got into his body via my right canine tooth."

She stopped walking. "Seriously?"

"Yes. It'll be in there at least long enough to trace the way to wherever his base is—and hopefully there we'll find a Shepherd. If I'm really lucky he'll live long enough for me to get a full read on their headquarters."

Miranda shook her head, chuckling. "You really are something else, baby. What am I going to do with you?"

He leaned in and kissed her. "Let's get to the hotel and hose you off, and then I'll be delighted to show you exactly what you can do with me."

Miranda's laughter rang out just as, behind them, the old half-demolished barn and the twenty-nine bodies inside went up in flames.

By the time Miranda climbed out of the motel room's minuscule shower, the filth scrubbed from her hair and the blood scrubbed from under her nails, she was feeling almost cheerful. She emerged from the steamy bathroom with her hair up in a towel turban.

The only available room had one bed and an armchair whose questionable provenance made both of the Pair a little uneasy, so David was sitting cross-legged on the bed with his laptop. He looked up and smiled at her. "The barn has burned to the ground and the fire's out," he said. "The Elite I had keeping an eye on it are on their way back."

"What did you do with Deven?" she asked.

"He's gone," David replied. "He was eager to get back to California before sunrise."

Miranda pulled on her spare set of clothes. She'd thrown away most of what she'd had on earlier. "I really need to stop getting staked," she muttered. "It's costing me a fortune in shirts."

"And to think you used to roll your eyes at my keeping a change of clothes in the car."

"Considering how high we are on the food chain, we sure do have a messy job." She paused. "Speaking of which . . . did Jonathan send the jet to Houston to pick Dev up?"

"No. There was a commercial flight out of Bush at twelve thirty—it was pushing it, but I'm sure the airline knows to hold takeoff until he's there."

"He was covered in blood," she pointed out. "Drenched. I know he didn't have extra clothes. There's no way TSA would let him through security looking like that, first class or not."

David had returned his eyes to the screen but told her absently, "He said he was going to stop in town and buy something."

Miranda couldn't help it; she burst out laughing and giggled uncontrollably until she had to sit down.

"What on earth is so funny?" he asked.

"This is a small town in Texas," she replied, wheezing a little. "The only place to buy clothes here that's open after sundown is Walmart. Just take a minute and picture Deven standing in line at Walmart."

David laughed so hard he nearly choked. "Oh dear God."

Still giggling, she found her phone, and when Deven answered, she said, "Tell me you're wearing sweatpants right now."

She could hear him rolling his eyes. "Don't you have a sister to hunt down?"

"Not until you tell me what you're wearing."

"Oh, for Christ's sake. The least offensive thing I could find was jeans and a T-shirt."

"What's on the T-shirt?"

"Nothing, it's just black."

"Liar!"

A sigh. "I can neither confirm nor deny the presence of Snoopy and/or Woodstock. Happy?"

This time she laughed until her stomach hurt; at some point, Deven muttered something in Gaelic and hung up.

Flopping back on the bed, Miranda said, "I needed that."

David smiled at her. "It's good to hear you laugh. Especially that little snort—I love that little snort."

"It feels good."

"Snoopy or no Snoopy, remind me to send that boy a fruit basket for getting you back to me."

Miranda moved over to him, shifting up behind him to wrap her legs around his waist and rest her head on his shoulder. "I wish you had been here with me."

"You do understand that if you uncover any additional estranged relatives, I'm going with you even if I have to hide in the trunk."

She grinned and kissed the nape of his neck. "So we're five hours from Austin . . . if we're going home tonight we need to leave soon. I still want to talk to Marianne, if I can find her, but I want to go home so badly I can taste it. What do you think?"

"Room two-twenty-one," he said. "As long as you don't take more than an hour, with the new window tint we'll have sufficient time."

Twenty minutes later, Miranda stood at the door to room 221—this time with her husband's assurance that there was nobody in the room but Marianne and Jenny . . . but flanked by two bodyguards, wearing Shadowflame, and aware of the three other Elite watching the door, just in case.

Marianne looked even worse than the last time she'd opened a door to Miranda's knock. Again, they stared at each other, then Marianne moved back out of the way to let her in.

Marianne's eyes moved from Miranda's face down to the sword she was wearing, but she didn't comment.

A room identical to the one Miranda had showered in presented itself as well as it could. The curtains were shut tight, and the rumpled bed held the form of a seven-year-old girl sound asleep in Minnie Mouse pajamas, her red hair a slightly frizzy halo around her head. Jenny didn't even stir—given the night she'd had, Miranda wasn't surprised. The Queen herself was looking forward to passing out and staying that way for as long as possible.

As Miranda swept into the room, she noticed the innocuous white box on the bedside table—sterile-packed syringes and, next to them, four vials lined up neatly.

Marianne followed her stare. "Don't you dare judge me," she said. "You don't know me."

Miranda just looked at her.

Uncomfortable under the Queen's steady gaze, Marianne sat down on the foot of the bed, crossing and uncrossing her arms, fidgeting. "I went back by the house and got some stuff," she said. "I don't want to go back again, but I don't know what to do about the old man."

"It'll be taken care of."

"Are those . . . people . . . going to come after me again?" Marianne looked over at Jenny. The little girl looked so vulnerable, and an expression Miranda imagined seeing on a mother bear passed over Marianne's features—the most emotion Marianne had shown yet. "They killed George. They cut off his head . . . they made me look at pictures so I'd behave. Told me all the things they were going to do to Jenny. And then they killed the old man and all I could think was, 'What a stupid waste of morphine.'"

"I can't guarantee they won't try to kill you again," Miranda admitted, crossing her arms. "But my husband has a contact in the U.S. Marshals who can get you into WITSEC, backed up by some of my own people as additional security. New identity, new home, new life for both of you."

"Why do you care?" Marianne asked, her voice hardening. "Why should you? Nobody in this family has ever done dick for you except Mom, and we locked her up and threw away the key. You can't possibly have any warm and fuzzy feelings for me after all this time."

Miranda regarded her sister in silence for a moment. "I don't, really," she said bluntly. "And the truth is, you're way better off far away from me. But another truth is . . . what happened to you and Jenny, and what happened to George and even Dad, at the end, is because of who and what I am. I know your life was already broken before I got here, but I made it a thousand times worse, and I want to balance the scale."

Marianne nodded, and Miranda could tell she appreciated the honesty. "That guy, with the other red necklace and the blue eyes . . . that's your husband?"

"Yes. When did you see him?"

Marianne tucked her hair back behind her ears nervously. "He knocked on the door earlier and said that you wanted to talk to me and if I tried to rabbit he'd wring my neck."

"He's very thoughtful like that. I'm leaving for Austin shortly, but you'll still have guards as long as you're here, and then they'll coordinate with the Marshals to get you someplace more long-term. There's an icon on your phone that will connect you directly to Marshal Ken Gregory. And you have my e-mail address as well."

Another nod. "Okay."

She looked at Jenny, and added, "You understand that there will be people watching you, and that if they deem you unfit or catch you with drugs, they'll take her into foster care in accordance with human law."

"Yeah . . . I get it."

Miranda opened the door, but before she walked out, Marianne called her back.

She turned to see what Marianne wanted; her sister had risen and was digging in her bag. "I want you to have this," she was saying. "I don't know why I took it, but I don't really want it. You might."

She handed her prize to Miranda: a small leather-bound photo album. "There's some stuff of Mom in there," she said. "Keep it, throw it away, whatever."

Miranda opened the front cover, and her mother's face smiled up at her.

"Thank you," she said softly.

Miranda closed the door behind her, and as she heard the locks being turned and flipped, she felt a weight lift from her shoulders she hadn't known was there. All this time she'd been carrying unfinished business around with her, waiting to feel some sort of closure, good or bad, with her family . . . and though there was no telling if she would ever see Marianne again, or that Marianne would even last six months without dying with a needle in her arm, she still felt like that last door had finally closed, the last connection to her human life gone.

She had expected that moment to feel sorrowful, regretful . . . but in the end what she felt was relief bordering on joy.

She crossed the motel parking lot to where the Escalade was waiting; most of the Elite had returned to the Houston branch in the vehicle that Miranda had arrived in. It would just be the Pair and Harlan on the way home.

David was waiting in the car, finishing up a phone call. "How are you?" he asked as she climbed in.

Miranda considered that. "Finished," she said. "I'm finished." He nodded, understanding, and she leaned against his shoulder and added, "Now get me the hell out of here."

Dawn was circling slowly around the last hour of night when, after a three-hour drive and an equally long flight on a slow and clunky 737, Prime Deven arrived back at the Haven in desperate need of about a week's sleep and clothes—any clothes—that actually fit.

As he walked down the hall he heard the outside shutters engaging. In a few seconds the beautiful views and courtyards of the Haven would be blocked from sight, the building closing in on itself, cool and dark and safe.

He found Jonathan in bed already, asleep reclining atop the covers in faded red flannel pants, with a huge hardcover book lying open on his bare belly. Deven knew he would have stayed awake as long as possible, counting the minutes until his Prime came home—knowing he was so far away, and hurt, but being unable to help, would have been a torment for any Signet, though it always seemed to be worse for Consorts than Primes.

He and Jonathan had talked briefly twice, once before the battle and again during the endless drive from Rio Verde to Houston. In that second call Deven had heard and felt the near-panic in Jonathan's voice from waiting to hear that his lover was all right.

It was a testament to Jonathan's endless patience that he hadn't come unglued when he realized the Elf had punted Deven halfway across the country without warning or discussion. Dev had honestly expected some anger there, but Jonathan had just said, "Miranda needed you."

Deven stood over him for a moment, listening to him breathe and watching his eyelashes flutter as he dreamed. He looked peaceful, so whatever he was seeing in there must not be precognitive.

Finally, he sat down on the edge of the bed and leaned in to kiss his Consort gently on the lips.

Jonathan made a noise and woke smiling. "How was your flight?"

"If there is a hell, it involves flying commercial."

The Consort yawned. "I checked in on Nico, like you asked—he was barely awake. I think he held out just long enough to know you were okay. Apparently that whole portal-building thing is like being hit in the third eye with a brick if you haven't seen the destination."

"Well, I'm glad he's all right," Deven replied, and if Jonathan heard anything more than friendly concern in the words, he graciously ignored it.

"And how's Miranda?"

"Much better. She went through so much today . . . and all for someone she doesn't even like."

Jonathan chuckled. "Family matters are never that straightforward. They're made up of layers of time, guilt, love, anger, and obligation."

"She said it was her fault."

"Taking on the burden of culpability not her own," Jonathan murmured. "Where have I seen that before?" He ran his hand from Deven's Signet down to his hip. "Incidentally, that is a magnificent ensemble you've got there."

"Oh, shut up." Deven laughed. "You should have seen me washing off dried blood in the men's room sink at Walmart.

The greeter at the doors about had a heart attack when I walked into the store—I think they told themselves it was a costume for some kind of horror film."

"I'm glad you got back before dawn . . . I was starting to worry."

"I told Wu to break every speed limit between the airport and here. I couldn't wait to get home."

"I can imagine not, if the alternative was the *Deliverance* Best Western."

"No, silly man. I wanted to get home to *you*."

Jonathan looked genuinely surprised. "Oh?"

"I've been thinking about this a lot lately . . . about us. I know I'm a disaster most of the time, and a spoiled brat the rest. But in spite of all my egregious faults, you have made me happier than I ever thought I could be. I hope you know what a miracle that is . . . that you are."

The Consort stared at him for a moment, then reached down and shoved the book off his middle, grabbed Deven around *his* middle, and hauled him down onto the bed, looking intently into his face. "You really mean that," he said, sounding faintly dazed.

"Of course I do." Dev brushed his fingers over Jonathan's lips, smiling. "You're my always."

Jonathan grinned. There was genuine happiness in his eyes, without a trace of the heavy emotion he'd been carrying around since all of this had begun. "Oh, darling, I hope you can stay awake for another hour, because you are about to get so laid."

"Don't you want me to take a shower before—"

Unsurprisingly, he never got to finish the question.

Eight

Three nights into her second stay at the Haven, Stella still didn't completely believe she was there. Everything after the wreck seemed so unreal she was sure she would wake up any minute now back in her apartment bedroom, startled out of sleep by her upstairs neighbor having loud arrhythmic sex with his girlfriend.

Instead, when she opened her eyes, she was in the same guest suite as before, left to her own devices inside the home of well over a hundred vampires who, for the most part, ignored her. She was the Queen's pet, not theirs; with the exception of the servants who fed her and kept her mini fridge full of Dr Pepper, and the two guards who alternated keeping an eye on her, she hardly saw anyone.

Last time, that silence had bothered her because she wanted desperately to know what was going on out there, but this time, it was a relief to be left alone. She just wanted to relax enough that she wouldn't have screaming nightmares about being hit by a truck and smashed into Witch-jam, trapped in a burning car and bleeding out, dying on the street, or ending up paralyzed. The worst dream was the one where she watched her father weep at her funeral. In her entire life

Stella only remembered seeing her father cry twice, once when her stepmother had died, and once a couple of years later when he and Stella had watched *Up*.

She knew how lucky she'd been not to die in that crash. The fact that it probably wasn't luck at all was deeply disturbing . . . people didn't walk away from crashes like that without a hair out of place. There had to be something else at work, and she had a feeling she knew what, or rather Who, was responsible.

Stella lay in the enormous bed wrapped in a safe cocoon of blankets, with Pywacket folded into a kitty loaf and asleep at the foot of the bed. She wished she'd taken Miranda up on her offer of a bottle of sleeping pills. An afternoon of oblivion without the crunch of metal echoing in her ears would be really nice.

How the hell did I get here?

She was an average, everyday Witch only a few weeks ago—a store clerk, average height, a bit on the round side, with a typically Austinesque fashion concept, perfectly happy with how things were. She'd come through a period of crippling depression thanks to music and was starting to reach a place where she could imagine doing something interesting with her life . . . a work in progress. Sure, her religious proclivities and her psychic gift put her in the oddball category, and with a homicide detective as a father her family life wasn't typical, but . . . how had she ended up the Pony Express courier between a deity and a bunch of filthy rich, gorgeous, sword-fighting vampires?

She'd accepted this role, whatever it actually was, that night during the Drawing Down, but it had yet to stop freaking her out. Maybe if she were sure of what she was supposed to do, she could get used to the idea.

She knew Miranda and the others felt the same way. They needed to know what they were here for—yes, to defeat Morningstar, but how?—and how exactly they were meant to complete their Circle, but the only being who had that information was Persephone, and they couldn't talk to her until they had completed their Circle . . . unless it was through Stella, who also had no idea how to do her job.

"Kind of crappy of you," she muttered. She'd developed a habit of talking to Persephone when no one was listening—

mostly complaining. She had no idea whether Persephone could hear her, or would care if she did, but there was something comforting about the thought that somewhere, out there, Someone was listening to her and might eventually answer. At the very least, Persephone probably thought she was amusing. That was something.

She sighed and felt her body beginning to finally relax after two hours of tossing and turning. The situation was frustrating to say the least, but she didn't have to figure it all out tonight. She could sleep tonight.

Her eyes drifted shut . . .

. . . and something startled her awake. Stella, suddenly freezing, flailed around like a drunken monkey for a minute, trying to make sense of things—why was she so cold? Why was the bed so hard? The air felt different, it wasn't shielded like she'd had it—was something attacking her?

She shoved herself up into a sitting position, gaping around her, heart pounding, breath coming in gasps.

This was not her room.

It was a study of some kind; there were bookcases and a desk, but despite the lack of dust, the place had the feel of a room that wasn't in use.

She had never seen this room before. She didn't even know what part of the Haven she was in.

As she got to her feet, turning in a slow circle, trying to understand, the question returned:

How the hell did I get here?

Less than two hours from Sacramento, coastal redwood trees stretched so high into the night that they seemed to tickle heaven as the wind wandered through the forest. The air was damp and cool, sound muted, a feeling of peace hovering like a ghost amid the massive trunks.

The sound of babbling water drowned out any lingering noise of civilization, and in the middle of the night, the only mortal nearby was the park ranger, who stood guard at the entrance and therefore didn't see two dark figures materialize just past the first bend in the trail.

Nico looked down at their joined hands. "That was interesting," he said, keeping his voice low. "Quite different from passing through a portal. What is the maximum distance you can reach?"

"If I'm at full strength and alone, and the destination is one I'm familiar with, I can Mist up to ten miles. Adding another person cuts that in half."

Nico's eyebrows lifted. "Amazing."

"You didn't seem as impressed with the car," Deven said with a smile.

"I do not think anyone was meant to hurtle over land at such speeds, especially along a winding road. It seems terribly dangerous compared to using magic."

"Snob." Deven gestured toward the path. "Come on."

The first time Deven had come to Muir Woods had been just after David left California; he'd had a Consort for only a few months, been Prime for only six more than that . . . back then he had believed, mistakenly, that if he showed weakness, Jonathan would reject him. He was desperate for someplace to be alone, someplace no one expected him to have any idea what he was doing. Here, the trees seemed to be saying, "Don't worry . . . you're not really in charge. We've got it all under control."

Leaning back against one of the trees, staring straight up at its faraway branches, he'd finally been able to untwist his thoughts. Here, alone among the redwoods, he had felt free for the first time in centuries.

After that he'd come here at least once every few months. The only person who knew exactly where he was was Wu, who drove him within Misting distance of the woods themselves. Jonathan said he didn't want or need to know the location—in an emergency, that was what cell phones were for. They respected each other's space.

Elf and Prime walked in silence for a while. Deven had debated with himself over whether to bring Nico here. He wanted the Weaver to see the beauty of the earth, but being alone with him in the middle of the woods made Deven deeply nervous. He wasn't entirely secure in his convictions about all of this . . . and if Nico were to kiss him again, he was afraid of what might happen. Here they were, in the most beautiful place Deven knew, and he with a legendary lack of impulse control.

He needn't have worried. Nico apparently could be an adult even if Deven couldn't. The Elf kept his distance without any hint of awkwardness, neither ignoring what had passed between them nor pressing the issue. If he was feeling any longing, he covered it well, and he seemed to have truly meant it when he said he would value Deven's friendship.

He could feel Nico reaching out to the trees with his energy, touching theirs, greeting them in whatever unspoken language Elves shared with the natural world. Periodically the Elf let his free hand trail along the bark of one of the giants and a smile played on his lips.

"You said you could hear them talk," Nico said. "What do they say to you?"

Deven chuckled. "Oh, they're not talking to me. I'm far beneath their notice. And it's not words so much as impressions they leave in my mind. I don't think I can think slowly enough to understand them."

The Elf only smiled and nodded in reply. As Deven had expected, Nico understood perfectly.

"What do you think?" Deven asked, gesturing at the woods around them.

Nico took in their surroundings with appreciative eyes. "This is a holy place."

A moment later, Deven asked, "This goddess of yours . . . what would she think of you being here, helping a godless murdering vampire?"

Nico looked at him sharply. "I wish you would not say such things about yourself."

"Why not? It's true." Though the words were harsh, his tone was matter-of-fact, which he could tell bothered the Elf. "It's funny . . . I tell my friends I'm an atheist, but that isn't really accurate . . . I'm an apostate, no longer welcome in either the house or the heart of God."

It was those same thoughts that had shoved him into the despair that Nico had healed him from, but now, it seemed things were back to normal; instead of wanting to curl up and wail, he could summon the distance he needed to keep walking.

Nico didn't like it. He was frowning, eyes on the path and hands clasped behind him. "You began to feel cast out by the Divine as a young human, when you realized that according to the texts of your faith you were damned to an eternity of torment—both because you had supernatural power and because you love other men."

"A great many people made it very clear to me."

"And after all this time you have not seen anything that would lead you to try to reclaim your belief—even though those who led your church were prone to human frailty and fallibility like anyone else? Can you not look past them to the God whose love informs the entire universe and is, more than likely, far wiser than the little children running the show here?"

"I didn't say I don't believe," Deven told him. "Belief and faith are two different things. I believe, sometimes at least, that God exists, but I have no faith that God has ever loved me."

Surprisingly, Nico didn't try to argue with him but said, "I am sorry you feel that way."

"I can tell you disapprove."

"Not to speak ill of your God, but . . . a Father who would cast his child into perdition for healing, or for loving someone, is a poor Father indeed. I cannot believe divine love is anything less than unconditional. I do not think you will ever be whole until you have found solace for your spirit . . . if you cannot reach out to your Father, perhaps you should seek another Parent."

"Oh, like who? Yours?" Deven paused and narrowed his eyes. "You're not on some mission to convert me to Elven religion, are you?"

Nico blinked, surprised . . . and then laughed. "Of all the gods to vie for your soul, I think Persephone will prove a much stronger contender than Theia. You are very much like us, whether you want to admit it or not, but somehow I do not think you would be content passively communing with the forest for all time."

"Smiling at squirrels and singing to flowers? Probably not." Deven smiled again, deciding now was a good time to change the subject. "But you approve of our forest, even if it's not as splendid as yours?"

"It is beautiful. They are so young."

"They're older than me."

Nico tilted his chin back and admired the distant view of the treetops. "The trees in Avilon are easily three times older, but there is something here that ours are lacking. We have seasons there, yet our world is essentially unchanging, static. Much like the Elentheia themselves, they do not evolve. Strangely, that tranquillity has always made me restless. This place feels more alive somehow, more vital, and in that way, more serene."

He lowered his gaze to meet Deven's, and the sudden emotion in his violet eyes made Deven shake inside. "It is wonderful . . . as are you, a creature of leather and steel, standing there in the starlight in a place where you actually feel at peace."

Deven felt himself flushing, and he held Nico's gaze until the heat became unbearable and he had to lower his eyes. "Nico . . ."

"I know," the Elf said, chagrined. "I apologize. I honestly am trying . . . but being here with you in this place is both paradise and purgatory. Here without the burden of all your cares, you are brighter than the sun."

"I haven't seen the sun in a very long time," Deven said softly. "I'll have to take your word for it."

Nico gave him a look of faint frustration. He moved closer and took Deven's hand, kissing the back of it before retreating again. "If I know you a thousand years, *i'lyren*, I will find a way to make you see what the rest of us see in you."

"Wait . . . what did you call me?"

He grinned a little mischievously. "It means 'my ghost,'" he replied. "Or, to be more precise, 'the spirit whose light is haunting me.'"

"So . . . Ghostlight."

"As I said, it suits you. Now . . . let us walk on, before morning steals the night away."

Deven shook his head, smiling wryly at the whole situation. "As you will it," he said, and followed the Elf deeper into the forest.

Dawn had cast its gauzy veil over the sky, and the Haven shut down—shutters on timers, metal walls clattering into place over breezeways, leaving the whole building in silence and a comfortable darkness.

Nico sat on the chaise he had come to think of as his own. He had been granted an override code to open the terrace door from his room, and he was careful to shut it behind him just in case one of the guards needed to come in. It would be the height of bad manners to accidentally immolate the staff.

His heart weighed heavily in his chest as he looked down at the two packs on the tiled floor at his feet.

It was time to go. He knew it was time. But to leave so much unfinished . . .

It would never be finished. He had offered his heart to Deven knowing that it would be rejected, but it still hurt more than he had believed possible.

The Prime was right, of course. Theirs was not meant to be a long-term romance, if it got even that far . . . at least, not as they were now. There would come a day, he knew, when he and Deven both would look at each other across a very different divide, and that time they might be able to cross it.

They would have to. Too much depended on this.

But for now, his work was done. He could go home.

Home. The thought filled him with longing, and he got to his feet, already drawing power up around him to build the portal. He would go home, and he would live in the safety and solace of his own world . . . until this one called him back again . . . for the last time.

Nico reached into one of his bags and pulled out a strip of paper, along which he had written out Deven's name; he slid the ring of Theia off his finger and tied the slip of paper to it, clearly labeling who it was meant for. The moonstone gleamed in the early light. He left it on the chair. Anyone who found it would know to deliver it . . . but he knew no one else would. The first hand to touch the ring would be that of its new owner.

He reached into his pocket and pulled out another object, this one a marked contrast to his ring: a black leather wrist cuff embossed with Celtic knotwork. Deven had left it during one of their healing sessions and never asked for it back. Nico had a feeling he owned quite a few. It was not a priest's ring, perhaps, but it was strangely far more appropriate to Nico, who snapped it on his own wrist with a smile.

"Ile amast amori est i'lyren," he told the empty air, pushing a touch of energy through the words so that if he were

dreaming, Deven might hear Nico's voice and, perhaps, smile a little in his sleep.

In the fantasy Nico had built for himself, that was exactly what happened: The sleeping Prime heard his declaration and whispered back into the darkness, "I love you, too."

But the reality dictated he raise the portal and go, and so he did, drawing power up from the earth and the forest all around, letting it fill his body and expand outward. He closed his eyes and brought up his vision of the Web, laying over it an image of where he was going: home. The solitary little house he dwelt in on the edge of Avilon, deep among the trees where whispers and stares couldn't follow . . . he held on to that vision, drawing it toward him, wrapping it in his consciousness as the warp and weft of reality parted to let him through . . . and with a blast of light and heat, Nico took up his bags and stepped out of the world of mortals, back home, where he dreamed of belonging.

In the first picture, Marilyn Grey was laughing, one of the girls on her knee; they both wore shorts in the summer sun, in the backyard of the house in Rio Verde. It was pretty obvious which sister was in the picture; her bright green eyes matched her mother's, and an enormous poof of red hair had fought its way out of a headband and stuck out in all directions.

The next page was a photo of the girls, playing in the sandbox. Marianne had used a set of plastic molds to very carefully construct an amazingly detailed sand castle, her tongue sticking out of the corner of her mouth as she concentrated on getting it just right. Meanwhile Miranda had dug a hole and was sitting in it with her bucket on her head, throwing sand in the air.

That about summed it up.

Most of the pictures were from that same era. Marilyn wore a wide variety of printed bandannas over her hair; the girls ran around barefoot with skinned knees. Her father wasn't in any of them.

Looking through the album, Miranda wondered if the voices had already come to her mother by then. Had she started to feel the first scrape of other people's emotions against her mind?

Was she still able to dismiss it somehow? Her face didn't betray any sort of fear or preoccupation. Here, at least, she was still 100 percent present, at least on the outside. They made cookies, pulled weeds in the flower beds, ran through the sprinklers. Everything was achingly normal.

When the Blackthorn had burned down Miranda's apartment, she'd lost her only happy picture of her mother; David had tried to find another, but since Miranda's had come from the only extant copy of Marilyn's psych file, and a variety of spectacular clerical errors had misplaced the photo on record at the DMV, both knew the only way to get more pictures of her was to go through the family. Miranda hadn't been ready for that before, so she'd gone without, but now she had an entire album full of her mother's face.

She had avoided looking through it for a few days after they got home from Rio Verde; for the moment she had just wanted to pretend none of it had happened and not think about her family at all. But the thought of seeing Marilyn again occupied her thoughts more and more until finally she took the album to her chair by the fire, sipped a glass of blood, and turned the pages slowly, smiling through tears at how adorable the sisters had been . . . how innocent and full of promise . . . how happy they had all seemed.

Miranda had grown quieter and more introverted over the years, a vague and unnamable sadness taking up permanent residence in her eyes. Marianne had gradually distanced herself from her depressive, weird sister. Miranda knew that things between her parents were never that great and behind the smiles was something far less than idyllic, but in a handful of moments frozen by the camera she could believe in the fairy tale of a happy family.

Miranda laid her hand on Marilyn's face. What would she think about her daughters' lives now? Marianne, ever the overachiever, was a drug addict; and Miranda . . . well, she wasn't exactly the poster child for suburban America either.

She heard the suite door open and shut, David shaking out his coat and hanging up The Oncoming Storm, and yawning. "Three more attacks," he said. "All in Europe. I managed not to say 'I told you so' to any of them, in the interest of diplomacy, but I thought it extra hard. Jacob actually called Western

Europe a . . . what phrase did he use? A 'barmy old codger.' I don't think Napolitano knew quite how to react."

"What about your tracker guy?" Miranda asked, raising her head. "Are you planning to send a team to their headquarters, or what?"

"Not yet. Right now he's giving me excellent insight into their daily movements. The tracker records eighteen different kinds of data, and the more I know the happier I'll be. I want to learn as much as I can about how they operate and let it record as long as possible before I send in a strike team to fetch the Shepherd—not just for our own edification, but to make sure the team stays safe."

He walked to the couch and leaned over her, kissing the top of her head, one hand on her shoulder sliding up to touch her face. "What are you doing?"

"Look," she said, holding the album up, open to the picture of Marilyn with Miranda on her knee. "That's my mom."

He didn't reply at first, so she turned her head and looked up at him. To her amazement, he had gone pale and was staring at the picture like it was a ghost.

"I know," she said. "She looks just like me. She's actually younger than me here."

Involuntarily, the Prime took a step back, still staring at the picture.

"What is it?" she asked. "David?"

Finally, he shook himself out of the trance, blinked, and looked down into her worried face. "I . . ."

His confusion scared her. "What? Tell me what's wrong."

David took a deep breath. "I don't know how, but . . . I could swear I had met her before. Not as someone who resembles you, but . . . I don't know how that could have happened. I would have remembered that when I met you later. But still . . . maybe the part of me that has always known you for my Queen sees that potential in her bloodline."

"Bloodline—" Miranda grabbed the book back and started turning pages, heart pounding. "The Morningstar soldiers that had me staked to the ground . . . they were saying something about killing Marianne and Jenny to wipe out the bloodline. Did you get a good look at Jenny when you spoke to Marianne?"

"No. We talked at the door, then I left."

"Okay, then. Here." She held up the book—a five-by-seven of Jenny from second grade that had been stuck in the back of the album, her bucktoothed little-girl grin infectious, her red hair in a Hermione Granger situation just as Miranda's . . . and Marilyn's . . . had been from time to time.

David stared at the picture for a long moment.

"What do you feel?" Miranda asked, afraid to hear the answer.

He frowned, tilted his head. "I feel the same thing I felt when I saw your mother," he said. "Recognition . . . as if we met at a party hundreds of years ago and were in the middle of a conversation when one of us had to leave. But I can't tell how much of that is the same thing, or how much is that she looks like you and you look like your mother. What do you think it means?"

"You don't happen to have a painting or anything of your son, do you?"

He shook his head. "Where are you going with this?"

"Bloodlines," Miranda said. "In the Persephone myth there was something about us being the descendants of the original Signets, the Secondborn. What if it wasn't speaking metaphorically? She made them out of humans like any other vampire, right? Those humans had families. Some probably had children."

"But that was two thousand years ago," he said. "By now that blood would be so genetically diluted it would be completely meaningless . . . well, perhaps except for yours." His eyebrows lifted. "You're the only one of us who still has family alive within a generation or two. Scientifically it's preposterous, but this is magic we're talking about, so who the hell knows? Maybe it's a mystical bloodline, not a genetic one, and can pass along far more distant family connections."

"They wanted to wipe my bloodline out." Miranda shook her head. "But it's not like if they killed me, Marianne or Jenny could just step into my place. Marianne's about as intuitive as a bag of wet flannel, and Jenny's in second grade. I don't know how all of this is going to go down, but I really doubt we have time to wait for her to grow up."

"Our blood may recognize each other, but that doesn't make us all interchangeable."

"Still, it has to mean something."

David looked thoughtful, closing the photo album and handing it back to her. "We have no way to know," he told her. "And even if we did, it wouldn't really change anything."

"I need to talk to Stella," Miranda said. "We have to find a way to get answers. If she's supposed to be our intermediary, there has to be a safer way for her to do it than Drawing Down. If she has to go into a coma every time they talk, we're never going to get anywhere."

She was almost expecting it when the knock came at the door a few seconds later.

She sighed. Of course.

The door guard poked his head in. "My Lady, young Miss Stella is here to see you—Elite Sixty-seven found her wandering in a daze around the corridor from here and thought it best just to bring her to you."

She and David looked at each other. "Sure," she told the guard. "Let her in."

The young Witch peered uncertainly around the door frame. She was disheveled . . . and still in her pajamas. Miranda had to smile; they were the same Hello Kitty pajamas she'd worn herself while in Stella's care.

"Sorry," Stella said. "I don't mean to interrupt, I just . . . something really freaky happened."

Miranda stood up and went to her, guiding her toward the couch. "Are you hurt? You're so pale."

Stella sank down gratefully and took a couple of deep breaths. "No, I'm okay." She seemed to remember where she was and looked around with interest. Miranda imagined it from her perspective. The bedroom of the two most powerful vampires in the South: What must it look like to her? Miranda tried to remember how she'd felt when she first saw it, but her own first impression was before she really had any idea who, or what, she was dealing with. The only memory that came to mind was calling David a "ninja computer programmer doctor," which turned out to be pretty damn close to the truth.

"So this is the inner sanctum," Stella said. Her eyes fell on Miranda's guitar, not three feet away, and she took another deep breath and swallowed. "This is too weird."

David had risen when Miranda did, but the Queen didn't

see what he was doing until he returned to the fireplace with a can of Dr Pepper, popped the top, and handed it to the Witch.

"Wow, how did you know?"

He smiled. "I know that look. It's the 'I just had some kind of psychic episode' look."

Stella guzzled about half the can, then looked embarrassed and held it in her hands for a while, fiddling with the tab with her thumb. "It wasn't exactly an episode . . . I guess it was sort of a dream? I don't remember any of it. I woke up on the floor in this totally random room around the corner. I thought I might be near the library, but this place is such a rabbit warren, who knows? But one of your guys walked by and saw me, and I guess I looked lost and whacked-out enough that he came to help."

"Which room was it?" Miranda asked. "What was in it?"

"It was just an office. I don't think it's even one you guys use. There was this huge leather chair, and the walls were lined with those bookcases, you know, the ones with the glass doors that open up and down?"

"Barrister bookcases," David supplied.

"Yes. Those. There was also a desk with nothing on it but a couple of knickknacks."

Miranda turned to her husband. "The empty study down from the music room?"

"Sounds like it. Most of my college textbooks are in there, but that's about it."

"The thing is . . ." Stella took another swig of her soda before continuing. "That was the third time this has happened . . . this week."

The Pair both stared at her.

"The first was the day after you were all out of town. I thought, okay, I'm sleepwalking. Weird, but not scary. Then two days later it happened again. It started to freak me out but I thought, maybe it's a coincidence, maybe I went sleepwalking again and that was the only place my brain could come up with since it had just been there. But then tonight . . . three times isn't a coincidence. Three times is a very special episode of 'what the fuck?' "

"And you saw nothing that seemed out of place or odd in the room?" David asked.

She shook her head. "The room was freakishly tidy. If there had been even a book out of alignment, it would have stuck out like a sore thumb. It was just a room. I didn't get any impressions from it like I might if something bad had happened there—there was nothing."

"I think we need to check out this room," Miranda said.

They all stood, but David said, "Let me meet you there—I want to stop and grab something that might help."

Miranda was still worried, watching Stella, that the girl might fall over; she might not remember what had happened, but the whole thing had definitely left her unsteady. She led Miranda down the hall and around the corner fairly confidently, and they wound up at the room the Pair had expected. Since it was in their wing, it was locked, and Miranda held her com up to it—

"Wait," Miranda said, frowning. "This room is locked."

"So?"

"So your com isn't authorized to get in here. How did you open the door?"

Stella shook her head. She had no answer to give.

It was just as the Witch had described: empty, silent. Miranda flipped the lights on for the human's benefit, but there was really nothing to see. "Where did you wake up?"

"Over here . . ." Stella walked over to stand away from all the furniture, slightly off center. "Same exact spot every time. I remember seeing this little splotch in the tile."

"Which way were you facing when you woke?"

A frown. "Well, now that you mention it . . . every time I was facing this way." She turned away from Miranda toward one of the bookcases. "And . . . okay, that's weird."

"What is?"

"The sequence of events was always the same. I woke up struggling, saw the bookcase, then started looking around trying to orient myself. But when I looked over here . . . every time, I noticed this book." Stella bent to one of the lower shelves and lifted its door, her finger falling on the spine of a thick, aged hardcover. "Maybe it was just because the cover's this funky shade of orange. I don't see what theoretical calculus would have to do with anything."

Miranda joined her and pulled the book from the shelf. It

was absurdly heavy. She opened it and flipped through, but all she saw were pages and pages of marginalia in a neat, slightly slanted hand she knew quite well. Nothing fell out of the book, there were no hidden messages—unless they were written in math, which David would have to judge. "Was there anything behind it on the shelf?"

Stella had knelt and was shifting the other books around. "Whoa."

"What do you see?"

"A mirror," Stella replied. "A tiny little mirror about two inches square, stuck to the back wall of the bookcase. What do you suppose it's for?"

Before Miranda could answer that she had no idea, David appeared; he had a small handheld device about the size of his phone that she recognized as a scanner of some sort.

She raised an eyebrow at him, and he said, "Ever since Ovaska, I've been working on a way to scan for psychic or magical energy to detect amulets and such and hopefully one day tell me what kind they are. Our regular technology—the kind we use in the sensor network, the kind in the tracker I stuck in the soldier—can't pick it up. I've tried dozens of methods and had no luck whatsoever. I couldn't find the logic."

"Magic isn't logical," Miranda said.

Stella laughed. "Of course it is. It's very logical. It's all cause and effect. If something seems to appear and disappear, that just means it went somewhere you haven't found yet. But there's an underlying order."

"Exactly," David said. "After you started telling us about the whole Web thing, and I started observing our abilities and incidents from that perspective, it started to make more sense." He held up the scanner. "This is the first version that has given me anything useful. I figure if there's something you're being led to see, this will either help us find it, or at least tell us if it's supernatural before we pick it up and play with it and get turned into frogs."

"Show him the mirror," Miranda told Stella.

The Prime bent and followed the Witch's gesture. "Well, now."

"Is there anything magical about the mirror?" Miranda wanted to know.

David held the scanner up to it and shook his head. "Assuming my readings are correct, no. It's just a mirror."

"Why would anyone slap a mirror in a bookcase?"

He examined it for a minute. "Odd . . . it's glued to the back wall of the bookcase, but it's not glued flat. There's something very thin underneath the bottom edge that's tilting the bottom out at a slight angle . . ." Something dawned on his face, and he straightened, looking around the room.

His expression became what she called his "in the Matrix" look; she could see him running through something as his eyes traveled over the walls. A moment later, though, he dug in his coat and pulled out a small flashlight.

She had long ago learned not to be surprised at anything he had in his pockets.

He glanced over at the light switch, and it flipped. The room spun back into darkness, and Miranda's eyes adjusted instantly, but she had to reach out and grab the Witch's arm to keep her from tripping as they got out of David's way.

David asked Stella where she'd woken up, and she showed him; he knelt there, turned on the flashlight, and aimed it directly at the mirror.

Miranda and Stella both gasped. The flashlight's beam hit the mirror, bounced off at an angle, shot across the room, and apparently hit another mirror, then another—the light zigzagged off almost every corner before hitting a bare spot on the wall, down by the floor.

"What the hell is that?" the Queen asked. "How did you not know this was here?"

"I never use this room," he reminded her. "I think the last time I was in here was to alphabetize the books a few months after I moved in. Why would I be looking for something this bizarre?"

"But what's behind that wall?" Stella asked.

"Let's find out." The Prime took a long look at the beam again, memorizing the exact spot where it ended, then reached over to the light switch with his mind and turned it back on. "Stay back a minute," he said, stowing the flashlight and approaching the spot. "I think the Signets are giving off interference that's mucking with the signal. When it was just mine I didn't really notice."

Miranda heard the little gadget beep several times, and David shook his head. "It's not registering anything. Whatever's in there is either perfectly mundane or shielded somehow."

The walls were paneled, and a wood chair rail surrounded the room; it would be pretty easy to take a panel out, stick something behind it, and replace it without it being obvious anything had changed. David felt around the panel for a moment, probably looking for a catch.

"I hope we don't have to saw it open," Miranda said. "I'd feel like a blasphemer damaging this woodwork." She went closer and added her hands to the search, pressing along the chair rail to see if it moved.

She was about to give up when she felt something under her fingers give just a tiny bit. "There!"

There was a soft click, and a section of the rail moved out a few millimeters, allowing the panel it held to tilt just enough to be removed.

She and David took hold of the panel and lifted it gingerly from its slot. Behind it were wall studs, and behind that bricks; she had no idea how the Haven had been designed or even when it was built, but there were cobwebs aplenty.

And right in between two studs, covered in dust, a box.

David's eyes gleamed with excitement. He lifted the box very slowly out of its hiding place and set it on the floor.

It was about the size of the calculus textbook that had led them here in the first place; carved out of ebony wood, it reminded her of the box the Stone of Awakening had come in—and the one her Signet had originally been kept in. There was some kind of writing carved around the edges, possibly Greek—Novotny's symbol-and-language database would make short work of it. A weird metal lock was built into the side, and though it was clearly very old, both box and lock looked rock-solid.

That wasn't the remarkable thing, though. The remarkable thing was carved right in the center of the box's lid:

The Seal of Elysium.

Nine

In her dream she walked around the streets of Prague, dressed stylishly for autumn, Vràna trotting along at her side, the dog's tongue lolling out in a smile and her tags jingling in the quiet night. The sky overhead held no moon, only thousands of stars that, if she stared up at them long enough, seemed to form a spider's web of faint threads of light.

It might have occurred to her that what she was dreaming had never once happened and probably never would—she had yet to set foot on the streets of her capital alone—but in the dream, at least, she walked like a woman with a purpose, hips swaying slightly, the wind catching the dark ribbons of her hair and trailing them out from beneath the hat she wore against the chill.

She stepped out into a picturesque old-town square that she wasn't sure really existed. The buildings around her opened up to offer a flirtatious peek between them, revealing a stone fountain and park benches, old-fashioned streetlights. The few people passing by were little more than shadowy shapes.

"Good evening."

Cora wasn't startled; every time she had the dream, she

was unafraid of anything. She turned toward the woman's voice, smiling. "Good evening."

There, sitting on a low wall that surrounded the fountain, was a young woman in a long black dress covered in a black velvet coat that trailed to the ground. She had a pale, oval-shaped face framed by a tumble of dark red hair much like the Queen of the South's, but rather than green eyes, hers were . . . well . . . for just a second they *were* green, though that might have been Cora trying to make something familiar of her; then, they settled on a disturbing, depthless black that also should have frightened Cora but for some reason did not.

Vràna padded over to the woman and sat down next to her, laying her gigantic shaggy head in the stranger's lap. Cora had never seen the Nighthound do that—she was loyal only to her mistress and affectionately tolerant of Jacob. The woman rested a hand on the dog's head.

"You are the Queen of this territory, are you not?" the woman asked. There was something so familiar about her voice . . .

"I am," Cora said.

The woman looked her up and down, smiling as if she'd just discovered her favorite daughter hiding in the garden. "Do you like being Queen, Cora?"

She frowned. "I had never thought about it." She sat down on the wall next to the stranger, considering. "I suppose I do—I feel like I have not really started yet, though . . . as if I had been convalescing from a debilitating illness and have only just risen from bed."

"An apt metaphor," the woman said with a nod. "But the time is soon approaching when you will have to leave the safety of your chambers and step out into the world. You barely know a tenth of what you are capable of, Cora. I hope that what you learn about yourself will be worth the lesson."

Cora stared at her, uneasiness finally reaching her through the odd reality of dreams. "I do not like the sound of that."

"The Web is in motion," she replied. "My son was kind enough to unlock the door, but it will take all of you to open. In the meantime we whisper through the door, trying to tell our secrets. If you would hear more, you must ask the Voice."

The Queen heard something rustling off to her left, and seemingly out of nowhere, a large raven soared across the square to land on the fountain, its broad black wings almost filling the sky. It hopped down beside the woman. A moment later, a second one arrived . . . and then a third. One was close enough that the woman could reach out and scratch its head; the bird made little noises of delight that were eerily human.

Cora heard more feathers and looked around the square, counting more ravens perched on lampposts, bobbing in the newfallen snow. Five, six, seven . . . there should be eight. She *knew* there should be eight.

Cora fought against the question for several minutes. She didn't want to know the answer, but she had to know the answer. "Who are you?"

"To you? A friend. To others? A Prime in my own right, perhaps; or a mother; or, in some cases, a hand waiting to be taken, a hope believed long lost. I am what each of you needs me to be."

Cora's heart was pounding. She could feel the dream beginning to unravel around her, details that had been so clear becoming misty and unformed. The woman before her remained fully present, but her dress and coat began to blur around the edges, becoming one with the shadows that had formed around the fountain, even in the dark of night. "What . . . what must I do?" Cora asked, her voice nearly swallowed by the wind.

The woman leaned forward and took her hand, sending a shock wave of energy through Cora's body. Their eyes met and held, and Cora could see the night sky overhead turning in the woman's eyes . . . containing the stars, containing the universe.

"Do not be afraid," she told Cora. "Love is stronger than fear, child. Hold on to it. In the darkness when you feel alone and small, remember you are a Queen . . . you were chosen for this, you of all your kind. You guard the heat of a will on fire . . . just let it burn."

Cora woke shaking, her skin fever-hot and her mind spinning, to the sound of wings.

"What do you mean, you can't open it?"

Dr. Novotny cleaned his glasses on the lapel of his lab coat, looking both sheepish and perplexed. "I mean we can't open it."

David frowned at the black box, which rested inside a Plexiglas enclosure and was currently finishing a busy day of tests, scans, and attempts to access its inner contents. "It's made of wood," David pointed out unnecessarily.

"I'm just as flummoxed as you are, Sire. We've tried everything—the box is held together with expertly made joinery, no adhesive whatsoever, so we can't dissolve the glue and dismantle it. We took thorough scans of the entire surface, and as you gave permission to break it if necessary, we even took a hammer to it. Hammer, pry bar, torch, laser . . . we've tried. It even seems to be fireproof. Not only is it not breaking, none of our equipment has left so much as a gouge on the surface."

"What the hell kind of wood is that?"

"I don't think it has that much to do with the wood itself," the doctor said, gesturing for David to follow him to the console, where he pulled up several screens of diagrams, scan results, and observational data. "The energy the thing is giving off is very strange."

"I didn't think it was giving off energy. I didn't get anything on my scanner."

"Your scanner needs work, then. It's definitely got an energy signature, but it's not a particularly active one. The closest descriptor is that it's humming very quietly."

"What about the lock? What kind of key does it take?"

"As far as we can tell, it's not a key at all; the hole is the approximate size and shape of the stone in a large ring. Your sire was a member of the Order of Elysium—do you recall if she wore a ring?"

"I don't remember." As Novotny fussed with the display for a moment, David quickly took out his phone and sent a text: *Elysium: do they wear rings?*

"As for the outer carvings, we had a bit more luck." Novotny brought up the scans of those, overlaid with translations of the language carved into the wood. "As suspected, it's ancient Greek, though it's a bit of an odd dialect. Still, it was easy enough to get through, and if the book itself is in the same language—"

"Book?"

Novotny smiled. "If you'll take a look at this scan, you can see that there's a slightly smaller rectangular object inside the box."

David crossed his arms thoughtfully. "It might just be another box. With another box inside it. The world's oldest and lamest practical joke."

"Well, maybe, except for one thing." Novotny pointed at one of the lines of translated text from the top of the box around the Seal of Elysium. "Herein lies the Codex of Persephone," Novotny read. "It's a book."

"How old is the box?"

"We ran carbon dating, but it's less than five hundred years old, so we couldn't get an accurate result. We're working on it. My deduction is that the Order uses that Greek dialect as their sacred language as Hindus do Sanskrit—the language is ancient, but the box itself isn't."

The Prime nodded slowly. "The book of rituals the Order's main Priesthood used was destroyed when the Priesthood was murdered, but there were other copies—partial copies. Hopefully this means the entire liturgy didn't die with Eladra . . . and moreover, hopefully this Codex contains information our Circle desperately needs."

"What kind of information?" Novotny asked.

"Any at all."

David's phone chimed, and he looked down at the screen: *Yes. Big oval, labradorite, carved silver band. Why?*

Do you know where we can get one?

A pause. *Any of the Order's living branches. Trouble is persuading them to part with one. Ring is given at initiation—it's the Priestess's badge of office, like a Signet. They don't exactly lend them out.*

If they're Persephone's Priesthood, doesn't that mean they have to help us?

You, they might. Me, not a chance in hell. I don't have contact with any of the cloisters outside California but I can send you a place to start.

Do that.

He turned back to the doctor. "I might have a way into the box—give me a couple of days. In the meantime, keep digging;

every little detail, no matter how seemingly insignificant, could help us down the line."

"Of course, Sire. Seemingly insignificant details are our business. I'll drop everything we have so far onto your server, and I'll call the minute we have anything new."

"Thank you, Doctor," the Prime said, and walked out of the lab, toward the elevators.

As soon as he was outside again, waiting for Harlan to arrive, David called California. "Who's your contact with the Order?"

Deven sighed. "I'm acquainted with several of the clergy through the Swords of Elysium—the closest is in Montana. I'll send you what I know about their location and maybe it'll lead you to someone willing to come and open the box."

"Are you all right? You sound . . . sad."

"It's nothing. Don't worry. What else did Novotny tell you?"

David related the latest.

Dev didn't sound terribly impressed. "So it's a book. Probably another copy of the ritual texts, which is good for the Order, but not really worth all this bother for us."

"But we don't know for sure. And we won't if we can't get the damn thing open. So send me that information and I'll get to work."

Dev paused, and David got a sense of him sitting outside—probably on the Haven terrace—and fiddling with something, a small object in his hand. "I might have an easier way," the Prime said with a sigh. "Look, I'm going to call for the jet. I'll be there by three. Have the box where I can get to it."

"But what—"

Click.

David looked down at the screen and shook his head. "Boy, one of these days you and I are actually going to finish a conversation whether you like it or not."

Then he pulled up Miranda's number.

"Hey baby," she said. "Anything good at Hunter?"

"Not really—but just to warn you, we're having a visitor in a few hours. Probably not for more than a day, but still, have Esther prepare a guest suite and get out the good bourbon."

"Oh," Miranda said. "That kind of visitor. Thanks for the warning. What do you have left tonight?"

"I'm meeting with my contact at the DOD. She has some satellite images of the Morningstar compound that will give me a better idea of their external security. Once I have that, we can raid the place without going in blind. I should be back in a couple of hours."

"Be careful. Love you."

"Love you back."

He hung up just as Harlan arrived but had to tell the driver to wait a minute; Novotny probably wouldn't be happy to give up the book in the middle of his analyses, but if by some chance Deven did have a way into the box, David imagined the good doctor would be overjoyed. He headed back into the building the way he'd come, wondering idly what the next important magical object would be—an enchanted sword? A pair of ruby slippers? The Ocarina of Time?

Once, he'd been absolutely sure he understood how his world worked. Primes, Consorts, Elite, Court, human allies: Everyone had a place, and everyone's role made sense. Everything ran like the gears in a clock, almost Cartesian in its utility, and Signet history backed up his beliefs. Primes died all the time and were replaced by new ones; vampire populations grew until an opposing force, either human Hunters or vampire authority, stemmed the tide. Then human populations grew until vampire numbers began to rise again—even with no-kill laws, the Shadow World provided a global check on mortal numbers, though it was no longer an efficient one. But still, everything fit together. Everything made sense. Life had order.

Or at least it had until he met Miranda Grey. She had brought more to his life than love, more than music, more than strength and the flash of red hair. Miranda was the flame that had set the world, not just his life, on fire . . . and however long it burned, whatever the endgame, he would walk into it thankful to have stood in her light.

In the space of a few short years, here he was, an entirely different kind of vampire, dealing with amulets that could bring back long-forgotten gods and turn humans into supernatural warriors . . . Witches who could speak with said gods face-to-face . . . and he himself had been resurrected from the dead. Now there was a magic book to contend with. What next?

"Just so you know," he said to the empty air in the elevator, "that was a rhetorical question."

There were times that Miranda could almost forget there was anything missing, but the minute she took up her sword to spar with one of the lieutenants, she had to do so around a sharp, almost incapacitating pain in her heart.

The Southern Elite was the best in the world. She had her pick of incredibly talented warriors to practice with and learn from.

But none of them were Faith.

There were a few who were actually better in battle than the Second had been, but they lacked her leadership ability, her teaching skill. A Second had to be more than just a fighter. He or she had to be someone the Signet could trust—someone in whose hands they could place the entire Elite. Right now, the South had no one like that, and no possibilities within the next five years at least.

Miranda finished her hand-to-hand session with Bax, retrieved Shadowflame, and called out one of the lieutenants for a quick match; Miranda was good, and knew she was good, but she was well aware most of the lieutenants could take her down pretty handily. She had greater strength, speed, and endurance, but none of that was an adequate substitute for skill and experience. All it meant was that she fell on her ass harder, faster, and more often.

She'd only been training for four years, after all. She hadn't just sprung up from the floor as a vampire suddenly able to win a war singlehandedly. She worked for it every night. Sophie, and later Faith, had both said the same thing: There would always be someone better out there.

As much as she hated working without Faith, she knew she had a lot to learn, and she couldn't stop training—even if she were willing to take to the streets of Austin without her skills honed as sharply as possible, she knew Faith would never allow it.

She hadn't been able to save her Second. Faith had died for her. There was nothing Miranda could do for her now except be the absolute best she could be in her friend's honor.

"You know it wasn't your fault," came a voice nearby.

Miranda, fresh from a shower in the locker room and busy pulling a comb through her hair with the aid of a powerful detangler, stopped what she was doing and turned toward the door. "You read minds now, too?"

Deven leaned sideways against the door frame. "Every time we work together using that Persephone connection, for the next few days I can read a lot more than usual, even through your shields. I got to listen to Cora and Jacob fooling around the other night. That was interesting."

He looked tired, she noticed—way better than he had after Rio Verde, but still, the light in his eyes was dimmer. Before she could stop herself, she reached out to him with her empathy, and without even dipping into the surface of his shields she had a pretty good idea what was wrong.

"Your boy left," she said. "When?"

"The day after we got back."

She heard sorrow in his voice for just a second before he covered it back up. Did he have any idea how hurt he was, or was he denying it as hard as he'd denied having feelings for Nico in the first place?

"I'm sorry," she said. She put her comb away, grabbed her sword, and walked over to give him a hug before pulling him along out of the locker room. "Whatever you say, I know you cared about him."

Deven snorted quietly, then let out a breath. "I'll get over it."

She didn't point out the obvious—that not once had she ever known him to get over anything—but said, "I know it's not really my fault . . . Faith . . . but I just keep thinking, if I had fought harder . . . if I had . . . I don't know. It doesn't do any good to play the 'if only' game, but I can't help it. I miss her so much." She looked at him. "What do you do, oh ancient one, when you lose someone who's a part of you like that?"

He grinned at the epithet. "Well, don't hide in a blanket fort with a case of whiskey and listen to Amy Winehouse. According to Jonathan, that's unhealthy."

She grabbed his hand and squeezed it. "We're just a three-ring circus of issues, aren't we?" Something hard she wasn't used to feeling cut into her finger, and she lifted his hand up and looked at it. "Nice ring."

It was a large oval, moonstone, set in silver that had intricate carvings all around the band. "It's kind of big for you," she noticed, and then it dawned on her. "That was Nico's?"

"Yes. He left it for me."

Miranda raised an eyebrow. "This looks the way you described the Elysium rings. Didn't you tell David they were sacred?"

"They symbolize the bond between the soul and deity. Why?"

Now both of her eyebrows shot up. "So he gave you his soul."

"Hardly."

She let the matter drop and studied the ring for a moment. "It looks an awful lot like it would fit in the lock on our magic box."

"That's what I'm banking on, yes."

"You said the Order of Elysium wears labradorite, though—isn't this a moonstone?"

"I'm hoping it won't matter. The two are very similar—moonstone is a colorless form of labradorite. If it doesn't work, at the very least we're no worse off than before. I told David he could try contacting the Order, but to be honest, I don't have much faith that they'll answer, after . . . what happened." He shrugged. "Nico was dedicated to a different deity, but he was sent here to help us, so it's worth a shot."

"Well, come on," she said. "I'm sure David's already waiting for us."

She was right, as it turned out; David was in his workroom, the carved box on the table in front of him, his feet propped up on a nearby chair as he scrutinized a series of satellite images on the screens in front of him. As they came in he was dragging one of the images to a mat that covered part of the table, which functioned as a sort of horizontal monitor and was used to create three-dimensional plans like the ones that had gotten them into Hart's Haven. David took the files his contact had given him, fed them into some kind of rendering program, and created a 3D map of the Morningstar compound that he could rotate, resize, and zoom in on. He had several spots marked that looked like guard stations.

He looked up and smiled, the light from the rendering

catching in his glasses. "Good, you're here. Let me save this and put it away."

Miranda grabbed her usual chair and pushed another one toward Deven, who took it without comment.

Finally, David moved toward the center of the table so that they could get closer on either side. He pulled the box where they could all reach it. "Well, Dev, what do you have?"

Deven slid the moonstone ring off his finger. "Don't ask," he said sharply to the question David hadn't asked yet. "Just see if it works."

David looked the ring over for a moment but surprisingly did as Deven said and didn't ask. He turned the box so the lock was facing them and carefully fit the stone into it, wiggling it just a little to make sure it fit.

He started to turn it . . . and couldn't. "Damn," he sighed. "I suppose it was—wait—"

Miranda could feel it even from her chair: The lock had begun to grow warm, and the hair on her arms stood up from some kind of charge that she could feel building in the air. "It's not going to blow up, is it?" she asked, pushing her chair back. "Damn it, you should have put it inside a blast shield!"

David didn't answer. He waited just a moment longer, then applied pressure to the ring again, trying to turn it . . .

. . . and Miranda heard a click.

David took the ring out of the lock and handed it back to Deven. The second the stone was removed, the side of the box fell open. He tilted the box and shook it gently to coax out whatever was in it.

With a soft slip of leather over wood, the book fell out into his other hand.

It was a thick, black-bound volume about the size of a standard sheet of copy paper, and its pages were yellowed with age, though the binding still held together perfectly. David put the box on the table and let the book rest on his knees, opening the cover gingerly.

The pages were thicker than modern paper and covered gutter to margin with slightly faded but even handwriting, diagrams, symbols. Most of the pages were illuminated with intricate drawings. "The outside of the box was carved with ancient Greek," David said, running a finger along what looked like a chapter title. "But this . . . what the hell is this? It looks like Greek, but . . . I can't read it."

Deven, sitting with his arms crossed, leaned an inch or two closer. "The Codex of Persephone," he read. "Being an account of the founding of our sacred Order, its laws and practices, and its symbols, as first set down by Priestess Caerna of Crete, in the year of the Great War; copied by hand in the year 1773 by the High Priestess Eladra."

David raised an eyebrow at him. "You can read this?"

Deven looked like he had a headache. "Of course I can, David. I'm magic. And that isn't ancient Greek—at least not the garden variety. It's Elysian Greek, the sacred language of the Order. The Order uses several dialects, but this one is only taught to the Acolytes, and only after initiation. Every High Priest or Priestess has to hand-copy the Codex before starting his or her own cloister . . . It would seem Eladra made two of them, and somehow this one ended up in your Haven. That's definitely her handwriting."

"Acolytes—is that what they call the people in the warrior class like you were?"

"No . . . an Acolyte is specifically someone training to be what Eladra was, to lead a branch of the Order."

Miranda and David both stared at him, but he didn't seem to notice and went on. "Still, it's not earthshaking, at least not for us. Nothing in the original Codex would really help us all that much—it's the Order's liturgy, not . . . hold on." Deven plucked the book from David's hands. He flipped through some of the pages for a moment, his expression becoming perplexed. "Once upon a time I knew the Codex inside and out . . . and this isn't it. Or, it is, but there's way more information in here than there should be. Some of these symbols . . . I've never seen them before. There are whole pages of them. I have no idea what we're looking at here . . ."

He looked up. "I need to take this with me and translate the whole thing. There's no telling what might be in here, but it's definitely more than just the Codex of Persephone, or at least it's not the Order's standard version."

There was a moment of silence before David said, "Deven . . . I'm going to ask you this question, and for once, I just want a straightforward, honest answer. You told me that your involvement with the Order was with the Swords . . . and you told Miranda that Eladra was your friend, as were the others you killed. But what was your real connection to the Order?"

Deven looked from one of them to the other, sighed, and said, "It doesn't matter anymore."

"That's not an answer," David snapped.

"Well, that's all you're getting," Deven snapped right back. "It has no bearing on what's happening now except that I know how to read this book and you don't. Since I'm stuck here until dusk, you can either let me take it and figure out which parts are relevant to us, or you can deal with it yourself and waste time."

Every time Miranda watched this particular death-stare match between the two Primes—which was often—she was convinced they were going to either start fighting or make out. In fact, it was neither; David just waved his hand dismissively, and Deven pushed himself up out of the chair, took the book, and left the workroom.

"Do you want me to go after him and find out the truth?" Miranda asked.

David shook his head and turned back to the satellite diagrams, setting the Codex box aside. "I suppose it doesn't really matter. I don't know why I keep thinking it's possible for the two of us to have a real friendship—honesty, trust, all of that madness."

"It's not," she replied, standing up and moving behind him to rub his shoulders for a moment. "I'm sorry, baby, but . . . you'll never just be friends. Not in the way you think you should be. Maybe you should focus on what you have, try to turn it into the best possible version of itself, instead of trying to be something you're not."

He looked up at her. "And how exactly do I do that?"

"Just meet each other where you are—let him be the fucked-up, emotionally damaged, manipulative little bastard you fell in love with, and don't try to control the outcome."

She kissed him, once on the mouth and again on the top of his head. "I'll let you get back to work."

She knew, as she left the workroom, that he'd be sitting there staring at those images for an hour or more, mind in a twist, before giving up and going to bed, but there was nothing she could do, really, except give him room to brood. Even after everything they'd been through, he still had a hard time dealing with emotions; anything that made him feel deeply scared him just a little. He'd try to think his way through it logically—even more laughable considering the situation. There really was no rationalizing his way through an emotional attachment to an ex he had a mystical connection to, who had at some point become his wife's best friend. Having a soul mate should have simplified things, yet as they all knew by now, the heart wanted what it wanted, and usually it wanted to misbehave.

Miranda opened up her senses, casting about the house to see if she could feel Deven; he and Jonathan always stayed in the same visiting dignitary suite, but since there were still a couple of hours left in the night he might be somewhere else in the Haven.

She had to smile when she figured it out: the study where the ice cream and liquor cabinet were, the same place she had stumbled across him that night years ago when she'd asked him about his tattoos and he had told her the story behind his loss of faith. Fitting, she supposed, to find him there now.

He didn't seem surprised to see her. This time, though, he wasn't drunk, but was sitting in one of the big leather chairs, cross-legged, the Codex open on his lap.

He said in exasperation without looking at her, "Why does it matter to either of you how I came by my knowledge? Can't you accept that I'm old, I know things, and that's it?"

"Because if you don't share what you know, we could waste a lot of time chasing our tails."

"If it were relevant, you would know about it," he retorted. "No one ever needed to know I could read Elysian Greek until tonight. I shouldn't have to lay my entire past bare just in case some piece of it proves of use to you."

She sat down. "All right, then. How about telling a friend about something that's obviously hurting you?"

He glanced up at her for just a second before averting his eyes to the book again, and she saw in his face that she was right.

She pulled her knees up to her chin. "It's getting harder for all of us to hold ourselves apart. Whatever the purpose of this connection, it's making us function almost like one big Pair—sharing strength, sharing emotions. It's still tentative, still uneven among all of us, but like you said, the more we use it, the stronger it gets. There's no telling how much worse it's going to become, but you're not going to be able to hide everything from everyone anymore . . . you might as well start with me."

Finally, the anger clouding around him seemed to fade, and he snapped the book shut and laid both palms on it for a minute, eyes closed.

He took a deep breath and said, "The woman who rescued me from the Inquisition and made me a vampire claimed that her Goddess had sent her to find me. She was a Priestess, she said, and was taking me to live in a safe place where I could study and live in peace . . . and one day take her place, not just at the head of her cloister, but as the leader of the Order of Elysium itself. Her name was Eladra."

Miranda's mouth and heart both fell open, and for a minute she couldn't find words. "Eladra was your sire," she said in a hushed voice. "You were her heir."

"She thought so. I couldn't accept it. I didn't believe in her Goddess, and the God I had loved had abandoned me to tormented death. I couldn't just jump ship from one religion to another without one hell of a conversion experience. I stayed there for a few years, trying to force myself to fit in. Finally, I ran. I never saw her again until the night I killed her . . . and all of my other teachers, and everyone who had taken me in and cared for me. Two centuries later I joined a branch of the Swords of Elysium anonymously on another continent because I wanted their weapons for the Red Shadow. Only members had access to their swordsmiths."

Miranda shook her head. The truth was no easier to accept now than it had been the night of the Awakening. "You killed everyone who mattered to you just to save our lives . . . and it didn't even work."

This time the smile was genuine, as was the pain beneath it. "No, Miranda . . . I was trying to *save* everyone who mattered. And not just for you two, but to try to stop everything that's happening now before it started. I can never make amends to Eladra—never thank her for saving me and giving me a home. But at least you're still alive, even though I failed you . . . and everyone else."

Neither spoke for a minute. She knew he was done talking for now. Her heart was full of a dozen conflicting emotions, but sorrow was the one that spoke loudest, and it urged her up off the sofa and over to his chair, where he looked up at her without speaking, then sighed and moved over so she could sit down.

Perhaps Nico had saved him from dying in despair, but it still clung to his back waiting for another chance to drag him down into the darkness. She couldn't do whatever it was Nico had done, but by God, if there was anything she *could* do, she would.

He was stiff in her arms for a while, trying to maintain the distance, and she just kept sending love and understanding along the link the whole Circle shared, and after what seemed like forever, she felt a slight shudder run through him, and he gave in.

Deven burrowed his face into her shoulder, one hand winding into her hair, and eventually Miranda grabbed a throw blanket hanging over the arm of the chair and covered them both with it. They ended up much as they had in the hayloft a week ago, but this time their positions were reversed; he lay against her chest, she the one with the strength, both of them looking for something they couldn't find anywhere else and might, just might, right here.

Miranda was finally starting to understand what their relationship really was: more than friendship, less than romance, deeper than either; mutual acceptance and comfort between two people who had, by a miracle, come to love each other through trial by fire. He had been her solid ground when David died, and her shoulder was the only one he wasn't afraid to lean on.

She didn't ask any more questions, didn't try to find the words to make any of it right; she just held on, and at least for that moment, it was enough.

Ten

Thread by thread . . . from horizon to horizon, softly glowing lattices of light spread out in every direction around her, and for a moment she was at its center . . . she was its center, and circumference, each strand plaiting itself around hundreds of others at the touch of her hand.

Infinite power flowed through her. Time itself lay still until she bade it to turn; millions of potential futures shifted and tipped. Within its endless transformation she could see so many lives playing out, their fates formed by the intersections and twists that branched out and touched others, then others, and eventually everyone and everything. Nothing was solitary, nothing happened in a vacuum. Every single choice made by every single being altered the Web in some way, from the flap of a bird's wing to the march of an army.

Her awareness shrank until she could see only her own part of the matrix, and by feeling along different strands she could sense her connections to those she loved, those she hated, those she had yet to meet. She existed in a ring of other microcosmic webs, seven others . . . one of which was still so far away she could barely see its edges . . . and one strand, brighter and stronger than the others, ran through them all.

Every two matrices were also bound to each other, except for the last two, who had not yet connected.

She wanted more than anything to touch them, to learn everything she could—in her own part of the lattice she could see the thread that made her an empath, and another that gave her musical talent. Just at a touch she could discover all of their secrets . . . but that wasn't why she was here.

Her eyes moved back to the quicksilver strands that connected each Pair. She wasn't sure what she was supposed to grasp about them, but she could see they were strong . . . yet brittle, in their way, if the right kind of power struck them in the right place. She had seen it happen, had felt it herself. From where she stood she could see exactly what a Bondbreaking would do, and what a miracle it was they had survived it . . . and miracle *was the right word given its source. Since then all of those connections had doubled in strength and were growing every day. Eventually, when that eighth web came close enough for them all to touch, the circuit among them would complete and . . . they would become what they were here to become.*

Over and over again, her attention returned to one of the silver strands; it felt as though her vision was being pulled to it, her subconscious trying to show her something about it . . . but it looked just like the others. What was special about this one? She held her hands over it, afraid to touch . . . following its line from one web to another.

As she stood examining the connections, figuring out how they worked and which way their energy flowed, she felt the telltale prickle on the back of her neck and the intrusive nudge of her gift . . . she wasn't alone. Someone was watching her.

Miranda blinked awake slowly, whatever she was dreaming sighing away into the polyphonic whisper of her subconscious. She would have thought it was a precognitive dream, given how her head was starting to hurt, but at least a few pieces of those always lingered; otherwise, why have them?

Her feet were cold, as was her face. She grunted and turned over to face David and borrow some of his thermonuclear warmth. For a second the weirdness in her mind evaporated, watching her Prime sleep . . . she remembered the first time, looking down at him on the couch as he began to have a nightmare about his first wife. Then, as now, he'd looked so human, vulnerable.

"Stop staring," he murmured without opening his eyes. "It's creepy."

She smiled. "I can't help it . . . you're just so damned cute."

One eye slit open and gave her a blurry glare. "Primes aren't cute," he said. "We're the embodiment of darkness. We inspire fear."

Miranda chuckled. "Oh yes. Especially Primes who sleep in flannel Iron Man pants."

Now both eyes opened, and he grinned. "I like the Batman pair, too."

"Millionaire genius crime fighter pants. Yep, I know how to pick a gift."

He shut his eyes again. "Go back to sleep," he said. "We don't have to be up for another hour."

She started to say something, but he had already drifted off again. She could let him have that last precious hour, or she could . . .

He yelped and scrambled backward. "Damn it, woman, your feet are freezing!"

"That's why I stuck them on you."

Rolling his eyes, he pounced on her and kissed her hard. She giggled around his mouth and was about to grab him by the millionaire genius crime fighter pants when over on the bedside table his phone rang.

She started to tell him to let it go to voice mail, but before the words came out something cold and heavy struck her heart . . . knowledge. "It's Jacob," she said.

He grabbed the phone just in time to catch the call. "Solomon." David sighed. "Christ, who died?" As she watched, his expression became something all too familiar. ". . . Oh."

The worldwide map of Signet territories was beginning to look more than a little unsettling. Australia was still leaderless. So was the Mideastern United States. And India.

David hit the command that would change Western Europe from blue to red. He sat back in his chair, staring at it—there were power vacuums opening up all over the world, and while he had never had any reason to consider what it would take to topple the entire Signet system, suddenly the possibility, though still far away from fruition, was far too real for his comfort.

He felt Miranda's hands on his shoulders as she came to stand behind his chair. "So Morningstar made itself a new crop of superhumans."

"Let's hope that's all they did. This time they had *two* Signets—imagine if they harnessed the power of both deaths at once. Either they just hatched an army or they did something even worse."

"How in the hell did they manage to kidnap a Pair? Jeremy was injured when they took him, and didn't have a Queen. Napolitano was a lifelong warrior and his Queen had at least a little training. He was a way more formidable force than Varati."

"All I know is their bodyguards were all found dead next to their limo—the driver, too. Just like Varati they attacked while the Pair was getting out of the car. Unfortunately it's going to be hard to get more inside information; one of the bodyguards was the Red Shadow agent who's been reporting on Napolitano for twenty years. Imagine that—not only did they make off with a Pair and kill a team of highly trained Elite, they took down one of Deven's agents."

"Does he have one in every Elite?" she asked.

"I have no doubt. Think of how long Lalita was here without us having any idea. We probably never would have found her out if it weren't for Ovaska."

"Wait . . . you don't think there's another spy here now, do you?"

David smiled. "Absolutely. In fact I know exactly who it is—I learned what to look for after the last time. I just haven't bothered calling her out because I prefer to keep her right where she is and watch her watching me. She might turn out to be useful at some point."

She didn't look at all surprised. "I swear to God, you two."

"He started it."

She smiled slightly, but her eyes were already back on the map. "Napolitano was in denial about Morningstar, just like most of the Council," Miranda murmured. "Even as strong as he was, that denial made him vulnerable. None of them want to believe humans can take us out like this. But Napolitano wasn't a rebellious upstart like some Primes I know. He was old guard, traditional. He'd been in power for ages. This has to get through to at least a few of the others."

David counted up the remaining territories and compared it to the calendar where he'd been keeping note of when Morningstar attacks occurred. "If the frequency of assassinations remains constant we'll all be dead before the year is out," he observed. "I know it won't be that easy for them now that more of us are boosting security, but . . . still . . . the math is not comforting."

"And they only have to kill one of our little group to ensure we can never pull out the big gun," Miranda added. "Whatever the hell the big gun actually *is*. Hopefully that much at least is in the Codex. Meanwhile we have to find Olivia's Consort . . . maybe we should hold a ball."

David laughed. "I don't think she'd be too happy with that idea. You do have a point, though . . . there must be something we can do to find this guy. Maybe there's a divination or a spell or something in the Codex . . . if nothing else we could ask Stella to do a reading of some sort just to give us some clue we can work with."

"I wonder how Olivia feels about all of this," Miranda said. "I mean, her Consort is her soul mate, so they're meant to be together, but it still sucks having so much riding on your love life."

"She's probably not too thrilled with the pressure, but a Prime without a Consort feels a constant, quiet emptiness that only one person can fill. We do our jobs, and we know we're where we're meant to be, but that space where *you* belong never stops aching. I haven't asked her, but I'm sure by now she feels it. I started to feel it the same day I took the Signet. I just didn't know what to call it for a long time."

They held each other's eyes for a moment, neither speaking, until the computer to his left chimed to let him know a call was coming in.

"That's Tanaka," David told her. "A few others will be joining in so we can all discuss additional security measures and precautions. It's probably going to be boring."

Miranda chuckled and kissed him. "That's my cue, then. I need to spend some time in the music room anyway—crazy anti-vampire cult aside, I still have an album to finish. Let me know when you're done."

As she passed by his chair and he leaned over to grab the mouse and start the conference call, he caught her hand again, and they smiled at each other, her love warming him inside and out and banishing at least a little of the anxiety he'd been feeling since Jacob had called. The world might go to hell around them, but as long as he could look up into her clear green eyes there was one sure thing in his life.

Olivia deserved to feel that same certainty. Fate or no fate, he hoped he could help her find it, and soon.

* * *

Comedy or tragedy,
I know you'll be the end of me . . .

There were a lot of unpleasant things in the Queen's world, but the thing that drove her craziest was writer's block. Enemies, she could fight; wounds could heal. Writing songs, however, was like trying to build a bridge out of smoke. Every time she thought she had a grasp on a song, it slipped out of her hands.

There was a reason she preferred playing covers. Writing new material was torture. Weaving together music and lyrics took confident hands, and hers were more than a little wobbly.

Suddenly, a flash of odd memory in her mind: threads of light as far as she could see, all crisscrossed and twisted around each other in what should have been chaos but was in fact an elegant, slowly-dancing order . . . her own hands reaching out . . .

The image was so powerful for a second that Miranda had to grab the edge of the piano to stay upright.

"What the hell . . ."

Stella had described the universe as a giant web . . . and Miranda had dreamed of a giant web . . . she remembered pieces of the dream, now, and though watching all those threads shift had been peaceful, underneath it was an urgency . . . someone was trying to tell her something.

She had a hunch who it was.

"Okay," Miranda said quietly. "So we can't talk to each other, but you can give me dreams . . . but if you're trying to make a point, I don't think I'm going to get it this way—tell Stella. Stella can tell me. Just . . . be a little gentler with her this time."

The music room was so silent a human could hear a pin drop.

Miranda let out a breath. "Invisible superbeing," she muttered, echoing David's dismissal of the whole concept of deity. "I guess it's not any crazier than talking to that painting of Queen Bess across the room. But if there's any way you could let me know you actually hear me, I'd feel a lot better about this."

Echo answereth not. The world was full of humans who believed in God even though they personally had no evidence to back up that belief and had to go on faith from the experiences of others. She at least had a conversation with an overly friendly raven under a tree. That was more than most people got.

She felt David approaching, and sure enough there was a soft knock a moment later. He opened the door partway. "Clear?"

"Yeah. I'm pretty much stuck for the night. How was your conference call?"

He came in and closed the door behind him, saying, "Surprisingly productive."

When he looked over at her, he paused. "What are you staring at?"

Miranda's breath had gotten stuck in her chest, hemmed in by her heart flying all around inside her rib cage. "What . . . what is that in your hand?"

He looked puzzled. "This? It was on the floor outside the door. I think one of the servants was dusting in the corridor. Why do you look so spooked?"

She couldn't answer. She could only stare at the object in question in mute astonishment:

A black feather.

"I had an idea," the Witch said, ushering Miranda into her room after the Queen knocked on her door. "It's pretty simple, and sometimes I just get gibberish, but it's only as hazardous as a tarot reading and might give us more concrete information."

"What, a Ouija board?" the Queen asked, sitting down where Stella directed her, on the floor in front of the table Stella had commandeered as an altar. It was almost exactly the same as the one she kept in her apartment, but this time Stella had added a careful drawing of the Seal of Elysium, as well as a plump pomegranate.

"Actually you're not far off. It's called automatic writing," Stella explained, joining her on the floor and busying herself lighting candles and a stick of incense. "I go into a light trance, nothing scary, and then just let my pen move over the paper, the idea being if Persephone has something to say she can use my hand to do it without having to nuke my brain."

Miranda watched her lay out a few sheets of notebook paper and a pen, which the Witch scribbled with first to make sure the ink was flowing. "And you can get good information like that?"

The Witch nodded. "It's kind of hard to do the first time, because your conscious mind doesn't want to give up control and you end up pushing the pen—just like with a Ouija board. But the cool thing is that whereas tarot is all symbols and can be interpreted wrong or misunderstood, automatic writing gives the spirit or deity or whatever a chance to say stuff flat-out without having to speak in riddles. Sometimes they still speak in riddles, but the chances of getting a direct answer are way higher."

"What do you need me to do?" Miranda asked.

"Wait until it seems like I'm pretty well under, then ask a question. Just see where it goes from there."

Stella had pulled a rather large book off one of the shelves in her room—a photographic coffee table book about horses—and rested it in her lap with the paper and pen. She and Miranda sat facing each other, and the Witch took a deep breath and closed her eyes.

Miranda wasn't sure where to look. If she sat staring at Stella it was bound to make the Witch uncomfortable, but she needed to know when she'd hit a trance state. Miranda settled for looking over at the altar but keeping her senses trained on the human to alert her to any energy changes.

There were, as before, strong wards on the room, but this time it looked like Stella had changed her strategy a little—

instead of just encircling the room with protective power she had interlaced that Circle with a matrix of energy that radiated out from the altar itself. There was a piece of polished labradorite the size of Miranda's palm sitting in the middle of the altar, and she could feel power thrumming within it; the Witch had harnessed the stone's energy, coupled it with her own, and was using it as the anchor for the structure she'd built. It was like the wards were now reinforced with steel beams.

Miranda was even more impressed with the Witch than usual—Stella had learned new ideas about how to work magic after the time she'd spent digging around in the Signets' bonds, and now she was adapting her own work to reflect what she had discovered there. Miranda wondered if Stella would have been strong or skilled enough to create such a thing when they'd first met even if she'd known it was possible.

Miranda felt, or heard, or both, movement in front of her, and she returned her gaze to the Witch, whose eyes were still closed. Stella's hand moved slowly to pick up the pen and hold it over the paper. Stella had been right; the trance hadn't caused a major energy shift in the room. It was definitely gentler than the Drawing Down.

Miranda cleared her throat. She felt a little silly, but not an hour ago she'd been talking to the empty air, so, "What do you want me to know?"

Stella's hand lowered the nib to the page, and Miranda watched, craning her neck closer to see if she wrote actual words or just scribbles. One letter at a time appeared on the paper, disjointed and irregular at first but then gaining confidence, becoming more legible.

It took almost a full minute to complete the first word:

YOU

Miranda read the word aloud, quietly, to encourage Stella, or Persephone, to keep going.

MUST

Sweat was pouring down Stella's face, but she seemed otherwise okay. The Witch's facial expression remained perfectly blank; the sweat was the only sign she was burning energy at all.

NOT

Miranda's heart began to beat faster with a sudden urgency.

Her nails dug into her knees, even a few seconds of waiting becoming too much . . . she could feel the import of the words, whether a commandment or an admonishment.

Stella's hand was shaking slightly. The next few letters became increasingly hard to read, but they were still clear enough.

BLAME

Now the Witch faltered, hanging on to the pen, and her trance, as hard as she could. Fatigue was wearing on her, threatening whatever connection she had opened.

Miranda watched, hand lifting to her mouth, as the last word formed haltingly, letter by letter, each taking a monumental effort.

Y OU R SELF

Miranda swallowed and read the whole sentence softly. The pen fell from Stella's hand and rolled off the book onto the floor; whether it was the plastic clattering or a coincidence, Stella's eyes snapped open right at that moment.

"What did you get?" Stella asked. She looked down at her lap and froze. "Fuck, that can't be good."

Before Miranda could say anything, her com chimed. She lifted her wrist closer to her mouth, still staring at the words in front of her.

"Star-two," she said.

"Miranda," David said, "I need you to come to our suite . . . right now."

She stammered for a second. "Why?"

"Please . . . just come. Now."

Miranda got to her feet and left the room—she'd thank Stella later—and took the short series of hallways back to her own, a strange combination of numb and terrified. She knew that tone in David's voice. It wasn't just the bad news tone, like the one she'd heard when Jacob called earlier that night; it was a tone that meant he had to tell her something he knew would upset her, something that had already upset him. He was trying to remain professional for the sake of anyone who might have been listening until he had her alone.

He was waiting in his chair in front of the fireplace, his laptop open on the coffee table, his face that long-cultivated mask of neutrality that she had learned to see beneath even before she was his Queen.

"Sit down," he said gently.

"What's going on?" she asked. "What happened?"

He took a couple of breaths to choose his words. "A few minutes ago I got a call from Ken Gregory of the U.S. Marshals. He had finished settling your sister and niece into WIT-SEC in El Paso. Everything went smoothly. She was supposed to check in with him once a day. Yesterday she didn't call."

There were already tears in Miranda's eyes, and she didn't try to stop them from emerging. That same bones-deep foreboding she knew far too well had gripped her as soon as she walked into the room. All she could do now was wait.

"Gregory sent uniforms to the apartment. There was . . ." He met her eyes. "There was blood in the living room, signs of a struggle. The Crime Scene Unit is still there now, but their initial finding is that there were two large pools of blood and that the amount was indicative of fatal blood loss. They didn't find any bodies, but . . ."

He passed his hand over his forehead, and she saw the mask crack; he'd been trying not to react, hoping it would keep her calm if he was calm, but whatever he had to say next was too much to let him feign complete stoicism.

He leaned over and turned his laptop toward her. "There was a flash drive placed very deliberately between the two pools of blood. There was only one thing on it . . . a video. Miranda . . . you don't have to watch this. I don't want you to. But you have to decide for yourself."

She was shaking inside and out. "Show me," she said hoarsely.

David closed his eyes a second, nodded, and hit play.

The video was shockingly clear, not the sort of shaky-camera, dimly lit thing she expected. It was in the apartment living room. There were four men in black, complete with ski masks: two standing in front, the other two holding a struggling woman and a little girl on their knees.

The camera zoomed in on their faces, the tears flowing down over the duct tape that silenced their screams. Their hands were bound behind their backs. There was a black eye forming on Marianne's face and blood already smudged on her shirt. Miranda would have bet her entire fortune that Marianne got the wounds trying to protect Jenny.

One of the standing men pulled a knife from his belt.

Miranda pushed backward, trying to put more distance between herself and what she was seeing, her entire being begging her to look away . . . but she couldn't. She had brought this down on her sister. She had to witness this.

Miranda felt David's fingers twine through hers, and she gripped his hand hard, tears streaming down her face as the humans who believed themselves among the righteous murdered an innocent mortal woman . . . and her seven-year-old daughter.

There was no sound. Marianne and Jenny died in total silence, Marianne's last words of comfort to her child lost in the cold silence of the recording.

The screen faded to black, and Miranda thought it was over, but Morningstar had left her one last message. A row of still photographs appeared across the screen, images she knew: Marilyn, Marianne, Jenny, and then a photo of Miranda herself when she'd still been human. One by one, a red X crossed out each picture . . . except for her own.

Miranda stared at the screen, her brain refusing to process the implications.

Finally, she asked very quietly, "Does this mean they killed my mother?"

David made an indefinite noise. "I was looking into that right before you got here . . . as far as I can tell from a quick glance through her records, no. She committed suicide; they're not taking credit so much as they're making a point . . . showing their intentions."

"Wipe out my bloodline," she said hollowly. "My mother had no siblings . . . my maternal grandmother is dead . . . and now . . . I'm all that's left." She leaned forward and closed the laptop screen, banishing the image from her sight, if not her mind. Even so, her words grew less and less steady, her temporary calm fracturing, falling apart. "They . . . they slit the throat of a seven-year-old girl . . . for the sake of their war . . . because of me. Of us. A world they had nothing to do with. How could . . . how could anyone look at that little face and just . . . she was *seven years old*!"

She shut her eyes, trying to stay grounded, but another image jumped into her mind's eye: a pen moving over a piece of paper, spelling out words.

YOU MUST NOT BLAME YOURSELF.

Miranda broke down sobbing, so angry and stricken she couldn't contain it anymore. Even if Marianne had been a stranger, or they'd hated each other, she didn't deserve this . . . to be forced to watch her own child's murder, to die in terror without even understanding *why*. And Miranda had sat smiling at a school picture of Jenny, chuckling at the familiarity of her out-of-control red hair and those leaf-green eyes, and the thought had come to her: Jenny might have had a gift like Miranda's. Miranda would have kept watch on her for just that reason, so that one day, if Jenny started to lose herself to her empathy, there would be somewhere she could go to learn how to control it.

She'd never liked children all that much, but that thought— all the things, from puberty to college to growing old, that Jenny would never get to do, just because a bunch of humans hated vampires enough to march to war through the blood of the innocent—made it so much worse. Marianne hadn't led a happy life, but she was doing the best she could for her baby, trying to make sure things were better for her. It was the same struggle played out millions of times across every human civilization, but the smallness of a single life still mattered. The fleeting rush of every human life *mattered*.

The people Miranda herself had killed had mattered to someone, somewhere, once.

David drew her close, wrapping both arms and presence around her to give her shelter; she felt him step in and add his energy to her shields so that if she couldn't hold them, they wouldn't collapse.

He didn't say anything at first, but as she started to calm down a little, she heard, "This is why I don't want empathy."

She let out a shaky breath. "I'm so tired of getting people killed," she said into his neck. "Just once, I'd like to actually save someone."

He didn't argue that she already had; he understood what she meant. Signets were the most powerful vampires on earth, but for all their power, their war never truly ended. Whether mortal or immortal, there were always those willing to prey upon others, to crawl out of the shadows and paint the city with blood.

"It's nearly dawn," David told her, kissing her forehead and then her puffy nose. "You should go on to bed. I have a few e-mails to send and then I'll join you."

Miranda lifted her eyes to her Prime's. "We have to stop them," she said quietly. "We're going to stop them."

"We will," he replied. "I give you my word, Miranda, we will." Then he smiled lovingly and kissed her forehead. "Just not tonight. Get some rest."

"Wait . . . stay here just a moment longer."

He nodded. She returned her head to where it had been, the spot it fit perfectly where neck and shoulder met. She could feel his pulse beneath her ear. He pulled her up and around to where she was mostly in his lap and held her tight again, love moving from one to the other along their bond, soothing some of the horror, helping her get a grip on the rage that wanted badly to claw its way out of her and lay all of Morningstar to waste whether she was strong enough or not.

Miranda felt an exhausted sleep lapping around the edges of her mind and didn't try to fight it. A day's sleep would help put some distance between her and what she had seen; then she might be able to approach it with calm, in a way that would help, instead of falling apart or accidentally projecting all over the Haven and sending the entire Elite into a depressive tailspin. She closed her eyes and let the warmth around her, the heartbeat against her cheek, and the quiet peace of the room draw her into the dark . . .

. . . where again, and again, she dreamed in threads of light.

PART TWO

The Ten of Swords

Eleven

Retribution came to Morningstar in the back of a laundry truck.

The guards at the compound's front gate were used to seeing the blue and white truck bearing orderly stacks of freshly cleaned, pressed, and folded black uniforms. With dozens of soldiers to clothe, the Texas base of operations received two such shipments per week, like clockwork, from a service located in Dallas.

The base itself was in the middle of nowhere, comprising precise rows of military surplus modular buildings, three Quonset huts as barracks, and one cinder block structure that housed the Shepherd and other officers. The huts were a recent addition—before they had discovered how to create effective soldiers, there had been few recruits, but now that they could use the power of a Signet's death to mind-wipe and program people, they could pluck humans off the street from any city, and the plan was to do so in waves. The month before, the ritual performed in Europe had created a hundred, and the next was planned for America. Most of that lot would go to Texas . . . their greater numbers meant more strikes in the cities, and that would draw out the enemy.

They were unaware that they had already drawn him out.

The same driver was always behind the wheel of the laundry truck—Jorge, an affable man who blasted the Dallas *norteño* station in his truck and was always laughing. He tried joking with the guards the first few trips, but they were stone-faced and disinterested in most facial expressions, so eventually he just went about his business, tried to be friendly and professional, and got in and out as quickly as he could.

The people at that place . . . they were wrong somehow. Only a few of them seemed capable of eye contact. They acted like military, but there was no indication what branch or why in hell they'd be out here. He'd done delivery routes to enough places like this that he decided it was probably better not to ask. He was getting a ton of overtime for this one because it was so far out of town; his family needed that money. So . . . best not to ask . . . but he still wondered.

He wondered, specifically, if he was going to turn on the news one day and see these guys in a standoff with the FBI.

When he arrived at work to take the truck out to the base, he checked it over as always to make sure what was in it looked like it matched the work order. Once about a year ago the guys had loaded a truck with the wrong order and instead of a load of scrubs a hospital got fifty hotel maid uniforms. Since then they all double-checked.

He went back inside to fill up his travel mug with coffee and flirt with Stephanie, the receptionist. He was out of sight of the truck for maybe ten minutes.

At the base, the guards checked his ID and waved him through like always. He maneuvered the truck up the gravel road to one of the modular buildings, pulling around to the side where two guys were always waiting to unload the uniforms, and parked. Wrong they might be, but they were fine with him ducking into the building, after he unlocked the truck doors for them, to take a piss after all that coffee on such a long drive. He got out, pushing the driver's-side door shut.

"Buenos noches," he called over to the soldier guys. They gave him a nod but, like the others, didn't smile or speak. "Let me get that." The keys rattled in his hand. The doors were secured with a padlock, then a sliding bar. Same routine every time.

The doors swung open.

A pair of dark blue eyes. A wicked smile.

A glowing red amulet.

A sword.

And behind him, a dozen others.

Something whistled past Jorge's head, and he heard both of the soldiers grunt—both fell to the ground, the hilt of a knife jutting out from their throats.

Panic as old as the human race seized Jorge, but there was nowhere to run. As they disembarked from the truck he started to edge backward toward the building, thinking if he made a break for it he could get there and yell for help. There were dozens of soldiers here. They must have lots of guns. These guys wouldn't stand a chance.

"Bring me the Shepherd," the dark man commanded. "Kill the rest."

Jorge bolted for the door, running as fast as adrenaline could carry him . . .

. . . and woke with a start at nearly three A.M. to find himself stretched out on the seat, the truck back in its parking spot at the empty, dark Dallas warehouse, the pink copy of his work order signed and dated like always . . . with absolutely no memory of how he got there.

In the eerie silence that shrouded the Morningstar base, the sound of boots striding along the road between buildings echoed loudly from one metal structure to another. The sodium floodlights cast an orange-tinted glow over the compound, obscuring the star-filled blackness overhead.

It was a surreal scene. Bodies littered the ground on either side of the road. They weren't all human. Some had slit throats, had penetrating wounds from a blade, or had been beheaded; a few had wooden stakes to the chest, usually at an angle to avoid the sternum in front and the spine in back.

At sunset there had been approximately seventy-five humans in the base, including all of the officers.

Now there was only one.

The first pyre had already been lit; that many bodies would take a long time to burn, and they needed to keep an eye on it. The impending autumn had brought rain to most of

Texas, but there was no need to risk a wildfire. It was the same protocol they'd followed at the abandoned farm in Rio Verde, but here, they didn't have to rush. No human authority would come out this far unless summoned.

The base was slowly starting to stink of burning flesh. Perhaps if more humans had occasion to smell a mass pyre, they wouldn't be so enamored of bacon.

As David walked through the carnage amid still-open eyes and skewed limbs of the remaining dead, his com chimed, the tiny noise almost explosive in the deep quiet of the night. "Star-one."

"We completed our sweep, Sire. No survivors found."

"And our casualties?"

"Five, my Lord."

"Send a team out to gather our dead and prepare them for sunrise somewhere far away from the humans. Transport will be here in twenty-six minutes—have everyone ready to go as soon as I'm done. Make sure all of their tech is loaded onto the second van."

"As you will it, Sire."

The single concrete building stood in the center of the compound. Four of the Elite were waiting outside for him and bowed at his approach.

"He's secured in his office," said Elite 41. "We searched the room for weapons and removed all communication equipment in case he got loose."

"Good. This won't take long."

He paused for a moment, reaching into his coat pocket to turn on the recording app on his phone, simultaneously looking in the small window set into the door. A nice office, considering the austerity everyone else lived and worked in. Collapsible metal bookshelves with a variety of titles—mostly on religion and military history. The desk was bare now, its computer already confiscated, and beyond it, trussed to his own office chair, was the Shepherd.

From the report he already had about the Shepherd in California, David wasn't expecting a crazed fanatic, but still, the man's unnatural calm after his entire garrison had been slaughtered put the Prime on guard immediately.

The human looked up as David came in, seeming neither cowed nor surprised at what had just walked in the door.

He was a fairly ordinary-looking man with sandy brown hair, hazel eyes, and the stern mouth of a man who rarely had much to smile about. He was thin but not very muscular, and it didn't look like he saw much more sun than David did. The Shepherd in California had worn clerical clothing, but far more casual; this one wore an unadorned black cassock.

David pulled a second chair over to the other side and sat down, elbows on the arms of the chair, fingers interlaced, and regarded the man in silence for a minute.

The Shepherd regarded him right back, unflinching under David's gaze. Either the strength of his faith had stripped away all fear, or he was an idiot.

Granted, the two weren't mutually exclusive.

Curious, David reached out his senses to get a read on the man's energy and emotions. There he met with a surprise.

Shielded. Interesting. Was he gifted in some way, or was it a precaution against a vampire or Witch using their gifts against him?

Finally, David asked, "Do I call you Shepherd, or do you prefer another honorific?"

At last the man spoke. "Shepherd will suffice."

David nodded. "I am sure you know who I am, Shepherd."

"I do. You're one of the eight archdemons."

The Prime laughed. "Archdemons? Is that really what you call us? That's adorable," he told the Shepherd sardonically. Then David sobered, tapping his fingers together. "Here's what I need from you, Shepherd. I need to know who's in charge of your organization. What master puppeteer pulls your strings? You must answer to a central authority."

The Shepherd raised an eyebrow. "Why? You don't."

"Not a temporal authority, no. Long ago we answered to a higher power."

"As do we. Each of us was called to duty by Almighty God; it just happens that he speaks through a man, a holy vessel who delivers the commandments of our Lord so that we, his chosen people, may carry them out and purge the earth of the demonic forces that have caused its ruin."

David had to restrain himself from snorting aloud. "You think vampires are the reason the world is like this? You've been reading the wrong history books, my friend. My people don't start wars. There are no vampire senators. We don't own corporations that destroy the environment. Making the earth uninhabitable would be rather counterproductive for immortals, don't you think?"

"There are more varieties of demonic plague upon this earth than just you," the Shepherd replied. "They will be dealt with as well."

"Witches," David surmised, holding up a finger. "What else?"

"You're a clever man," the Shepherd told him. "I think you'll figure it out on your own."

He chose to ignore the comment. "So does this leader of yours have a name?"

"We call him the Prophet."

"And he's just a man like you?"

A slight smile. "He is just a man like any of us, another of God's children . . . and yet much more."

"How much of this more-than-a-man's plan are you made aware of? Does he trust his Shepherds with the endgame?"

"We know what we need to know, when we need to know it."

"In other words, no." David considered for a moment. "So . . . your leader receives the word of God and relates it to you, or relates the parts he wants you to know. In order to carry out this word, you conscript soldiers and turn them into robots."

The Shepherd shook his head. "Our soldiers join us of their own free will and offer themselves up to the cause. In that way they are just like yours; but ours are men, not demons. They must be given power by God to defeat you."

"Well, they're doing a bang-up job." David crossed his arms. "Yes, you've killed Primes—in ambush. You needed two dozen warriors at each attack to get the job done, with crossbows, and still only half of them came back alive. In straight combat, your people have fallen by the dozen every single time. Now, don't get me wrong, they're good. Very good. I've killed a lot of them, and I'd say they're at the same level as some of my midtier Elite. But if you really want to take us all out, you're going to have to do better. In the meantime just look at how many lives you're wasting."

"They are all blessed men. They will be greatly rewarded in heaven for their sacrifice."

David recognized that kind of talk, as well as the faint gleam in the man's eyes. It wasn't the kind of thing said by a man who had a lot to lose; it was what you would hear before someone hijacked a plane and killed hundreds of people to earn a place in heaven.

A thought occurred: "Is there a way to reverse the . . . gift . . . you've given your soldiers? Can you turn them back into normal people once all of this is over?"

"No."

"That's a shame."

The Shepherd smiled. It was a sincere smile, but there was something nasty underneath it. Was it really fanaticism he was seeing, or was it sociopathy? "Victory has its costs . . . as you will no doubt learn. Our God is vengeful, as are we."

The Prime nodded once more. "Here's another question: What is all this bother over our bloodlines?"

For the first time, the Shepherd looked genuinely taken aback. "Have you not found your Codex?"

"Wait . . . you have one, too?"

The Shepherd leaned forward as much as he could in the zip ties that had him bound to the chair. "We are opposite sides of a coin, our people and yours. The moon and the sun, returning over and over to fight for the heavens. You will find far more similarities than differences as all of this unfolds."

David started to contradict him but thought better of it and temporarily shifted his line of inquiry. "Where did you find your Codex?"

"We had contracted one of your number to perform certain tasks for which, at the time, our people were ill equipped. She infiltrated the Haven in New York to fetch the Codex for us so that we could begin preparations. After that, her mission was to bring us a live Signet, but her thirst for vengeance killed her."

Marja Ovaska. "No," David corrected. "My Queen killed her. But why didn't you have Ovaska bring you the other artifact as well? You needed it to create your army as much as you needed a copy of the ritual."

"Hart didn't have it back then. He acquired it about eight

months before his death. With a few careful nudges, Jeremy Hayes delivered both artifact and Signet to us."

"You still haven't told me what our bloodlines have to do with this."

"It is not for me to know," was the reply. "I was ordered to wipe out the women of that bloodline. The rest of your family lines died out long ago; we've been looking over the entire globe and found nothing."

David stared at him hard. "Did your organization have anything to do with the death of Marilyn Grey?"

The human blinked, clearly perplexed. "No. We were only in our earliest formative stages then. It wasn't until we found our own Codex that we knew what had to be done."

That, at least, would be a comfort to Miranda. Even though the reports of her mother's death were detailed and precise, and there was nothing untoward about it, she was afraid that she was responsible for the death of her entire family. It was true that she was the only one left. They had done a quick search for cousins, aunts, anything . . . but there were none. Even the two cousins her own age Miranda remembered playing with had both died. He could understand why she thought Morningstar might have engineered the whole thing.

He had quite firmly disagreed, however. There were medical records, death certificates, and newspaper obituaries for all of the deaths, and they were diverse enough in cause and location that if it was a cover-up, it was massive. In reality human beings really weren't that good at large-scale conspiracy; someone always talked. David knew, based on the video they had left, that Morningstar wouldn't cover anything up. They wanted Miranda to know what they had done.

This man had ordered them to kill Marianne and Jenny and record the whole thing. Even military officers in the middle of a war would do anything possible to avoid taking innocent lives . . . especially those of children. Yet the word had come from on high, and the Shepherd had followed it without question.

Perhaps it was fanaticism *and* sociopathy.

What David really wanted to know was where the Prophet had come from and where he was holed up, but he knew, both by observing the Shepherd's reactions and by intuition, that the Shepherd didn't know any more than he had said already.

The Shepherds weren't going to be of much use; they could try torturing one later, but David didn't think it would do any real good. Information in Morningstar was apparently given out in miserly doses; it was no wonder the soldier Deven had interrogated hadn't had much to say.

No . . . they were going to have to go up the food chain.

That meant this interview was over.

David stood up and returned the chair to its original spot. "Thank you for being so forthcoming, Shepherd. I think I've kept you tied up long enough."

The Shepherd's eyes fell on David's sword. "Are you planning to cut my head off?"

David smiled, and this time, he finally got a response: Staring up at him the Shepherd paled a shade, and the vein in his neck began throbbing visibly.

"Oh, no," David told him, watching the fear build. It was one thing to know your adversary was a vampire, and quite another to see his eyes turn black. "That would be a terrible waste . . . after all, it's the new moon."

Miranda fell back against the alley wall with a moan, letting the man slide slowly to the ground. The blood raced through her body, and though the effect wasn't as extreme as the first time, she still felt renewed strength filling her every cell.

Last time they had waited far too long. This time, it was the night of the new moon, and neither had been feeling anything like they had before—Miranda noticed she was a little off, her responses slower, but it was nothing like last time. She could still think straight, choose a target with more deliberation.

She stared down at the body with contempt. This one was a loathsome excuse for a man. She had caught him leaving a church, and his thoughts and emotions were so disgusting she might have killed him regardless. His mind was full of a nine-year-old girl . . . and not with the love of a parent for his child.

The Queen didn't normally feed on men—she still had a visceral reaction of fear and revulsion when a strange man got too close to her, and given how intimate feeding could be, she had long ago decided to stick with her own sex. But this time . . . perhaps it was because she still had the image of Jenny tied up and crying burned into her mind, but she had dragged the man into the alley and not bothered trying to soothe him as she tore open his throat.

Miranda looked around for a suitable place to leave the body. There was no Dumpster here, unfortunately, but the church had a little bit of land attached to it, and when she'd cased the place she'd noticed a storm drain. That would do for now. She held her hands over the body and concentrated, reaching into herself and *pushing*.

It vanished.

The Queen sighed, straightening her coat. She hadn't wanted to leave the Haven tonight. She had wanted to stay near a computer screen and watch the raid unfold on the dedicated network David had built for the mission. He'd spent two weeks finalizing the details for this, making sure everyone he needed was in the right place at the right time, paying off one of the employees of the laundry company to get them into the warehouse and the truck, making sure everyone on the strike team had memorized the layout of the compound and knew where the highest concentrations of humans would be at that precise hour. He wasn't leaving anything to chance, he said.

She was still worried. She hadn't wanted him to go—why couldn't he run the raid from the Haven and have the team bring the Shepherd there? This was a battle he didn't have to fight himself, yet he wanted to send a very clear message to the rest of Morningstar. She could have joined him, but the Queen had had quite enough of that sort of thing for a while. If she raised her sword it was going to be here in Austin.

It was probably just as well she hadn't been home for the fighting. Anxiety was already making her stomach hurt. The distraction of hunting had kept her from getting too crazy. She hadn't sensed anything amiss along the bond; in fact, she'd felt grim satisfaction from the Prime . . . and then the wave of energy she already recognized. A battlefield was a good place to be when you had to drink someone to death.

Her phone rang. "Hey, Dev."

"Feeling better?"

"I guess." She started walking back toward the street where she was supposed to meet Harlan. "Good tip about the church."

She had finally told Deven about the new moon, and in typical Deven fashion, he hadn't expressed the slightest regret over the deaths; instead he had immediately suggested that since the new moon fell on a Saturday that month she should stake out a Catholic church to catch the postconfessional crowd the night before Mass.

"Ninety-five percent of the people there will be genuinely penitent over fairly pedestrian sins, but the rest want an audience," he had said. "Murderers especially—if they get away with it, they have to brag, and they think a priest who can't see their faces is ideal."

"But won't they have looked into the law and know they could still be arrested? Texas doesn't have confessional privilege."

"TV and movies make it seem like every criminal is a mastermind, but the truth is, most of them are depressingly stupid."

All she had to do was wait behind a tree, scanning people's emotions. Deven was right—nearly all of them were good people who went into the church feeling bad about something and came out feeling better . . . but it didn't take five minutes to find what she wanted.

"Have you heard anything from the raid?" Deven asked.

Miranda waited at the corner for the *Walk* sign to light, standing among a group of humans on various nighttime errands. Several were on their phones, too, but she was willing to bet they weren't talking about vampire warfare. "Not yet. I'm heading home now to check the network, but if anything had gone awry I'm sure he or one of the Elite would have called. How's the Codex coming?"

"It's . . . weird."

"You've had the thing for two weeks—I thought you'd have it all translated by now."

"Well, I'm getting there, but there are a lot of symbols I've never seen before, and they're key to understanding the text, so it's going more slowly than expected. Unfortunately the sections I haven't been able to finish are the ones that seem to apply to us."

"Of course they are. This is our luck we're talking about."

"Fair point." He paused. "Look . . . I know you're having a hard time with killing humans. But there are thousands of people like the one you found tonight. Organized crime, drug dealers, pimps, Congress—lots of things besides vampires slink around in the darkness. We walk among the unrepentant every night. You will never have to take an innocent life, Miranda. You have to shift your perspective or guilt is going to eat you alive." She could hear him smile ruefully. "Trust me. I used to be Catholic. Guilt is my heroin. But guilt never made anyone a better person, and neither did shame. You are a good person. You're doing the best you can to do what's right in a painful situation. Do you hear me?"

"Yeah," she said, smiling at the words, the smile almost reaching her heart. "I hear you."

"Good. Here endeth the lesson. It's been so long since I last lectured David I was afraid I had gotten rusty."

Miranda grinned. "How can you be so wise and so fucked up at the same time?"

"Most wise people are fucked up. You don't gain wisdom from pleasant experiences, after all—you buy it with pain."

She had to chuckle at the wording. "You should write greeting cards," she suggested. "Cards for vampires could be a lucrative niche market. You know—Lordy Lordy, Look Who's Five Hundred Forty."

He laughed. That made her feel better; she rarely got to hear him laugh. "Go home," he said. "Put on something slinky and wait for your adoring husband to return from his service in war."

Miranda snorted a bit loudly; a woman walking past where she stood let out a little yelp of surprise. "I'm going to put on yoga pants and fall asleep on the couch," she replied. "How about you put on something slinky and drag that big burly blond of yours off to bed."

"I don't think I have anything slinky, but I might manage the second part. Good night, love."

"Good night."

Perfect timing—she was less than a block from the rendez-vous point, and she could see down the street that the limo was already there. As appealing as the idea of sleeping was, she knew she wouldn't; she would sit by the computer, her insides in knots until her phone rang and she knew it was all over and David was either ensconced in a hotel in Dallas to pass the day or on his way home to his Queen.

Twelve

He walked in a slow circle around the training ring, scrutinizing the tall man who stood at its center.

The man waited, looking straight ahead, standing essentially at attention except with a long fighting knife in each hand. He was beautifully built, with impressive but not overly bulky muscles beneath the complexion of a man from the Middle East. Dark, slightly wavy hair that would have been absolutely gorgeous long; eyes to match, so brown they were nearly black, unyielding but full of keen intelligence, quick to take in detail. Facial hair kept close to the skin.

"I am satisfied with the results of your final assessment," the Alpha finally said, stopping in front of him. "I believe your training is at an end."

In an ordinary world, this man would not have been intimidated by someone of Deven's stature, vampire or otherwise. And truth be told he *wasn't* intimidated, exactly—Deven could tell. He had never been defiant, but he didn't avert his eyes in the Alpha's presence and asked more questions than the others usually did.

Deven trusted his gut, and it said this man was exactly what he needed. Most people who stood where the man was standing were afraid of him, and he liked it that way, but given this one's abilities he was willing to accept respect and obedience.

They could work on fear later if it became necessary.

Deven removed a flash drive and an envelope from his coat pocket and handed the drive to the man. "Your first assignment," he said. "I'll warn you now—it's beneath your skill. Everyone starts off with a similar job so I can see how you perform in the field before you are sent out on behalf of clients. This location guarantees you won't be bored, even if on paper it seems pedestrian." He held up the envelope. "Your cover ID, boarding passes, and additional credentials you probably won't need but should have just in case. You have the number to call if you run into trouble or have questions. Are you prepared for deployment?"

The man sheathed both knives on his back and took the envelope. "Yes, Lord Alpha."

"Very well then. I expect your first report Friday of next week. Now . . . this is your last chance to back out. The minute you are designated and step outside this room, the only release is death. Your contract is as immortal as you are."

He didn't move.

"Good," Deven said. "Kneel."

The man obeyed, his eyes never leaving the Alpha's face. Deven stood over him, taking a knife from his belt, and drew the blade across his own index finger, both of them watching silently as blood welled up in the cut. Deven touched the man's forehead, tracing a waning crescent moon in blood. The man probably wouldn't feel the low-level current of energy that uncoiled from the blood and bound him to his fate.

"You belong to me now," the Alpha said. "Rise as your first designation: 1.3 Alizarin."

He took a step back to allow the Agent to stand, caught his eyes, and added with a slight smile, "Welcome to the Red Shadow."

The night was quiet, with barely a wind to stir the trees; cricket and frog songs were the only constants. The slightest sliver of moon had appeared in the sky, though it was obscured at the moment in a bank of cloud that had arrived on the leading edge of the autumn's first front.

Deven had been out on the Haven terrace for an hour, sitting cross-legged with the Codex on his lap, one hand resting on its cover, the other toying with the moonstone ring he still couldn't put away.

Once he had loved spending time on the terrace, staring out at the forest, and he still did, but . . . it was different now. A soft melancholy had grown over the walls and twined around the columns like ivy.

He couldn't be out here now without thinking of Nico.

He finally had to admit it: He missed the Elf terribly—and not just for romantic reasons. He hadn't realized, until they met, just how badly he longed for someone to connect with who understood what he was and what that meant.

He also knew he should be glad Nico was gone. A world apart, Deven couldn't be tempted to do anything stupid.

I have enough. I don't need an extracurricular Elf to complicate things. When I fall in love people get hurt. I only want one man, and I have him.

To distract himself he shoved the ring back into his pocket and returned his attention to the Codex, where it was supposed to be.

He hadn't been lying when he told Miranda the damn thing was resisting translation. Entire sections were written in symbols; it looked like some kind of runic alphabet, though he was familiar with the Norse Elder Futhark and with the Celtic Ogham and this was neither. If he had to describe it to someone, he'd say it looked like the bastard child of Norse runes and Sanskrit.

Not once in his time with Eladra had she ever mentioned the Order using anything like this. His best guess was that the first Signets, the Secondborn children of Persephone, had their own sacred alphabet—something they could use to keep their inner workings secret from any but the highest-ranking Priestesses of the Order.

If that was true, he had no idea what to do about it.

The parts that were simply in Elysian Greek were simple enough. They comprised the texts and rituals he was familiar with from the Order, along with a retelling of the myth of Persephone and Theia.

He'd always liked the Order's version of the story. A lot of mythological scholars claimed the two sister goddesses had been enemies—one darkness, the other light, one a huntress and one a healer. But by the Order's reckoning it wasn't opposition; they complemented each other, two halves of a whole. They bickered like siblings always did, but they loved each other.

Deven sighed, frustrated. The fact was he was going to have to send the Codex back to David only half translated. David might be able to find another High Priestess willing to help, or he might be able to use that ridiculous brain of his to analyze the symbols, identify the patterns, and crack the code. Hell, he'd probably write some kind of program that would do it for him. Novotny could have handled the Greek, but it would have taken longer, and there probably would have been translation errors, missed nuances. Elysian Greek was complicated—it gave the finest Greek scholars migraines with its convoluted metaphors.

According to David, Morningstar had a Codex, too. Deven wondered what language it was written in.

He closed the book and sat back, his left hand still on the cover, fingers tracing the Seal of Elysium. He thought of the Cloister he had destroyed . . . it wasn't the one where he had lived, but they were all very similar to one another in layout and design. It had been so long since those first days that he could barely remember what life had been like there, but some things were still clear: the sound of voices lifted in hymns that had been sung since long before the time of Christ; the smell of beeswax candles and ritual incense. And above all, there was the peace that saturated every corner of the Cloister, the peace from which he had fled.

Eladra had tried so hard to help him accept that peace. But what he couldn't make her understand was that he had spent his human life in a place much like the Cloister—but one that was full of fear, not love—and after years of torment in the name of God, followed by a month of being slowly and brutally murdered in the name of God, the thought of devoting himself to any religion felt like another violation on top of every other he had endured. He had been burned by the fire of God so many times that he was terrified to touch anything warm. He had still believed then, but he wanted nothing to do with God—any god.

She tried to show him that this was different . . . that he was exactly the kind of child Persephone loved, and that none of her earthly representatives would ever hurt him . . . but he had not believed her. She was fighting a battle already lost.

He'd tried to pretend that the only reason she cared was the prophecy that had led her to turn him in the first place . . . but no, deep down he knew better. He had known the moment he woke to immortality, months of agony and a terminal fever finally banished from his body, with her beside him, her eyes full of kindness and her gentle hands washing blood and sweat from his face, that she loved him as her own child, just as he knew that he had broken her heart when he ran away.

If only he'd taken a moment to tell her . . . anything . . . to apologize, to thank her for trying to save him. He had slaughtered them all as quickly and efficiently as he could without letting himself feel anything. In the end, after all she had done for him, Eladra was just another target, another mission completed.

Deven pushed the Codex down to the foot of the chaise and put his head in his shaking hands. "I'm sorry," he whispered. "I'm sorry. I'm sorry."

"All right, now, stop that," he heard, jolting him back into the present. He looked up to see Jonathan approaching with an expression on his face at once stern and concerned.

"You know what will happen if you dwell on the past," the Consort admonished him. "You can't do this to yourself."

"I didn't do it to myself," he said softly. "I did it to her."

Jonathan sat down next to him, putting one hand on his thigh, the other on his face. "You said Eladra knew what her fate would be. She chose to turn you, and by doing so, knowingly accepted what would happen. At any point she could have told you that part of the prophecy, could have tried to change things, but she didn't."

Deven laughed humorlessly. "So you're saying my killing her is her fault."

"No. I'm just saying you didn't betray her." Jonathan pulled him close, this time eliciting a small but genuine smile. "And tearing yourself up over it isn't going to change what happened—all it will do is kill you. Do you think she'd want that?"

"You don't think the matrix the Elf built is strong enough to withstand the power of a good hard vampire mope?"

"I don't think you should tempt fate, baby. Besides . . . you've been sad long enough. What did Nico tell you to do when your emotions get all weird?"

"Breathe, ground, and consciously let go."

"Well, then, do it."

The Prime closed his eyes and grounded as firmly as he could . . . but letting go wasn't as simple as it sounded. Those old feelings were desperate to stay wrapped around him, like Spanish moss, slowly choking the life out of him. Nico had given him protection against that fate, but the memories and emotions were never going to go away. Still, he tried, for Jonathan. After a moment he did feel better.

Deven sighed and rested his head on Jonathan's shoulder. "You've been so good to me," he said, eyes closed. "I wish I had more to give you."

Jonathan was quiet for a while, both of them listening to the midnight symphony going on all around them. He seemed to be debating with himself over something, and while he did, Deven relaxed against him, the relief of his solid presence like the front that had blown in and softened the sky.

Then Jonathan drew back, and Deven blinked and looked at him curiously. "What's wrong?"

Jonathan's words were just about the last thing he was ever expecting to hear. "Let's get married."

Deven stared at him, incredulous. "What in the . . . what now?"

"I'm serious, Deven. It's legal now—let's do it."

"But . . . why? You've never brought this up before."

Jonathan's expression and voice were both perfectly sincere, leaving Deven feeling even more bewildered. "I've been thinking about it for a long time," the Consort admitted, sounding a touch sheepish. "I just knew you'd think I was insane—and maybe I am. I know it's just a silly piece of paper issued by human authority. But this war we're facing, the way everything keeps changing, it's . . . what if you break again, and the Elf never comes back, or he does but you're too far gone to repair? I don't know what's going to happen to all of us, but . . . even if we win, I know that the world we're left with won't be the same one we know. To me, in all that uncertainty, a silly piece of paper means everything."

"But we don't even have real legal identities; why do you care about legal marriage?"

"Because . . . I never thought the day would come that I could," the Consort said. "Did you ever think you'd be able to marry one day?"

"No." Deven smiled a little. "I never credited humanity with the ability to evolve that far. But those rights are for the people who fought for them. I've never done a damn thing for anyone's cause but my own."

"It's not just about the young. It's about all of us."

"So that's why? To celebrate human government taking a moment not to be completely repulsive?"

"No . . ." Jonathan kissed the top of Deven's head, bringing another smile. "Just for once, before the world goes to hell, I'd like to know I had some part of you that no one else ever had."

"My soul isn't enough?"

"You didn't give it to me freely, Deven. The Signet split you in half and joined you to me. I want you to bind yourself to me of your own free will. I want to be your choice."

"You really are serious about this," Deven said, frowning, shaking his head. "I didn't realize it meant that much to you."

"It does."

Again, he leaned against Jonathan with a sigh, closing his eyes for a few seconds before saying tiredly, "Well, then, you're not doing it right. You should be on your knees—you know how I love you on your knees—and have a ring or something."

"I don't have a ring. I'll get you one." There was a smile in his voice. "Diamonds?"

"Only if they match my tiara."

Now the Consort sighed. "Fine . . . if it will convince you I mean it . . ."

For all that he thought he felt so indifferent toward the idea, Deven found he was still astonished when Jonathan shifted off the chaise and knelt in front of him, making them almost the same height for a moment. As Jonathan took his hand, Deven felt his heart flip over, breath catching in his chest.

He's really doing this. Good God, he really is.

Their eyes caught and held until Jonathan asked, "Will you marry me?"

For a moment he couldn't move, couldn't speak, couldn't react at all. Then Deven leaned forward until their foreheads touched, clinging to his hand for dear life. One tear, then another, and a third beaded on their joined hands, and Deven didn't know which was stranger: the fact that he was crying, or the words that came out of his mouth.

"Yes," he said softly. "Yes."

"What?"

Miranda's head popped up at the uncharacteristically obvious surprise in David's voice as he came into the suite, phone to his ear. If he was letting that kind of reaction show, he had to be talking to one of their Circle. Bad news, then. They never got good news these days.

"All right . . . what's the date?"

Miranda tried not to listen in, not so much out of politeness as because whatever it was, she'd rather hear the whole thing from David at once. She went back to tweaking the vocal line for one of the last two songs she hadn't finished; things were going well in the studio, but she didn't want their recording time to go over schedule, which would eat into Grizzly's other clients' slots and cause him a world of issues with temperamental musicians.

Miranda heard David say Jonathan's name. That meant it probably wasn't another dead Prime—it was usually Jacob who called those in, since Jacob had a lot of connections with the Signets outside the United States and Deven liked to pretend he didn't have spies in all their Elite.

"So is this going to be a big thing, or . . . ?" David was walking around the room, his version of pacing. She had no idea how to interpret the look on his face. "Okay, good." Finally, he cracked a smile. "So which one of you is wearing white?"

Miranda's eyebrows shot up. What the hell?

"What about security? This is kind of a huge risk, you know. No, you're right . . . still, send me blueprints of the building so I can look for problem areas. Then we'll talk specifics."

She gave up and put down her guitar, pulling her knees up to hug and watching him wander around. He seemed awfully agitated, but not angry. Empathically she was getting a weird mix of emotions that, like his expression, was hard to analyze.

"All right . . . yes, do that. I will. Oh, and . . ." He took a deep breath, and just before he hung up he said, "Congratulations."

He stared down at the phone for a second before looking up at her. He'd ended up at the fireplace with one hand on the mantel; he hadn't even taken the time to remove his coat and weapons when he walked in.

She just looked at him and raised an eyebrow.

Now he was almost smiling, shaking his head, bemused. "We are cordially invited to attend the wedding of Prime Deven O'Donnell and his Consort Jonathan Burke, at ten P.M. on September thirtieth, at the Sacramento County courthouse. Drinks and amusements to follow."

She was aware her mouth had dropped open. "What in the . . . what now?"

David nodded. "You heard me right."

Her stomach tightened. "Tell me Jonathan hasn't foreseen their deaths."

"He says it has nothing to do with precognition, but that he's wanted to ask since the Supreme Court ruling and didn't think Dev would go for it. Then the other night Deven was having some kind of emotional episode, and Jonathan realized he really has no idea how long Dev will last before he falls apart again. He didn't want to end up regretting that he didn't at least propose, even if Deven said no."

"I thought this was all fixed," Miranda said, staring into the fire. "I thought it would be at least a year or two before they needed help again."

"I don't know, beloved. I'm beginning to think . . ." He

trailed off before saying, "I think all of this may be a bandage on a wound that can't close. Deven swears that it wasn't as big a deal as Jonathan says it was—he was dwelling on the past, which Nico told him not to do at least for the first few months, and as soon as he pulled out of it he felt fine again. But if it's barely been a month since Nico left, and he's already having problems . . ."

"You think he's too broken to heal," Miranda concluded for him, her heart aching. "You think the best we can do is help him stay alive until Morningstar is dealt with. And you think deep down they both know it."

David nodded. "I wonder what it would take to get the Weaver to return and stay at the Haven full time so he can take care of problems as soon as they arise. If the cracks aren't allowed to get bigger, they'll be easier to fix."

"Like a hospice nurse." Miranda gestured for him to come join her, and he shucked his coat and tossed it on his chair before sinking onto the sofa at her side. "So what did they say about the wedding? How many people are we talking about here?"

"Only the seven of us. They've got a JP willing to come in late at night, and then afterward there'll be some sort of celebration. Needless to say security is a big concern. We've been asked to bring additional Elite. Deven says he has a plan— one that I'll appreciate—but is waiting until he can get a look at the building plans to run it by me."

She watched him curiously. "You're not happy about this."

"All of us in one place? No, I'm very much not happy. If Morningstar gets wind of it, all they have to do is attack us the same way they have the others. They could take the entire Circle out at once—hell, if they get any one of us, we're screwed. Granted, if we're expecting it, they'll have a hard time succeeding, but still . . . it's dangerous. We're going to have to plan very carefully."

"Baby . . . that's not what I mean."

"What do you mean?"

She smiled and ran her hand down his arm. "They're getting *married*. Legally. It's kind of definitive, and it's a level of commitment you never reached—and never could. I know you don't really want to be with him anymore, but that doesn't mean this won't hurt. That's usually what happens when one's ex ties the knot."

He frowned. "I'm not hurt."

She just looked at him. Unsurprisingly, he looked away. "I know for a fact that he was hurt when you got married," she said. "Not begrudging you happiness—he helped get us together, after all—but it's your heart comparing what is to what used to be, and what will never be. Part of you has to mourn that. It's okay."

David didn't confirm it, or deny it; instead, he noted, "There was a time, not that long ago, when you would not have felt that way."

"Weird, isn't it?" She smiled, scooted closer, and kissed him. "If you'd told me back then how we would all feel about each other now, I would have kicked you in the head."

He laughed quietly. "That isn't where you would have kicked me."

"Maybe not." She swung around onto his lap, grinning, and gave him a long kiss, winding her hands around his neck.

Their eyes met. "I'm a lucky bastard to have you," he said.

"You're also wearing way too many accessories for this party." She reached down and began to unbuckle The Oncoming Storm, leaning back to deposit the sword on the coffee table, followed by a throwing stake and two knives, letting her hands linger where they would. He watched her, not speaking, eyes sparkling. "These also have to go," she added, and moved down to the floor to attend to his boots. Luckily they weren't the knee-high lace-up pair, so it didn't take half an hour to get them off.

She looked up. Now she could read his expression perfectly. She climbed back up and took her time sliding his shirt up and off. The second she had tossed it on the floor, he put one hand on the small of her back and the other on her shoulder and pulled her back in, his mouth taking hers hungrily. His hands worked their way into her clothes and had them off her in a few well-practiced moves.

Miranda pulled her lips from his and turned her attention to his neck, biting lightly here and there while she reached down and felt for a zipper.

He pulled her hand away and said a bit breathlessly, "Remember what happened last time?"

Miranda made a pained face, touching the back of her head, remembering how much the coffee table's corner had hurt. "Good point." She stood up, took a few steps back, and unhooked her bra, turning to walk away as she held out her hand and dropped it on the floor. She looked back over her shoulder and smiled, quoting, "Take me to bed or lose me forever."

He was there in less than a breath, hauling her up into his arms, returning her smile and answering, "Show me the way home, honey."

She giggled as her back hit the comforter and her Prime separated her very quickly from her panties. She was about to offer up another line from *Top Gun* when his mouth left her lips, but with kisses taking a slow, circuitous route from her neck down over her breasts, then over the landscape of her belly, she forgot what she had intended to say, and reflected, for just a second before all thought was licked right out of her consciousness, that she was lucky, too . . . lucky to be married to the world's hottest nerd . . . lucky that she was about to spend the rest of the night and probably until noon being shagged senseless by said nerd . . . and above all lucky to have found the one place in the world where she, with all her strangeness, fit perfectly, with someone who fit perfectly with her.

Thirteen

Miranda had never seen the Haven of the West before; in fact, the only other two Havens she had seen were Hart's old one—which Olivia had abandoned and had demolished to show the New York Shadow World that things were going to be a little different now—and the beautiful old castle near Prague where they had taken part in the Magnificent Bastard Parade to honor Jacob and Cora.

She was surprised at what she saw when they climbed out of the car and stood before the absolutely gorgeous Mediterranean-style villa outside Sacramento. Even from outside she could hear the silvery chorus of fountains beyond its walls and smell the deep odor of thick forest; the Haven stood near a cliff, its back facing a wildlife sanctuary.

Its location was genius, from a security standpoint. It could only be approached from the front without some serious climbing gear, and motion sensors were hidden all along the cliff face to trigger both alarms and flood lights. There were security checkpoints at three locations between the Haven and the highway, giving the Elite plenty of time to organize in the event of an invasion. Every person allowed in was on a list of approved personnel or expected guests. Having seen her own Haven attacked, she approved of the seeming paranoia.

She was still staring when the double front doors opened and the Pair arrived to greet them. She laughed merrily, caught up in a dual hug. "It's good to see you, too," she said.

David took her hand, and they followed the Pair up the steps into the Haven, followed in turn by two servants who had grabbed their bags and Miranda's guitar.

Inside was just as lovely as outside. There were a surprising number of courtyards and open walkways, considering the place was populated by vampires. Jonathan pointed out the extra shutters and metal doors like the kind used over storefronts—at sunrise the only places they couldn't access were the courtyards. There were also tunnels, like the ones in Austin, connecting the Haven itself to the buildings that stood on either side and housed the Elite's living quarters and training facilities.

Every Haven was different. Some, like Prague's, had been built as human dwellings and then altered to suit vampire tenants. Others, like this one and the one in Austin, had been designed and built by vampires from the ground up.

They arrived at their guest quarters, an airy and spacious suite that felt much bigger than it was because of high ceilings and lots of windows letting in both moonlight and the sea-scented breeze.

"This is beautiful," Miranda said. "It's just . . . wow."

"Since David's already been here, perhaps you could give Miranda a tour," Deven said to his Consort. "Meanwhile we can go over the security plans. Jacob and Cora will be here in an hour, and Olivia closer to dawn."

"Absolutely," Jonathan said, offering his arm to Miranda, who curtsied and took it. The two Primes headed down the hallway in one direction, the two Consorts in the other.

This Haven was only about half as big as hers, but the lay-out was a bit more organic; the Austin Haven looked confusing to new people but was actually laid out in a very simple geometric grid that split off from two main hallways that, in turn, split off from the front entrance. What got people lost was the fact that many of the hallways looked the same. Here, the halls and rooms were more like tree branches.

At one point they walked down a long hallway lined with weapons. "The Gallery of Pointy Things," Jonathan said grandly, sweeping out his arm. And while there were quite a few gorgeous specimens on display, from all over the world and a variety of time periods, it didn't seem like quite as many as she had expected Deven to own.

She said as much to Jonathan, who laughed. "Come with me."

He led her to a very short side corridor that dead-ended in a locked door, which opened into a downward flight of concrete stairs. At the bottom, there was another door—this one with a security panel. The whole setup reminded her of David's server room.

Jonathan grinned at her and fed the panel a numeric code, then touched his index finger to a small scanner. The red light over the door changed to green, and Miranda heard a deep metallic click.

The door slid open to the side—the effect was very *Star Trek*, and she wondered if David had been involved in the security measures. Jonathan beckoned for her to follow and hit a switch that brought up the lights one by one.

She crossed the threshold and gasped.

"Okay, this is more like it," she said.

They were in a rectangular room whose walls were lined with drawers and niches . . . dozens and dozens of niches, each one displaying a weapon of some kind. Swords, daggers, crossbows, axes, spears, knives of every possible description . . . most of them she didn't recognize, though there was an entire bank of swords that looked very much like the ones she, David, and Deven all carried. Whereas the weapons in the Gallery represented most of history, what was in here was obviously meant to be used; most of it was of modern design, dozens of styles of each type.

"What does this do?" she asked, patting the top of a small machine that looked like it belonged in a woodshop.

"It's a stake sharpener," Jonathan said with a grin. "Much faster than doing it by hand—there's another one in our Elite armory."

"Do the Elite get their swords from here?" she asked, wandering around the room and gently pushing in drawer fronts, which caused them to click open. Each weapon had a card beside it detailing its type, country of origin, year crafted, designer or smith, and its name if it had one. Most of the finest-looking swords, which were on the wall instead of in drawers, had names; smaller pieces didn't. She read them to herself: *The Darkened Star. Silver Rain. Shadowbreaker. Stormfire.*

Jonathan was smiling. "The Elite have their own armory. This is Deven's private collection—he's used every single one of these. Many of them were custom made for his hand. A few he checks out to Red Shadow operatives when they need something special. That's why we're underground—this is millions of dollars we're looking at, and some of his most valued possessions. Needless to say they had to be kept someplace fireproof and secure."

Hearing that, Miranda felt a little guilty being here without Deven; it was like she had gotten past his shields and was poking around in his head.

"David has a room like this, only it's full of servers and computer equipment," she said.

"We have one of those, too. As you can imagine, your Prime insisted on climate control for our system. In fact, there are three subterranean rooms; the third holds documents, what few archives we found when we got here, and a few other things Deven wanted kept secure."

They took the stairs back out; the door to the armory slid shut as they left, and she heard the lock reengage as the light turned back to red.

"Now for something completely different," Jonathan said. "Down this hallway is our suite, but when you're back in yours, look for a door that leads outside; it'll be behind a curtain you can pull back if you want. It leads out here . . ." He led her to a pair of French doors, and out.

Again, she gasped. The view was quite literally breathtaking.

She walked up to the wall that stood between them and the cliff and stared out in silence for a while. She loved the Texas Hill Country and loved her Haven, but to live in a place with this view . . .

"All those trees," she said. It didn't feel appropriate to speak louder than a reverent whisper. "You know . . . this feels exactly like the sort of place Deven would live."

Jonathan chuckled. "Do you think so?"

"Yeah. Are there big forests in Ireland? I can't remember."

"I think places like this are in his blood."

Miranda put her hands on the wall in front of her. "Blood . . ."

Jonathan seemed to be waiting for her to say something, but when she did, apparently it wasn't what he was expecting.

"My sister," she said. "Her daughter. My bloodline. I just wish I knew what it meant. I know in my gut the answer is in the Codex, but Novotny hasn't had any luck translating that runic alphabet, and even David couldn't work it out. He's sent out messages to any contact he could find who might know an Elysian, but there hasn't been a word yet. So we're just . . . waiting. We're always waiting."

He reached over and put a hand on her shoulder. "It wasn't your fault. Nobody forced these madmen to declare war on us."

"What do you think it means?"

"I do have a theory. I don't think we're interchangeable, but . . . suppose a Pair of us were Bondbroken, leaving one alive and going mad. What if somehow the empty space in the Circle could then be filled by someone else of the dead Signet's bloodline—not as a replacement for the dead, but as someone to fill the gap in the Circle long enough for us to defeat Morningstar? That's a lot of ifs, but if there were even the *possibility*, Morningstar would have to hunt down anyone who could potentially fill that empty space. Otherwise killing one of us wouldn't guarantee victory."

"But now it will," Miranda said with a nod. "Now we're all we've got." She stared out at the trees for a while before adding, "Maybe it's just as well. If Jenny was the only one, that means she'd replace me, which would mean I'd be dead. Even if somehow David survived that and wasn't insane, I can't imagine making him live without me. I know what that feels like. I survived his death, and I was willing to keep going, but . . . if some random guy had shown up wanting to take his place, even without bonding to me directly . . . I don't think I could have lived that way."

Jonathan shook his head. "It seems to be an awful lot for Persephone to ask of us . . . it wouldn't be fair, or right. But I guess there are a lot more lives in the balance than just ours."

Miranda suddenly realized she'd brought both of them down with her brooding, when they should be celebrating. She shoved the thoughts of Morningstar away; there would be plenty of time to deal with that after this weekend. For just a couple of days, maybe they could all simply enjoy each other's company.

"Okay, enough of that," she said. "Let's get back to the matter at hand. Tomorrow's your wedding, Mr. Burke. Do we get cake?"

He laughed. "No, none of that. Really, the ceremony's barely going to be worth putting on a tux. After that Deven wants to go dancing—there's a hunting ground in the city that's already Signet affiliated so it'll be easy to secure."

"That sounds like fun," she said. "I'm still kind of amazed you got him to do this."

"I honestly thought he'd say no," Jonathan admitted. "But at the time . . . seeing him go through that again, thinking it was going to get worse . . . I had to try."

"How is he now?"

"He's been fine since then. I know I overreacted, but when I think of watching him fade away again, I panic. I would do anything to save him from that . . . but all I can do is be a battery for this power-web Nico made to hold him together. I feel utterly helpless. In that moment all I could think of to do was propose. Silly as it sounds now, damned if he didn't say yes."

She watched the emotions play over his face. "I guess he was pretty surprised."

"That's putting it mildly." Jonathan grinned, his levity returning. "Don't tell him I told you this, but . . . he cried."

"No way!"

"Yeah. Then he dragged me to bed for nearly five hours of very intense and enthusiastic sex. I could count the number of times that's happened on one hand. He's been way more affectionate in the last couple of years, but still, this was different. Apparently the promise of a ring lit him on fire."

"You really got to him," Miranda said. "Good for you."

She heard another door open behind them and turned in time to see Deven and David emerge from the house. David came to stand behind Miranda, wrapping his arms around her and watching the view with her for a moment; Deven and Jonathan did much the same.

"Do you feel reassured?" Miranda asked.

David actually nodded. "We made some adjustments, but the plan Dev came up with is rather inspired."

"So shouldn't you guys be having wild bachelor parties or something?" Miranda looked over at the Pair. "Strippers, booze?"

Deven smiled. "I can see naked men any time I want. And I have better booze here than I could get at a strip club." He tilted his head back to look up at Jonathan, giving the Consort the opportunity to kiss him on the nose. "What about you?"

Jonathan gazed down at him adoringly. "I'd rather be here with you. Not to mention with our friends, who've come all this way to watch me make an honest man out of you."

The Prime laughed. "No ritual in the world could do that, my love."

Miranda couldn't help but grin broadly at the two of them—she so rarely got to see them being cute. Pretty soon Jacob and Cora would be here, and . . .

"Guys," she said, "We should make sure Olivia doesn't feel weird being the only single person here. It's got to be hard enough already, being Prime alone."

David kissed her ear. "I'm glad you thought of that, beloved. I guess that means shagging out here on the terrace is off limits."

"Oh, I don't know," Miranda replied. "A lot of people would enjoy watching that."

"Like who?"

Deven and Jonathan each raised a hand.

Miranda giggled. "See?"

"Hell, let's do it right," Deven said. "We'll all come out here, throw down some tarps, and have a nice orgy."

"Not tarps," Jonathan suggested. "Twister mats."

They were all laughing when the Haven Steward called Deven. *Sire, the Pair of Eastern Europe has arrived.*

"Thank you." Dev took Jonathan's hand and pulled him away from the wall. "Come on, love, let's go say hello and get them settled." As they reached the door, Deven called over to them, "We'll pick up the Twister mats on our way back."

* * *

When they left the Haven the next night, David took a moment to scan each of the two limos for explosives; Morningstar didn't usually use them, but a bomb would have been an ideal way to eliminate any of them instantly, and they did seem to get blown up on an alarmingly regular basis. He even did a quick visual inspection to satisfy his own nerves.

The courthouse was full of Elite, and the Signets all Misted from the car into the building so there was no way they could be shot disembarking as Varati had been. It wasn't without its costs: Olivia wasn't a strong Mister yet and ended up being very loudly sick in the ladies' room when she materialized.

David smiled sympathetically at her when she emerged still faintly green. "You'll get used to it," he said. "It looks like you've got pretty good control already. It's just the vertigo that you have to conquer."

Despite her nausea, Olivia gave him an appreciative look. "You look really hot in a tux."

He grinned. "Not so bad yourself, Prime."

She was wearing a lovely forest green dress that set off her gray-green eyes and even had her dreads pulled up elegantly, showing off the intricate tattoos all over her shoulders.

Before either of them had a chance to feel awkward, the courthouse door opened and one of the Elite guards came in with Cora's Nighthound, who did not respond well to Misting. He handed off Vràna's leash to the Queen, bowed, and went back outside.

Cora, too, looked beautiful in her shining royal blue with her dark hair falling down over her back, and he told her so in Czech, which made her blush. "Thank you, my Lord."

Even surrounded by such beauty, it was Miranda who made his heart skip. She had chosen another dress in the same violet shade as the one she'd worn to the Council ball, and just like that night, neither of them could look away from each other. She walked up to him, and they joined hands.

"Are the boys ready?" she asked.

He looked around; Jonathan was talking to the justice of the peace, but Deven was nowhere in sight. It felt a little strange to be in an empty government building at night—it was just them, their numerous guards, and the JP. David walked over and asked Jonathan, "Where'd he go?"

"There's a little room over there where the bridal party usually waits," Jonathan replied. "I think he went in there to have a panic attack."

The courthouse had a chapel, but Deven had said "absolutely not" to that, so they had opted for another room set aside for nonreligious weddings; it was small and fairly unadorned, with a few seats and, against the back wall, a studio piano that looked like it had been constructed at the same time as the building. The room was big enough for perhaps twenty guests. In this case there were five guests and a dog, or, as Jacob had told the human security officer, a "service animal."

David followed Jonathan's gesture and poked his head into the little side room, which was lit with candles and lined with mirrors, all showing nothing but the opposite wall.

Deven stood staring into one of the mirrors. When he heard the door open he turned toward David. "I just needed a minute."

David came to stand in front of him. "Cold feet?"

He shook his head. "It's funny . . . this is the one rite of passage I never expected to take part in. I know we've been together for sixty years, so it's not as if we weren't already committed, but . . . it just feels different, somehow. I don't think it really hit me until we got here. I'm getting married, David. *Me*. I have no idea what to do with that."

David laughed, understanding perfectly. "Believe it or not, I felt the same way, and it was just me and Miranda with Faith as a witness. We weren't even dressed up—she said she didn't care about a wedding, she just wanted a marriage. I kept telling myself it was just a human convention, that it was our Signet bond that mattered . . . and I was wrong. It *was* different. Not more important, or stronger, just different."

They stood facing each other for a moment, David reaching up to straighten Deven's Signet, then smooth out his lapel, before smiling a little and saying, "Sometimes I wonder how things would have been different if we'd had a chance to do this."

Deven raised an eyebrow. "Would you have asked?"

"I don't know. Perhaps . . . or I might have spared myself the disappointment. Even then I knew I was far more emotionally invested in us than you were."

"What makes you so sure of that?" Deven asked, genuinely taken aback.

"I just knew." David smiled again, this time with a touch of regret. "Up to that point I had never loved anyone the way I did you. After you became Prime and your Signet didn't light for me, I knew our days were numbered. If I couldn't be your Consort, I might have settled for being your husband, whether for a year or a hundred . . . but eventually Jonathan would still have come along."

Deven caught his hands and held them firmly. "If you thought for a minute that I didn't love you as much as you did me, then I was a failure from our first night together. I know I never gave you what you deserved. I wish . . . I wish I could make it up to you. I've never forgiven myself for hurting you."

"You never forgive yourself for anything," David reminded him. "But I forgive you. And the truth is . . . deep down I've known since the night I met Miranda that your breaking my heart was the best gift you could have given me. It just took me a while to understand." He leaned in and kissed Deven softly, and they were silent again for a minute, holding on to each other as they had so many times before, before David sighed and stepped back. "I'll see you out there."

He had his hand on the doorknob when Deven said, "David . . ."

David paused and turned back. Deven was smiling almost wistfully, his eyes shining in the candlelight as he said, "I would have said yes."

Something in David's heart felt like it let go of a long-held breath. He returned the smile, nodding, and left the room, closing the door behind him.

* * *

Forever is so very long, my love
And ours is not an ordinary fairy tale . . .

The room's having a piano was a coincidence, but Miranda couldn't resist sitting down in the last couple of minutes before things got underway.

Then she rose and stood next to Jonathan, while David stood

next to Deven—they'd been asked to be best woman and best man, respectively, each handing over a ring at the right time.

She watched, smiling, thinking of that night she and David had stood in front of an old man who looked an awful lot like this one, with Faith looking on. They'd been wearing exactly what they would have any other night, long coats and swords and all. She didn't remember any of the words; all she remembered was being happy, smiling up into David's eyes, wondering what she was getting into . . . even though she already knew.

"We are gathered here tonight . . ."

Her face had probably looked a lot like Deven's did as the justice of the peace began his lines—the Prime looked a little surprised at himself, being where he was, but also much happier than she'd ever seen him. Once or twice, she thought she saw his eyes start to tear up, but it was gone as quickly as it came and could have been a trick of the light.

She glanced down at the rather large gold wedding band she was holding. It was enormous; Jonathan had the sort of fingers usually found on people who ground bones to make bread.

She turned the ring in her hand and noticed for the first time it was inscribed inside the band in incredibly tiny letters: *"Doubt thou the stars are fire; doubt that the Sun doth move . . ."* The second half must be carved into Deven's ring. *"Doubt truth to be a liar; but never doubt I love."* That, for some reason, brought tears to her eyes, and she was sniffling when she stepped forward to hand the ring to Deven. He squeezed her hand gently when he took it.

"With this ring, I thee wed."

Miranda looked over and caught David's eye. He smiled, and she felt love and appreciation from him, warming her from the inside out. She returned it as well as the smile.

As Jonathan had promised, the ceremony was very short; rings, brief vows, and that was pretty much it. It was interesting watching the officiant—she could tell by the pauses before pronouns that he hadn't performed a lot of same-sex weddings, but he was perfectly glad to be there, and his smile was genuine as he concluded:

"By the power vested in me by the state of California and

the county of Sacramento, I now pronounce you, Jonathan and Deven Burke, joined for as long as you both shall live." He grinned, the expression lighting up his wrinkled face so much that Miranda started giggling. "Now, kiss!"

Deven was laughing as Jonathan grabbed him and spun him around, kissing him passionately. They ended up standing in each other's arms, and everyone else came up and hugged each other, then the Pair. They both looked absolutely blissful, neither entirely willing to move away from the other.

"All right," Jacob said, "What sort of amusements did you have in mind for the rest of the evening? A champagne toast followed by moderately awkward ballroom dancing?"

Deven's smile turned mischievous. "Not a chance," he said. "You all brought a second set of clothes—go change. We're going clubbing."

The others had already walked out of the room, but Jonathan lingered to pay the JP and have him sign the marriage license, and Deven stood there watching him for a moment before lowering his gaze to his left hand, where the ring now encircled his finger.

David had suggested platinum, which was what his and Miranda's were made from, but Jonathan had made one of his few serious requests in the whole situation and asked for gold. Theirs was already a nontraditional wedding, he had explained; he wanted one traditional thing.

The officiant left with a parting grin and wave, and Jonathan came back over to where Deven was standing, holding up the calligraphed piece of paper. "Look," he said. "We're official."

"There it is, in black and white," Deven murmured, touching his name . . . his old name, then the new. It was going to take a while to get used to the change, but he'd been adamant about it—that, he said, was *his* traditional thing.

"Come on," Jonathan said. "We should get changed—let's just grab the little waiting room next door."

Deven tucked the license in his bag and brought it along, shutting the waiting room door.

He had his coat and shirt off before he felt Jonathan's eyes on him and looked back over his shoulder. "You're getting distracted, husband."

Between one breath and the next Jonathan had hold of him and shoved him back against the mirror—not hard enough to break it, thank God—and was kissing him hard, hands already trying to get the rest of Deven's tux off.

Jonathan said in his ear, "Say that again."

Deven knew exactly what he meant, and grabbed the Consort's hair and pulled his head back so their eyes met. "Husband," Deven said.

A growl, and they were kissing again, this time headed down toward the floor—it was probably filthy, but neither especially cared in that precise moment. That was why soap, and dry cleaning, had been invented.

"We do have someplace to be," Deven panted, though it took quite an effort to remember how to speak English with Jonathan doing what he was doing.

"They can wait a few minutes."

"Just a few . . . we'll have to hurry."

"Then shut up and let me get down to business."

Deven laughed, rested his head back against the dingy industrial carpet, and surrendered without a fight.

Fourteen

The club was called La Caccia, and it was similar to the Black Door in both form and function, just a bit smaller. Even half a block away, waiting for the limo to make its way through traffic up to the front doors, Miranda could hear pounding bass, and there was a line outside that snaked around the building.

David was tense next to her. He claimed he was only worried about the security plan. She let it go at that but said, "Oh, come on—it's their first quickie as a married couple. Cut them some slack."

The plan wasn't going to collapse from a half-hour delay arriving at the club; a far bigger hazard for the vampires was the trip back to the Haven. Not only was it possible for Morningstar to attack the limos and take out enough tires to cause an accident and leave them vulnerable, it was imperative that no one find the Haven itself.

Dozens of Elite had been deployed for tonight, and the club itself, which was already watched over by tight security to make sure its human patrons weren't injured by its vampire patrons, would have fifty extra guards inside and outside the building, even on the roof.

"Baby, relax," she said. "You're making me twitchy. I just

want to let my hair down for a couple of hours, and I can't do it with you throwing off sparks."

He leaned his forehead on his hand. "I'll try. But this is a—"

"Bad idea," she finished for him. "I heard you the first twenty times. But we're not in charge, remember? We're here for our friends."

The other occupant of their limo smiled at Miranda. She had a sneaking suspicion that Olivia wasn't fooled by David's behavior either; yes, he was worried about their safety, but there was more to it than that. The look on his face when Deven reappeared freshly changed and pretty obviously post-coital was a dead giveaway that the wedding had affected David more than he'd let on . . . just as she'd warned him it would. He probably didn't even realize it.

"So how's the Elite-building going?" Miranda asked, hoping to change the subject. "I heard you found a Second."

"Yes," Olivia confirmed. "Her name's Regan. For some reason—and I know this will surprise you—I've been getting a ton of female recruits."

"That's awesome."

"It is. We're about sixty percent women right now, but Regan's running another trial this weekend and she said it's all men. I'm hoping we'll be up to the numbers I want in another month."

Miranda frowned. "So you don't want so many women?"

"All things being equal, I couldn't care less what sex they are. I don't hold a sword with my vagina, so why should it matter? But I'd rather keep a fairly even ratio for now so that people don't accuse me of preferential treatment of women because I'm a woman." She rolled her eyes. "There's already talk that I'm building some kind of Amazon army. You know, aside from all of us, the Council is nothing but a bunch of useless old morons."

"I agree wholeheartedly," Miranda said. "Besides, in battle I think a vagina would be a much better weapon than a penis. They're way less fragile and most men are already afraid of them."

Olivia laughed. "Point taken."

The car pulled to a stop, and one of the Elite waiting

outside the club opened the door for them; here the doors and the street were much closer together, and it was just easier to walk in than to Mist. Olivia had expressed relief hearing that part of the plan.

Miranda's main worry for the time being was Cora; she didn't know how the shy Queen would react to a place like La Caccia with so many people in such a tight space. But as soon as they were in the building, Deven gestured for them all to follow, and he and Jonathan led them through a door to the left of the main entrance, where a long hallway wrapped around the side of the club and brought them to a back room up on the second floor.

Outfitted with comfortable chairs and a couple of tables, it was the ideal place to leave Vràna, who obviously couldn't come out into the crowd. There was even a small bed in the corner and a door she suspected led to a private bathroom.

Jonathan saw Miranda looking around and leaned close to say, quietly, "We've fed in here quite often, among other things. Dev has this tendency to try every drug that crosses his path, but his favorite tends to make him . . . affectionate, let's say."

"Which one is that?"

"There's a designer brand of Ecstasy called Euphoria Twenty-one that's made specifically for vampires."

"That door leads out into the club," Deven was saying, indicating the one on the opposite wall. "Cora, you're welcome to stay here the whole time, or come and go as you please if you find the crowd overwhelming."

The Queen, who had been visibly nervous, relaxed immediately. "Thank you," she said, kissing Deven on the cheek. "I knew you would think of me."

He smiled at her. "If there's anything we can get you that will make your evening more comfortable, just say the word."

Jacob took his Queen's hand and said, "Why don't we go out with the others for a few minutes, so you can see what it's like in there, and then we can come back if you like. I'd hate for you to miss out."

She nodded. "I will go . . . as long as you stay with me."

"I always do," Jacob replied, kissing her hand. Miranda

loved the way Cora smiled at him; when they'd first met, Cora had been so terrified of everything, especially men, that Miranda had wondered how she would ever be able to love her Prime without fear. She should have known that Jacob would be so good for her—not only was he a gentle man with a quiet disposition of his own, he had limitless patience and understood that in their lives there was no need to hurry. That patience had paid off beautifully for them both.

Jonathan opened the door, letting the noise of the club flood in, and they left the room and ventured into the fray.

Just like the Black Door, La Caccia had two levels; looking out over the first level, Miranda saw that the dance floor was packed and the bar a whirl of activity. She glanced over at Cora—the Queen's eyes were wide, but she held on to Jacob's hand and didn't bolt.

Jacob apparently caught Miranda's thoughts; she'd forgotten he was a telepath. "Don't worry," he said as he led Cora past her toward the stairs. "She's braver than she lets on."

He winked at Miranda, and she noticed that while Cora still looked like she might jump out of her skin, the closer they got to the dance floor the more she perked up.

"Well, come on," David said over the noise, wrapping an arm around his Queen's waist and kissing her ear. "Let's get that hair of yours down."

She dragged him down the stairs and into the crowd, where the energy of human and vampire blended together into one desire-filled roar. All around her vampires were courting their prey, drawing them close, hands on hips and shoulders. The smells of sweat and blood were intoxicating, and she let herself be swept up into it.

She saw whom she wanted immediately: a college-aged girl done up in Goth, with black lipstick and hair streaked with bloodred. She was lovely, healthy, and having a great time with her friends; she also had no objection to dancing with a woman, so Miranda sidled up next to her and gently prodded her mind to get her attention.

"Wow," the girl said. "Hey, aren't you—"

"No talking," Miranda replied. "Just come with me."

She was aware of David watching as she slipped back into the rhythm, this time with the girl pressed in close. Miranda leaned her head toward the girl's shoulder, letting her hair fall around to block the view as her teeth lengthened and she struck.

The girl stiffened for only a few seconds, and then she was moving again, and Miranda held her close, drinking deeply and quickly. The human tasted like youth and clove cigarettes, and Miranda released her with the usual mental commands.

She was unutterably grateful that since she had started killing on the new moon, the rest of the month it was as easy as it had always been to let her humans go. If she'd had to fight that impulse every night forever . . . she probably would have lost her mind.

David moved up and kissed her, and she tasted blood on his lips as he did on hers. She sucked it off his tongue and put her hands on his shoulders. "Feeling better?" she asked.

He kissed her again. "Some. I'm going to get a drink—I need to loosen up."

"I support you, good sir, in your alcoholic endeavors."

Grinning at her silliness, he made his way back through the crowd, just as someone else made his way toward her. She was surrounded mostly by mortals until a familiar immortal energy met hers and a hand curved around her waist.

She smiled. "Shouldn't you be dancing with your husband?"

Deven spoke in her ear so he didn't have to shout. "He doesn't dance. Trust me, it's a good thing. He's got all the grace of a giraffe on meth."

"Speaking of meth . . . I didn't know you had a drug habit."

He drew her back against him, and they rejoined the music together, the hand on her waist sliding down to her hip. "I wouldn't call it a habit," he said. "More of a hobby."

"Looking for an escape?"

"Sometimes. I toned it down after Jonathan and I Paired— he doesn't like the way I feel when I'm high. I try to use a bit more discretion these days."

He held up his other hand just enough that she could see the little zippy bag he produced—two white pills, each marked with the number 21.

"Is that that Euphoria stuff Jonathan was telling me about?"

"It is indeed." One pill disappeared. "Regular Ecstasy is in and out of our systems in half an hour. This lasts two full hours—long enough to have a fantastic time, but short enough to end by last call. It's also a much cleaner high."

"What does it do to you?"

"Haven't you ever had Ecstasy?"

"I wouldn't know where to get that kind of thing even if I wanted it. I'm guessing that stuff is a little harder to find than most."

"There's only one dealer in Sacramento and it's two hundred dollars a pill."

"Two hundred dollars? Good Lord."

"Worth every penny."

She could feel his energy changing. Parts of him that were always on guard relaxed a little, and the happiness he'd been feeling since the wedding deepened into something dark and sweet . . . and seductive . . . that wound around her like vines, tendrils of it making her shiver. Her own energy responded to his strongly, which she wasn't expecting, and she drew in a fractured breath.

He turned her around so they were facing each other. "Trust me," he said. "You're safe. I won't let anything hurt you."

She watched, spellbound, as he took the other pill and placed it on his tongue . . . and then, before she could react, he kissed her.

The thought of spitting the pill out never even occurred to her. She swallowed it, giving him an irritated look that he apparently thought was amusing.

Miranda felt another familiar presence and looked over to see Cora and Jacob on the edge of the crowd, dancing—far enough from the center that Cora wouldn't feel trapped. Cora looked like she was having a good time, and Jacob was clearly enraptured at having his Queen doing a little bit of butt-shaking.

Olivia, too, had found someone to dance with—David. Miranda's eyebrows shot up when she realized it was him. He glanced over at her, as if checking on her, and smiled.

She shot him a thumbs-up and looked away so he wouldn't feel weird and could return his attention to his partner. She didn't want him to think she was worried, or that she didn't trust him; she wasn't, and she did. She also didn't want his friendship with Olivia to be strained because of jealousy, hers or otherwise. Miranda didn't want a repeat of Faith any more than David did.

She looked around again, frowning. "Where's Jonathan?"

"Feeding," was the reply. "Or possibly fucking, I can't tell."

She stared at him. "On your wedding night?"

He laughed. "It didn't change anything, Miranda. The same rules still apply. You know how much feeding turns us on—just like you know that back before he met you, David shagged every human he bit. Jonathan's always been the same way. It's perfectly natural. Now relax . . . you should be rolling any second now."

She started to say something, but before the first word was out, she felt it. A wave passed through her body, igniting every inch of her skin; suddenly the air felt like it was stroking her, even as she breathed it in and out. Her clothes felt softer, the weight of her hair on her neck was unspeakably wonderful . . . sounds grew quieter, their edges worn down and blurry, though she could still understand words perfectly if she tried.

And though she would have been horrified ten minutes ago, she could feel her shields thinning out. They didn't open, and didn't even come close to falling, but let in way more than usual from the people nearest to her. It was strange and made her heart pound, but it was manageable.

She let herself reach out and taste their emotions, pushing away anything negative and drawing in the happiness, the arousal. Everything from falling in love to enjoying a particularly well-made margarita gave her more; she wrapped herself up in it. It felt like an endless psychic orgasm, without all the thrashing and screaming of the usual variety.

She closed her eyes for a moment, just feeling, but when she opened them again she gasped.

"What do you see?"

Miranda shook her head, unable to find words for a few seconds, and she blinked hard, hoping it would disappear—to no avail. "Threads," she said, her nails digging into his arm. "The web of light—it followed me here."

She could see it as clearly as in her dreams, light reaching out in every direction, connecting every single person in the club, from the human patrons to the Elite guards to the bartender to Cora's dog. She could see it, and feel it, energy moving in slow rhythm with the music that surrounded them all, new connections being formed and others dissolving.

"I shouldn't be seeing this," she said, a note of fear entering her voice. "This isn't my gift. I don't understand why I keep seeing this."

His arms encircled her reassuringly, and he said, as if such things happened every day, "It's nothing to be afraid of. You're getting a glimpse behind the curtain of reality—it must have something it wants you to see."

She nodded. It had never occurred to her to think of the vision as something with its own consciousness, but if Stella was right and the manifest world was the party dress that a deity wore to dance with its creation, there must be a specific purpose to the dreams, and if she tried to get her fear out of the way maybe it would say its piece and go.

She let out a slow breath and tried to just let the vision do as it would, without latching on to any of it; she grounded herself as much as she could and let it flow, in and out, shifting with the heartbeat of the club. Her near-panic subsided little by little. It was only nature—she didn't need to fear it. It reached out to her like an old friend, as if there had been a time, long ago, when she had been intimately familiar with every last strand.

And this time was different; it wasn't trying to take her anywhere or push any knowledge into her mind. It just wanted to dance.

Miranda closed her eyes, leaned into the dark strength of her partner, and released all control over the night, her sense of individuality dissolving as if she had become a single strand in that tapestry of light, crossing and uncrossing a thousand others, enjoying the deep and ages-old connections between her and those she loved—a perfect circle, or getting there, held in the gentle sway of the hands that had fashioned the Web, hands that were guiding her toward something she would worry about tomorrow . . . tonight she reached out to her Circle, seven hearts all in love with each other and waiting for the last . . . and for one shining hour there was only love, and music, the feeling of hands on her body, and the mingled beauty of humanity and immortality all around her.

After he turned Miranda over to her Prime, Deven returned to the room where they'd left Vràna; he expected to see Cora there, but she must have gone back out again with Jacob. He had the room to himself, except of course for the dog; it was quite a relief after all the sensory stimulation beyond the door. He flopped into one of the chairs and closed his eyes, summoning the energy to push the drug through his system faster. It was close to the end anyway, but he didn't want to wait.

He felt something big and shaggy bump against his hand, and smiled, scratching Vràna between the ears.

David had been rather put out that Deven got his wife high, but the way she shoved her Prime back against the wall and practically swallowed him whole seemed to make David more amenable to the situation. Deven had instructed him to take Miranda up to one of the back rooms and give her whatever she wanted for the next hour; they'd both enjoy themselves even more than Deven knew they already did. Cora and Jacob weren't the only Pair he'd caught sexual echoes from. A few years ago that would have bothered him, but now, it was almost comforting—any of them feeling happy made him feel better along the connection they all shared. Tonight, there wasn't an ocean separating any of them . . . the whole Circle, almost, in one place . . . it felt right, and good, and he knew he would miss it when they all parted.

A while later he heard the door open and shut, felt who it was, and smiled. "I was hoping you would come after me."

"What are you doing?" Jonathan asked, folding himself onto the floor at Deven's feet. Vràna let out a canine sigh and padded back over to the corner.

"Getting sober."

"Why? I thought you loved that drug."

"I do. But I was down there trying to decide whom to glue myself to next, and I realized the only person I wanted tonight was you. And I don't want to be high with you . . . not tonight."

The room started to feel normal again. The barriers in his

mind drew shut, and in a few minutes his skin just felt like skin, the air just felt like air. It was always disappointing to come down off E21, particularly when the levels of dopamine and serotonin plummeted after the drug had used them all up—that was the reason it wasn't sold to humans. The serotonin dump was so severe it would drive most mortals mad, if not straight to suicide. He was very careful to regulate the drug trade in Signet-affiliated businesses—police raids were an annoyance he didn't need.

He opened his eyes and looked into Jonathan's. "There," he said. "It's all me again."

Jonathan laid his hand on Deven's knee, and Deven traced over the ring, adding, "You know . . . I thought I was just doing this for you, because I've done so little to make you happy all these years. But it turns out . . ." He lifted Jonathan's hand and kissed the ring. "I loved marrying you tonight, Jonathan. And I love that we're married. Thank you for asking me."

The Consort returned the gesture. They smiled at each other. "Thank you for saying yes," Jonathan said.

"Let's get everyone back up here . . . I want to go home."

Jonathan found Deven's phone and sent a group text. Then he sent another, this time to their drivers. "The limos will be here in twenty," he said.

First back were Jacob and Cora; the Queen was flushed but smiling and looked as though she'd had a drink or two. A few minutes later Olivia arrived—her clothes were in something of a disarray, suggesting that after leaving the dance floor when David left her, she'd gone off and found someone else to pass the time with.

Miranda's and David's clothes were not in disarray, but energetically it would have been hard to miss what they'd been up to. Miranda was just barely still high; by now she'd be feeling like herself, just a little fuzzy, and hopefully her visions would have ceased not long after she hit the peak.

He had the sudden intuitive flash that she had been having those visions for a while now, and that she hadn't told anyone about it, not even David. She wasn't a Weaver—what on earth could she possibly need to see in there? The possibilities it suggested were not pleasant.

Deven's phone alerted him to a text. "The cars are out front," he said. "Is everyone ready?"

Nods all around.

"Twice in one night," Olivia said, looking queasy at the thought. "Consider my willingness to barf all over Sacramento your wedding gift."

"I was hoping for a gravy boat," Jonathan replied.

"Do we all know exactly what to do?" David asked.

"We've been over it fifty times," Jacob pointed out. "I think we're good."

"All right," Deven said, standing up. "Let's go."

Seven vampires walked out of the club and got in the limousines with an Elite escort that lined both sides of the path from door to door. Two cars pulled away from the club and headed down the street, bearing east toward the highway and then south out of the city.

Deven looked out the window around the street. "Okay," he said. "Go."

Their driver, a longtime Elite himself, obeyed with a "Yes, Sire."

David let out a breath. "That's a relief," he said as the club building grew smaller. Eventually they turned onto another street and it totally disappeared from view. "How far out are they?"

Deven spoke into his phone. "Location? Good. Any signs of pursuit? Keep me posted." He looked over at the others. "Halfway across town. Ramos is pretty sure they're being followed."

"Which means they've been watching," Jonathan mused. "I wonder if they were at the courthouse, too, or if they just knew we'd be at La Caccia."

"No telling," David said. "If they already had surveillance on the club, it's possible they didn't know where we were before that and just saw us arrive—it can't be that common for two limos to pull up there. They're unabashedly conspicuous."

"That's what makes them an ideal decoy," Jacob said, all the way in the very back seat with Cora asleep on his shoulder and Vràna riding happily with her tongue hanging out. "They're a lot more comfortable, though. I haven't ridden in a van since I was an Elite."

A block away from the club, where there was an urban church with two large passenger vans parked on the street, a third van went completely unnoticed. Two by two, figures appeared from the shadows . . . if one looked closer, one might see they had on similar clothes to the vampires who had taken the limousines but weren't nearly as heavily armed. It was almost as if the limo passengers expected an attack.

The limo drivers were to take a long and meandering route through town before leaving Sacramento toward the south . . . while the van went straight out of town and made for the Haven, to the west. If the limos could shake their pursuers before they reached the city limits, so much the better.

"How can we be sure they didn't spot the fake us?" Miranda asked. "We know based on the stuff we found at the Texas base that their tech isn't nearly as advanced as ours, but all they'd need to know that wasn't us was a pair of binoculars."

"Well, we can't be absolutely sure, but I think the fact that they're following the limos is a good sign." David turned slightly in the seat so that the Queen could lean on him. She looked pretty exhausted, and in fact was asleep within five minutes.

Olivia was conked out, too, and Jonathan, who had called shotgun so he'd have more room, was starting to nod off. It would be only three thirty when they got back to the Haven, giving everyone plenty of time to shower and unwind before bed.

David was looking forward to falling over onto the mattress and not moving for a while. He wasn't sure how he felt about tonight. He was willing to admit that Miranda's suspicions were right—she hadn't said so tonight, but he knew she thought he was upset about the wedding. But just as Miranda had said, he had to mourn that loss—a loss that had happened sixty years ago and was still not remotely healed. There were so many layers to their history; every time one scarred over, another started bleeding . . . hell, he hadn't even bothered taking the bandage off until after he met Miranda, and thanks to his decades of denial the Queen had been left with wounds of her own. She was just wise enough not to let them fester.

But if Deven's getting married would help close that door and finally convince David's heart it was over, maybe he could finally let go. He was tired of hurting over something that should have been long over with.

He stared out the window, not really seeing what passed by, thinking that humans were lucky, in a way. They had to age and die, often horribly, and their lives were so brief . . . but they had one distinct advantage over vampires.

They had only one lifetime to live with their regrets.

Everyone was grateful to arrive back at the Haven; even Vràna looked much happier once she was out of the van.

Deven checked his phone again; the last text he'd received had stated that they were pretty sure they'd lost the car that was tailing them and would be heading to the Signet-owned warehouse where they could leave the limos for the day and get some rest before returning the following night. He wouldn't feel at ease about the whole thing until he heard they'd arrived.

In the meantime, the guests headed off to bed, most exchanging hugs and a few kisses. As soon as David and Miranda had vanished around the corner, Jonathan took Deven's hand and pulled him toward their suite, giving him a mischievous grin as he did so.

Right outside the Signet suite, Deven finally got a text: *Arrived. All clear.*

"So," the Consort said, closing and locking the suite door behind them, "I suppose this is our one-day honeymoon."

"I suppose you're right."

"Then you had better go clean up so I can get you dirty again."

Deven grinned, pulling off his shirt with a yawn. "You know chances are we'll just fall asleep."

Jonathan came over and kissed him. "Not this time," he said. "I'm not letting today slip away. After today we can both do what we want, like always—but today you're all mine. I want to remember every moment—and trust me, Mr. Burke, I intend to make every single one memorable."

Deven couldn't help it—he smiled, damn near beaming, at the name, which gave him a surge of what he realized had to be real happiness. Jonathan was right; they had to grab it and hold on while it lasted. "All right," he replied. "I'm all yours." He headed toward the bathroom, but stopped and said, "Just do me a favor . . . have Marta bring up a really big pot of coffee."

Fifteen

Night descended over the Haven and revealed a shining three-quarter moon; its cool blue-white light bathed the terrace, spilling inside through the windows, while the wind wandered aimlessly through the trees. It was a quiet, serene night, and a welcome respite for the seven Signets who had passed the day curled up asleep . . . or occupied in other ways.

Deven leaned in and nuzzled Jonathan's ear to wake him. Jonathan grunted and said, without opening his eyes, "You have clothes on. I don't approve."

"You can sleep in for a while longer if you like," Deven told him. "I saw Olivia off—her flight departs at ten, so she hit the road an hour ago. Jacob and Cora are about to leave as well. I tendered our official good-byes to all three of them— they understood your absence. David and Miranda will be here until midnight."

"I'm meeting with the limo team as soon as they get here," Jonathan murmured. "I'm getting up."

"I can do that," Deven said. "Go back to sleep."

"No, no . . . Thomas asked me last night to come to the debriefing since it's an evaluation of the Elite's performance.

As Second he wants me there as the commanding officer. It won't take long."

Deven stood, but Jonathan reached out and took his hand before he could walk away. The Consort's eyes opened, and he held Deven's, smiling softly. "I love you," he said.

"I love you, too. Now take your time . . . I know you're still worn out."

"I keep forgetting how athletic you are. I'll be lucky if I can walk." Jonathan's eyes had drifted shut again.

"Is that a complaint?"

He grinned. "Absolutely not, my Lord."

Deven squeezed his hand, shaking his head. "You're incorrigible."

"Who wouldn't be, with such encouragement?"

He rolled over as Deven left the room, pulling the pillow over his head, which meant he'd be up within ten minutes.

Deven left the suite through the terrace door, stepping out into the cool evening with a contented sigh. He had expected to be the only one up and about this early, but a feminine figure stood by the wall, watching the forest sway and shiver. Even if he hadn't already known who it was, the large furry shadow next to her would have given her away.

"My Lady," he said. "Do you mind if I join you?"

She smiled. "Not at all, my Lord."

"You two are due to depart soon—is everything ready?"

"Yes. Jacob is making sure our things are safely stowed in the car. Truthfully . . . while I had a moment, I was hoping I might find you out here."

"Oh? Why?"

Cora bit her lip, torn. "I do not wish to interfere in your private affairs, but . . . I have been worried about you for some time now."

He had to smile at that. "Everyone is worried about me," he pointed out. "You're in good company."

"I have somewhat different reasons," she replied. Seeming unsure what to do with her hands, she put them on the wall the way most people did. "I am worried . . . about your soul."

Deven's heart sank. "Cora, please don't—"

"Not in the way you think," she insisted. "I have no sermon for you. I would be both foolish and incredibly presumptuous to think you have not heard it all a thousand times. But you must know . . . Jacob and I are less bound up in the Circle as we live so far away, but I have been able to feel your sorrow and pain trying to live without faith. I do not care what you believe, my Lord. But you must reawaken that part of you, or all the magic and strange creatures in the world will not save you."

He blinked. "Strange creatures?"

She blushed a little. "A few weeks ago, I was in meditation, and I felt something over here in California by virtue of the Circle connection. I could feel something being done to you—magic. I felt a presence, and that presence greeted me as a friend."

Understanding, he nodded. "You met Nico."

"I believe so." She cast a glance around them, though there was no one else outside, and said, "I know he is not mortal. I could sense it. I am not sure what he is—I did not know there were possibilities beyond human and vampire."

He debated for a moment whether to tell her, and decided of all their friends she was the least likely to blab it all over the Circle. "He's an Elf," Deven said, expecting her to express some kind of incredulity.

She didn't. She simply nodded. Then she looked at him keenly, and he knew what she was seeing. "You are, too," she said. "At least in part."

"Yes."

Cora reached down and rubbed Vràna's head with one hand. "When I was here in my mind, I got the strangest sense that I had seen him before. Since then I have thought about it many times, trying to remember. Almost the moment I stepped out here and saw your forest, it came to me."

"Go on."

"The first night I met you, you touched my hand, and I saw something . . . a young man. He had long auburn hair and deep violet eyes, and was watching me—you—with such love, my heart could barely contain it. It was gone in a second, and I thought I had imagined it."

Deven's heart had tightened more and more with each trait she described. "That was Nico," he confirmed. "That was definitely him. But Cora . . . he's gone. Back to his paradise and to his people. Even if he returns to heal me again, I don't want to love him. It hurts too much . . . and I've hurt too many people. I'm not going to cause Jonathan any more pain than I already have."

Cora gave him a sad smile. "Do you think love can be switched on and off at will like an electric light?"

"No. But I know it can be walled off, pushed aside."

"You mustn't do that," she said earnestly, her lovely face grave. "The way to open the spirit is through love. It is through love that we are redeemed, made whole." Cora returned her gaze to the trees for a minute before she asked carefully, "Do you pray, my Lord?"

Deven sighed and leaned on the wall. "No, Cora. I do not."

"Would it bother you if I prayed for you?"

His first impulse was to snap at her that she should mind her own goddamned business . . . but he found that, after that first knee-jerk reaction, it didn't bother him at all. If it had been anyone else, he might have felt differently, but he understood Cora's motivations; she was his friend, and she was only offering love. Whatever his past, he couldn't help but be touched. "No." He smiled faintly at her. "Pray to your heart's content, my Lady."

She was unsatisfied but didn't push. "Thank you." Quickly, probably before he could change his mind, she came up and gave him a kiss on the cheek. "I believe my Prime is calling to me; I shall go now. I hope we all meet again soon."

As she walked away, he replayed her words in his mind. First Nico, now Cora. It almost felt like they were in collusion. He hadn't had so many people nosing into his religious life since he had a religious life.

He heard someone come outside and knew immediately who it was. The Queen of the South joined him at the wall.

"You're not worried about my soul, too, are you?" he asked.

She gave him a long blink. "No more than usual."

"Good."

Rather than asking the obvious question, Miranda just asked, "How was the wedding day?"

"Exhausting."

"That's it?"

"No." Deven leaned on his elbows, staring down at the

ring. The question came out before he could really think about it. "Do you ever wonder why people love you?"

The Queen moved closer, extending a hand to cover his. "There is no why," she told him, her tone brooking no argument. "They love you because they're them and you're you—flawed, tired, sad, strong, loving, all of it. Love doesn't need a why."

She sounded so certain that he almost believed her. He put an arm around her waist, and she leaned on him with a smile. "What's His Lordship doing?" he asked.

"Most of our stuff's already in the car," she replied. "I think he's anxious to get home. He's up at the front of the Haven watching Jacob and Cora drive off. What about Jonathan?"

"In the garage talking to the Elite who posed as us in the limos and the lieutenants who led the security details last night."

"I feel like I should be doing something useful," Miranda chuckled. "But it's so nice out here, and there's never enough time for any of us to spend together. We should get your Nico to move here so he can teleport us back and forth."

He didn't reply, and neither spoke again until Miranda lifted her head, frowning. "Do you hear that?"

"Hear what?"

"It sounds like an alarm clock," she replied. "Kind of a—"

Deven felt the vibration a split second before thunder tore through the night.

They both looked toward the sound in time to see the far end of the building explode, shooting chunks of the walls and clouds of debris into the air. He heard Miranda cry out in fear and felt her grab his arm as a second explosion rocked the foundations of the Haven, followed by a third, and a fourth—the noise was horrific, the shaking and pitching of the ground under their feet exactly like an earthquake.

The wall in front of them fragmented almost in slow motion, but by the time the wave of stone and wood reached them, time had sped back up again.

The force of the blast threw them both off the terrace, over the side of the cliff. He felt repeated impacts with the cliff wall—the dull crack of a broken arm, broken ribs—as he and the Queen crashed down toward the forest floor.

The last thing he saw before blacking out was one final explosion bursting into the sky . . . and then he slammed into the earth, and the world went dark.

"David!"

Miranda came to screaming his name, unable to think about anything but finding him, getting to him. The panic was far beyond sane—seconds later logic asserted itself and she acknowledged that neither of them was anywhere near dying, and the thought was almost enough to keep her calm.

Up atop the cliff she could hear chaos; people shouting, alarms going off, the sound of something spraying that could have been a sprinkler or a water main. Every minute or so there was a thud as a chunk of wall tumbled down to the ground. Miranda looked around and saw that debris had flown over with them, flying into the trees and actually taking one down. The splintered trunk shone pale and stark in the moonlight.

She turned over and sat up, trying to find her phone. By a miracle, it was still in her pocket. Her entire body hurt, battered and bruised from the fall, and she had to force her fingers to cooperate on the screen.

He answered on the first ring. "Miranda!"

"Are you all right? Where are you?"

"I was out front. Most of the explosions blew toward the back—I'm a little banged up but okay."

She looked over to where Deven lay unconscious on the ground. Blood was oozing out from under him. "I need you," she said. "I need help with Deven."

Before she even finished "I need you," David materialized out of the air a few feet away; he toppled forward onto the leaf-strewn ground, coughing, and she saw that when he'd said "banged up," he was putting it mildly. None of his injuries looked serious, but he must have been hit hard if he could barely manage a Mist.

They both took hold of Deven and gently turned him over. "I can't fucking believe we got blown up again," Miranda said, hearing the note of hysteria in her own voice and trying again to ground. "What's it like up there?" she asked David as he took a quick inventory of Deven's wounds. It looked like the Prime had been hit by flying glass; there were lacerations all over him, and their tumble down the cliff had been far worse for him than her. A piece of wrought iron was sticking out of his stomach, causing the bleeding. David pulled it quickly before answering her question.

"A nightmare," David answered. He was beyond shocked, almost beyond words. She'd never seen him look quite that bewildered. "The main building is nothing but a pile of rubble and broken walls. Anyone who was still in there is either dead or trapped—that's all the guards, most of the servants. One of the Elite buildings is fine; they weren't rigged to blow but the other one got hit with so much debris it's half gone."

Deven groaned and opened his eyes. He was badly hurt, but Miranda knew he'd be fine as soon as they found—

"Jonathan," Deven said. "Where is he? I can't . . ."

"He was in the garage, wasn't he?" Miranda asked. "That's a concrete building—it might still be standing."

She met David's eyes. The answer was written on his face.

Before she could say anything else, she heard a phone ringing—Deven's. David found it first. "It's him!"

He hit talk and put it on speaker, holding the phone close to Deven.

"Where are you?" Deven asked, trying to sit up and failing. David moved behind him, helping him upright. "Are you hurt? I can barely feel you."

The answer came slowly, in hoarse and ragged breaths. "Baby . . . it's okay."

Suddenly a memory struck Miranda—kneeling next to Drew in the empty classroom while he bled out onto the floor and said a whispered good-bye to a sobbing Kat. *Oh no. Oh God. No . . .*

"Tell me where you are," Deven said again.

". . . trapped."

"Where? David and Miranda can Mist you out, we just have to know where to look—"

"It's too late."

They all stared at the phone. "Jonathan, don't be ridiculous," David said in a very calm voice. "We can Mist you— but only if we know where you are."

". . . don't understand . . . I'm not . . . I can't feel any-thing . . . pinned . . . I got my hand to the phone, but that's all I've got . . . I think . . . something's gone . . . I can't feel it . . ." His voice started to fade.

Panic had entered Deven's voice. *"Where are you?* Damn it, Jonathan—"

"Miranda."

She had her hands pressed to her heart, so far past fear that she could barely force her mouth to move. "I'm here."

"Promise me . . ."

She waited, but there was nothing else for a few seconds, and she cried, "Jonathan!"

"Promise me you'll save him."

Deven was staring at the phone, shaking his head slowly back and forth, and he whispered, "That's not how it works . . . we go together."

"No."

Again, they all stared.

Miranda could feel Jonathan dragging scraps of strength into his body with all that remained of his will. "You know what to do, Miranda. Promise me."

She started to deny having any idea what he meant . . .

"Oh, God . . ." she said softly. "Oh God."

A matrix of light appeared in her mind, millions of con-nections beckoning to her . . . but this was no dream.

It was real.

"That's what it was?" she all but screamed. "All this time, *that's* what I was learning?"

"I want . . . your word."

"You can't ask me to do this!" she exclaimed. "Don't you know what this will do to him? To us? I can't, Jonathan— don't make me promise!"

"It's the only way . . . has to survive . . . everything depends on this."

Heart and mind frozen, she looked down at Deven. As Jonathan weakened, so did he, and he had his eyes closed, breathing labored . . . waiting.

She tried to reach Jonathan with her energy, to give him . . . something, anything. Life support. Anything—even just to let him know he wasn't dying alone there in the dark, far from any comfort. She managed to find him with her mind and began to cry when she realized he was right. There was no healing strong enough to save him. They could still try to Mist him out, but he was so weak that he would die in the attempt and they would lose both of them . . . or . . .

"Please," he said. She could barely hear him. "Please."

Tears were running down her face as she leaned toward the phone and whispered, "I promise."

"Good . . . that's good . . . th . . . thank you . . . Deven, baby, if you can hear me . . . I love you. You were my always . . . too."

"I'll be right behind you," Deven told him with a soft smile through tears, touching the screen of the phone as if he could touch Jonathan through it. "Just wait for me."

On the other end of the line she heard a clattering sound that she realized was the phone falling to the ground.

The rest was silence.

Beneath them the ground began to tremble. It wasn't severe and lasted only a few seconds, but it was enough to erase any doubt.

Deven gave a cry of pure, agonizing desolation that tore Miranda's heart in half, then lay still against David, surrendering, knowing what was coming. He was ready to go. She could feel it. There was nothing left . . . only one last bridge to cross.

Miranda lifted her eyes to David. "Do it," he said. "Whatever it is, do it."

"Anchor me—"

She closed her eyes, and immediately the vision of the Web appeared as it had in her dreams for weeks. And just as in the dreams, she could see it—the Circle, as it existed now. That strand she had been staring at for hours in her sleep shone in her mind's eye . . . but its light was fading, slipping away. She knew what it was now . . . and she knew what to do.

Miranda braced herself against David's power and reached into the matrix.

She took hold of the fading strand and *pulled*, dragging it closer, drawing one end of it back away from the edge of death.

"No!"

She heard the desperation in Deven's voice, heard him struggling; she couldn't open her eyes, but she shook her head, tightening her grip on the bond. "David, hold him down."

Deven was fighting her with his energy, too—what power he had left he tried to use to wrest control back from her and follow his Consort into death. But he was weak, and growing weaker; and she had her strength and David's. Even a grief and shock-stricken Prime had no chance against the will of the Thirdborn.

Iron determination took hold of Miranda—from where, she didn't know—and she took a deep breath and snapped the bond in half.

She didn't stop to find out how he reacted. She wasn't finished.

Purely by instinct, she felt her way around the Circle until she found what she needed. She had no talent for this, only what she had learned in her dreams, but it turned out a delicate touch wasn't required when one had brute strength.

She heard David's voice, almost cracking with fear. "Hurry. I'm losing him."

Miranda couldn't stop to think about what she was doing. She knew the consequences would be dire, and she might destroy everything right now with her novice's hands . . . but she had promised. And she knew, even without that promise, that this was what had to happen.

She took the end of the broken strand . . .

. . . and joined it to their own.

She started pulling energy from David to pry their bond apart just enough to slip that strand in, then close it and seal it. It was messy and wouldn't hold forever, but it would hold for now. She pushed the energy back into a flow, and though it shook and wobbled, it moved along the bond, from one, to two, to three.

As soon as she let go, she fell back out of the vision and into her body, breathing hard and drenched in sweat. Her head was already pounding, and she knew she was going to pass out, but first she had to be sure . . .

David had Deven's head in his lap and was staring down at the fallen Prime, whose Signet was dark. They waited, neither able to speak, as the minute stretched out . . .

A faint light kindled in the Signet's depths. As she watched, heart in her throat, it began to pulse gently as it brightened before growing steady again. All of the wounds on his face and arms began to close, and then to fade away; she could feel her own doing the same.

At first she didn't understand what was different, but a shudder ran through Deven's body, and she realized what it was.

His Signet was an emerald.

Or, it had been.

Now it shone red.

He drew a gasping breath, eyes opening, and struggled backward in fear—he might not have been dead, but it had been close, and suddenly being dragged back into his body had to be terrifying. He stared around at them, uncomprehending, until his eyes fell on the phone that lay beside him.

One hand reached over to the screen, fingers touching it lightly, shaking. Miranda saw the screen light up, saw *Call Ended*.

There was only one way to describe what happened then.

Deven shattered.

He sank back onto the ground, body racked with sobs, curling up in a ball with his hand still on the phone, gripping it so hard the screen cracked. Miranda remembered what he was feeling. She recognized the sound as those sobs broke into a thousand pieces and became screams of despair, of abandonment. When it had been her voice, Deven had been the one to bring her solace.

David was crying, too, but managed to pull off his coat and lay it over Deven, adding his own arms to try to offer comfort to what could not be comforted. He lifted anguished eyes to Miranda's. "What have we done?"

She fell over onto the ground, suddenly too weak to move. She could feel energy being pulled from her—when it was just David she was connected to, she didn't feel it at all, but now the circuit was precariously off balance, trying to stabilize itself. She didn't fully understand the implications until she shut her eyes and, briefly before she passed out, saw the Web . . . saw what she had done to it. Their bond, and the Circle, had been remade.

The Pair was now a Trinity.

The still-intact Elite building had become triage for the wounded, while those Elite who were unharmed or already healed combed through the wreckage of the Haven, looking for survivors or any belongings they recognized.

Miranda sat quietly on a cot—one of two dozen that had been set up hastily in the main training room—and watched the activity around her, numb, and glad to be numb.

Exactly one survivor was pulled from the ruins. A cheer went up when they found her, and another when they got her free; they brought her in and laid her out on one of the cots, giving her blood and encouragement. She was a servant, by the look of her torn and dirt-encrusted clothes; she found herself hugged by everyone around her and was soon healed and asking to go back out and help.

Miranda found herself thankful for sheer dumb luck: David had already sent their Elite home, so none of them were in the bombing; and their luggage was already in the car out front and thus had survived. The car's windows on the passenger side had been broken by shrapnel, but everything in it was intact.

Thirty-eight bodies had been found, primarily in the Haven itself but a few in the second Elite building who had been near to the blast. Those bodies were being shrouded and laid out in rows for the sunrise.

"My Lady."

She looked up at the Elite standing solemnly in front of her. She hadn't heard him approach. "Yes?"

"We found this and thought it best to bring it to you."

He held out his hands, offering her a sword. She took it gingerly and nodded her thanks, then slid the blade out of the sheath to confirm its identity—by some miracle, like its owner, Ghostlight had survived.

It had to have been in the Signet suite, but those rooms had been demolished, not even leaving a wall to mark where the Pair had lived. All of their possessions, everything they'd collected or treasured over the long decades, gone in an instant.

Miranda couldn't help but think about Faith . . . they had found the hilt of her sword, but it had blown apart, while Faith herself was essentially vaporized.

Too many bombs . . . too much fire, too many lives blown into dust. Why did it always have to be an explosion? Why couldn't any of them die in peace, held by the people they loved as they sighed their last breaths? Why did it have to end in blood and fire?

She knew the answer, of course. This was what they had signed up for—a violent death with only one comfort . . . and that comfort was far more fragile than any of them had ever known. For centuries Pairs had died together, but it seemed that era was ending—just in time for her to have become Queen. Such bitter luck.

She laid the sword down on the adjacent cot, alongside its bearer, who had yet to regain consciousness. She hoped he wouldn't until they were away from here; this was not where he needed to wake up.

A moment later David returned, dusty and subdued. He took a bottle of water from a nearby cooler and came to sit down next to her.

Wordlessly, he held up what he had brought back from the ruins: a cracked, soot-smudged Signet.

"What do we do with it?" she asked softly, taking it from him and wiping the stone with a clean spot on her shirt. There was blood on the chain, the blood of one of her dearest friends. Her hands began to tremble.

"I don't know." David sounded defeated. "We . . . we found him. They're trying to get him out, but a concrete pillar had fallen and crushed him, and the walls of the garage fell on top of that. No one in there survived. It was . . ." He looked away, and she saw the impossibility of tears in his eyes again. "There was no way we could have saved him. He wouldn't have survived a Mist. There wasn't much left down past the abdomen . . . he couldn't feel anything because his spinal cord had been severed, thank God. I don't even know how he lived long enough to make the call. When I think that . . . he was alone in there, Miranda, in a concrete tomb with no light but the phone and twenty feet of rubble between his dying breaths and freedom. He died down there alone." He put his head in his hands.

She threaded her arm around him, and he around her, and they held on to each other. "Not alone," she said. "He heard our voices right until the end. He knew Deven was safe. That had to count for something."

He didn't reply, just shook his head. She had never seen him like this—he'd taken charge without hesitation, but out of the eye of the surviving Elite he looked like an orphan wandering around a war zone.

"What about the bombs?" she asked. "Is there any evidence?"

If anything, the question seemed to make him feel worse. "It's my fault."

"How can it possibly be your fault?"

"They got the idea from us. The only nonvampire staff allowed past the gates are the groundskeepers—they come once a week during daylight, in a truck. It's always the same team—they have to scan their IDs and fingerprints and there's a camera watched by a day guard inside the house. The humans had all been background checked and vetted. Morningstar must have brainwashed them and sent them in with the explosives, knowing that since they were regular visitors they'd be let through. There's no telling how long they had control . . . or how long those bombs were there waiting. They wanted revenge for their soldiers and their Shepherd . . . and they got it."

"We thought we were so clever," she murmured. "Decoy limos, wild-goose chases . . . the thought never occurred to any of us that they might already have found the Haven."

She reached down to touch Deven's face and was relieved to see he'd warmed up a little. Her eyes fell on his left hand.

"Jonathan's ring," she said. "We can't leave it here."

"I have it," David replied quickly before she could start to worry. "It was lying near him. The left hand was . . . mostly gone."

Miranda resisted the urge to cry again. She was so tired, every time she cried it felt like her head was about to split open. "What are we going to do?"

"Go home," he said. "We'll go back to Austin . . . after that, I don't know. Let's just take it one step at a time."

"When can we leave? We need to get out of here before he wakes up. He'll want to see the body."

"What makes you so sure?"

She met his eyes. "I did. Even Bondbroken I couldn't really believe you were dead until I heard Deven say he'd seen you—but I still wished I could, to make it real to my mind. And you were in one piece, not . . ."

"You're right. We can't let him see that. I just want to do one more round of the Elite and make sure they're organized. The Second is dead, but there are several high-ranking lieutenants who can run things for a while. Let me check in with them, and then we'll go."

There were too many questions they had no way to answer. There was no precedent for this. Should they leave Jonathan's Signet here? With whom? Would whoever came along to take over the West have another one made?

She couldn't think about it. One step at a time, she told herself. First, get home.

Maybe then they would figure out the second step.

David's phone rang, and he groped after it halfheartedly. "Solomon."

Miranda didn't want to listen. She wasn't sure she could take anything else falling apart.

"Oh, God."

Damn it. She shut her eyes. When he hung up, she said wearily, "Jacob calling with another assassination?"

"No." Something in his tone made her open her eyes. "Jacob and Cora never made it to the airport," he said. "They're gone."

Sixteen

Cora fought her way out of oblivion, forcing herself to open her eyes even though her eyelids felt like they each weighed a ton.

At first her surroundings made no sense. She lay on a tile floor, freezing cold; directly in front of her was a metal door. The chamber she was in was empty of furniture and had no windows.

She didn't understand. The last thing she remembered was being in the car, on her way to the airport with Jacob and Vràna. They'd gotten stuck in traffic because of an accident ahead, and the driver took an alternate route. Had they stopped? Had someone attacked the car?

"Jacob," she said, her quiet voice echoing off the tiles. "Jacob!"

Very, very softly, she heard to her left, "Cora?"

She crawled over to the wall and pressed her ear to it. "I am here."

"Are you hurt?"

"No, are you?"

"No. Do you remember what happened? We were in traffic so long we missed our flight, so we stopped to have a quick hunt and they got the drop on us. I think we were sedated."

"But where are we?" she asked.

"My guess is Morningstar headquarters."

"Can you Mist?"

"I tried," Jacob said. "These cells are shielded. Clearly they know their audience."

Cora swallowed hard, the reality of their situation beginning to sink in. They had been captured, were now imprisoned . . . and everyone knew what Morningstar did with Signets.

She struggled against paralyzing fear. "What should we do?"

"Wait," he answered. "That's all we can do for now. That and pray."

"Did you see where they took Vràna?" she asked.

"No. She's a smart dog—she probably pulled a Lassie and ran all the way back to the Haven for help."

Cora didn't really understand the reference, but she was too shaken to say so. She pulled her knees up to her chin, trying to get warm and trying not to cry. In addition to her present fear, she could feel something . . . a great, gaping chasm of sorrow in her heart. She knew it wasn't hers, but if the room was shielded . . . either the shields weren't as strong as they thought, or whatever was happening in the outside world was terrible enough to reach her even here.

Distantly, she heard men's voices, growing closer. They were coming.

She heard the cell door next to hers open, heard a struggle. "Get the other one!" one of the men yelled.

Keys rattled outside and the door swung open. There were four men outside, each one holding a crossbow loaded with a wooden stake, all of them pointed right at her.

"Try to fight and we'll turn you into a fucking pincushion," one of them said.

They dragged her out into the corridor and pushed her down the hall. She couldn't see Jacob anywhere. She couldn't try to escape if she didn't know where he was; if she left him behind they would surely kill him and end her anyway.

The hallway opened up into a large room full of people. Row after row of black-clad soldiers sat on wooden pews lined up in front of a broad stone altar.

The men hauled her up to the front of the room and grabbed her by both arms to hold her still. She pulled in her energy and tried to Mist, but this room, too, was shielded—whatever went on inside was protected and hidden from the outside. That suggested to her addled mind that this place was still in the city; if they were out in the country like the Haven, they wouldn't be so keen on keeping their activities concealed. In fact, each area she'd been dragged through reminded her of the courthouse they had been to—shabby, decades old. This might be an abandoned school or something similar.

She was trying to distract herself from what was coming. It was working until a second group of men entered the room, this group bearing Jacob.

They held him at stakepoint, forcing him up onto the altar and onto his back, where they shackled him down and roughly took his Signet, laying it on a nearby table.

She knew they must have threatened to harm her to get him to cooperate. He was not a man of rash action—he would wait for an opportune moment, taking his time to assess the situation before acting. She hoped he had a plan.

Seeing him chained there, Cora nearly fainted from the intensity of her fear but held herself up by inches—she wasn't going to embarrass Jacob or herself by swooning like a Victorian lady.

Jacob turned his head and caught her eyes. She could feel his love for her reverberating from one end of their bond to the other. She refused to look away. If they were going to die, the last thing either would see was the other's eyes.

A man in cleric's clothes came forward. The Shepherd. Her English wasn't quite good enough to follow everything he said, but he was delivering some kind of sermon, and she caught words like "demon" and "lake of fire." The next part, though, she did understand, and suddenly the sadness she had felt earlier made terrible sense.

"As you all know, brothers, tonight we celebrate our victory over the Archdemons. The judgment of God has rained down upon them, turning their fortress to ash, and when silence fell, two of them lay dead. This war is won, my brothers—but now comes the most important part. We must lay to waste all of the remaining demons who walk the earth, starting with their leaders and finishing with every last vile beast of their kind. Tonight we will begin our new chapter by taking the power of these two remaining Archdemons, and with it we shall bring in more to our cause . . . hundreds more. Let us pray."

Cora wanted to wrestle her way out of their grasp and shake the Shepherd, demanding to know whom they had killed. If a Pair was dead . . . there were only two possibilities.

The Shepherd shifted from prayer into intonation, reading something from a large leather-bound book with symbols all over it. She felt a crawling, slimy energy from the book, whether part of some spell or due to the kind of people who had used it.

He took up a large bowl and set it down on the floor next to the altar, then said quietly to Jacob, "Fight me, and before we kill her we'll pass her around and make sure she's begging for death."

The Shepherd seized Jacob's arm and yanked it out to the side where it hung over the bowl. She saw the knife in his hand a second before he sliced it across Jacob's wrist, and blood began to drip down from the cut, splashing into the bowl.

Cora thought she understood—they would use the blood to create their warriors, but to activate the spell they needed a Signet's death, and they intended to use a Bondbreaking. That way she would be alive a little longer, and they could repeat the blood ritual with her death as a catalyst.

She watched, helpless, as the Shepherd laid the Signet at the head of the altar six inches or so from Jacob's head. She saw the hammer nearby, and sheer panic swept her up in its fist; she began to struggle in their grasp, harder and harder. The Shepherd barked something about holding her still, then yelled to Cora, "Make one more move and I gut him!"

He took the knife and held it over Jacob's midsection. They were going to die regardless—she had to try. She jerked sideways one more time and very nearly wrested herself free.

The Shepherd's mouth tightened into a severe line, and he plunged the knife down all the way through Jacob's stomach. The Prime didn't scream, but he let out a strangled cry. Blood flowed out of the wound and over his side, coating the white stone with red.

Cora stared at the blood, and suddenly something inside her . . . snapped.

All the noise in the room faded away, and her fear evaporated beneath the fire of something else entirely: anger.

How dare you? How dare you hurt my friends, even kill them, and then try to take our power? How dare you lay a hand on him? Or on me? How dare you . . . human!

She felt her body temperature rising. She breathed hard, glaring at the Shepherd through a red haze of growing rage, imagining she could take her strength and hit him with it, make him hurt the way her friends had hurt.

The Shepherd saw the look on her face and went pale, grabbing the Signet and the hammer and backing away from the altar. He darted over to the wall and held the Signet up against it—the hammer swung toward the stone—

Cora felt her rage rising up through her body, and she welcomed it. She let it wash through her, and *pushed*, screaming, *"NO!"*

The Shepherd burst into flame.

He shrieked, trying to bat the flames out on his clothes, but they leapt up over him too fast, and the fire consumed him. The Signet tumbled out of his hand and hit the floor.

Cora felt the men behind her drop their grip, and she spun around toward them, *pushing*.

All four ignited at the same time. They ran for the exits, screaming, but didn't reach them before they were completely immolated. Meanwhile all of the other soldiers were shoving each other, fighting their way out of the room in a panic, while each pew went up in flames as they cleared it.

The more she pushed, the easier it was, and soon she was surrounded by fire, the intense heat like balm on her skin. She breathed in the heat, loving how it felt, what it promised.

"Cora!"

She turned to see Jacob trying to jerk his arms hard enough to break the chains. She came back to herself and ran over to what remained of the Shepherd's body and, not far away, found a ring of keys he had dropped next to his knife, and Jacob's Signet. The latter she shoved into the pocket of the coat she still had on, and she kept the knife in her hand as well while she unlocked the shackles.

Unchained, Jacob sat up but wavered; he'd lost a lot of blood.

It was a pity he couldn't just drink it back and be fine again—he would need a live human.

But she was not about to leave that bowl there for them to use in their unholy games.

One last push, and the blood began to burn.

"Come on," she said, shouting to be heard over the din of screaming and the roar of the flames. She pulled Jacob along with her, past the crowd of soldiers trying to organize themselves to put out the fire, down the hall, running until she saw an *Exit* sign in one of the corridors.

Jacob threw himself at the door, and it shuddered and opened. Thankfully, it was dark out—the whole escape would have been cut very short if it were still daylight. In the distance, as they ran, she could hear sirens approaching the building.

They ran as fast as they could until Jacob's blood loss caught up with him and he had to stop and rest. She helped him sit down on a bench and started looking around for suitable prey.

She felt his eyes on her and looked down into his face.

"What the hell did you just do?" he asked. He was staring at her like she had become some new, wild creature . . . and in fact, she felt like a wild creature. She was thankful he wasn't afraid of her. "I've never seen anything like that."

"I do not know," she answered, sitting down next to him. "I was angry . . . they were hurting you. I wanted them to stop."

"Does that always happen when you get good and pissed off?"

She smiled a little. "No . . . I do not remember the last time I was good and pissed off . . . at least, not enough to hurt people." She took his hand. "No one has ever tried to harm you in front of me before . . ." Something new and strange had taken root in her, and she concluded, the fire now in her voice, ". . . and no one ever will again."

The adrenaline was beginning to wear off, and she began to wonder herself: *What had she just done?*

Suddenly, she remembered her recurring dream . . . the raven woman . . . those last few words:

You guard the heat of a will on fire . . . just let it burn.

* * *

So Cora was a firestarter.

That was a new one.

David set his phone aside and put his face in his hands for a moment, sweet relief breaking through the storm clouds. At least something had ended well.

Aside from reeling at Cora's gift suddenly waking up, and grieving when David told them what had happened in Sacramento, they were completely unhurt. The California Elite searching the city for them also found Vràna—the Nighthound had returned to where her mistress had been taken and was, apparently, sitting there the entire time, waiting for her to return.

Olivia was the only one of the Circle who had gotten home without incident. He could tell she felt guilty. When he told her the news, she had offered to come to Texas and do . . . whatever she could, which unfortunately was nothing.

There was nothing anyone could do.

His phone rang, and he leaned back with a sigh. "Lieutenant Murdoch—report."

"Most of the territory is quiet, my Lord Prime, except Los Angeles—two warring gangs have taken advantage of the situation and are tearing each other apart all over the city. Our numbers simply aren't great enough to put them all down."

"Are these gangs only fighting each other, or have they become violent toward the local population?"

"Only each other so far, my Lord."

"Well, then, let them kill each other. If the conflict spills out into the Shadow District as a whole or threatens the human citizens, I'll pull more swords from Seattle—work on keeping it contained, and let me know the second anything changes."

"As you will it, Sire."

After they hung up, David rubbed his forehead wearily. He rose from his chair and left the workroom without doing whatever it was he'd intended to do when he got there. There wasn't much point—he couldn't focus. Neither of them could.

It's only been a few days. Give it time.

He returned to the suite and hung up his coat. It had been a long night, after a sleepless day; aside from fielding phone calls from half the Council, he was trying to coordinate cleanup and recovery efforts, and there was also the little matter of having become, essentially, Prime of half the United States.

The West and the South were adjacent, so for the time being, he had taken control of all of it. That way the West wouldn't degenerate into all-out war; he kept the Elite organized like they already were, reallocating a few of his own from some of the less populated areas of the South and putting them under Lieutenant Murdoch's command. His reputation would hold things together . . . for now.

That was what most of the calls were about. The Council didn't care who had died; they just didn't like what he was doing. They considered the Western Signet dead. He should by their rules let the West descend into chaos until a new regime arose. Instead, he was breaking the rules, presuming that he had the authority to simply claim someone else's territory and, in their words, create his own empire.

He had told them, one by one, with the exception of those two or three whom he still respected, to fuck off in no uncertain terms. After all of their denials, even with the evidence staring them in the face, they still refused to believe that mere humans could be a real threat. Even though Jacob Janousek was well liked in the Council, they pretended not to hear that he had been attacked, nearly killed. One of the most powerful Pairs on the planet had fallen, and they looked the other way.

It was a losing game, and up until now it was one he'd been willing to play.

He was done playing.

When Tanaka called with his condolences, David told him, "I'm sorry, old friend . . . if you ever need my help, you need only ask . . . but I hereby sever all ties with the Council. They're on their own. They've made their bed . . . now they can die in it."

Tanaka hadn't been surprised at all. David sensed that a full-blown dissolution wasn't far away, and that it might just be Tanaka himself who declared it. Even without Morningstar attacking them all directly, the Council was falling apart. He might have been impressed with how vampire history was unfolding if he could have summoned the energy to give a damn.

David crossed the room and knocked lightly on the far

door. Rather than a verbal reply, the door opened a few inches by itself, and he slipped into the dark little room, closing the door behind him.

"Any change?" he asked.

Miranda shook her head. She was sitting on the bed, and surprisingly, Stella was with her. The young Witch was staring intently at the sleeping figure in the bed—doing something with her Sight, he realized.

David joined them, taking a spot at the foot of the bed. Miranda reached for his hand.

They had agreed as soon as they got home that the best thing would be to put Deven in the mistress suite for now. Neither of them wanted him to wake alone.

Miranda had hardly left his side all week. David knew it was as much guilt as it was worry. Jonathan had all but held a gun to her head, but still, she had chosen to act on her visions and do the unthinkable. She knew that she was violating Deven's free will—he wanted to die, and denying him that when his Consort was dead was utterly monstrous. She knew what it was like to be left behind, her soul torn in two, but that hadn't stopped her. . . and David was glad it hadn't.

Stella opened her eyes, shaking herself a little. "Jesus," she muttered. "I mean, just . . . Jesus."

"What did you See?" Miranda asked.

The Witch looked down at Deven. "The matrix that Nico guy built . . . it's beautiful. I've never seen magic like that in my life. The power it would take to make something like that is staggering. I don't know how a mortal could possibly control that kind of power. It's so elegantly crafted, it's breathtaking . . . or, it was."

Miranda nodded. "I figured as much."

"The way it was designed, it ran on a sort of low-voltage current of Jonathan's energy. But now . . . when you . . . when the bond broke, the matrix fractured and fell apart. There are pieces of it left that could possibly be repaired, but for the most part, it's gone. So everything that was wrong before is wrong again—and his soul mate is dead. The kindest thing would be to kill him, but you can't."

"But we can't go on like this," David said. "He's sucking both of us dry."

"That's mostly because of the shattered matrix—it's still drawing power, but since it's busted that power is leaking out all over the place. I think the first priority would be to plug those leaks; from there we can figure out your options."

"Can you do that?" Miranda asked. "Plug them, I mean."

"I don't know. I've never done anything like this before. But I have to try, otherwise this is going to kill all three of you." Stella stood up and stretched. "Let me do a little research—as soon as I have a useful idea I'll let you know."

"Stella . . ." Miranda looked reluctant to say anything but went ahead anyway. "Do you know anything about Speaking Stones?"

"I know that they're used for a kind of benign blood magic, where the person doing the calling anoints the stone with blood, and it calls out to anyone with similar blood. Witches mostly use them for finding family members. It's nearly impossible to do if you don't know the person you're calling. Why? Oh . . . right. You want to call Nico."

"We know you can help," the Queen told her. "But when it comes to actually fixing the bonds themselves . . ."

"You want to bring out the big gun. I totally agree. I'm not going to claim I can do more than I can do—like I said, I can probably stop the two of you from energetically bleeding to death, but you're going to need a lot more firepower to fix the real problem." Stella gave them a reassuring smile. "We're going to figure this out," she said. "I'm not giving up on you guys."

She left, and he and Miranda just sat for a while. David kept searching Deven's face, looking for any hopeful sign; he looked like he was in such pain, even unconscious.

Finally, she unfolded herself from her cross-legged position, groaning at how stiff she was. "I've got to get some sleep," she said. "Would you take over for a while?"

"Of course."

She kissed David gently and headed back into the suite for a shower and what he hoped would be a long nap. He was worn out, too, and if he was going to stay in here, he might as well try to rest.

He stretched out on the bed next to Deven and closed his eyes, laying one hand on Deven's chest to feel his heartbeat.

Once, long ago, they had slept that way every day—without intending to, each had sought out the other's pulse, and they slept with palms against chests, hands curved around wrists or throats. An outsider would likely have thought they were trying to strangle each other. The irony hadn't been lost on David.

He didn't realize he'd drifted off until he felt something against him shift; his eyes snapped open, and he propped himself up on his elbow, looking down, watching for something, anything.

He hadn't imagined it. One of Deven's hands twitched. A moment later, his eyelashes fluttered and very slowly opened partway.

David's heart clenched. Deven's eyes were lifeless, lightless. He didn't seem to know where he was at first, but eventually he turned toward David, who offered a tentative smile.

After what felt like an eternity, Deven managed to speak in a harsh whisper.

"Kill me."

David looked away, eyes burning.

"If . . . if you really love me . . . don't make me live like this. I'm done . . . I want to die. Please just let me die."

David met his eyes again. "I can't."

"Please . . ."

"I can't, Deven. You're bound to us now. If you die, we die. We're trying to find a way to fix it, but for now, at least . . . you're ours."

"But how . . . how could you do this to me? How could she . . . after what happened to you . . ."

"It wasn't her idea," David replied as gently as he could. "But how could either of us deny a last request, especially if it meant saving you?"

"Last request . . ." His eyes closed, tears starting to fall. "Oh God."

"I'm sorry."

David thought he was about to break down again, but after a moment he said, "Go away. Leave me alone . . . please just go away."

"Dev—"

"Go!" Lightning seemed to flash in Deven's eyes, and David knew what was coming before he saw the extended hand—a massive shove of power slammed into him and threw him off the bed, across the three or four feet of open space and hitting the wall hard enough to crack vertebrae.

"I'm not asking," Deven snarled. "Get out."

David pushed himself up off the floor, barely able to move through the pain in his back, but it was already healing as he got to his feet, retreating toward the suite door. He paused, wanting to say something—wanting to say so many things—but there was nothing he could say to make any of this better.

David left the room, leaning back against the door and breathing in the warm, comforting air of his own suite. He drew in what strength he could and forced himself to move, undressing and crawling into bed beside Miranda, who stirred and woke when she felt him near.

"It was all for nothing," he said softly. "All of it . . . even if we find a way to stabilize the bond, the Circle can never be completed now. We'll keep fighting, and they'll keep picking us off one by one . . . and once all the Signets are gone there will be nothing to stop the entire Shadow World from tearing itself apart."

He met her gaze and saw the truth there; Miranda, too, had all but given up. "Maybe we should just let it all go, then," she said, though he knew she didn't really mean it. "Maybe we should kill him. Then we could all go . . . and be free of this."

David took a deep breath. "No. We can't. Not if there's even the slightest chance we can find a way to destroy Morningstar. We can't leave our people to fend for themselves against those bastards. Not yet."

She didn't argue. He knew she agreed, and that one way or another they would find the strength to go on. For now she got as close to him as she could, and they held on to each other tightly, both so tired they couldn't think, but neither able to sleep.

For days Deven lay unmoving, even when there were others in the room. They fed him, and he swallowed obediently but gave no hint he heard them speaking.

The Witch was there as well, discussing the situation with failing hope: even if all the energy leaks were repaired, even if the three of them could be balanced, the reality was that two Thirdborn could not be bound to a regular vampire. They simply were not compatible. The place where Miranda had fused them together would soon start to crack; when that happened, without a way to reseal the bond, they were all dead. They could try bringing him across, but he was weak, and the chances of his surviving the transition were slim.

He stopped listening after that.

Everything had gone numb, which was a nice change of pace. It gave him enough clarity to understand that it didn't matter what the others did; dying wouldn't solve anything any more than living would. There was no reason to go on, because there was nothing to go to. There would be no one there on the other side to walk with him into eternity.

It didn't matter who had "saved" him or what their motivations were. What it came down to was a cold, bitter truth.

Jonathan hadn't wanted him.

He was gone, and he had refused to let Deven follow even though he knew what he was leaving behind—he knew what kind of pain he was forcing his Prime to endure. They had watched Miranda try to gather the scattered pieces of a broken life when David died, but even knowing what she had suffered, Jonathan had not only forced his Prime into that same black lake of desolation, he had held Deven's head beneath the water until he drowned.

The reasons were irrelevant. The truth was still the same. Jonathan had left him—the one person who was never supposed to, the one constant, the only promise that mattered . . . gone.

If they wanted to keep his body alive so they could continue to fight a war they were going to lose, that was fine. If they gave up and killed him and they all ceased to exist, with nothing after but eternal oblivion, that was fine, too. It made no difference to him. Everything he was, everything that mattered, had died in that explosion. There was no coming back this time.

It was already over.

Miranda stared at her hands on the keys for a long time before she stopped trying to make herself play.

After everything they had survived, their lives came down to this: waiting to die.

Each passing night dragged them further and further into the dark—they both tried to hold the balance, but no matter how they shielded or how much they fed, Deven was killing them, and there was nothing anyone could do. As strong as Stella was, she wasn't strong enough; she'd said it herself back when David and Miranda had been split . . . no Witch could remake a soul bond.

She shut the piano and pushed herself away, leaving the music room. The entire Haven felt like a tomb; the oppressive, leaden atmosphere was straining the limits of her shielding. She had to get away, even if she couldn't go far.

Autumn had arrived with a vengeance in central Texas. The nights were already chilly, and wave after wave of storms had blown over them since they'd made it home. She had on a jacket, but the air still hit her like a punch in the lungs; uncaring, she broke into a run, getting away from the Haven and stumbling into the gardens.

She dropped onto a bench. She knew this spot quite well; she and David had walked here back when she was still human.

She had lived through so much. She had changed so much. And unless Persephone decided they were worth another miracle, none of it made any difference.

Stella had attempted some kind of summoning spell, but she had no idea what she was trying to summon; that kind of magic required either knowing where the intended target was or at least knowing the target well enough to have some kind of connection. Still, she tried.

The Witch had tried to help with the energy leakage as well and had made some progress—she'd figured out how to patch several of the biggest holes, which at least gave Miranda and David some of their strength back. It helped Miranda to figure out that half of what she was feeling wasn't hers; she was absorbing emotional information from two people now, multiplying what she had to control. That didn't stop it from being awful, but it did make her feel less despairing; the impulse to give up wasn't hers, and knowing that helped her fight it . . . to a point. They were still being dragged toward the abyss, but Stella had bought them time.

Now Miranda closed her eyes and imagined she could

reach out far enough to find Nico, wherever and whoever he was. "Please," she murmured, tears coming to her eyes for the thousandth time in two weeks. "Help us. Help him."

She sat in silence for a while listening to the wind and the night birds, looking across the grounds, toward the only place she had ever really felt was home. Within those walls was everything that mattered to her—her family, her music, her people. After everything she had survived to get here . . . Miranda's eyes narrowed, and she sat up straighter, her hands gripping the arms of the bench so hard they shook.

"No," she said softly, this time addressing Persephone. "I'm not giving up. To hell with your war—I won't just lie down and die after everything I've been through. Maybe this will kill all three of us . . . but I'll go down fighting and come out swinging on the other side. You can help us or not, but if you want us to fight for you, we need more than dreams and feathers. So put up or shut up."

The night's continued silence swallowed her words, offering silence back as her answer. She shook her head, anger burning hot in her chest—it was almost a good feeling, knowing she was still capable of something besides mourning.

Wait—

Miranda grew still, sure she'd felt something—a change in the wind, perhaps. She looked around with her heart pounding, the stubborn little part of her that refused to accept the inevitable straining for hope, for the possibility that just maybe . . .

Suddenly the hair on the back of her neck stood up, and she felt something like an electrical charge building in the air. She was on her feet in seconds, sword drawn by reflex, turning in a slow circle and scanning the treeline for any movement.

And there, only about ten feet from her bench, she saw something. A patch of the night seemed to grow denser, contracting into a single point that then expanded again, this time in a watery circle of glowing violet-white light.

Miranda's heart lurched to a halt. She remembered that feeling . . . she had seen this before, as she lay staked to the ground in an empty farm building waiting for the sun to scorch the flesh from her bones. She remembered it . . . remembered what had happened next . . .

The light inside the circle grew brighter, and she felt a kiss of wind—wind scented with evergreen, not yet touched by autumn's chill.

There was one final blast of light, blinding her so she had to shield her eyes with her forearm . . . and then the energy evaporated, the night just as it was before.

Slowly, she lowered her arm.

Green eyes met darkened violet.

Miranda gaped at the young man who had appeared in the middle of the garden, her mind finding it impossible to make sense of him. He had dark auburn hair that fell down almost to his waist; he wore a midnight blue cloak over a sort-of-medieval-looking outfit. A strange tattoo of spirals and swirls ran down along one side of his face. He was incredibly beautiful, even otherworldly, and stared at her calmly, kindness in his eyes.

That was when she noticed his ears.

"I am Nicolanai Araceith," he said in a gentle voice.

"Nico," she said, still not quite able to process what she was seeing. "But . . . you're an Elf!"

He lifted one eyebrow. "I know that."

"You're supposed to be extinct!"

He smiled. "I am supposed to be a lot of things." He stepped forward, moving closer to her, and though she wanted to back away, she couldn't. "You are Miranda Grey, Queen of this territory, are you not?"

She nodded.

"It is a pleasure to meet you. Now, please . . ." He turned his head to look at the Haven, then looked back at her, urgency in his expression. "Take me to him."

Seventeen

Though he had stayed away for days, keeping busy and trying not to think too much about the future, David found himself returning to the mistress suite and sitting on the side of the bed again, unable to look away.

The gold band on Deven's finger was loose; he was growing thinner. None of them could seem to feed enough—David had mentioned to Miranda, just broaching the subject, that they might have to kill again before the new moon if they wanted to maintain even enough strength to function at minimal levels. She had been so upset by the idea that he hadn't brought it up again . . . yet.

"I brought you blood," he said into the heavy silence. "Flowers seemed so cliché."

He wasn't expecting an answer and didn't receive one, so he went on. "The West is still quiet. Eventually I'm sure someone will challenge my authority, but for now it's calm. And . . . the crew out at the site got the ground cleared enough to reach the underground vaults. They're bringing everything up and packing it for storage. There are also a few other things they found intact, or mostly. There was . . ." He had to take a deep breath before continuing. "They found a signed first

edition of *Les Misérables* where your suite used to be. The
edges are charred, but it's still in one piece. I don't know if
you'll want it, but . . ."

David trailed off, bowing his head.

He was working hard to keep himself together for the sake
of his Elite, and to help maintain calm among the Circle—not
to mention that he refused to give the Council the satisfaction
of watching him fall apart. But the emotional distance he had
prided himself on for so long had crashed down around him
like the walls of a collapsing building, and for the most part
he saved his energy for dealing with the outside world and
spent the rest of the nights in a daze. He felt like he had come
home a different person . . . an older, sadder person who no
longer cared about the things he had once devoted himself to.

He'd been trying to comprehend why, if she cared about
them at all, Persephone had let this happen—he knew there
was still something preventing her from intervening directly,
but she had spoken to several of them in their dreams, given
premonitions . . . why, he wondered over and over, hadn't she
warned them?

It took him a while to get it, but when he did, he had nearly
broken every glass object within a twenty-foot radius before
he reined his mind back in.

She *had* warned them. Or, more specifically, she had
warned Jonathan.

Everything he had said while he lay buried in the wreckage made sense once David understood that Jonathan knew he
was going to die.

David couldn't guess how long he had known, but he had a
feeling it was quite a while. He might not have known exactly
how it would happen, or where, but he must have had a firm
idea of when—why else would he propose to Deven out of the
blue? That proposal had brought them all together and provided an opportunity Morningstar couldn't resist—was that
the plan all along, that Jonathan would set the whole thing in
motion himself?

And whether she was trying to help them or simply shoving them toward the fate she had planned, Persephone had
given Miranda the knowledge she needed to save Deven's life.
The dreams had since stopped, and Miranda claimed she

could no longer reach the vision of the Web where she had worked that night; but David had a feeling that if she were ever to reach for it again it would be there. She had blocked it out, not lost it.

On top of everything else, Stella had told him about her tarot reading. The Ten of Swords . . . a man in torment, bleeding to death in the dark. A sacrifice. Miranda had interpreted it as the humans they had to kill on the new moon . . . but she'd been wrong. Stella thought the Two of Swords represented Deven, and the Queen of Swords was Miranda; Deven, a sacrifice, Miranda . . . and the Eight of Pentacles, the spider.

As soon as he saw the web of light on the card he shook his head, sick inside; yes, she had tried to warn them as well as she could, but she couldn't stop what they began with their choices. At any point during all of this Jonathan could have shared his knowledge. He had chosen not to, accepting his own fate, even though they could have stopped it if they'd known.

Or maybe they couldn't have. Maybe if they'd stopped the Haven's destruction, they would have walked into another trap later. Maybe there could be a thousand means but only one end.

He didn't blame Jonathan, exactly, though he was angry at the Consort for his silence—but he knew how hard it was to have precog and know what was going to happen. An ability like that took its toll. He imagined Jonathan walking around acting like everything was fine when he knew that night was approaching . . . the way he had known that Deven and David would crawl into bed together and nearly destroy everything three years ago. David had no idea how he would deal with that kind of power. He couldn't judge Jonathan for his choices.

But he was still angry.

There was a soft knock on the hallway door. "Come," he called.

Miranda was pale as she entered the room, and her expression set off all his internal alarms. "David . . . there's someone . . ."

Before she could finish the thought, he saw there was someone behind her, and froze. Whatever emotion he'd been feeling evaporated into thin air so that pure, unabashed wonder could take its place.

The creature that walked into the room was not human, nor was he a vampire. Like their kind, he gave off an air of agelessness, though without the darkness that dwelt in a vampire's every cell. An enormous aura of power surrounded him under perfect, precise control, but it was not the power David or Miranda had; it was spun out of moon and star. And though he looked young, the equivalent of a human in his early twenties, he was certainly *not* young. Whatever he was, he'd been working magic for longer than David had been alive.

He fixed his eyes on David's, and there was something familiar about . . .

Purple. They were purple.

David lowered his gaze back to Deven, then looked up again.

"Good evening, my Lord," their visitor said. He had a calm, reassuring voice with a musical accent and moved with the grace of a young wild animal . . . a deer, perhaps, gliding silently through the woods.

David stared at him, unable to tear his eyes away. "You're Nico."

"I am."

The only thing David could think to say, which immediately made him cringe inwardly, was, "Nice ears."

Lame it might be, but it earned him a sweet smile from Nico. "Thank you. I grew them myself." He sat down on the bed and gazed at the vampire who lay there. Deep sadness touched his face and his voice. "Oh, my love . . . I am so sorry."

"Can you fix this?" David demanded.

Nico looked up at him gravely. "I will know more once I have looked more closely into what has happened here."

He reached over and gently took Deven's hand from David's. Their fingers touched as he did so, and David felt a jolt—similar to static electricity, but a less physical kind of buzz, like one aura recognizing another.

"Do you have any idea why he hasn't woken again?" Miranda asked.

The Elf frowned. "He probably cannot. With the combined trauma and the energy imbalance he would essentially shut down—it is the body's way of preventing death from psychic burnout, even in vampires. He may go in and out of lucidity until this is all dealt with one way or another."

Nico took both of Deven's hands in his own and closed his eyes, sinking into a trance state within a matter of seconds.

Miranda edged over to stand behind David, rubbing his shoulders. "Stella's spell reached him," she explained quietly. "He didn't know exactly what happened, but he knew he was needed. I was sitting in the garden calling to him, and he felt it and used my thoughts as a homing beacon."

"Reached him . . . where?"

She sat down next to him, close enough that she could speak without distracting Nico. "A place called Avilon," she said. "It's like a parallel world. Anyone who survived the genocide of their people hid there, and they sealed it off."

David stared a moment longer before he turned to her and said, "Elves."

"Apparently they're not as extinct as we thought," Miranda said, and then to Nico: "What do you See?"

"A terrible shame," he replied. "I was quite proud of my work. At least I know it took a broken soul-bond to destroy it."

"But can you stop the leaking?" she asked. "Can you keep all those broken places from draining us?"

Nico smiled faintly. "Of course I can. Here."

David felt something change—somewhere deep within all three of them, a surge of energy moved through, and within minutes the feeling of being slowly bled dry faded. David gasped, and Miranda did, too; suddenly he could think a hundred times more clearly, and the pervasive hopelessness that had been grinding them under its heel dialed down about 80 percent.

"I would recommend you feed soon," Nico said. "It will help replenish your lost strength. But that, I fear, was the easy part."

"Does that mean you can help us?" David asked.

The Elf sighed. "Yes . . . but I would prefer to discuss it with you elsewhere. If he wakes it would be best if he didn't hear what I have to say." He looked over at them. "If you would come to the guest room where the Queen has installed me, perhaps in an hour? I would like a few minutes alone here to try to shore up some of the remaining matrix."

David and Miranda exchanged a look and nodded. "All right," David said, rising. "Call if you need anything."

"I shall."

David couldn't call what he felt hope, exactly, but at the very least, he felt a lightening in his heart for the first time since the California night had erupted and turned their world to ash and rubble. He could tell she felt it, too; she took his hand and led him out of the mistress suite, back to their room where they could call for blood and with any luck start to feel like themselves again.

In the silence that followed the Pair's departure, Nico returned his gaze to Deven's drawn, ashen face and had to fight not to shed tears.

"I did not know it would come to this," he whispered, brushing his fingers over Deven's lips. "I only knew what my part would be. And I thought we all had more time. Years. I had no idea that . . ."

He thought of the tall, broad blond he had spoken to on the terrace that night: his good humor, his fierce love for his Prime, and the underlying sadness that Nico understood now, too late. He should have recognized it. He'd been feeling it himself for a long time.

He had spoken a half-truth to the Pair. He *could* try to strengthen the few remaining threads of what he had created. He would certainly like to. But it would do no good.

In reality, he had wanted a moment alone with Deven, just to catch his breath and try to come to terms with the full extent of what had happened. He had never seen damage like this . . . and he had never, ever seen a vampire try to Weave. Miranda's work was adequate to keep Deven alive, but it was dangerously clumsy, made with force and desperation but not skill. A big part of what he would have to do involved just undoing what she had done.

Yet the fact that she had done it at all with no experience whatsoever was miraculous. Magic at that level was something only a few Weavers could aspire to. She had mentioned having dreams of the Web, and that she had learned what to do without even realizing she was learning it. That could only be divine intervention. It would have taken a century or more for Miranda to learn the right way, but in the time she had, she'd learned an effective way.

If Miranda had that much favor from Persephone when the chasm between Goddess and vampires was still so wide, the potential the Queen held was more immense than any of them knew.

He felt the fingers he held tighten almost imperceptibly and stared into Deven's face, waiting.

It took the Prime—or whatever he was now—a moment to find the energy to open his eyes, and when he did, he drew an astonished breath. "Nico?"

"Yes . . . I am here."

Deven almost smiled. "I knew you would come. I knew you would make it right."

Nico touched his face but said only, "I am here to help all of you. You must trust me, *i'lyren*, as you trusted me before."

Again, that flicker of a smile, and Deven's eyes closed again as he drifted back into sleep.

Nico leaned down to kiss him softly, then rose and left the little room, which he was fairly sure adjoined with the Pair's dwelling. The Queen had shown him to a small suite down the same hallway—guests usually stayed in another wing, she said, but she knew they were going to need him to stay close.

The guards he passed stared at him, wide-eyed, and he smiled. *Ah, yes. This again.*

The room was comfortable, though not as beautiful as the one in California had been; there were fewer windows in this Haven, much less light and air. His two bags sat on the bed where he'd left them.

He thought back to the lecture he'd received from the Enclave when he returned from California to Avilon. Several of the members had ranted at him for quite a while about how dangerous it was to set foot in the mortal world, how he had no business helping vampires, how his duty as a Weaver was to his own people, and how he must never, ever do such a foolish thing again.

He had arrived back in Avilon weary and heartsick, already missing the Prime he had fled. Needless to say, when the Enclave demanded he appear before them, he was in no mood.

He knew that both Kai and Lesela had tried to explain the situation to them, just as he knew they wouldn't listen. So as soon as the lectures were done, he looked the High Elder of Avilon straight in the eye and asked in a steely, cold voice, "And what exactly are you going to do about it?"

The answer was what he thought it would be: nothing.

In truth, he'd been waiting his whole life to make the High Elder make that face.

Nico opened the first bag, shaking his head. He busied himself unpacking to pass the time, and before long he heard a knock.

The Prime and Queen swept into the room and took a seat by the fireplace, where there were two chairs; he considered pulling the desk chair over for himself, but really, he was far too nervous to sit still. The best he could do was try not to pace. The Pair waited expectantly for him to gather his words.

In any other situation Nico would have taken far more time to admire them; the Queen was exceptionally beautiful with her riot of bloodred curls and her perceptive green eyes, and every inch of the Prime was written in nobility, power, and intelligence. He could certainly imagine them commanding the loyalty of hundreds of warriors. It was easy to see why Deven loved them both so much.

Finally, Nico said, "Here is how the situation stands. Problem one: The three of you are Signet-bound to each other, but such a bond was never intended to contain three souls. All things being equal, it would eventually drive you all mad."

"But all things aren't equal," Miranda observed.

"They are not. Problem two: The two of you are Thirdborn. Your energy and his are not compatible at such an intimate level. Because of your combined strength the bond would hold together for a while, but in time it becomes another imbalance, with the same result. Problem three: Deven's sanity has been all but destroyed. The trauma of Jonathan's death, the violence of their broken bond, and the shattering of the matrix have left his mind in ruins. This is particularly dangerous for you, my Lady, as your empathic gift would cause you to lose more and more of yourself to the black hole of his psyche—in fact, it speaks to your strength and talent that you have not lost your mind already."

He leaned against the side of the fireplace, arms crossed. "Then there is problem four: your Circle. There is a new empty space in it; even if your Trinity could survive as it is, that empty space would ensure you will never reach your full power, the power needed to eliminate the threat of Morningstar."

"You can't help us there," David said tiredly. "The last scion of any of our bloodlines was killed last month, and she was of Miranda's line, not Jonathan's."

Nico nodded. "In a situation like this one, hypothetically the wisest course would be to unbind you, closing Deven up as an individual and restoring you two as a Pair. Then a scion could step in, also as an individual. It would not be nearly as strong as a Circle made up of Pairs, so there would be limits on how much you could do as a group, but victory would still be highly possible."

"There's nothing like that you could try? Why not?" the Queen wanted to know.

"Problem three." Nico paused, letting them think about it.

David shook his head. "If we let him out of the bond, without someone to hold him here, he'll kill himself. There's no question about it."

"I can rebuild the matrix to save his mind, but it requires a battery—a powerful vampire with an intimate and very strong connection to him."

"So the only thing that will save him is a Consort," David said. "No other connection would be deep enough to power the matrix, and no other connection would stop him from committing suicide. He wouldn't do it if someone else's life is at stake."

"You *think* he wouldn't," Miranda told her Prime. "But we don't know for sure."

"The question is moot anyway," David pointed out, the impossibility of their situation clearly beginning to wear out what resolve he had left. "Even if we had someone of Jonathan's bloodline, they wouldn't be a true Consort. We get one soul mate. That's it. If we fit a new person in, it would have to be as an individual, like Nico said . . . and the fact is, there are no more scions of Jonathan's line. They're all long dead."

Nico was quiet for a long moment before he said, "No, my Lord . . . they are not."

The Elf watched them, and they both stared at the Elf, and nobody spoke for a minute.

David broke the silence. "What are you talking about?"

Miranda knew before he even replied, but she waited, praying she was wrong.

"When I first met him, I saw that Jonathan's precognitive gift was exceptionally strong. I was curious as to where it had come from. Often such gifts speak of distant Elven blood. But I did not wish to pry, so I thought nothing further about it. Then, not long after I returned to Avilon, I began having nightmares. I saw horrible things that I cannot even describe, and all of you were in them. I had never even seen your faces, but I dreamed you."

The Elf's eyes grew haunted as whatever gruesome images he'd seen in his sleep paraded through his mind again. "To reassure myself I went into the Web and looked for all of you. I thought perhaps if I saw you were all well, I could sleep again. But something caught my eye, and even though I knew it was an intrusion, I followed the threads before me until I ran into the last thing I expected."

"What was that?" Miranda asked.

"Myself."

David's eyebrows knitted together. "Come again?"

"As I had suspected, generations ago, one of Jonathan's female human forbears lay down with an Elf and rose up with a daughter. That particular Elf, Kael, already had one daughter, a full Elf who had fled to Avilon. So while Kael's half-human child grew up, married, and had children and grandchildren of her own, his fully Elven child grew to maturity and, two hundred years later, gave birth to twins."

He smiled a little. "Multiple births are practically unheard of among my people. It was said the twins were born under a dark star, for one was born with black hair and the other with dark eyes. The twins were whispered about, and inspired fear, though neither earned it. It did not help that they were among the most powerful ever seen in Avilon. And then there was the prophecy . . . a woman named Lesela, gifted with prophetic talent, saw the death of the dark-eyed Elf. She said that he would first give his heart, and then give his own life, to stop the destruction of three worlds."

Miranda saw the resignation on his face, and beneath it a deep alienation; despite having a twin, he had been lonely his entire life, living in the shadow of his own potential darkness. She took a deep breath and said what they all already knew. "You're the scion."

The Elf nodded. "I can unbind the three of you and then bind Deven to me. Not only can I power the matrix, I can continually adapt it so it will never break again. The two of you will be whole again, and the Circle will be as it was."

"But . . ." Miranda sat forward, hands clasped. "Deven wouldn't want that. We'd be forcing it on him."

Nico gave her a look that actually made her lean back. "You did not trouble yourselves with that before," he said sharply. "Why now?"

Miranda's eyes filled, and her face burned with shame. "I was doing what Jonathan wanted," she said. "There wasn't time to debate."

When she raised her eyes again, the Elf's expression had changed, and he walked over to her and touched her head. "I am sorry," he said. "My words are undeservedly harsh considering the love behind your actions. Miranda . . . none of this is what any of us wanted. You did what you had to do. Jonathan's last wish was for you to save Deven. But he is not saved. You put a tourniquet on a gaping wound that I alone can heal."

The weight of his hand was more comforting than she expected; a faint current of energy seemed to radiate from him naturally, and it helped keep her from losing control of her emotions, though her shields had been trembling off and on since they had come home.

David spoke up sharply. "You're forgetting one very important little fact in all of this."

Nico nodded. "I have not forgotten. Believe me, I have thought of little else."

Miranda caught Nico's gaze again, and he said, "I am already immortal, like you. But that alone is not enough."

Realization hit her. "To do this . . . to save us . . . we have to turn you." She shot David a look of disbelief. "Is that even possible?"

David leaned his head on his hand. "It will have to be."

"David . . . we *can't* do it. If one of us sires him, he'll be Thirdborn like us. We can't do that to him. I won't. Not to mention it would be pointless unless we turned Deven, too."

The thought of the Elf killing humans every month to survive was appalling. It was bad enough imagining what the transition might do to a creature like him—unleashing that kind of darkness, letting it take him . . . if she pictured him with eyes that went black like theirs, she felt physically repulsed by the mere idea.

David felt her growing anguish. He reached for her hand. "It doesn't have to be like that, beloved. We can drain him, and then feed him someone else's blood. We'd be the instrument of death, but not his sires." He looked up at Nico. "But it would have to be someone at Signet level or higher. Otherwise we risk blocking off parts of your power."

"Shall we call Olivia?" Miranda ventured. "She's probably the closest."

"No, she isn't," David said. "We have a Signet right here."

Miranda looked up at the ceiling, running her hands back through her hair. "God . . . so not only are we going to force him to live—we're going to force him to sire someone. Remind me again why we're the good guys?"

"Sometimes we can't be the good guys," David said. "We just have to be the lesser evil. And you know as well as I do that creating a blood bond will make it less likely that he'll commit suicide and kill them both."

She frowned. "But it won't really be a Signet bond. I mean, you can bind yourself to him, but you can't *create* a soul-mating. You can't just turn yourself into a Consort. It would just be an energetic connection . . . right?"

But David said, "It can't just be an energetic connection. To power the matrix they have to have a deeper bond than that. Is it even possible to force something like that when it's supposed to be determined by a higher power?"

Nico looked away. "What you speak of—creating a soul-bond and imposing it on someone—is nearly impossible. It is also an egregious violation of natural order and free will. Your actions that night were born out of desperate circumstances, but to do the same thing in a calculated, premeditated way . . . splitting open someone's soul to fit your own into it violates everything I was ever taught." He looked back at them. "And it is exactly what I intend to do."

Eighteen

The autumn sun shone down over the Haven grounds, show-ing an entirely different kind of landscape from the one that appeared after sunset. Most of the flowers there were night-blooming, but there were still plenty of wildflowers bursting open in the morning light. Dragonflies and butterflies flitted over the gardens, and a few deer picked their way out of the forest and over to an open lawn to graze. Deer would venture into the open during daylight only if they knew beyond doubt it was safe.

Nico walked along the garden paths, touching the plants on either side, listening to the murmur of green growing things. This Hill Country was so different from where he had lived, but it still sang. Just as in California, there was a youth and a wildness to it that he found comforting.

He stopped at a stone bench and sat down, tilting his head back to let the sun warm his face. He tried to memorize that feel-ing . . . the brightness . . . the intensity of color all around him.

It was the last daylight he would ever see.

He tried not to think about what he was about to do to him-self, or to Deven. He tried to simply enjoy the morning, soaking it in.

Footsteps approached, and he lowered his head and looked along the path to where a young woman was walking in his direction. Her eyes were on the ground, an air of confusion and unhappiness around her. He realized, watching her draw near, that she was no vampire.

She was nearly upon him when she noticed anyone was there. She yelped and jumped back, hand going to her chest. "Fuck, I didn't see you there! Nobody else is ever . . . out here . . ."

He stared at her, and she stared back. "You are human," he said.

She nodded slowly. "And you're an Elf."

He returned the nod. "Nicolanai Araceith, at your service."

"So you're everybody's savior," she mused. "They're supposed to fang you up tonight, right? I guess that's why you're out here."

"Everyone's savior," Nico repeated, shaking his head. "I wish it were so simple."

She looked ashamed for saying it. "Sorry. It can't be easy having so much depend on you."

He smiled. "Walk with me," he said, rising. "You are the first human I have ever seen up close, and unless I am gravely mistaken you are the Witch, Stella—I would like to hear your perspective on what has passed here."

She turned a little pink. "Really? I mean, I'm not . . . you're like ten times more powerful than I am. I don't see what good it would do to ask me about it."

"Oh, surely not ten times," he teased, offering his arm. "More like five."

"So what did you say your full name was? Something about a lanai? What does that mean?"

He chuckled. "Our first names are given by our parents, and we choose the second ourselves when we come of age," he said. "Nicolanai translates to 'shadow of the forest,' but with a connotation of the color of shadow among the trees at the moment dusk turns to night. My mother thought it described my eyes."

"And the second part?"

"*Ceith* is 'night,' specifically the dark and silent time around, say, two A.M. *Ara* is a shortened form of *aranae*, which is both our term for Weaver and our word for 'spider.'"

Stella froze. "Spider."

"Yes."

She shook her head with a humorless laugh. "The Spider, the Weaver . . . of course."

He observed her surreptitiously as they took the winding path that made its way around and through the extensive Haven grounds. She was exceptionally bright, and though he had no idea what was considered beautiful among human females, he thought she was lovely—very different from the willowy gazelle-like Elven women. If she were to go to Avilon, if everyone stopped fearing her for being human, she would likely have her pick of lovers; to them she would be exotic and mysterious, although *mysterious* was not a word he would use for Stella. She wore her heart out where all could see it, expressed her opinions with conviction. He liked her.

She also had a thirst for magical knowledge and obvious talent; if he survived the next few days he might offer to show her more about Weaving, as Elves had done for Witches hundreds of years ago.

"Just so you know . . ." She grew uncomfortable for a moment, looking off at the Haven. "I think what you're going to do to Deven is awful. But it's the right thing to do."

Nico sighed. "He will hate me for it. And probably the others, too."

"Probably. But not forever. He won't be ready to replace Jonathan for a long time, but—"

"I have no intention of replacing him," Nico said, a little more harshly than he intended. "That is not what this is about. I could not replace him if I tried, and even if I could I would not want to. Even taking the same role, even if Deven's heart healed, it would never be the same. It is unlikely he will ever love me—especially not now. I am prepared to live with that."

"But how can you live forever as a soul mate to someone who doesn't love you?"

"It does not have to be forever," he said sadly. "It only has to last until the war ends."

Stella had tears in her eyes as she told him, "None of you

deserves all of this. Miranda and David are amazing people. So's Deven, in spite of what he thinks. And you . . . I don't know you, but I got to spend time with the magic you'd worked. You can tell a lot about someone from seeing how they create. There was so much love in every thread."

He smiled at her again, and kissed her hand. "That is what we do," he said. "We strive to bring the love of our Goddess into everything we make . . . even the awful things."

She paused. "You know . . . a while back Miranda and I were talking about how you make a vampire, and . . . you're going to need blood when you wake up. Human blood, the fresher the better. If it's okay with you I'd like to give you mine."

They held each other's eyes. "You do not have to."

"I know I don't. I'm the only human here, but if I said no, they'd find another one in town without any problem. But I tried to help with magic, and I couldn't do much. I'm limited. I can't do the things you can do. I can't make all of this better. At least let me do what I can."

He nodded, then leaned forward and kissed her lightly on the lips. "I would be honored."

Stella blushed furiously, but smiled. "Okay, then."

As they resumed their walk, Nico knew without a doubt that whatever Stella might think of her abilities, her work was far from over . . . and by the time she returned to live in the human world, if she did, *limited* would be the last word she would ever use to describe herself. She would learn how great her own strength was, how much she had to offer.

He could only hope her lessons would not be as painful as his.

The atmosphere in the mistress suite had not changed since David had been there last. It was hard to breathe in a place so saturated with pain . . . but he had to come. He was drawn back there inexorably again and again like a moon in orbit around its planet . . . or like a dog waiting to be kicked.

Depending on how long it took the Elf to recover from the transformation, in a few days the Signet bond would be reworked again and he and Miranda would be a Pair once more. It was definitely for the best . . . but in the back of his mind, in a place so selfish he'd never speak of it to the others, was a part of him that wanted so badly to just fix what they had . . . to keep Deven as part of them, and perhaps someday . . .

He sighed. Not only was it selfish, it was foolish. David wasn't usually given to such self-indulgence. And yet . . .

And yet here he was again, losing Deven to someone else. He understood it had to be this way, and realistically a Trinity was a bad idea on so many levels, virtually guaranteed to end up hurting Miranda, who mattered far more . . . but just like everything involving Deven, it still made him ache.

"David . . ."

David's breath caught at the sound of that ragged whisper. "I'm here."

His voice was thready and sounded so young. "It hurts."

"I know it does."

"It's my fault." Deven's eyes opened a little, and they were clouded with both pain and confusion. "You left me . . . Nico left me . . . Jonathan left me . . . I'm the constant in this. I just . . . I'm wrong. I broke it."

David had to take a deep breath to hold back tears. *Damn it.* "I'm here . . . and Nico's here . . . and I know wherever he is, Jonathan loves you. He wanted to save you. We all do."

"It's too late." A tear ran down Deven's face. "I deserve this."

"No." David held tighter, just barely keeping the tremor out of his voice. "I won't give up on you. I won't."

Just the faintest of smiles passed over Deven's lips. "Stubborn bastard."

"Some things never change."

A shiver ran through Deven's slender body, and he murmured, his voice becoming more vague, "Is it already time for shift?"

David sighed and played along. "Not for a couple of hours. Go back to sleep."

"Can't be late again . . . people will talk."

"Let them talk."

Again, the smile. "Love you, *Ó Lionáin*."

"I love you, too." He sat up slowly, careful not to jostle Deven and wake him up all the way; it was especially important he stay asleep tonight. "Sleep . . . I'll wake you when it's time."

As Deven drifted off again, David heard a voice from the door: "Are you ready?"

He raised his eyes to his Queen, who saw the look on his face and came to him immediately, putting her arms around him.

"Oh, baby, I'm sorry," she said, kissing his forehead. She touched his face, wiping tears away with her thumbs. "I know how hard this is."

David took a long, deep breath. "If I ever see Jonathan again I'm going to kick his fool ass."

She stood in front of him and he put his arms around her waist, resting his head against her. She didn't ask for any explanation—didn't need one. They were both running on the very edge of what they could bear. In that respect he was thankful they were going to split the Trinity; he and Miranda would have a chance to breathe again without the constant pull of someone else's fathomless grief.

Finally, when he thought he could put his mask back on for Nico, David rose from the bed, giving Deven a parting kiss on the cheek. *Forgive us. Even if it takes a thousand years, forgive us.*

The Elf was waiting in their bedroom, looking terrified but determined. Miranda asked, "I understand Stella offered her blood to you, Nico?"

"Yes," the Elf said softly. "It is a good choice—a Witch's blood will be very strong."

"How long after you finish the transition will you be ready to rework the bonds?" David wanted to know.

Nico shook his head. "I am unsure, my Lord. It will depend on how long my recovery is. I may have to do it in stages. Also there is a particular configuration of symbols and energies I require to do Weaving at this level—this is not your average magic. I will need considerable protection."

"Why didn't you say so earlier?" Miranda asked. "We can get you anything you need."

"I have what I need. I have Stella. She is as we speak setting up the room to my specifications. Then she will come and feed me when I wake."

"Sounds like everything's in place, then," Miranda concluded. "Are you two ready?"

They nodded.

"Let's go."

Nico's eyes were on Deven's inert form as they returned to the dark little room, the three of them sitting down, Miranda cross-legged close to Dev so she could reach his arm easily, Nico between her and David.

They all stared at each other, and David nearly laughed—it was like agreeing to a threesome without anyone knowing how to start. They had opted to drink from the Elf together to speed up the whole process, but Miranda still wasn't used to feeding on men of any sort, even one who wasn't exactly a paragon of human masculinity. She wasn't threatened by him, just . . . uncertain.

David took pity on both of them and moved closer to Nico, drawing the Elf against him, baring one side of his throat. He could feel Nico's pulse racing, and between that and the scent of his skin, warm and alive and touched with something that reminded David of either trees or cookies, or perhaps both, David's teeth pressed into his lip, wanting. He reached past the Elf to take Miranda's hand and beckon her closer as well. She leaned in and nuzzled Nico's throat, taking up the other side, and without either signaling the other, Prime and Queen bit down hard, eliciting a strangled cry of pain from their prey.

Nico's body tensed as if he were going to struggle, but he held himself there with a strength of will that surprised David. Indeed, he was amazingly strong in a lot of ways—David could feel, as he and Miranda pressed into the Elf and their hands slid around him to help him feel secure . . . or possibly trapped . . . muscle in his willowy frame, and a solidity that he wouldn't have expected from a being of light and healing.

Of course, as soon as the blood flowed and David got his first taste of it, he realized he had badly misjudged the Elf. Light and healing were well and good, but what infused his blood was much darker, far more sensual. He tasted like a long night of sweaty sex in front of a bonfire . . . like wild animals and the serpentine roots of a tree through the earth.

Miranda moaned softly and reached over to wrap a hand around David's neck. He could feel her taking deep and intense pleasure from the blood, just as he was—neither of them wanted to stop. Nico was incredibly strong, and the energy in his blood hit them both like a freight train after so many days of feeling so enervated.

We're going to kill him . . . have to stop . . . I don't think I can.

Fortunately Miranda had enough sense left to know it was time, and she lifted her head with a snarl. Her lips were bloody, her eyes pitch-black. "Stop," she said.

Despite 350 years of learning to control himself, David resisted her—she had to grab his hair and pull him back. To wrench his attention away from the Elf, she clamped her mouth on David's, and they took a few seconds to lick the blood from each other's mouths before the Queen turned back to the matter at hand.

"If we weren't otherwise occupied I'd have you right here," David said to her quietly.

She smiled. It was a predator's smile, and it made his body burn even hotter. "Later." She had already lifted Deven's arm and turned it up to expose the wrist. Not allowing herself to hesitate, she bit him, holding her head so that her second fangs wouldn't add extra holes.

The Elf lay limp between them, barely breathing. "Drink," David told him as Miranda held Deven's arm to his mouth.

Nico obeyed readily enough, though he was so weak it was hard to detect him swallowing. When Miranda took the wrist away his eyes immediately closed, but he was still breathing raggedly—even under the euphoria of blood loss, he was afraid to let go.

"It's all right," Miranda said into his ear. "We're with you, Nico. You're safe. Just rest."

A moment later, the Elf's breath stilled. That pounding heartbeat had dwindled over the past few minutes, and finally it halted . . . for now.

The Queen looked dazed. "Good God."

David nodded in agreement. "I read somewhere that vampires were partly responsible for the Elves' extinction—if they all taste like that I can see why."

"And he's so strong," Miranda added. "If we were already at our normal strength, blood like that could last us for days."

The Prime lifted the Elf up himself, and Miranda followed them into the suite, where he laid Nico out on the bed and they sat down to wait. They could have returned him to his guest room, but since no one knew how bringing an Elf across would work, they'd agreed to keep him here where one of them could be with him at all times.

Miranda joined David, leaning against him. She kissed his neck, then bit lightly. David held back a groan.

"Do you really want to have sex in front of a dead Elf?" he asked.

She looked chagrined. Mildly. "I suppose not. How long will he be gone?"

"It's hard to say. With humans it's a matter of minutes, but when I turned you into a Thirdborn you didn't breathe for ten. The blood has to wake up and prevail against death."

He barely had the sentence out when a violent tremor ran through Nico's body and he sucked in a breath, eyes flying open, panicked.

"It's all right," he said, he and Miranda each taking a side and holding him down so he wouldn't injure himself or them. "You're safe and cared for. We're going to send you to sleep for a while so you won't feel anything."

Nico didn't seem to understand him, but the comforting tone of his voice worked where the words themselves did not. Nico took a deep breath, and David felt him grounding himself. The fact that he could ground at all in this state was impressive.

But when David tried to push the Elf down into unconsciousness, he met with a problem.

It didn't work.

"What the hell . . ." David concentrated, summoning some of the extra energy Nico's blood had given him, and tried again. Nico fell asleep . . . but came out of it in less than a minute.

"Let me try," Miranda said. Her brow furrowed. "Why isn't it working?"

"I don't know. He's not consciously resisting. It must be his Elven blood meeting the vampire blood—it's going to be a fight, no matter what. We assumed that it's possible to turn an Elf, but . . . what do we really know for sure?"

Miranda didn't have a chance to answer. Nico jerked away from their grasp to turn on his side, and the first swell of pain hit him, hard—he cried out, clawing at the bed, and David felt him go cold, then hot.

David saw tears in Miranda's eyes and knew their source. She remembered what this felt like. It was one of the worst experiences of her life—just thinking back to that day in Kat's bathroom was enough to make her rock back and forth and tremble.

There was nothing they could do; they tried again and again to knock Nico out, but to no avail. Instead, Nico writhed in agony for hours that turned into days, without relief, and they could only watch helplessly as tormented moans built steadily into screams.

During the Burning Times, Elves were dragged into the dungeons of the Inquisition and had to endure torture of the cruelest kind; every depraved method men had ever concocted from white-hot brands to sexual sadism was visited upon them. Many of the Elves who had survived that era and now knew peace in Avilon bore scars that even magic could not erase. But since then, the newer generations had lived in safety, and as they could never know disease, they rarely experienced significant physical pain.

Those first few hours of misery scrolled out into one day, then two, then three. The pain came in waves, pounding against the shore of his body over and over again. He felt every moment of the transformation—his entire digestive system realigning, parts seeming eaten by acid; his jaw changing shape, actual bone breaking itself and healing, breaking itself and healing. His eyes felt like they had been stabbed with a thousand needles, and the sensory changes that started in his brain made his head hurt so badly he went into seizures.

The worst part was that he couldn't sleep. No matter how horrible the pain was he couldn't pass out; so on top of being ripped apart from the inside, he was so exhausted he wanted to give up and die.

Still, he held on, finally clinging to the one thing that would persuade him to fight: Deven. He couldn't wrap his mind around a war right now, couldn't stay alive for something so lofty as the notion of saving the world. He needed something immediate, something he could imagine the touch and taste of. It took no effort to call forth the memory of that one stolen kiss—in his mind he invented a time in the future when Deven was healed and might look to him, if not for love, at least for comfort. Even that possibility was worth the fight.

At last, the pain seemed to lessen its hold, but in its wake came fever. His body was fighting the change with all its strength, and though it was losing, it would not go gentle into the night. He burned, his skin raw as if he'd been in the glaring sun for a full day; even the lightest touch made him scream. The skin blistered and bled before it finally healed, but at some point an infection of some kind took over.

Nico knew he was dying even as he lost hold of his thoughts about Deven and tumbled into delirium. He had been a fool to think he knew the mind of the Goddess; the prophecy had predicted his death would save three worlds, but what did that really mean? As soon as he realized Jonathan was dead he knew it meant he would become a vampire . . . but what if he was wrong? Perhaps death simply meant death. In the state he was in, he couldn't ponder philosophy. All he could do was keep breathing, and that much was getting harder. He was so tired . . . all his strength, and he wasn't strong enough for this.

"Nico?" he heard through the fog of pain in his head. It took a moment to recognize the voice. It also took a moment to recognize his own, as torn and hoarse as it was.

"Stella . . ."

He felt the weight of her body on the bed next to him. "It's just you and me," she said. "It's really still too soon for this, but everyone agreed you need all the strength you can get."

He heard her gasp, and the smell immediately leapt up over him: blood. The smell was so strong he was nauseated.

"Here," she said, holding her arm over his mouth. A single cut ran across her wrist. "Come on, sweetie, you need to drink."

Nico stared at the wound, which hadn't started dripping just yet. The drops of blood were so bright, so intensely red they made his eyes hurt. And even though the smell still sickened him, his stomach lurched and he felt . . .

Oh Goddess . . . my teeth.

Tentatively, he wrapped his hands around Stella's arm and drew the wound to his mouth, licking very lightly for a taste.

A part of him wanted so badly for it to be disgusting—to prove to himself and affirm what the Enclave had said, that he had no business here, that he couldn't possibly be the chosen one for this. If he couldn't be a vampire, his role here was ended.

His stomach twisted around itself trying to make him understand that yes, this was what he needed, *now*. He took another careful lick, and another, before pressing his lips to the wound and actually trying to suck.

He heard Stella moan. He lifted her arm enough to say, "Am I hurting you?"

"No . . . God, no."

Hot, thick blood filled his mouth, and as he swallowed it coated the raw inside of his throat, sending strength to all parts of his body and soothing that fire that kept trying to burn him alive. He could feel her heartbeat in the blood, felt it beginning to slow down almost imperceptibly, until it fell into sync with his own.

He knew that signal by instinct. He pulled his mouth away and turned his head, breathing hard.

She was so close to him, the comfort of her presence so real and caring. He laid his face against her shoulder, expecting her to object, but instead she grew warm—flushing—and held tighter. Her voice was a little unsteady. "There . . . that wasn't so bad."

At her words, he began to tremble, and she kissed the top of his head and took his hand. After a moment, as he calmed, he realized he was drenched in sweat and suddenly freezing. The blood had broken his fever.

Another voice piped up at the door: "Good evening, Miss Stella—how is our patient?"

Nico didn't recognize the voice, but Stella seemed familiar with their visitor. "Hey, Mo . . . I think he might be doing better."

A shadow fell over him, and he looked up blearily into a cheerful brown-skinned face with lively dark eyes and a beard. Nico didn't really know what to make of beards, and the vampire's face and demeanor were novel enough to distract him, for a moment, from his own misery.

"Here everyone calls me Mo," he said. He had an accent different from any other Nico had heard. "I am the Haven medic—odd, I know. You would be surprised how much work I have to do with the Elite getting themselves injured and our Prime and Queen being poisoned, shot, staked, murdered, blown up, and knocked into various comas. I cannot say I know much about Elf anatomy, but I'll do my best."

Mo examined him quickly and efficiently, still talking, probably to help with the distraction. His voice and accent were very soothing. "I have seen many crossings, but never one this rough. Human nature is usually ready to give itself up to vampire nature. Apparently Elven nature is another thing altogether."

A third voice: Miranda. "What do you think, Mo?"

"I think perhaps the worst is over. The important thing now is that he sleeps. If he doesn't drop off on his own in the next hour, give him this—aim the needle for a vein if you can."

"Thank you, Doctor."

"How are you feeling, my Lady?"

A sigh. "Terrible, to be honest. He's not actively draining us anymore, but the emotional drain is wearing me out. But hopefully it's just for another couple of days."

"And you, Miss Stella? Feeling weak or dizzy?"

"No," Stella replied. "I feel fine, actually."

"Good, good. Now go and eat—you may feel fine but we cannot have you passing out in an hour and bashing your head on the furniture."

Nico felt Stella's presence, and then Mo's, retreat from the room, leaving him alone with the Queen.

She sat down next to him. "You look like hell," she said, kindness in her words. "I was really worried we were going to lose you there for a while."

"So . . . was I. Still not sure."

He felt something cool on his forehead; she'd brought a wet rag and used it to sponge the sweat from his face. He could feel her need to do something, anything to help. Guilt, he realized, for doing this to him.

He tried to ask where the Prime was, but weakness was overcoming him quickly. *Goddess, let me sleep. Just let me sleep.*

After the hell of the last few days, just lying there feeling his temperature slowly dropping and the gentleness of the Queen's touch was a relief too profound to describe. He even managed a tiny smile, in the midst of sliding gratefully into the dark, when he heard her voice again and felt the velvet-soft nudge of her empathic power helping him down as she sang him to sleep:

> *Don't you dare look out your window, darlin',*
> *everything's on fire*
> *The war outside our door keeps raging on . . .*

* * *

"*Rise, child. Have no fear. You belong to me now.*"

His eyes opened reluctantly, blurry at first, then sharpening to a knife's edge. His vision took in the entire room in a single glance, noting every detail. Except for the area before the fireplace, everything had a faint blue or gray cast to it, and it was as if the shadows had a light of their own, for as he looked into them everything was visible.

It took a moment to understand he could see in the dark.

Nico sat up slowly, fascinated. Where was this? Yes . . . the Pair's room. He had been in this absurdly soft bed for four days, most of it in agony. Now, though, his body felt strong, and as he lifted his hands and looked at them, they seemed somehow more real, more than three-dimensional.

And while there was a sleepy quality to how he felt, at the same time paradoxically he felt more awake than he had in his life. A continuous stream of new sensory information was flowing into him: sight, scent, sound, touch, all intensified.

Touch . . . his skin was on fire again, but this time not from pain. He wanted nothing more in that moment than to feel another's flesh against his, to taste sweat, to lose himself in someone's body.

And he was hungry.

He climbed out of the bed with care, expecting to feel weak from so long lying down, but the second his feet hit the floor he felt he could run a thousand miles without pause.

He'd been stripped of most of his clothes—or had pulled them off with the mad need to relieve his fever. They were folded on a chair nearby. The fabric felt different, softer but with so much more texture than he remembered.

There were guards flanking the suite door, but he leveled a look on them—the same one that had always made the Elite in California clear their throats and look away—and they didn't comment on his passage.

Once out into the hallway, though, he really had no idea where to go. After turning the corner to get out of the guards' line of sight, he stopped and shut his eyes, listening . . . for what, he wasn't sure, but he knew it was there somewhere.

Hundreds of lives surrounded him; he could feel them, hear them moving around. They all had a certain family resemblance, of a sort; an undertone in their energy that he found comforting . . . except one.

He was drawn to that one for an entirely different reason.

He followed it along another corridor toward a door that stood partway open. The smell of old books wafted from the doorway, and as he got closer, so did a faintly sweet scent, something like vanilla and brown sugar. Peering carefully around the door frame, his eyes confirmed what he'd already known: It was a library, rows and rows of books in all descriptions with cushioned nooks for reading spaced between shelves.

He caught movement—a shadow under the nearest row.

Bright red hair caught up in a bobbing ponytail; a sleeveless shirt showing off a spiderweb tattoo; and clunky black boots under wide-legged pants with a variety of pockets. She was softly shaped, with a pale and slightly pink complexion. He could hear her pulse all the way from the door.

The Witch stood on tiptoe to put away a slim blue volume and ran her finger along the shelf, looking for a specific title. She was humming and had no idea anyone was there until he had moved up behind her and was no more than a foot away. The warmth and sweet scent from the back of her neck made his upper jaw ache.

She turned around.

Before the scream could pierce the library's contemplative quiet, he had his hand over her mouth and gripped her arm with his other to keep her from bolting.

When she saw who he was, she sighed, relieved . . . until

she got a good look at him. Her eyes grew wide, and she stepped back; he let her go, as there was nowhere for her to run, and sure enough she backed into the shelf.

"God, Nico . . . you look . . . different."

He tipped his head slightly to the side inquisitively. "Do I?"

He moved in closer, almost touching. Her hands reached back and sought something to hold on to, but all she met were books, her nails scraping over the spines. "I was just in here doing some research for Miranda," she said. "They've got this book with some weird runes in it that I thought . . . um, thought they looked familiar." She swallowed hard, staring up into his face with a strange mix of emotions that were both innocent and decidedly *not*.

"Everyone here has strange eyes," he observed quietly. "I only ever saw violet until I came here."

"I don't know if you knew this, but . . . right now . . . yours are silver." Stella gave him a weak smile. "I guess that means you're hungry."

"I am indeed." He leaned down until their lips were nearly touching, and on her breath he could taste the cinnamon candy she'd been sucking on before he found her.

She stiffened slightly when she felt his hands move around her waist, but once she realized that was all he was doing, she relaxed visibly—so trusting, even knowing what he could do to her. "Well, I . . . I offered you my blood, and you can still have it, just . . ." In the second before their lips met, she breathed, "Please don't hurt me."

Stella's hands shot forward from the shelves and took hold of his shoulders, perhaps with the thought of pushing him away, a thought that morphed rapidly into its own opposite.

Considering how young she appeared, the way her nails dug into his upper arms and her breasts pressed against him was somewhat surprising . . . but then, he knew the others underestimated her, thought of her as little more than a girl. He knew better, and when she pulled back and leaned her head over to expose her throat, one hand wrapping around the back of his neck to pull him in, she was anything but a child.

He was afraid that he wouldn't be able to operate his own teeth, but it turned out his instincts had no intention of waiting another minute. His canines slid down and curved, the motion painful in a delicious and almost sexual way, and he whispered into her neck, "This will hurt . . . forgive me."

Her entire body tightened as he bit down, and she struggled for just a second—that fear was far older than logic. Teeth withdrawn, he lowered his mouth to the wound.

He knew he was giving off some kind of aura that was affecting her strongly, but right now he didn't really have any control over it; that would come later, he supposed, when he was used to this. She moaned softly and rocked her hips against him, and he got a better idea of what it was doing to her.

Her heartbeat began to slow . . . slower . . . slower . . . he knew he should stop, but taste and power both fought against reason.

Suddenly, a hand seized his shoulder and tore him off Stella, who sagged against the shelves, panting.

"That's enough!"

He turned on his assailant and hissed.

Miranda's face went paler with shock when she saw his face. "Jesus."

Again, instinct took hold. He could sense her strength, and the glowing red stone she wore whispered of authority older even than he. Power mantled around her like great dark wings—not quite threatening, but suffering no disobedience.

They stared each other down.

Finally he averted his eyes and slowly knelt, begrudgingly offering his submission.

Miranda glanced at the Witch. "Stella, are you okay? I'll call Mo."

"I'm all right—really, I'm fine."

The Queen looked at him again and spoke sternly. "Wipe your mouth, Nico. Only animals leave a mess."

He heard another voice beyond the doorway, this one masculine, dark. "Did you find him?"

"Yes," Miranda called. "He came after the only human blood in the Haven."

"Shit—" The voice's owner appeared, and again Nico felt twin urges to snarl defiantly and bow low to the ground in deference, choosing to remain where he was and meet his eyes directly. "Holy God."

They both looked him up and down. "I didn't think I'd be

able to tell so easily," the Queen said. "I thought since he was already immortal it wouldn't make that much of a difference."

"It was there already," the Prime mused. "We just couldn't see it until now. But I felt it when we drank from him."

" 'Born under a dark star,' " Miranda said, coming forward and touching Nico's face. "You won't ever see this, Nico, and it's hard to explain, but . . . you look like a hunter now."

David came into the room and gestured for Nico to stand; he echoed the Queen's motion, then turned Nico's head from one side to the other, his deep blue eyes betraying something that might have been desire.

"He really is striking," the Prime said with a slight smile. "Especially now. It was all white light and celestial harmony before."

"Why don't you get him back to bed," Miranda told her mate. "I'm taking Stella for a quick check with Mo—don't argue," she said to the Witch. "You're a lot paler than you were last time. He probably took more."

"I don't think it's that," Stella said quietly, but the Queen was too busy helping her up for the words to register.

"Come on," David said, taking Nico's hand and pulling him out of the library. "That's enough excitement for one night."

Instead of going to the Pair's suite, David led him to his own room; Nico followed him obediently but reluctantly. "I think you can have your own bed now. After this sleep you should be yourself again."

I am myself. He didn't say it aloud, but he could tell the Prime heard the thought.

"No, you're not," he said. "Turning brings out the darkness in you, but once it's finished you're still basically who you were—right now you're all hunger and hormones. Case in point, the way you're staring at my ass."

Nico had to smile. "It is a lovely ass."

He smiled back. "I know. Now, to bed."

The Prime tucked him in, still smiling, and kissed him on the forehead.

Nico caught him and kissed him hard on the mouth. "Stay," he said softly. "Stay with me."

They held each other's eyes for a moment, and he could see some temptation there, but then David chuckled. "So many reasons no." This time, he bestowed a light kiss on Nico's lips before turning off the light. "Sleep, Nico."

Nico shrugged inwardly. Worth a try. He burrowed into the blankets, and though he expected to be awake for a while, within minutes his body remembered what it had been through in the last few days and shoved him off wakefulness and into the placid waters of oblivion.

Nineteen

Stella waited anxiously, wiping her clammy palms on her ritual robe. She had no idea what to expect when the Weaver arrived; it had been two nights since the library and the only communication she'd had from him was when one of the Elite delivered the request for her to come to the ritual room.

"Are you sure you're comfortable with this?" Miranda asked before she left. "You were pretty freaked the other night—I won't leave you alone with him if you're even a little bit worried."

Stella laughed. "You said he's back to normal, whatever that is. If he tries to eat me I'll call you."

Despite her bravado she was still nervous and busied herself rearranging things on the altar even though she'd arranged them four times already.

She heard a soft knock and turned to see Nico waiting outside in the hall. "May I enter?" he asked.

She nodded.

He was wearing flowy Elf clothes, which she guessed were ritual wear; the whole outfit was dark blue, making his ivory skin stand out even more. Again, the change in him was obvious, though what exactly had changed wasn't; there were shadows in his eyes that hadn't been there before, and his features seemed to have sharpened slightly. His voice had also altered, becoming just a little softer, like being caressed by the feathers of a bird's wing.

Good Goddess almighty, he was hot.

Stella frowned at herself. None of that now. She could fantasize later when it was just her and her . . . personal appliances. Right now there were more important things to do.

Nico closed the door behind him and leaned back against it, staring at the floor before he lifted his gaze to her.

"Forgive me," he said.

His eyes lit on the two pink marks on her neck. They were almost gone already, but their ghost remained. His expression became anguished, and he looked away again.

"It's really okay," Stella told him, licking lips that had gone dry when he walked in. "I gave you permission, remember? Besides, you weren't exactly in your right mind."

He closed his eyes. "I fear I do not have a right mind anymore, Stella. Everyone said that when I woke I would feel like myself . . . but how can I? I can feel it in my veins, in my skin. Part of me is terrified of myself, of losing control . . . of being this thing I have become. But part of me . . ."

She knew what he was saying. "Part of you likes it. Wants it. And that scares you, too."

Nico pushed himself off the door and came to the altar, looking down at it with eyes cloaked in sorrow. "I knew I would die. I did not know I would wake again. I know that I was born for this, but . . . how can I be an Elf, and a . . ." He took a deep breath. "An Elf and a vampire, too?"

She couldn't help it; she had to help, even if she couldn't. She put her hand on his arm. "It'll take time," she said. "It's a lot to deal with—there's not exactly a handbook for this kind of thing."

He smiled. "I am sorry to whine at you, Stella. You have already borne enough of this situation. I admit I find you easier to talk to than anyone else here . . . perhaps because as a Witch you understand at least a part of what my life means. Or perhaps because we are both alone here of our kind."

"I'm honored," she said, and she meant it. Before she could second-guess herself, she hugged him tightly, and after a second or two he hugged her back. To her surprise, his hands started to slide around her waist, to pull her closer . . . then released her, suddenly self-conscious. Was it possible he was attracted to her, too? She would never have believed it from anyone else. Men had looked right past her her entire life, and yet here was this Elf . . .

"We should get started," Nico told her when they drew apart. "This will likely take most of the night."

"What do you need me to do?"

"I do not need anything, actually. I was hoping you might want to observe—you already have considerable talent at Weaving, and there is much more you could do with the right knowledge. I . . . I could teach you, if you wish to learn."

She could tell her surprise was evident on her face—he looked worried, probably that he had crossed another line. "You would do that?" she asked. "Really?"

He nodded, finally looking amused. "It is a time-honored tradition. Long ago, Witches were essentially human Elves— they worshipped our Goddess, practiced our magic. Most of that knowledge is long lost. We have an opportunity to bring it back."

Stella was already grinning. "Hell yes!"

"Good. Join me, then, in the center of the Circle."

They sat down facing each other on the floor, and though she was expecting some sort of complicated protection spell like a Witch's Circle Casting, he simply bade her to close her eyes and awaken her Sight. She did, and watched in rapt fascination as he touched the floor, and row by row, radiating out from where they sat, the symbols she had painted began to glow white in her mind's eye.

"Shift into your vision of the Web," Nico instructed.

A moment later, her mind lurched and turned—suddenly the Web in front of her doubled, tripled, quadrupled in size, and she could see a hundred times farther than before. The threads of light appeared in subtle shades of moonlit white and silver, but now she could see pale blue ones as well, and the ones she had already known about were brighter.

She would have been afraid—that much power, spread all around her, was overwhelming—but she could feel Nico's presence as if he were standing behind her with his arms around her. She understood, then, that she was now looking through his eyes, seeing the Web as a true Weaver saw it. How in the hell did he get anything done with all of this before him? It must have taken years to learn which threads were what, and how they interacted.

"Centuries," Nico said aloud. "I first apprenticed when I came of age at sixteen. That was about five hundred years ago."

She gaped at him—or, gaped toward him. "You're *five hundred* years old? Do Elves go crazy when they get old, too, or is that just vampires?"

She heard him laugh. "No. We are made differently. And our lives, for the most part, are far more tranquil. Now . . . just relax, and watch; ask whatever questions you need to."

Stella returned her attention to the task at hand. Nico was already spinning the vision around to find the Circle of Signets within it. The eight places were still there, but now instead of one empty, there were two. The second empty place was in the middle of a bunch of twisted threads, and one of the Pair bonds was glowing a faintly sick color, its light irregular. She could see where Miranda had welded Deven into their bond; the joining was already starting to corrode.

She stared at the empty spot for a moment. Jonathan belonged there. It didn't feel right without him—no, not right at all. "Where is he now?" she asked softly.

"I do not know," Nico replied. "If you look where he used to be, there are faint traces of that connection—an afterimage. A soul cannot be destroyed, but it changes form. Where he is now depends entirely on where he chose to go."

"Can you tell from here who belongs in the eighth slot?"

"In most other situations, I could. But this Circle is different. In any other potential relationship I could find the cord from one to the other and follow it to that person's life-web, but here, it is shrouded from me, the way the true depth of the Web is normally shrouded from you."

"Is there anyone who could see it?"

"Yes," he said, smiling. "Persephone. But I can tell you this: It draws nearer every night. Intuition tells me that the Lady Olivia will have found her Consort before the year is out."

He talked her through the basic makeup of the Circle's web, much of which she had figured out on her own and was proud to hear confirmed. The theory wasn't complicated, but knowing which threads to move and which ones to make stronger depended on maintaining the greater balance. It was a hybrid of magic and physics that demanded extensive knowledge of both.

She could see why it took centuries to learn what he'd learned. She, in her limited human Sight with only one life span, might as well not even try.

"Nonsense," Nico told her. "You have already done remarkable things, and you will do many more."

Seeing the intricacy of it all made the task ahead even more daunting to Stella. Right now, the Trinity was joined and David and Miranda were still fairly balanced themselves—it was Deven who was pulling everything off. Once he was disconnected from them and their bond resealed, they would be back to normal without much ado. Deven himself, on the other hand, was a mess.

"Once the bond is cut, the trick is to cauterize the end so it will not bleed out. Once that is done, and he is a whole individual again, I will begin work on our bonding. That will require an even more careful touch or we will end up in this same situation. Then I can rebuild the matrix around Deven's mind so that when he wakes up he will be mentally fit again."

"And you can do all of that in one night?"

"In theory, yes, but this is far more complex than most of the work I have done. I may have to put in the groundwork for the matrix and then finish it in stages as I did before. That would be a reasonably safe place to stop for the night and finish tomorrow if necessary."

She watched him begin to gingerly pull the strands apart, laying them out so he could see what was what and start shoring up the wobbly threads in Deven's part that had been pulled loose.

It was incredible. He made it look effortless, but she knew for a fact that just shifting a thread even an inch took an immense amount of power and control. She'd only been able to plug a few leaks because it didn't really require much Weaving, just energy stuffed into the gap. Nico's work was elegant, like a dance.

Hours passed while he realigned the sections and created new threads that were simply there to wire others together. Becoming a vampire didn't seem to have harmed his abilities at all; in fact, she could feel a lot more of his emotions and thoughts being this close to his energy, and right now as he worked, he was completely himself, happy in the way that people were only when doing what they were born to do.

Finally, it was time to break the bond; it lay bare with plenty of space around it so that cutting it wouldn't damage anything else.

"Are they going to feel it?" she asked.

"Certainly. When it is first broken it will probably hurt."

Stella fell silent. She didn't want to distract him. He was running his mental hands along the bond, looking for the right place to break it.

She saw him look over to Deven's life-web, felt his regret. Then, as she held her breath, Nico took hold of the bond and fed power into it until it burned so brightly she was blinded—

—she heard it snap—

Instantly energy was bleeding all around them, shooting out of the three severed places. Nico didn't miss a beat; he grabbed the two ends of the Pair bond and fused them together, then spun around and seized the end of Deven's. She could See him pouring energy into the cord, pulling it around until it caught itself like a serpent biting its own tail and soldering it shut. He Wove a thinner thread out of himself and wrapped it around the welded spot to keep it together while the energy flow reestablished.

Stella's heart skipped; she could feel him weakening. The toll of the past few days hadn't completely healed, and even with all the strength he had regained, he was burning so much of it there definitely wouldn't be enough left to finish all the work he had to do.

Nico understood that, but he was far more concerned with his three Signets than his own welfare. Deven's thread was taking a lot out of him—the Prime was an abyss of damage, and though Nico didn't intend to fix it all at once, he couldn't leave all of those frayed ends to leak even more energy into the ether.

The whole thing played out in mere minutes. Stella felt

Nico falter—he was almost at a safe stopping place, but not quite—and without hesitation she said, "Here! Take this!"

She threw him a line of energy, and he snatched it up gratefully to make one last pass over the two bonds, feeling for weak spots and potential leaks. Then he used what she gave him to close up his own energy, and simultaneously they both fell back out of the vision and into the ritual room.

Stella came back to herself with the cool wood of the floor against her face and Nico lying in front of her, unconscious.

She wrestled herself upright and spoke into her com: "Star-two."

Miranda was breathing hard, and she sounded shaken. "Are you okay?"

"Yeah—Nico's out, though. He should probably be put to bed."

"I'll send in the guards to help."

"What about you, are you all right?"

Miranda paused. When she spoke again Stella could hear tears, as well as awe, in her voice. "Yes," she said. "Yes . . . we're okay."

The second the power hit, Deven sat bolt upright in bed, gasping awake.

He could feel it—something was different. Something felt . . .

Another shock wave of energy ran through him, and another; his mind tumbled around itself, trying to find any solid ground, but for a while it felt like he was spiraling through the night sky with nothing to hold on to.

Finally, he hit dry land and sat panting, hands clenched in the sheets, not understanding what was happening.

It took a moment for him to realize what he was feeling.

Nothing.

Those two presences that had been rubbing him raw with their concern and affection for days now were gone from his mind. He no longer felt them dragging him closer, trying to reach him. He finally had what he wanted.

He was alone.

It's gone. They're gone.

I'm free.

For the first time in weeks he could feel his own mind again. He could reach into himself and find . . .

He froze, and memory came rushing back.

"Baby . . . it's okay."

Deven covered his face with his hands . . . the stark horror of it, feeling the immense crushing pain in his lower body and realizing what it meant . . . those last few halting words, extorting a promise from the Queen and then . . . then . . .

". . . if you can hear me . . . I love you . . . you were my always . . . too."

"No," he whispered, pleading for mercy the way he had so many times. "No, no . . . God, please . . ."

But he was long past God's help. And Jonathan was gone.

Gone.

He had died in the ruins of their life together—the home they'd shared for sixty years, the bed where that very afternoon they had made love for hours to celebrate . . . celebrate . . .

"By the power vested in me by the state of California and the county of Sacramento . . ."

It was all gone. Jonathan was gone, and he had left Deven behind—had all but forced Miranda to trap him here, to turn the one true thing he'd ever possessed into a mockery of itself, as if by pasting him into their bond he could forget what he had lost and they could have a merry threesome for all time.

There was nothing now. No home, no Consort, no place for a broken-down Prime who had never belonged anywhere, until he found the other half of his soul . . . and now he would never belong anywhere again.

He sobbed quietly into his hands for a moment, overcome with so much pain it drowned out the whole world.

And then, the thought arose again, realization stabbing through the sorrow:

He was free.

The cold that he had clung to for days settled back around him like a cloak. He stretched out his senses, groping around the Haven until he found what he was looking for.

The grief threatened to rise again, but he shoved it down with sudden anger—there was no time to bawl like a baby. He had work to do and he had to hurry before the others knew he was awake. There was only one thought that mattered: *End this*.

He had absolutely no doubt that whatever they had done to free him from their clutches was only temporary—they must have a plan for him, another path to force him down at knifepoint.

Not this time. He forced himself out of bed, into clothes; he picked up his sword without looking at it, afraid of what he might feel if he thought about anything too closely. He had to hurry before the ice in his heart fractured and left him bleeding on the ground . . . and before they realized he had gone and tried once more to cage him.

They would not take him alive again.

Nico woke almost immediately after Stella and one of the Elite helped him back to his room. He was exhausted, but it was always difficult to sleep for the first few hours after intense Weaving; as soon as he'd regained consciousness he was up and in the shower.

Hunger pulled hard on his body as he put on clean clothes. It was normal to be ravenous after such work . . . but now, that hunger was different, centered in his jaw, in the feeling of sand in his veins. He felt dry on the inside, painfully itchy.

He knew that he couldn't live off donated blood forever if he wanted to maintain his strength, but the thought of going into the city was still too frightening. He couldn't imagine stepping into the teeming mass of humanity, with all its fear, until he had learned better command of his new senses. He didn't want to lose control and hurt anyone . . . and he was closer to that possibility than he had admitted to the others.

Nico held on to the back of a chair with both hands, steadying himself. They all thought he was just as strong and capable as he had been before—he had even managed to fool Stella into believing it, when she was standing in the Web with her mind pressed to his. Powerful she may be, but she was still young and inexperienced, and she would see what he wanted her to: namely, himself, in one piece, unafraid.

And there was more work to do. He couldn't put off binding himself to Deven. If he waited long there was too much risk that Deven would wake before it was done. Nico couldn't bear the thought of force-bonding Deven with the Prime aware of the violation, but moreover, Nico wasn't sure he was strong enough to bind them if Deven tried to fight it. He had already used too much power on too little rest.

There was no alternative, though. In an hour or two he would crash for most of the day, but then, as soon as he woke, he had to act . . . before his conscience and his heart stole away what remained of his courage.

Over on the bureau, a small carved box waited: Jonathan's broken Signet. He would need it for the binding, though he was almost afraid to touch it. It was a holy relic, a symbol of love and sacrifice . . . and pain. He hadn't even opened it since Miranda had brought it to him.

For now he focused on what was easily fixable: his hunger. The room he was in had a small refrigerator and microwave, whose uses he had learned back in California, and the Queen had told him how long to warm the bagged blood to make it reasonably palatable.

He turned toward the fridge, but before he could move, something seized him around the neck and hauled him backward so hard he choked. The cold edge of a blade pressed into his throat.

There was a low hiss at his ear, even as a scent he knew very well reached him and he realized, horrified, what was happening.

"All right, Weaver," Deven said, his voice ice cold, his sword's blade cutting lightly into Nico's skin. Nico was too frozen with fear to struggle, but if he had, he would have been beheaded in seconds. "Now that you've done what you intended to do to me . . . you're going to do something *for* me."

"It's done," Miranda whispered, sitting on the edge of the bed. "He really did it."

David was upright now but still on the floor where he had fallen the second they both felt the bond snap—that same agony they had felt when he died overcame them for just a few seconds, and they had reached for each other in sheer panic. But then the pain vanished as if someone had cut the power to it, and Prime and Queen passed out from the relief. She had woken to Stella's voice asking if she was all right.

Miranda and David stared at each other. There were no words, really—that endless drain they had been feeling for days, the constant pull of grief threatening to suck them down into its maw, had just . . . gone. There were no more energy leaks, no sense of continual hunger to offset the loss. Everything that had gone wrong the night she put her hands on their bond was quickly shifting, becoming right again.

She felt strong, complete. Herself. And yet . . .

"I feel . . ." She trailed off, looking for the right description. There wasn't one.

David nodded. "So do I."

She would never have believed it possible, but she felt . . . sad. Neither of them had believed they should keep Deven in their bond, even if they could, but it still felt like she had lost something vital . . . something that could have been wonderful, if only things were different. It was like losing a limb she hadn't known she had, and now she could feel its phantom pain.

"I'm sure it will fade," she said. "You can't be bound to someone without it leaving a scar . . . right?"

"I don't know." He smiled. "But I do know I'm going to give that Elf one hell of a kiss."

Miranda chuckled. "Give him one for me, too."

Before he could reply, Miranda's com chimed, and she heard a raspy, weak voice half whisper, "He's gone."

Miranda frowned. "Nico?"

"Deven . . . he attacked me. He's gone."

David was already on his feet and out the door, and Miranda got up and followed him, both skidding to a halt at the entrance to Nico's room. David threw the door open, and Miranda gasped . . . she saw blood.

Nico lay on his side on the floor, one hand pressed to his abdomen. He was ghostly white and panting from the pain.

"Just relax," Miranda said, peeling his hand away. The wound was deep but already starting to heal; he must have been far more tired than they thought, as slowly as it was closing. "What happened?"

"He . . . he woke after the bond broke . . . put a blade to my throat and forced me to build a portal from here to the city. Then he stabbed me so I wouldn't be able to go after him."

"Where did he go?" David demanded. "Did he tell you the exact location?"

"It was in his mind. A large, empty building . . . I think you call it a warehouse. I could hear, in his thoughts: one hour till dawn, repeated over and over."

"Oh God," Miranda said. "David . . ."

"We have to get there now," the Prime said. "Do you have the strength to send us to the same place?"

"Probably not. But if you can Mist, I can show you where to go."

"I can reach that far," David said. "What do you think, beloved?"

Miranda took stock of her reserves and how far it was from the Haven to Austin. "I think so—if you can help me."

David called Harlan and told him to head for the city in the Escalade with the anti-UV-tinted windows; if they were caught in town by the dawn they could at least get someplace safe without being hurt. "I'll send you a location as soon as I have it," the Prime said. "Just get on the road."

"On my way, Sire."

Miranda helped the Elf sit up; he looked awful, blood-soaked and pale, but there was grim determination in his eyes. "Go," he said. "I will be fine."

The Pair stood and took each other's hands. "Show me," David said.

Miranda barely got a mental image of one of the warehouses in East Austin before the room dissolved and her consciousness lurched hard, spinning her through space farther than she'd ever gone before—she'd never tried Misting more than a couple of miles, but something about David's telekinetic gift boosted how far he could go. It was so draining he rarely did it, but there was no other choice this time; by the time they got to town in a car and found the warehouse it would already be sunrise.

The world seemed to warp and bubble around her, as if someone had dropped a stone in the calm surface of reality. She tumbled forward into David's arms, her stomach pitching, nauseated.

She straightened and looked around—they were indeed on the street in front of a warehouse, one she recognized vaguely but had never entered. It was very near the building where David and Faith had died; that must be how Deven knew it, from the days he and Jonathan had spent protecting the city while she was missing.

"Come on," David said urgently, grabbing her hand and taking off for the door.

He opened the door slowly, an inch at a time, to avoid making noise; Miranda caught a whiff of musty air that smelled like paper, and the sign on the interior wall confirmed it: a document disposal company.

"Roof," David murmured. "Sun exposure."

Miranda's heart was pounding. She could already feel the oncoming dawn, and since the day she had become a vampire she had feared that tightness in her skin, the atavistic need to hide in the dark. But she remembered, too, the morning she had fallen asleep with Deven in the hayloft. He had taken care of her, given her courage. The thought of him here, waiting for the sun, so empty and tired of being alive . . . regardless of the Circle and the war, she didn't know whether to hope they found him in time, or not.

They took the stairs as quietly as they could and reached the door to the roof.

"Be careful," David said to her. "Remember, he was willing to stab Nico—he's not rational. He'll hurt you."

"I don't care," she replied. "Let's go."

At first, all Miranda saw beyond the door was a flat concrete plane, and it gave her a sense of déjà vu that nearly forced her to freeze—she remembered being dragged up stairs just like these, out onto a roof just like this, where her life had come to a violent, screaming end and the night had erupted into flame . . . always explosions, always fire.

David didn't hesitate, though she knew he was remembering, too. He walked through the door out onto the roof—

—and went flying, as out of nowhere, he was kicked in the chest.

Miranda ran out, already drawing Shadowflame, but she had to halt . . . there was a foot on David's throat, holding him down on the ground, and a blade hovering just over that.

"Deven, no!" Miranda yelled. "Don't—"

He looked up at her, and the words died in her mouth. There was nothing familiar in his lavender-blue eyes, no warmth, nothing of the Deven she knew. There was only rage and pain, focused on a single goal: death.

"Do you think you can kill me, Dev?" David ground out. "Go ahead and try."

Deven gave him a look of disgust. "What did you hope to accomplish by coming here?" the Prime snarled. "Did you think you would reason with me, tell me you love me, that the Circle needs me for its war?"

Miranda tried to sidle around to the right to get behind him, but Deven caught her, shaking his head and tilting a finger back and forth, scolding. "Take another step and I cut his head off," Deven told her.

David Misted out from under his foot, reappearing a few feet away. He had his sword out before Deven could react, and dove in, the need to incapacitate the Prime and get him out of the open air driving him to go on the offensive.

Of course it wouldn't be that easy. Even with a second's lag time Deven was impossible to surprise; he was already waiting for David's sword, and metal struck metal with inhuman force.

Miranda knew better than to jump in—she was good, but she was nowhere near their level, and she'd just get hurt. Instead she pulled two of her knives.

Focusing her inherited telekinesis on them, she threw both, using the gift to steer them toward their target. One struck home, hitting Deven's sword arm and driving in up to the hilt.

He didn't miss a stroke but pulled the knife and tossed it carelessly over the edge of the roof. The other one missed him but nearly hit David and struck a metal plate that was leaning near the door hard enough to bury its blade.

The two Primes fought each other all over the rooftop, and in any other circumstances Miranda would have been spellbound. She'd never seen them fight each other before, and it became clear very quickly that almost every time she'd seen David in battle he was using only half his skill. He didn't hold back against his teacher . . . but the advantage wasn't his. He only wanted to win, not to kill. He had to be careful. Deven, on the other hand, had nothing to lose.

She could smell dawn coming. They had perhaps thirty minutes before the sun was high enough to kill them. Miranda, no longer confident in her aim with the two of them moving so fast, looked around for some other way to trip Deven up, but there was nothing on the roof, not even trash.

There was only one thing she could do, and she hated herself for doing it, but there was no time, no choice; she summoned her empathic power, working it into an image drenched in emotion, and threw it at him.

She saw the impact and for a moment was sure it had worked. He stumbled slightly, his face going blank for a second as the ammunition she'd used hit home.

Jonathan.

But to her shock, not only did he resist the energy, he took hold of it and threw it back at her.

She should have known that he would get some measure of empathy from her and David, but she hadn't realized it would be so strong. Being able to sense emotion was far more common than being able to use it as a weapon. A wave of pain struck the Queen, and she cried out and fell backward as her mind filled with image after image: *David's death, Faith bound to barrels of explosives, Jenny and Marianne . . .*

Miranda fought with all her strength not to collapse beneath the onslaught. No one had ever used empathy against her before, so she'd never fully realized the kind of damage it caused. Despair and fear clawed at her heart. She had to drop onto one of the low brick walls that divided the roof into sections, breathing hard, holding up her shields with everything she had.

But even though Deven had turned the power back on her, it did what she had needed it to do; he had faltered, and that lapse in attention was sufficient to give David a second's advantage. His sword got past Deven's defenses just once, but it was enough.

Blood splattered all over the roof as a laceration opened Deven's midsection, just below the ribs. He staggered back, his sword clattering to the ground.

It wasn't a grave wound, just a bloody one that had to hurt like hell—no worse than the one he'd given Nico.

David stood still and watched him, expressionless. When he spoke, though, his voice was anything but impassive. "Please, Deven . . . come inside. There isn't much time . . . just let us help you. I know how much this hurts—"

Pale eyes full of cold fury lifted to David's face. "Do you?"

Miranda came forward to stand by her Prime. "I do."

Deven shook his head. She could feel him trying to speed the wound's healing, but he was still weak and could only stop the bleeding. His words were halting, dragged out of him by anger. "No, you don't. That was different . . . he didn't choose to abandon you—he came back from the dead for you."

She noticed, with the part of her mind that was petrified of the rising sun, that the stone in Deven's Signet was green again. Another part of her mind felt the air shifting, the hair on the back of her neck standing up, her skin tingling . . .

"Jonathan wanted you to live," she said, ignoring the change in the air. "He didn't abandon you. He knew he was going to die and he made sure you could survive without him."

"I didn't want to survive without him," Deven snapped. "He *knew* that. He was the only thing keeping me going for years—I couldn't die because of him. But now . . . now there's no one keeping me here. I'm free to do what I should have done hundreds of years ago . . . free to die as I should have before Eladra ever turned me."

"If you die, we're all dead," David reminded him desperately. "We need you. Without you we can't win."

"Do you really think I care?" Deven almost laughed. "Do you think that has any meaning to me now? We're already done for, David. The Circle will never be whole . . . I'll never be whole. There will never be anyone who can fill that emptiness."

"Yes, there will."

Miranda turned toward the voice. She had felt the portal building, but not its opening; they were both too focused on Deven.

Nico stepped out onto the roof calmly and joined them. Ashen, his clothes soaked with his own blood, he had somehow found the strength to come here even lying wounded on the floor—scraping together every remaining remnant of his power for a one-way trip.

"Ah, yes, my offspring," Deven said with loathing in his eyes. "Here to take Jonathan's place, to step in as if you could ever be his equal."

"I do not want to replace him," Nico replied. He started to list sideways, and Miranda moved closer and caught his arm; he leaned on her heavily as he spoke. "Nor could I. But there is a hole in the Circle that must be filled."

"Well, now there will be two holes," Deven corrected. And even through his anger, she could hear it: Emotion was seeping back in through his defenses. She could feel him fighting it. He was trying not to break down, and failing; Miranda's heart broke for him. She wanted more than anything to put her arms around him.

There were centuries of loss, a dozen lifetimes of wandering alone in the dark, in his words as he told Nico, "I don't care what you have planned. I don't want you . . . and I don't want to live. I won't take another life with me . . . I've already taken too many. But now I'm free, and I can set this right. Please . . . just go inside. This is what I want." He turned pleading eyes on David. "Just let me go . . . David, it's time for you to let me go."

Miranda looked over at David, expecting him to respond, but before he could say anything, he drew an astonished breath, his eyes widening, staring at Deven. Miranda followed his gaze and her heart froze in her chest.

"Nico . . ." She spoke quietly. "I thought you didn't have time to make the new bond."

Nico, too, was staring in obvious disbelief. "I did not."

Deven seemed to finally notice their expressions and followed their eyes. He let out a strangled cry of denial.

His Signet was flashing.

"No," he whispered. "No, no . . . no . . ." What strength he had left failed him. Slowly, shaking, he went to his knees in front of them, shaking his head.

Nico stepped closer to him, reaching into his robe for something. He lifted an object from his pocket, reverently, and held it flat in both hands so that they could all see it.

Jonathan's Signet.

Its stone was healed . . . and it had come back to life, its emerald light rekindled, pulsing in exact rhythm with its mate.

Miranda couldn't speak—neither could anyone else. But she turned her eyes to Deven, and saw his face . . . saw him lose all his fight, lose everything.

His eyes closed and his head bowed as he realized what it meant.

That one moment of freedom had been taken from him. He had lost his only chance. It had come down to the same decision as always: let the rising sun reduce him to ash and murder the one bound to him, or go on living . . . unable to shed the weight of centuries that it seemed would never end.

And in spite of everything, even in the face of the hollow, deathless years to come, there was still only one choice.

He stood, nearly falling over several times but ignoring their offers of help. Deven wavered on his feet, then steeled himself and took the half-dozen steps to the Elf. Without saying anything or looking Nico in the face, he took Jonathan's Signet and fastened it with shaking hands around Nico's neck.

The two stones began to pulse faster, and then to shine steadily. Miranda could feel it—both of them opening up fully, that circuit Nico had so carefully created in Deven splitting and joining seamlessly, on its own, the way Primes and Consorts had come together for hundreds of years.

Miranda understood, though understanding didn't make it any less heartrending. Dea ex machina: In the end, Persephone had taken the burden of forcing a bond on Deven out of Nico's hands. It was her will, not theirs, that made two into one . . . and thus the matter was settled.

Pairing was supposed to be a joyous thing; often born out of what seemed from the outside like love at first sight, the realization of having found one's chosen, perfect partner always inspired at least a moment of bewildered, incandescent happiness. Even the vilest Prime could know that feeling if he ever found his Consort.

Nico felt it. She could see it in his eyes. But he wisely held back his reaction, for an emotional outburst might be enough to shatter what little was left of his new Prime into a thousand jagged shards . . . shards that Nico would have to somehow put back together again if he wanted them both to live. One impossible task at a time was quite enough.

Deven didn't meet Nico's eyes. He just crossed his arms protectively over his middle, where the wound from David's sword was still closing, and walked away, back to the door and out of the rising ghost of morning.

Twenty

"All right," David said, "here's the deal. I refuse to let three quarters of the country descend into anarchy. I understand your concern, but your opinions are inconsequential to me. If I decide I want the entire Shadow World, I'll have it, and there's not a damn thing you can do to stop me."

The rest of the Council were stunned into silence, except for Tanaka—there was a particular breathing pattern the Japanese Prime had that meant he was secretly laughing. Tanaka had been the one to broker this phone call, a last chance for the Council to coax David back into their fold, but David was fairly sure Tanaka had mostly done it to amuse himself. It was a well-established fact that once David Solomon made up his mind there was no swaying him.

"But Lord Prime, please try to see it our way," said Central America. "This consolidation of power appears rather threatening from the outside. The U.S. is vast—no one Signet can control that large a population."

"Hide and watch," David responded. "Prime Olivia is firmly in command of the East. As soon as Prime Deven has recovered and is ready to reassume power in the West, I will gladly surrender it. Right at this moment, however, the South,

West, Midwest, and Mideast are all under my control. And if you should grow careless, Alvarez, Downing—I'll cheerfully take Mexico and Canada, too. If any of you had listened to me when Morningstar first appeared, you might not be hiding in your Havens watching those of us with balls and brains save the world. Now, if you'll excuse me, that's enough of this nonsense for one night."

David ran his finger along the screen, dumping Prime after Prime off the call until only he, Olivia, and Jacob were left.

"Do you think they'll try to depose you?" Olivia asked.

"They'll have their own problems soon enough," David replied. "Even by my lowest estimate Morningstar has to number over a thousand by now. Besides, if they try anything, we can just have Cora use her Fireball Power on them."

Jacob snorted. "Good thing she's not in the room right now," he said with a bit of chagrin. "She's still trying to come to grips with it—she'd never killed anyone before. At the same time, though, she really wants to learn how to use it. I've been putting out feelers for a pyrokinetic to come train her. Believe it or not, they're rare."

"Are you sure she'll be all right?" Olivia wanted to know, concern in her voice.

"She's . . . determined," Jacob said. "Ever since that night . . . something's changed. It's a good change—like all of a sudden she realized she has a right to defend what's hers, and the tools to do it with. Cora likes structure, guidelines—once she has a set of defined steps to start from, she'll work her way through it."

There was a pause in conversation, as no one wanted to ask the obvious. Finally, David took pity on them.

"There's nothing new to report here," he said. "We have to be patient . . . it's only been six weeks. Right now everything is still too new, too raw—you don't get over losing a soul mate quickly, if ever. We just have to give it time and have hope."

David watched the others hang up, thinking: They had to have hope. Most of the time that was all they had.

Deven had retreated so far into himself he hardly ever looked anyone in the eye. Most nights no one knew where he went, and he had shielded himself against Nico so strongly the Elf had a hard time sensing him at all. As David had said, too much had happened in too little time, and now that killing himself was no longer an option Deven had to learn to live again, in a world without his first soul mate, his husband, who had gone to his death knowingly and left Deven behind.

Nico had rebuilt the matrix around Deven's mind, and that tiny bit of energy it took to keep it stable was one of the only forms of contact Deven allowed his Consort. Nico, for his part, was still trying to adjust to his new life in this strange new place, and though he was learning quickly—his English was even starting to pick up contractions and slang—David often saw him out in the gardens, touching the plants, sadness in his eyes, looking so lost. David remembered that handful of days that Miranda had blocked her Prime out and slept in the mistress suite, and the misery it had caused them both . . . and that hadn't been nearly as strong as the shields Deven had slammed down between himself and Nico.

Deven's recovery was up to Deven now, and Nico was the one who needed help. David, Miranda, and Stella had silently agreed to do whatever they could to keep him going.

In fact, one of the Prime's intentions in coming to the workroom was to fetch the Codex. The pages of symbols still eluded them, and even a translation program based on one used by Army intelligence couldn't crack it. Stella had mentioned that Nico knew something about runic alphabets from his magical studies. He might have some idea what the runes in the Codex meant, or at least what language they were in, and having a project would be good for him.

David logged out of the system and picked up the book, headed for the one place he knew he was almost certain to find the Elf.

It was an unseasonably warm night, cloudy, with the promise of a cold front the next afternoon. Outside the Haven the crickets and frogs held noisy court punctuated by the occasional objections of an owl. The paths were lit softly, and his eyes easily picked out the dark shape resting quietly on a cushioned chaise back among a bower of moonflowers.

David paused, stricken by the beauty of the tableau. Nico's fine, silken hair fell all around and over the seat, one ear poking up through it; he had taken to wearing darker colors and tonight was in forest green, every inch an Elf down to his bare feet. But Elf though he was, he was something else, too, and it was written in the line of his body, the way his fingers curled on the cushion, even in the way he breathed. He didn't seem so much like a deer now as a young wolf curled up in its den.

Strange . . . they had known the Elf for only a month and a half, and David had not wanted to like him when they met. By the time Nico had the Signet around his neck, though, they had all taken him into their fold without question . . . above and beyond any other urges the Elf might inspire—and there were plenty of those—there was just something about him that cried out to be loved. David wasn't the only one who felt that way, either—in fact, the only person who didn't was the person the Elf was bound to.

"Nico?" David spoke softly and sat down beside him, touching his shoulder. "Are you awake?"

One violet eye opened, then the other. "Yes, my Lord?"

"I brought you this—I heard you might be able to help us translate the rest of it."

Nico sat up, recognizing the book in his hands, interest sparking in his eyes. David handed it to him and watched as he turned the pages. Nico lamented, "I know a few lines of human Greek from the epic poetry kept in the Avilon library, but this dialect of the Order's is strange to me."

"That's fine—we've got translations from Deven for most of that part. What we need help with are the runic symbols, mostly in the second half of the book."

Nico paged through gingerly, admiring the illuminated text: the intricate border illustrations of pomegranates, ravens, serpents, and dogs shaped remarkably like Cora's Nighthound, all bound up in what looked like knotwork but, on closer inspection, revealed itself to be interlocking threads of a web that radiated out from the top inside corner of each page.

When he came to the first page covered in the runic symbols, Nico stopped, eyebrows shooting up. He gave a delighted laugh that startled the Prime. "This is what you couldn't read?"

"Yes. We compared them to a number of runic alphabets from several Norse . . . what's so funny?"

Nico grinned. "There is nothing Norse about these symbols, my Lord." He tilted the book toward David. "This is Elvish."

"What the hell is Elvish doing in a vampire Codex?" David asked.

"Perhaps I'll find out when I read it."

David watched him for another moment before asking, "How are you?"

A weary smile. "About the same." The Elf closed the Codex and held it in his lap. "Thank you for asking."

Unable to hold back any longer, David reached over and took his hand, squeezing it as he spoke. "I know you feel alone here, Nico . . . but you're not. We may not be Elves, but we care about you. I care about you."

Nico looked down at their joined hands, then up at David, searching his eyes. "What . . . what do you mean?"

David chuckled. "Nothing like that. But I would like to know you better, and to help take care of you while you're here."

"You do not have to take care of me," Nico told him, but there was gratitude in the words. "I am not a child."

"Yes, we do. We all take care of each other. You're not an exception—you're one of us now. You're hurting, and none of us can fix it . . . but we can give you what you need, so that you can give Deven what he needs . . . time. And one day soon, one way or another, you'll crack that wall he's got between you."

Nico lowered his eyes, which were shining with tears. "I wish I could believe that. I wish I had hope."

"That's all right," David told him, drawing the Elf gently into his arms. Nico buried his face in David's shoulder and wept softly, hands clinging to the lapels of David's coat, pressing into the Prime as hard as he could, as if wishing he could dissolve into David and leave the world behind. David kept hold of him, kissing him on the forehead and, once or twice, on the lips, giving him something strong to cling to in the storm. "It's all right," the Prime repeated, stroking Nico's hair. "I can hope enough for both of us."

Almond-scented steam rose from the bubble-laden surface of the water, thickening the air and making everything sleepy and sweet. Her head rested back on a waterproof cushion, her hair held up on top of her head and out of the suds, though a few tendrils insisted on having a soak with the rest of her. She lay back with her eyes closed, smiling slightly, more relaxed than she'd been in weeks.

Earlier that evening she'd finally wrapped her last recording session. In a couple of months she would lead her new album by the hand to the national playground and watch it run off to swing with the other children. For once, her precognitive gift told her something good: Musician Miranda was about to become very busy, and this time Queen Miranda was just going to have to work around it.

Maybe she could even avoid getting shot.

She felt David arrive at the suite. Strange . . . since that night they had been re-bound together, their connection was doing some odd things. She felt hyper-aware of David now at much greater distances and with much greater detail than ever before. She'd always sensed him, felt him in her mind, but now she could feel him inside her, just under her skin, and while it was definitely weird . . . she loved it. It was like he was always holding her, always caressing her from the inside out, so that when they actually touched it felt like they'd been struck by lightning. That was another thing to ask the Elf: whether anything had changed during his work, or if it was just another step in their journey together as a Pair. She didn't want to lose it, but she was curious why it had appeared.

And one more thing . . . a few nights ago, in the city, she'd been leaving a show and heard something pitiful in the alley . . . it turned out to be a kitten, or at least most of one. The poor creature had one leg mangled, her ears chewed off, her tail broken . . . but she had come to Miranda without hesitation. Miranda carefully got her into the car, though she knew it was futile . . . but then . . . something in the Queen, something hovering deep in her belly, raised its head and demanded a chance to help. Shaking her head with disbelief at her own temerity, Miranda held her hands over the kitten . . .

. . . and healed her.

Deven had claimed that his healing talent was not a vampire one, so it couldn't spread throughout the Circle . . . but now she had a gray and black meowing refutation of that claim. Miranda had pushed energy inelegantly into the cat's body, but that had done the trick, and her leg was sound, her ears were healed, her tail straightened.

Now that kitten had happily claimed a corner of the royal bed, kneading the sheets with her little pine-needle claws and emitting a purr way louder than a body her size should have been capable of. David wasn't all that keen on the idea at first, but he didn't have any real objections either, so the Queen now had a cat. Some nights when Miranda took long soaking baths, the cat would perch on the side of the tub watching her human do such a bizarre and senseless ritual. Tonight, however, Miranda's bath was feline free.

That brief, nightmarish time bound as a Trinity had mutated their powers even further. She wasn't even sure what to call half of it. She wanted to know if Deven felt the changes as well, but there wasn't much point to asking, even if she could find him. He'd just vanish without speaking to her.

She missed her friend. She wanted him back . . . she wanted both of them back, but only one could ever return. And though her empathy and her instincts begged her to do something, anything, she knew the only medicine for Deven was time.

After another hour, when she was nice and pruny, she pulled the drain stopper with her toes and stretched languidly, enjoying how the heat had made her muscles let go of the tension that had become habitual over the last few months.

Pulling on her robe without tying it, she returned to the bedroom. Esther had been there; the fire was roaring against the winter cold that had already made its way into the Haven days ago despite the single night of temporary warmth outside, and the bed had been turned down to reveal the thicker comforter and extra blanket Esther knew they would want.

She smiled. A pair of socked feet were sticking off the arm of the couch. There were black boots on the floor beneath.

A welcome, and reassuring sight: her husband sprawled on the couch asleep, laptop still open on the coffee table, an empty wineglass that still smelled faintly of blood next to that. Three and a half centuries old, a rebel Prime who had broken with the Council and now ruled all but one territory in the United States, one of only two of his kind and sired by the

Goddess of Death . . . napping in a vintage-style college T-shirt that said *University of Gallifrey.*

And right there in the middle of his chest, a sleeping kitten.

She couldn't have loved him more in that moment if she'd tried.

Miranda reached up and took the clip out of her hair, letting it fall down around her shoulders. She grinned to herself and sat on the edge of the couch, pushing her robe off. She nudged the cat onto the floor with one hand. The kitten gave her an indignant look and turned away to lick herself. Then Miranda leaned down and kissed her Prime awake.

He made a half-growling noise and opened his eyes a slit. "I'm asleep," he said drowsily. "And I'm dreaming there's a beautiful naked woman within easy pouncing distance. I can't possibly be that lucky."

She flicked her tongue against his earlobe. "How lucky would you like to be?"

Now his eyes opened all the way. "Wait . . . didn't I marry you?"

"As a matter of fact, you did." Miranda took one of his hands and placed it on her thigh, where it began to wander of its own accord, his nimble fingers tracing spirals over her skin. "It's late," she said. "Are you done with whatever it was you were sleeping through?"

"Done enough. Besides . . . I don't think I could concentrate on code right now."

She smiled, then leaned close and said very softly into his ear, "Take me to bed or lose me forever."

David wound his fingers through hers, all the worry and sadness they'd been carrying around for months falling away, for a while, leaving just the two of them, one heart beating in two places. He smiled and replied, "Show me the way home."

"Hey, Lark. I'm just checking in . . . I really miss you. Maybe I can sneak off into town one night this week and we can do a movie or something. I'm just craving actual human company. Give me a call, or e-mail."

Stella stuffed her phone back in her pants pocket with a

sigh. She didn't know if Lark was avoiding her calls or they just had bad timing; at this point either was equally likely. She'd barely spoken to her best friend since she'd come back to the Haven—her life had been sucked into a vortex of weirdness and she felt like she was living outside time, in another dimension.

She went back to what she'd been doing when the impulse to talk to Lark struck: dusting and rearranging the altar in the ritual room. It hadn't been used since that night she had watched Nico work; he hadn't had a chance to make good on his offer to teach her. She didn't blame him. He did have a lot on his mind.

She was just so lonely. Everyone made it clear she was wanted here, and that they cared about her, but with so much going on, there was no time to eat ice cream with Miranda or learn Weaving with Nico. The closest she got to either was eating ice cream while entertaining extremely vivid fantasies of licking it off the Elf's neck. She had seen him only a couple of times since he'd taken his Signet, and she wanted very badly to seek the Elf out, to offer . . . well, whatever comfort a silly young human could give an immortal . . . whatever he needed that she could find a way to give.

Most of the items that had been on the altar were back in her room already, since they were from her personal shrine; there were two large pillar candles, a bowl of salt and one of water, and a slowly desiccating pomegranate remaining.

The thought occurred: She might not be able to do much Weaving, but she could go in and look, have a peek at the Circle and see how things were shaping up. She was curious what all the bonds looked like now, especially the one between Nico and Deven. It couldn't hurt to do that, could it, as long as she didn't touch anything or dig around? They'd trusted her with far more than that, and if she wanted to learn that kind of magic, she needed to spend more time studying.

Excited at the prospect of having something new to do, Stella grabbed a big cushion and dropped it on the floor, then dropped herself onto it cross-legged. She took a moment to ground and center, a bit annoyed with herself; she'd been neglecting her meditation practice lately, and that almost certainly had something to do with how unhappy she'd been. With all these supernatural beings around her, staying grounded was even more important.

"Bad Stella," she muttered. "Bad Witch, no broomstick."

Taking a deep breath she closed her eyes and started to reach inward to draw up the Web . . .

. . . but something . . .

Her eyes popped open. Something wasn't right.

The energy in the room felt strange all of a sudden, charged with static electricity that made her arm hairs leap up on end. She shifted into her usual Sight, the less sophisticated vision she'd always relied on before.

What she saw . . . what the hell?

Stella was on her feet, pushed by a swell of power in the center of the Circle that felt unlike anything she'd ever experienced. The way it was swirling slowly around the room, gathering in front of her, made no sense to her eyes or her Sight. The air in the room grew hotter, each breath feeling sharp in her lungs.

She would have run, but the energy was between her and the door. She had nowhere to go, and she was about to lift her com to her lips and yell for help, when . . .

The power condensed into a single point, then blew outward with a nearly audible snap like a flag unfurling. Energy rushed out from the center, the force of it nearly knocking her on her ass. The single point grew until it was a circle of light, and another blast hit her, this one of wind.

The door was closed. There were no windows. Wind? From where?

Stella stood transfixed, too petrified to move, as the light became brighter and brighter, ultimately flashing bright enough to send stars dancing through her brain.

A moment of intense heat—

—and it was gone.

Stella had her hands over her face and took them away slowly, her heart racing so fast she couldn't even feel individual beats.

Oh . . . my . . .

A face she knew, but without its warmth—staring at her with cold eyes, seeming made out of shadow and fire—jet-black hair, shining like a raven's feathers, falling down like a cloak over black robes that reached the floor.

Those eyes burned into hers . . . filled with wrath and power that had no interest in discretion or diplomacy . . .

. . . violet eyes.

A voice that she knew was normally low and melodic snapped at her like a bolt of lightning, as commanding as any here she'd ever heard, and Stella was so afraid she could barely comprehend the words.

Every syllable was knife-sharp and hell-dark.

"Where is my brother?"

FROM *NEW YORK TIMES* BESTSELLING AUTHOR

Yasmine Galenorn

HAUNTED MOON

AN OTHERWORLD NOVEL

There's a new Fae sorcerer in town—Bran, the son of Raven Mother and the Black Unicorn—and Camille is the unwilling liaison between him and the new Earthside OIA. With cemeteries being ransacked and spirits being harvested by a sinister, otherworldly force, Aeval sends the D'Artigo sisters to rescue the missing wife of a prominent member of the Fae nobility. Their search leads them to the mysterious Aleksais Psychic Network and, ultimately, to face the Lord of Ghosts. There, Morio and Camille must undergo a ritual that will plunge them both directly into the realm of the dead.

"Yasmine Galenorn is a powerhouse author; a master of the craft."
—*New York Times* bestselling author Maggie Shayne

galenorn.com
facebook.com/AuthorYasmineGalenorn
facebook.com/ProjectParanormalBooks
penguin.com

M1312T0513